NIGHTSCRIPT

VOLUME SEVEN

———◆———

EDITED BY C.M. Muller

CHTHONIC MATTER | St. Paul, Minnesota

NIGHTSCRIPT: *Volume Seven*

Tales © 2021 by individual authors. All rights reserved.

FIRST EDITION

Cover: "Banshee" by Jana Heidersdorf

Additional proofreading by Chris Mashak

This anthology is a work of fiction. Any resemblance to actual events or persons, living or dead, is entirely coincidental.

Nightscript is published annually, during grand October.

CHTHONIC MATTER | St. Paul, Minnesota
www.chthonicmatter.wordpress.com

CONTENTS

Feast Your Eyes on the Yawning
      Monotony of Humdrum Rot | *Clint Smith* | 1

The Passing | *Joshua Rex* | 21

When Sleep At Last | *Douglas Thompson* | 30

The Summer King's Day | *Timothy Granville* | 42

Roadkill | *Elin Olausson* | 57

It Looked Like Her | *Gordon Brown* | 67

Little Gods To Live In Them | *David Surface* | 74

We Are The Gorillas | *Douglas Ford* | 91

The Body Trick | *Alexander James* | 100

Feed | *Jason A. Wyckoff* | 115

'Neath The Mirror Of The Sea | *Rhonda Eikamp* | 123

Clipped Wings | *Steve Toase* | 138

The Cardboard Voice | *Tim Major* | 150

The Validations | *Ashley Stokes* | 165

A Perfect Doll | *Regina Garza Mitchell* | 183

Madam and Yves | *Marc Joan* | 190

The Delf | *Danny Rhodes* | 202

Where the Oxen Turned the Plow | *Charles Wilkinson* | 214

Feast of Fools: A Heartwarming
      Holiday Romance | *LC von Hessen* | 230

Feast Your Eyes on the Yawning Monotony of Humdrum Rot

Clint Smith

———◆———

Two rental vans pulled into the parking lot of Mooring Cove Inn, their headlights swiping the exterior of the novelty hotel. The frigid water of Lake Michigan delineated the hips of this port village, where tree-needled hills slid down into slim inlets. Moonlight shone on the surface of the harbor, tracing the curves of the town's convoluted coves.

Seven passengers in the first vehicle, eight in the second. Technically, Ben Gibbs was not supposed to be here tonight. Truth told, despite this being a New Year's Eve, Ben had no place of particular consequence to be on this night of December 31, 2000. A trip back home would, humiliatingly, have to wait.

The driver of the lead van, and coordinator of this post-wedding retreat, was Garrett Harper. His wife, Melinda, was contentedly situated in the passenger seat. The parties in the vans had attended the nuptial ceremony and its requisite reception, the occupants exhibiting a wide spectrum of sobriety, with one of the drivers, Garrett, claiming to be in total control. It'd been ten years since he'd seen either Garrett or Melinda. *Spring of 1990*. Of course, they all looked older now. *No*. The preservation of Mel's youthful features was fascinatingly distracting. In the interior's darkness, Ben, between passing bars of paltry light—and cautious of the driver's eyes in the rearview mirror—would snag a peek at Melinda, glimpsing the soft lineaments near her eye socket, sloping to her cheek, the lithe swipe of jaw.

Up until an hour ago, Ben had been ignorant of the old lodging's existence, but now saw that Mooring Cove Inn was exactly as Garrett had succinctly described: a pirate ship converted into a touristy hotel. Craning his neck to get a better look, Ben saw that it was weirdly true. Some sort of massive wooden ship—a merchant vessel or brigantine—had basically been bisected at midship, with the breach now housing a three-story, retrofitted bulk of rooms, its architect imitating the antique aesthetic of the ship itself. Elongated due to the anachronistic insertion of the guest quarters, the ship's wide stern and glassed-in rear gallery had been transformed into an ornate portico, creating an impressive edifice; diametrically, the forecastle and its long bow extended out over the harbor.

This, Ben thought, eclipsed the classification of local curiosity—*this* was a gimmick made manifest. From the back of the van, one of the giddy girls, with inebriated eloquence, said, "It's like someone jammed the House of the Seven Gables into the middle of The Flying Dutchman." Ben was unacquainted with the references and also unacquainted with the girl, but thought someone had called her Erin.

One of the guys back there said, "Now *this* is fucking fantastic."

Garrett brought the van to a stop under the carport's awning. "All right," he said, "I'll go check in." He swiveled in the driver's seat, addressing Ben. "Come in with me, man."

Ben hesitated a tick too long. "Yeah," he said, "why not," uncoordinatedly nudging past knees on the bench seat to get to the sliding door. Ben's breath immediately fogged in the night air, and as he passed the passenger side window, he could not help but flinch a glance at Melanie—a slow blink there, a subdued stall, her features possessing the suppressed fluidity of submergence.

Ben sidled up alongside the friend he'd not seen in nearly a decade.

"*Shit,*" Garrett bristled, "cold as hell."

Ben winced, looking up toward the hotel's roof, noting at its center three tall masts. Small accent lamps were trained on wide, square-rigged sails, the wind's steady susurration rippling the time-tattered sails and rousing the sagging ratlines. In the sky beyond, the moon glowed within ribcages of clouds. What was likely intended to be majestically amusing, Ben now found to be flamboyantly eerie.

The spacious swath which served as the hotel lobby played more like a maritime museum than a kitschy vestibule. On the far end of the chamber, a robust fire seethed in a cobblestone hearth, its light licking the mahogany flesh of leather reading chairs. Above the mantel, the wood-paneled wall was decked-out with an assembly of paintings and sea-centric weapons: a blunderbuss, a pair of cutlasses, a boarding axe. Affixed centrally from the ceiling by a set of chains was an oversized wooden steering wheel, which had been craftily repurposed as a chandelier.

Ben gazed at the space, pleased by the sudden dissipation of his pretensions, imagining that if he were twenty years younger, a ten-year-old Ben would be giddily captivated by the opulence of pirate paraphernalia.

The front desk was vacant. Garrett, without hesitating, yanked the roped clapper of a counter-mounted bell, a veneer of verdigris covering the novelty. As the echo faded, Garrett cocked an elbow on the counter and regarded Ben. "Man, I'm really glad you joined us."

Ben's smile was small. "I didn't really have a choice." He eyed the spacious lobby and its high-seas trappings. A nearby shelf boasted an octant, other brass gadgets. "I should be thanking you for permitting a stowaway."

That day, Ben had traveled 250 miles to attend the wedding of a childhood friend, the couple having planned it this way: an unconventional Sunday ceremony with the intention of memorializing the indelible marker of New Year's Eve.

He'd traveled solo, hesitant to attend in the first place, certain that an ensemble cast from his formative years—both genuine friends and dubious acquaintances alike—would make an appearance. Of course, Garrett showed up. Ben had heard Garrett and Mel, to his dismay, had gotten married several years earlier. He thought she had more self-respect, would have been able to detect what was underneath. *Who knows—*

maybe Garrett's changed.

Ben had been alone in a pew when Garret and Mel walked in, his heart ticking a bit when he saw her, even from a distance. But seeing them together, as husband and wife, soured Ben's perspective. Garrett and Mel waved at Ben as they took their seats on the opposite side of the sanctuary. The old gang, in one form or another, was back together.

At the reception, Ben did a heroic job of integrating himself, but it was a socially torturous thing to behold. Forgoing goodbyes, he attempted a discreet getaway at the reception for a roundtrip retreat home, only to sink into a frigid car that wouldn't start; and, adding to this indignity, it was Garrett—he and his wife and his band of companions on their way to a pair of rental vans—who'd spotted Ben and his pitiful vehicle in the parking lot.

Garrett insisted, explaining that he'd made reservations at a lakeside village about an hour west—this hotel somewhat of a Great Lakes destination, charming in its touristy tawdriness. "At least come with us to the hotel," was Garrett's rationale, "you can party with us for a few more hours and figure shit out in the morning."

Ben, reluctant but quite literally without a viable alternative, agreed.

Now, standing here at the hotel's front desk, Garrett hissed, dismissive. "Man. Don't mention it. Like how many years has it been?—five . . . six?"

It was the first time they'd been alone all evening. He fixed Garrett with a hard look, his smile fading a bit. He self-consciously withdrew his left hand from the front desk countertop, those crooked fingers that had, a decade earlier, healed so poorly. "Ten."

Garrett exhaled, wagged his head. "So, what's with the day-to-day? What line of work you in?"

Ben cleared his throat, accessorizing his occupation to bring some dignity to it. He failed. Still, Garrett raised his eyebrows. "That sounds great, man. Good for you."

Ben was afraid to ask: "How about you?"

Garrett shrugged, sophisticatedly explaining that he was now in league with a multinational company specializing in medical devices and research-based pharmaceuticals. "Right now we're working on selling the *in vitro* diagnostics divisions, but that's down the road, you know." Ben nodded as though he were not debilitatingly ignorant of this minutiae. Garrett back-jabbed a thumb over his shoulder. "This place is supposed to have a bar on the other end of the hotel. Who knows"—Garrett edged in on Ben, voice low—"maybe you'll get lucky."

Ben laughed, returning to his appraisal of the ornate lobby. "Funny."

"No, seriously," said Garrett. "What about Erin? She's single. Or at least tonight she is."

Ben inhaled, understanding he meant the Seven-Gables girl from the van. "Oh. Sure. Maybe."

"Yeah." Garrett made a face: *Bummer*. "She's a smart girl, but a forgettable lay."

Ben's eyes zagged to Garrett's. After a second: "Just joking, man."

A rustling sounded from the lightless corridor behind the front desk, then a young woman emerged; she was wearing a uniform—a cross between peasant blouse and dirndl—which she was in the process of smoothing as she approached her station. Smiling. Her cheeks were flushed. Her name tag read Bethany. "Good evening, gentlemen. Welcome to Mooring Cove Inn."

"Reservation for Harper," said Garrett. Ben thought he saw Garrett give the buxom young lady a graceless once-over. "We should have a block of rooms..."

Ben, from the fray of his periphery, noticed a tall figure slither out of the back-office room, disappearing in the gloom of the corridor, nothing more than a slender swipe of coverall gray, then: shadows.

When he sensed that Garrett and the front-desk girl were wrapping up, Ben cut in: "I'd like to reserve a room as well." He went for his wallet but Garrett stopped him.

"No way—it's taken care of. We have plenty of rooms. You can have your own." And just like that, Garrett, with smirky gallantry, handed over a gold credit card to Bethany.

Slowly, Ben slid his wallet into his pocket. He doubted he had enough money on his own credit card to get the car fixed. His mouth was dry. "Thanks, man."

Garrett's face flexed. *What are friends for?* "I'll get my department to expense it."

Bethany was inspecting the wall behind her comprised of old-fashioned, room-key alcoves; she removed a number of brass keys and addressed Garrett: "All right, Mr. Harper, we have a block of ten rooms along the lower starboard tier." She indicated a stairway. "And if it interests you and your party, The Gull's Wing"—she pointed—"has a special, New Year's menu and a full bar."

Garrett scooped the faux-antique keys from the countertop. "Yes," he said, "I believe we're very much interested in a drink."

As Ben tentatively pulled away from the front desk, he watched Bethany return to the dark corridor, and as she neared the threshold to the back office, a long arm extended, fingers clasping the young woman's wrist. Instead of eliciting alarm, Bethany exhaled a giggle as the sinewy arm tugged her over the threshold.

THE GULL'S WING was the hotel's restaurant and adjoining tavern. Situated in the ship's reconstructed and expanded galley and retrofitted forecastle (and still adhering to the wood-and-brass, seafaring aesthetic), the spacious suite—glassed-in by tall windows along the converging walls of the port and starboard bow—overlooked the lake below, the marina's dark water reflecting constantly-morphing mercury tines of moonlight. Ben thought if he allowed his mind to wander, it would actually be easy to imagine that the structure was gently cleaving across the harbor.

They'd hastily acclimated themselves to their quarters a short time earlier (Ben, as promised, was granted with his own room), and now the road-trip attendees and locals alike filled the bar with raucous life, anticipating the encroaching hour of midnight and its commencement of a new year.

The new year, however, was poised to begin with Ben scrambling to find a tow-truck to retrieve his car from the church an hour away, and the likelihood of securing a mechanic who was willing to tinker with it on New Year's day.

Not long after ordering drinks, Garrett ringmastered his troupe toward a small dance floor, mingling with the existing contingent of strangers. Ben discreetly separated himself, half-watching Mel as she earnestly interacted with her friends—the quirk of a familiar smile . . .

how she peeled a panel of hair over her shoulder . . . the tick of her hips as she listened intently to someone trying to speak over the music. She was and always has been, he thought, the kindest and most lambent creature he'd ever known.

Mel's dark eyes hitched directly in line with his.

Ben looked away, steering himself toward the bar. He asked the bartender for a phone book and a cup of coffee. The bartender said she'd have to make it fresh, but she'd bring it out to him; from somewhere below, she hefted and handed over a sooty directory.

Ben spotted an empty booth on the far side of the room; he wove between tables and a series of wooden stanchions. An elderly man was seated at one of these tables, clearly inebriated, his bald head bobbing over a scattering of files and paperwork. Though dressed managerially, the old man offered a vagrant's smile.

A tight nod from Ben.

Quieter over here, Ben slid down into the booth, giving the tavern-side of The Gull's Wing another glance before cracking open the phone book.

Ben'd barely begun his search when he absentmindedly eyed the wood-paneled wall next to him. Along the lacquered surface of the shiplap-style wood were a cluster of smooth holes—not unlike the damage, albeit diminutive, from a shotgun blast. No. This was something else. The perforations had slightly different diameters. Ben expanded his appraisal to the ceiling, the decorative trusses. Though interspersed and nearly unnoticeable among the dark whorls of varnished grain, the schizophrenic honeycomb-holes were now quite conspicuous.

Ben returned his attention to the wall. Frowning, he raised his hand to the wood, gently running his fingers over the punctures, meditating on the contagious nature of rot.

"Terado worms," came a slurred voice.

Ben flinched, yanking his hand away from the wall. The elderly drunk who Ben had seen sitting alone at the nearby table now stood a few feet away, holding a half-filled pint glass. A little more harshly than he'd intended, Ben said, "Excuse me?"

The old man used his bald brow as a pointer, indicating the small patch of holes on the wall. "That right there is the work of terado worms." He was evidently waiting for Ben to respond.

"Oh," said Ben.

"Well, terado worms is one name for them, depending on how smart you want to sound. Pileworms is another. But their more common name is naval shipworm. Detestable creatures, really. Mind if I join you?"

Ben's jaw was loose. "Uh, well—"

The old man rested his glass on the table and sank down on the opposite side of the booth. Rheumy eyes. "They're not even worms, really," he continued, as though they'd been chatting for hours, "they're just little mollusks with a, oh"—he curved his fingers into crescents—"a shell on their head to bore into wood." He took a sip from his pint. "You might notice those little holes, but you'd never know they'd penetrated until the wood was just crumbling to pieces." Ben was now only listening peripherally as he assembled an excuse to extricate himself. "They secrete this chalky casing to protect themselves—these long, wormy siphons. You know what those casings are called?"

"Uh. No."

"Crypts." Amber light glinted off the old man's head as he nodded, polished off his pint, and brushed a finger over his lips. "Vile animals."

Ben was about to dismiss himself when the bartender arrived with both the coffee and a fresh pint. "Here you are, Mr. McLean."

The old man thanked her as she retreated. He chuckled. "I'm less of a regular than a fixture at this old place." Then—with an air of almost regal sobriety—extended his hand across the table. "Name's Ennis—Ennis McLean."

After a cautious assessment, Ben shook. "Ben. Gibbs."

"Well, Mr. Gibbs. I apologize about the intrusion, but, I wagered, a fellow bachelor could benefit from some companionable conversation as the clock winds down."

Fucking strange. A presumptuous observation from this elderly man, but nevertheless accurate. Ben couldn't help but glance at his own left hand, the swervy pinky and ringfinger. Ben took a sip of coffee. Hot, hideous. He looked directly at Ennis. "How do you know," he waved a hand, "about these shipworms?"

"Ah. My firm used to represent the family who opened this place back in, oh, '58 or thereabouts. It's been sold several times in between, updated, of course; but we oversaw the installation of the original ship, or at least significant portions of it." The man explained that the original proprietors had salvaged some massive craft, that they'd hoped to exploit Great-Lake lore with the intention of making the hotel a Midwest landmark. "The Great Lakes are a graveyard."

Ben looked past the tables, out toward the tavern's dance floor. Mel was still holding court with the road-trip party, but there was no sign of Garrett. "I see," Ben said.

"You know," Ennis said, "simply staring at that fetching young woman won't lure her to you."

Ben shot the old man a bloodless look, but its durability didn't last; he cast down to his coffee, took a sip, winced. Ben mumbled, "She's married."

Ennis immediately made a noise—something between cough and laugh. "You mean that lech who's been ignoring her all evening?"

He had Ben's attention again. He licked his lips. "Garrett."

"Ah. Garrett." After taking a drink, Ennis said, "When you've been in this tavern as long as I have, you begin to see patterns." Music thumped over in the bar. From the mounted televisions, there was a shot of Times Square crowds preparing for the oncoming countdown about an hour from now. "So tell me," Ennis said, "what's the pattern that brought you together with this Garrett and his rowdy revelers?"

Ben now felt as though he were having a conversation with a well-meaning elderly relative as opposed to an alcohol-addled octogenarian. "They're my friends. Well, Garrett and Mel at least. I don't know most of them." He explained how he'd been invited to the wedding of a childhood friend, how he'd traveled from Sycamore Mill to attend, how the occasion had engendered a small reunion. "My car broke down, so Garrett"—Ben twitched fingers toward the clique of partiers on the small dance floor—"and his friends offered me a ride."

"And so?"

Ben chuckled. "And so, now here I am in a gaudy hotel tavern talking to a stranger."

Ennis grinned, compressing the already pronounced wrinkles at the corners of his eyes. "No. What's the *real* story?"

Ben took a deep breath, suddenly wondering if he'd conjured this elderly entity to simply rid himself of this regrettable baggage.

Ben didn't allow time to lapse, figuring this was the fastest method to dismiss the old fellow. "We were all pretty close when we were kids, teenagers, really. For the last two years of high school, we had this idea of abstaining from a traditional spring break trip—forgoing the drunken beach routine—and volunteering with a non-profit, helping to build houses for needy families." The old man across the table quirked a smirk. Ben couldn't help but chuckle. "Yeah, I know—pretty idealistic for a bunch of juveniles—"

Ennis chortled: "The *Adolescents of La Mancha.*"

Ben frowned. "Huh?"

"Never mind. Please, continue."

"Even though most of us went our separate ways after high school, we kept up the tradition for a couple years during college. But, by that point," Ben's hand went to the coffee mug, which was empty, "we'd all just . . . changed." Ben, now uncomfortably aware of the unease he exhibited, changed tack. "Like I said, we tried another reunion trip, the traditional spring break build with Homes of Hope. But they'd been together for about a year at that point."

"Your two friends over there?"

Ben nodded. "A surprise to everyone, really."

"So what's the dilemma?" Ennis said.

Ben scowled. "Just, at the time, neither seemed content, or even at peace, with each other."

"And *that's* your central grievance?"

Ben took a deep breath, providing Ennis with an honest but shorthand version of what happened on that final trip—the laconic scrawl on the back of a blurry postcard.

It was spring break, 1990. All in their early twenties by then, each now mapping the boundaries of what would be their lives. They argued a lot, Garrett and Mel, and had adopted a savviness when severing these altercations when anyone wandered into their vicinity.

About midweek, Mel had injured the palm of her hand—a nasty laceration which she insisted was not severe enough for medical attention. Still, she concealed it from the foreman.

Later that night, at the church-hostel, Ben was restless, and as he was returning to his bunk, he was certain he smelled smoke. He walked outside, finding Mel sitting on a picnic table skirting the woods, a blanket wrapped over her shoulders, the cherry's pinpoint ember occasionally floating up to where her mouth would be. Ben approached. She whispered, "It's lonely out here." The night noises were steady. "Come and keep me company."

The picnic table creaked as he settled down next to her. His eyes had adjusted by then. "You all right?"

West Virginia night had settled over the woods like a black net. She exhaled, a grin behind the smoke. "Fine." She offered the cigarette.

Ben accepted, took a drag, returned it. "How's your hand?"

Mel snorted. "Bloody, but not bad." Ben clicked on his pocket-size flashlight. Mel peeled back part of the gauze. Blood had dried burgundy, but her hand seemed fine.

The next question was at the trench of Ben's lips—his tongue flexing with a question—but Mel obliged in a feat of telepathic trickery. "Garrett's never really going to change," she said. "Growing up has just made things worse—the internships, the fucking fraternity, the *real* world is just peeling away what he really is." She inhaled, exhaled smoke. "Garrett's always been coddled, but there's something else inside of him that's just... *spoiled*."

In the wake of their conversation, Ben dwelled on what he'd missed—what Mel had been hinting with such subterranean articulation. His suspicion gave dimension to trauma—*Abuse*, though whether mental, physical, or both, he could not quite enunciate. In the years that followed, Ben regretted being so polite that night.

Mel finished the cigarette, butting it out on the bench. Their talk drifted, an hour passing with ease. At some point, they returned to her injured hand.

"Thank you," she said.

Ben laughed. "For what?"

"Just," night noises, "for being the same Ben I've trusted since we were kids."

Ben laughed, speaking with little tact. "We're not going to be able to talk like this when you and Garrett get married and disappear into suburban bliss."

Though she'd finished her cigarette, Mel exhaled as though she were expelling something from her lungs. "Garrett will never commit to anything conventional, he's made that clear. We'll be in our fifties and still"—she forked fingers into quotes, scratching the air, no humor in her voice—"*having fun*."

The insects had created a discordant cipher, its music cushioning and compelling Ben's thoughts, and in their discursive intimacy, a sort of clandestine intoxication had seized him. "Well," he said, "if you're not married by the time you're thirty, then I'll propose."

Ben waited for Mel to rejoin his laugh, but a silence followed, lingered. Eventually, Mel reached down and clicked on the small flashlight, peeling back the gauze to expose the laceration. She smirked—something complexly playful and solemn. "Swear it," she smirked, "swear it as a blood oath."

And in that state of sentimental euphoria—he slid his hand into this pocket, withdrawing a small folding knife. He opened the blade, placing the cutting edge against his thumb. He expected Mel to waver—tell him to stop, that it was a joke—instead, he took a swipe, drawing a line of blood. He looked at Mel, her eyes glittering in the flashlight's feeble bouquet, her expression challenging. Ben extended his hand which she clasped, pumping his palm with emphasis. "'You got a deal," she said, letting go. "No going back now."

The next morning materialized with the group closing in on the final phases of the build. As it happened, Ben and Garrett were on the roof of the house, laying shingles. Whatever tension had been braided between Mel and Garrett appeared now to have dissipated. A tacit happiness permeated the day, and it felt, to Ben—up there on top of the house, laughing under the straight-on afternoon sun—like the old days.

Overlapping hammering wove with music from a radio on a sawhorse somewhere below. Ben crouched side-by-side with Garrett, both mock-singing with some song, both shifting shingles into position.

The hammer came down on Ben's left hand, which had been splayed for balance. There was a peculiar pique in the pain—a severity which instantly registered as a fracture.

Sunlight flashed. Ben clenched his teeth, wrenching his body, his sneakers scraping the shingles, conscious that he must stop himself from sliding off the roof. Garrett was stammering then: a stuttery string of apologies. Wincing, Ben peeled off his work glove. Two fingers on his left hand, the pinky and ring fingers, were extravagantly broken.

Ben felt Garrett's hand slide over his shoulder, his friend's silhouette casting a cloak of shade. "Oh, god, oh, man—are you okay? I'm so sorry, man—it was an accident."

Later, after a prolonged trip to the town's clinic, Ben was driven back to the church-hostel, his hand in a crisp splint. Before dinner, Garrett had approached Ben, offering a bottle of water, comedically unscrewing the cap. "Seriously, man," said Garrett, "I feel awful."

Ben shook his head, "Really—just a mistake, dude. No hard feelings."

Garrett's expression didn't change as he continued staring at Ben.

Ben laughed. "I swear, man."

Garrett, still eyeing Ben, took a sip from his water bottle. His tone dipped when he said, "Oh, you *swear* it do you, playboy?"

Ben looked at his friend, ticking over his now-spiteful expression. As preoccupied as they'd been the night before, Ben imagined how easy it would have been for Garrett to eavesdrop on the two of them. And here, a confirmation: it was still Garrett, but there was something else there now: a sophisticated veneer of nastiness. Then again, maybe not. Maybe it'd been there all their lives.

Ben nodded a few times. That was that, and *that* was over a decade ago.

Now, the old man across the table spoke. "Would you do it again?"

Ben inwardly shivered. Hearing Ennis's voice reeled Ben back in from his regrettable digression. "Would I do what?"

"The builds—the non-for-profit trips."

"Oh. No, I'm afraid not." Ben smiled. "A young man's game."

Ben glanced out over the bar, it's too-small dance floor. He spotted Mel, but, again, no sign of Garrett.

"Well, if you're going to make your move," said the old man, a jocular taunt, "all the elements are in alignment: unrequited affection, a blood pact, the threshold of a new century."

Ben flexed a frown. *A new century?* Ennis chortled, waved as if to dispel something complicated, spluttering something about the Gregorian calendar and the debatable existence of "year zero."

Ben shook his head. "Speaking of a young man's game," he said, "I'm afraid it's time for me to turn in." He stood, then, stretching. "It's been nice chatting with you, Ennis."

"And you."

Ben remained on the restaurant's perimeter, skirting the possibility of being noticed as he made his exit.

"*Ben!*" Mel's voice, calling out over the music; he stopped short and turned, watching her trot over. Panting a bit, she said. "Where're you running off to? Going to hide in your room or something?"

The tach of Ben's pulse eclipsed the drumming music. Despite this, he smiled. "No. Just forgot something."

The nectar-colored light made her skin look warm—her cider-tinted eyes. "Liar."

Ben exhaled. "I'm just going to turn in, you know? Not really my scene."

She tilted her chin up a degree, the unspoken acting as awkward insulation in their intimate space. Mel's lips parted, but Ben's nerve disintegrated; he blurted, "Where's Garrett?"

Mel's eyelids fluttered; she used a finger to drag an errant strand of hair from her forehead. "I don't know. I—I haven't seen him in a while." There was something detached in her intonation, a subcuticular code that Ben did not have the wits to readily decipher. "I'm afraid he's not going to be back in time for the countdown."

Ben's lips were numb. He finally looked at his watch. *11:47.* "All right— let me hustle down to the room and see if I can find him, okay?" And now Mel, nodding, appeared uncharacteristically stricken. "I'll hurry."

It was quiet in the lobby, the only movement coming from the fireplace's leaping light. Ben glanced at the vacated front desk and the rear-office corridor beyond. Still dark back there, but Ben thought he caught the discreet hush of some sort of intimacy—Bethany and her rangy companion getting an early start.

Ben steered into the stairwell, dropping down to the lower level of rooms. Throughout his twisting descent, he heard the growing volume of voices in the distance, the countdown echoing from the tavern—*twenty-seven . . . twenty-six . . . twenty-five*—he checked his watch. *How can it already be midnight?* He sped up, skipping every other step. And then, with his hand on the railing, his heart hitched as he heard the final sequence: *five . . . four . . . three . . . two . . . one!*

The lights in the stairwell tremored and snapped off. Having not yet reached the lower landing, Ben lurched to a halt. Instead of the expected sounds of New Year's exuberance, there was nothing, just the sudden gasp of silence. He blinked in the darkness, hearing only his labored breathing. Nearly a minute passed before his eyes began to acclimate. Up ahead, he could distinguish a languid, amber glow. Ben emerged at an intersection that should have led to both his room and Garrett's block of rooms, instead he was confronted with a passage that looked more like the thoroughfare of some wood-paneled cellar, the walls of which were dimly lit by quaking flames in sconces.

He shuffled on, trying, and failing, to recall what the hall had looked like earlier—*all wrong*—*this is all*—

There was a figure up ahead, crumpled and slinking along the lower coving of the floor. Cautiously, Ben edged up on a young woman, her face obscured behind tousled hair, but the top of her dress had been ripped, exposing her pale contours. He knelt, his hand uselessly hovering over her shoulder. He could smell the alcohol coming off her now; she did not appear to be in pain, but rather in the throes of . . . something else. She evidently registered his presence; Ben saw the glint of her lower lip as she slur-purred, "*You . . . promised.*"

A muted clunk from one of the nearby rooms. Ben rose, seeing now a stronger light coming from a threshold. Slowly, Ben entered. It was not Garrett's room, but there he stood: Garrett, rifling through the interior of a large piece of leather luggage, muttering to himself; his dress shirt—some vintage, ridiculously frilly garment—was unbuttoned to the sternum.

Ben moved into the room—the antiquated aesthetic more pronounced here: wall-mounted, liquid-filled lanterns seethed light. On the wall hung a column of cutlasses and gilded pistols. Nothing was as it had been before—the perceptive trick of the centuries-old veneer made Ben dizzy.

"Ah," said Garrett with tangible glee, and Ben watched him tug a bundle from the leather trunk. The brief flash of jewelry.

"Jesus, man," said Ben. "What—what the hell are you doing?" Garrett ignored him, pocketing some old-fashioned paper currency. Ben stepped closer. "What about Mel?"

Garrett's brow furrowed. "Who?"

Ben clenched his teeth. "Melanie—your *wife*."

Garrett chuckled, gathering his things. "Oh. Her. Well, let's just say that these little . . . dalliances . . . are on the margins of her purview and should remain there. Surely I can count on your discretion, Benjamin."

"What about—?" Ben feebly waved a hand at the room's door, the young woman just outside the threshold.

Garrett flitted a hand. "We've finished for the evening." He smirked. "You're welcome to her." Garret made a move for the doorway, but Ben stepped up square, placing his mangled left hand on his friend's chest. Garrett stopped, regarding Ben's crooked fingers. "Whose handiwork is that? Oh"—he looked up quickly—"I remember now." But then Garrett's expression shifted; he now appraised Ben with sober and sincere curiosity. "Did *she* send you?"

Ben shoved Garrett, who responded with instant viciousness, using his forearms to thrust Ben against the wall, rattling the array of antique objects.

Garrett produced a gleaming knife, slyly repositioning himself, shifting to block the threshold. Back against the wall, Ben said, "You're a real piece of shit, you know that?"

Garrett shrugged, and for a moment, his expression fluctuated between grin and grimace. A sneer won out as he said, "I should have just shoved you off that fucking roof."

Garrett began to rush forward, the knife peaked over his head, but he faltered, suddenly swerving his attention to the floor. The girl from the hall had scrabbled into the room, and was now clawing at Garrett's arm and waist. "*Please . . . please,*" she mewled, "*you promised . . .* "

Garrett thrashed to free his arm, but Ben bolted, swiping one of the pirate pistols from the wall behind him. Garrett tried to raise the knife but was too late. Ben, clasping the barrel of the pistol like a hammer, side-armed the bulbous brass pommel against Garrett's temple.

Garrett's body convulsed and collapsed in a heap on the hardwood floor. Now the half-clothed girl crawled on top of Garrett. "*Don't touch him . . . he didn't mean it . . .*"

Garrett dropped the pistol and hurdled over the couple, sprinting down the hall and bounding up the stairwell, still absent of electric light. The lobby was dark but was fussed by firelight from the fireplace, the room hysterical with twitching shadows.

Ben hit the corridor to the Gull's Wing. Slowing now, he felt his way along the passage until he emerged into the main chamber. Through wide windows which overlooked the harbor, robust bars of moonlight sheeted the restaurant's surfaces with soft illumination. With the chairs overturned and resting on the tabletops, the quiet space appeared to have been closed for hours. Ben crept in further, his eyesight acclimating to the murk. Ben rounded into the tavern and jittered to a stop.

There were, he saw now, dozens of people present, pressing themselves into nooks and corners, some crouched down beneath tables. Burrowed in their shadows, it was as though the half-obscured figures were performing some mockery of hide and seek, or in the midst of preparing to jump out and scream, *Surprise!*

Movement, then, on the verge of the room. Ennis McLean, evidently not noticing Ben, emerged from the darkness, arms raised in front of himself, his long fingers flexing and wiggling as if over unseen piano keys. He was whispering. Ben realized now that they were *all* whispering.

And then the old man stopped in the middle of the dance floor, his gaze rotating slowly to fall on Ben. The elderly fellow was grinning, the sharp wings of his mouth, contorting the features into an indecent imitation of agreeability.

Ennis raised a finger, aiming the too-long appendage directly at Ben. The old man's mouth opened wider—an abhorrent, oblong cavity. And then with a gurgling, violent heave, gouts of gray liquid surged from the old man's mouth, splattering on the wooden dance floor. The excretion was alive with a veriform lashing, ropy lengths struggling against their own hagfish-like viscosity.

Then, simultaneously, the hide-and-seek figures flinched and came rush-crashing forward toward Ben, shuddered, pivoted, and scrambled for the exit.

With footfalls only yards behind him, Ben tore through the dark corridor, continuing his acceleration through the lobby. Then, beyond the rear of the front desk, a tall figure lunged from the darkness. Unclothed from the waist up, there was the flash of gray skin as the figure attempted to vault over the front desk, but instead hit the counter with a pulpy impact—rotting ribbons of lacy flesh hung over an angular, calcified carriage.

Ben pounded down the stairwell, whirling on the banister's newel caps to gain momentum. Finally, he was at the lower floor, turning left toward his room. Ben raced down the dungeon-like corridor, fumbling for his key—he shouldered the door, which yielded, but not before catching the lurching, disjointed locomotion of his ghastly-complected pursuers.

He shoved the door shut, a quaking hand rattling the chain latch into place. Chest heaving, Ben backed away. Pounding then: dozens of knuckles, fingernails sounding as though they were scoring the wooden door. Ben wheeled on a small, unrecognizable room, a wall which no longer contained a contemporary window, but rather a row of round portholes. The circular glass rattled, and then Ben saw the water—the rhythmic emergence of black waves cresting the glass. The beating continued, intensifying as what sounded like more pursuers gathered against the door.

What meager moonlight could be seen through the porthole slowly diminished as the waves crept higher. Ben staggered, the floor now listing against a crashing tide; staggering for balance, feeling both nauseous and drowsy, he pitched sideways, sagging to the floor, caught between the dualized hammering against the door and the waves which malleated the very air.

Lying on his side, Ben's eyelids fluttered. He watched the portholes, the serrated swells of black caps eclipsing the night. There came then the yielding peal of splintering wood, and a concussive exhalation overtook him, extinguishing what was left of the light.

FRIGID, BEN QUAKES awake. Still heaped on the floor of his room, but the space is as it had been in its original state. The curtains are partially drawn over normal windows which permit joyless, gray light. The cusp of dawn. Ben finally stands upright. Sore, he limps cautiously toward the door.

Intact. The brass chain still affixed in the lock. Through the peephole, the corridor is empty. Holding a breath, he opens the door, and after a tentative, swivel-assessment, steps into the hallway. A stiff-gaited Ben Gibbs proceeds down the hall, toward the stairwell; mounting the steps, he smells smoke, hears the somehow comforting echo-pop of burning wood.

He hesitates at the lobby threshold before easing in. From behind the front desk comes the growl of percolating coffee. There's an attendant there, a tall young man. Ben, unblinking, crosses into the lobby. The young man looks up, smiles. "Good morning, sir. Did you sleep well?"

Ben blinks finally. "Not exactly."

The young man says, "I believe some members of your party are out front." His long arm extends, gesturing toward the lobby's entrance.

Ben turrets his attention to the wide front doors. He hobbles over, and through the glass now sees a yellow cab, Mel at the curb, her arms crossed over her chest, clearly trying to stay warm.

Garret, as though for balance, has one hand resting on the roof of the cab, his other hand bracing his temple. Their exchange fogging the air between them.

Then Garrett notices Ben through the front doors—he smiles, though wearily, and waves for Ben.

Ben, with the cautious composure of a clenched fist, approaches. Garrett is pale, perhaps even febrile, but his smile and voice are bright. "Hey, man. Happy New Year."

Ben glances at Mel, the raw, low-lying clouds. "You—you too. What—"

"Garrett's going to the hospital," says Mel. "He hit his head sometime last night—we're worried it's a concussion."

Ben scrutinizes his friend.

Garret cuts in, "Ambulance is a little excessive, I think." He attempts a careless bearing, but winces. "Must have partied pretty hard. I'll be fine." Garrett leans over and kisses Mel on the cheek, then offers a hand to Ben. "I'm really glad you joined us, man." Garrett eyes Ben, his mouth working without sound; he pulls Ben toward him for an awkward, half-hug embrace, then lowers himself down into the back of the cab. Garrett waves feebly behind the glass as the car pulls away, the yellow vehicle and its taillights growing indistinct in the clutches of the morning mist.

He flinches when Mel speaks. "We missed you at the countdown last night."

She's smirking. A familiar thing, for a moment: an invitation for either tender consultation or playful sarcasm. Ben blinks, now detecting something wholly *un*familiar: the slow sluice of anger toward her. He stares. "Where were you at midnight?"

Mel says nothing for a stretch, their silence insulated by the hushing gnash of the nearby lake. Eventually, Mel breaks eye contact with Ben and again rubs her upper arms for frictional warmth. She sniffs—an aspect of petulance as opposed to a consequence of cold—and creeps in on Ben. Inches between them. Her chest meets his and, with eely fluidity, moves her mouth to his ear. She speaks, sounding congested, husky with lust and phlegm. And then Ben feels the oystery spill on his neck, chilly liquid coursing down to his clavicle. "Come inside," she says, "and keep me company."

The Passing

Joshua Rex

"You are here to watch me die," the old woman said.

She did not look near death, at least not to Klaus. Nor did he understand why, of all the children gathered downstairs in the parlor, he alone had been summoned to his grandmother's room in the attic of the five-floor Zauberstab fachwerkhaus which she occupied like its brain—or, in keeping with her nickname, *eine Wespe*. Whether or not she actually resembled one Klaus didn't know, for none of the children had ever seen her.

Klaus had been playing Elfern with his cousin Ingrid, and was turning over the King of Leaves card when his mother appeared in the doorway between the dining room, where all the Zauberstab elders had gathered, and the parlor. She held a lantern at her tapered waist and around her wrist hung a large iron ring loaded with barrel keys. She was pale as the face on the cameo at her throat. The grandfather clock along the west wall, steady as a strong heart, ticked several long moments before she spoke. "Klaus, die Urgroßmutter Zauberstab would like to see you."

His cousins looked up, each regarding him with identical expressions of trepidation.

"She wants to see *me*, mother?" Klaus said.

"That is what I said," his mother replied sharply. "Come, *gerade*."

The staircase was of dark wood and creaked like the hull of a galley on a roiling sea. Klaus had never been beyond the first level of the family house. In the upper floors the shadows seemed to gather like smoke, obscuring the archaic furniture and window coverings. The rooms were tomb-sized, filled with breath-smothering dust. The objects Klaus was able to glimpse in the steadily decreasing light seemed incongruously old, as if by mounting the stairs he was walking back along an ink-drawn timeline on a leaf of ancient vellum.

On the landing of the third floor his mother drew a match from her chatelaine, struck it, and lit the lantern, the flame swelling warmly on the wick. Klaus gasped as the corridor filled with faces. His ancestors' paint-crackled visages stared at him imploringly, some so vividly rendered they seemed to be peering through midnight windows, their hands or elbows resting on the edges of the frames as if they were sills. He thought that he might actually know some of their names. He was always asking his mother about his *Vorfahren*—particularly those on her side (his father knew little, and cared little, of his own Baden heritage). The portraits were so lifelike it was eerie to think that only a moment ago they had been looking into darkness. His mother was mounting the next set of stairs, the cadence of her steps even and unequivocal as the grandfather clock. As she moved the light went with her, again shrouding the faces. Klaus scurried up after her, glimpsing more family members on the subsequent levels. His mother moved quickly and so he was allotted only an ephemeral peek, but he noted that the likenesses became smaller and less ably wrought—austere, with crude lines and sparse coloring. They were also very, very old: rendered on wood panels and plaster rather than canvas. As the lantern light trailed along them it glinted off facets of bright, saturated color and gilded contours: jewels, gems—even a few crowns.

The fifth level was a single, long passage. The floor was carpeted—or coated—with what felt like moss. Klaus's footsteps became muted and his mother's trailing skirts hissed as they dragged along it. Ahead on the far left was a low, arched door—rich gold-brown in color, streaked with what looked like resin, and deeply scored. As his mother approached it she lifted the key ring and after several moments of nervous fumbling and sorting, she isolated one and slid it in the antiquated lock. The mechanism turned with a grinding *click* and the door opened, slowly and ponderously, revealing the first three steps of a narrow, winding stair. A smell like moldering leaves wafted down from the space above, accompanied by a hoarse yet stalwartly voice.

"*Komm herauf, Junge.*"

The words, and the way they'd been spoken, reminded Klaus of a witch from one of the *Märchens* his mother would read to him. He looked at her now, his expression one of panic in the dim lantern light. She knelt, brushed his tow-colored hair back with one quavering hand and held his face. Her eyes were moist as they brazenly scanned him, as if trying to memorize every detail. She reached in her pocket and drew out a small black book and a necklace of dark beads. Klaus recognized these, though he did not understand why they were being given to him now. She placed the necklace over his head and put the book in his hand. Then she pulled him to her and held him in a desperate embrace, pressing her lips to his forehead before turning him toward the door. "Oma Wespe is waiting," she said. Her words were strangely flat, belying the prior ardent display of physical affection.

"You will wait for me, yes?" Klaus said, his eyes moving to the lantern. The thought of walking back alone in the black through which they'd just passed seemed incomprehensible.

"Go on," his mother said sternly.

Klaus glanced back several times as he started up, making certain that she had not left, that the *light* had not left. His mother appeared calm, though her expression seemed deceptively impassive. As he approached the top step he heard the door close—and lock—behind him. He had a vision of her in that moment retreating hurriedly through the hour-woven shadows, lantern swaying, the twisted wooden furniture and the countenances rendered in tempera and oil flashing like things illuminated by lightning as she fled.

"Come, come . . . your mother has not left you," the voice above beckoned. It seemed to draw Klaus toward it, up the remaining stairs. The stink of rotting leaves grew more pungent, combining with the sweet scent of the aged rafters into a sort of cloying musk. Klaus became aware of his thundering heart, beating triple-time in relation to the cadence of his shoes scraping dryly on the steps. His fear was extreme, but he found that he could not account for it, for inscrutable as Oma Wespe was—as frighteningly as his relatives depicted her in their (presumably) apocryphal tales concerning the old woman's startling intuition (the way she seemed to know *everything* about them)—she was still his grandmother. His *great-great-great* grandmother, astoundingly. And she had, after all, favored him over the others with her gifts—like the black book the size of a deck of playing cards with EDDA embossed on the leather cover (the language so arcane and the fraktur font so ornate Klaus couldn't tell if it was a collection of verse or stories or spells), and the equally enigmatic necklace of ash tree beads arranged rosary-like on a silver strand which ended in a small wooden horse. The passage of these precious family artifacts to a nine-year-old boy had caused a fractious and acrimonious schism among the elder Zauberstabs. Klaus had heard his mother relaying to his father Oma Wespe's words as she had entrusted the objects to her great-great granddaughter, to be given to Klaus. *"You must be cautious with him at all times, Johanna: the boy is a Root, and the others like the gnawing dragon. He is the only living Zauberstab able to bear the Green Crown. He is vital to you all . . ."* Klaus had held the items only once—in his bedroom with his parents standing side by side before him, regarding him with uncharacteristic apprehension. After a few moments of bewildered examination, Klaus had handed them back to his mother who, reaffirming as if reading from a decree that they were and always would be *his*, placed the items in a bureau drawer and locked it. He had not seen them again until now.

But emerging on the top step, Klaus felt all at once ridiculous at having been so afraid. What *had* he been expecting? Certainly someone more imposing than the plain old woman seated in a plain old chair. The room was likewise as ascetic. There was a simple bed beneath a diminutive square window under the eaves. The window was occluded by a wooden shutter which was latched with a single bent nail crooked through a metal loop. The bare, pitched space was lit only by three tallow tapers stuck on the spikes of a crude, wrought-iron candelabrum standing on a simple wooden table to the right of the chair. Oma Wespe herself was gnarled and mummy-gaunt, with a thick white mane of wild, clotted locks glazed with a dull sheen the color of green lichen. The candlelight projected a silhouette of her hair onto the slanting ceiling above where she sat. Strangely, the shadows were inverted, casting an image of what appeared to be the bent branches of an immense winter tree. Her dress was somewhat contemporary (within the last quarter century or so) and was the flat black of full mourning. Her eyes, in contrast, were so thick with cataracts they seemed to glow like twin moons. She was staring ahead, as if considering a piece of exceptional art or music, but there was no painting to be seen here, nor pianist performing some hauntingly emotive sonata. Blind as they appeared, the eyes shifted, locating Klaus. A smile began to open like a widening crack across her desiccated face.

"Willkommen, young Herr Zauberstab," the old woman said.

"Herr *Baden*, Oma," Klaus said meekly. "My name is Klaus Baden."

"Ah, names . . . so many of them. They are grafted on and change and vanish. They are celebrated and disowned and revered and bastardized. They carry honor or infamy. Men marry and consume their wives' identities like they do everything else. But the fruit borne of the marriage bed is derived from the heartwood of separate trees—of father *and* mother. *Baden* may be the appellation written in the village records and pronounced by your father's tongue, but it is only half your blood—and for our purposes tonight, decidedly the lesser half."

"Purposes, Oma Wes—Zauberstab?"

The split grin closed slightly. "I see Ratatösk continues to carry his aspersions up and down the Tree. But it is fair, I suppose, for one to expect creatures of legend to look as they are rumored to appear. Tell me: do I look like a 'wasp' to you, *mein Kind*? " The boy shook his head and the cracked smile gaped once more. She held out a hand, pale and coarsely honed like something whittled, gesturing toward the bed. "Please, sit."

Klaus reluctantly crossed the room. The wooden necklace beads rattled as he settled onto the hard mattress. The blanket was brittle as an old tarp and stunk like *Fürze*. He wondered how she could live up here, without any books or games—without anyone—and only that feeble light. She reminded him of one of his mother's dolls that he'd discovered in the attic of his own house. The dingy cloth-and-yarn thing, missing an eye and with its thread mouth unraveling at one corner, had been seated alone before a tea set, the table latticed with web, the corpse of a fly filling the tiny cup before her. How long she had sat there, shut away in silence—a thing intentionally forgotten in order to be rediscovered later? Klaus's heart began to drum once more as he thought of his mother sliding the key in the battered door below. She had *re*-locked it after he'd gone up, hadn't she...

The old woman was looking him, still as that stowed doll and with the same canted grin, her eyes like white cocoons. Klaus asked why she wanted to see him, and that was when she had told him that he was there to watch her die. He had backed away slightly, his feet dangling off the bed. "But you don't look ill," Klaus said. It was true. Wasted and shrunken as she appeared, her posture was nonetheless upright, her speech fluent and articulate, her folded hands steady.

"It is not a matter of illness, but *time*," Oma Wespe said. She'd let the last word drag, disgorging along with it breath which corroborated the room's decaying leaf stench. "I am like a yew, you see, hollowed at the core after a long life sending down tendrils of regeneration to the native soil. Many I have sent—none more important than you, Klaus. But my powers of renewal are spent."

Despite a welling of pride, Klaus frowned. Scores of Zauberstabs had held prominent positions in the local government, the duchy, even the Reichstag. Bürgermeisters, lawyers, parliamentary representatives. Even the Fraus and Fraüleins of the family had established successful capital ventures beyond their duties of motherhood. His own mother, for instance, was the proprietor of their village's most profitable dress shop—income requisite, alas, to support Klaus's father's tavern bill as well as her ever burgeoning family. "But I've done nothing," Klaus replied. "I am not even a good student. I was whipped by my teacher for my low marks in history..."

Oma Wespe laughed; the sound was sonorous and had a slight ringing quality, like tonewood or a gently-struck bell. "I have faith that you will flourish when you are presented with something worth remembering.

Have you read the book I gave you?"

Klaus looked down at the black tome. He parted the pages slightly, shamefully. "I cannot understand it."

"Would you like me to tell you what it says?"

He nodded, closed the book and started to give it to her but the old woman held up a hand. "I have it here, you see," she said, pointing to her head, "every letter, every texture. It is yours now to assimilate."

"But how will I learn?"

"Follow along as I speak."

Klaus turned to the first page, his eyes moving across the lines as the old woman told a tale of a tree connected to the sky by its branches and to the soil by roots which reached deep into worlds and wells. She told of a dragon called Nidhögg who gnaws at those roots; of a great eagle with a hawk between its eyes who sits at the summit of the tree; of four harts which chew its leaves, and a squirrel that runs up and down the trunk, telling the dragon what the eagle sees. She told of the tree's sinuous might and resiliency, of the weight of eons it had been made to bear. She told of the people who had hung from it like ornaments. And as the old matriarch spoke, as if enunciating an invocation, the Gothic letters, beveled and curved like bars of hammered steel, became legible to Klaus. He glanced up at Oma Wespe, unable to suppress his joy. The withered woman's eyes were closed. She was still, but the branch-like shadows of her matted hair were swaying slowly on the ceiling, transformed by an un-felt wind into the turns and loops of script which flowed into words, and those words were names—hundreds of thousands of them—bifurcating infinitely as the silhouettes began to spread upwards, vine-like, along the roughly-hewn rafters. As they reached the apex of the roof the latter seemed to vanish, the sloping sides parting to reveal the sky into which the tendrils rose until each tip was touching a star. At the same moment there was a snapping like splintering wood, and then a noise like a fat tail dragging.

Klaus looked down from the light-studded tree fingers to the floor where a trio of slick, pseudopodian roots, thick as a man's leg and covered in spasming feelers, was emerging from beneath the hems of Oma Wespe's dress. His grandmother's face had become featureless—a shriveled, shrunken tuber, imploding as it sunk through the dress's neck hole. The roots, caked with russet clods, slid like sightless vermicules across the floor toward Klaus, rearing as they reached the bed. Klaus kicked backwards on the wretched coverlet but the appendages bound him easily—one holding each leg while the third slid along his sternum and impaled him through the mouth. It widened his trachea, branched into his lungs, the root hairs elongating, becoming engorged, usurping the bronchioles. Rhizomes and radicles proliferated from this bulbous core, exploring every inch of his interior atlas: fingers, toes, winding through his gut, supplanting his vertebral column and ribs, gulping spinal fluid and stomach acid, quaffing blood. The twin feelers binding his ankles laid him supine, moved up his body and penetrated his ears. They pierced his brainstem, split into peduncles, erupted into trillions of filamentary shoots which appropriated his neurons, plugged into his axon terminals, and stretched to the tips of his dendrites. They transformed the lobes of his cerebral hemispheres to fertile cambium into which was inscribed the chronicles of millennia—millions of names and dates and images and narratives.

Klaus sat up, aware now of phantom extremities descending from him, permeating the dead grain of the floorboards and the squared studs and the raw bracing beams, tunneling through the wattle and daub, and reaching deeper still into the motherland itself, fecund with the mool, the saponified flesh, the pitted bone, the teeth of his ancestors pebbling the earth like barren seeds tucked beneath the soil. He knew the *Vornamen* of the people in the pictures populating the halls below, could feel them looking at him, trapped within their frames. He sensed his mother's disquiet as she waited on the other side of the battered lancet door. He felt his living family members dangling from his prehensile boughs—his uncles and aunts and grandparents and cousins downstairs, waiting for him to descend, waiting for the reassurance that they and their progeny were safe to cross the continents and the oceans without fear, that those alien loams or brackish waters would not dilute the blood or sever their far-seeking limbs. Waiting for confirmation that, through him as it had been through Oma Wespe, the three blind roots clutching the ballast below the foundation would remain firmly fixed.

He drank their emotions, drawing them up through the walls and transpired them like vespers into the ether, past the moon-parted clouds to the whirling coruscations where the hallowed dead crowded the stars.

Klaus knelt on the bed and opened the window. The wind soughed as it entered, the clean air carrying with it the singed accent of some fire safely distant. He walked to the chair where Oma Wespe's dress lay unoccupied and crumbled. He folded it with care; it was a relic now, a bequest to Zauberstab posterity.

Below, he heard the door unlock and open.

"Klaus?" his mother called. Her tone was formal, oddly reverent. "Would you like to come down now?"

Klaus carried the book to the table where the taper flames fluttered in the night breath. He placed the little volume on the surface, then removed the necklace and coiled it atop the brittle leather cover, centering the horse so that it stood within the pile of ash beads. *Yggdrasil*, he whispered, running his thumb along the breadth of the tiny equine. It was the oldest tale—the one from which his roots drew their deepest draughts—but it was not the only story. There would be manifold fresh shoots to quench, and it would be his privilege to sustain that prideful thirst for the long century to come.

Cradling the dress in his arms, Klaus blew out the candles and started across the room toward the stairs, finding his way with ease through the black.

WHEN SLEEP AT LAST

Douglas Thompson

———◆———

TODOR HAD HATED the Sassars since he was a child, and now that Senator Drest had won the election he felt as if his time had come at last, his views and resentment vindicated. Todor's father had been a hunter too, in these bleak hilly borderlands, and had passed on to him all the skills that he and his wife Zorana now used to put food on the table each week: deer and squirrel and occasional wild boar. He respected the deer and admired their beauty, strength and grace, and yet he felt no remorse when he shot and skinned and butchered them. He chose his targets carefully, understood the principles of conservation, always avoiding juveniles or pregnant mothers, choosing instead the males of a certain age whose glory days were probably gone and who he might be doing a favor anyway, letting their lives end with a bang rather than a long sordid decline as the young bucks progressively wounded them. Todor understood that he was part of nature.

So much for deer, but as for Sassars: Todor felt they should each know better than to enter border land and attempt to pierce the boundaries of his beloved and hard-won homeland. Back before independence, how they and their children had lorded it up when he was young: coming up here with their families and taking all the best jobs. Todor's own father had lost out on the promotion to senior lecturer that he should have got at the university, lost out to some loud smarmy Sassar git with a posh accent who'd gone to the right school. That was the saddest and most galling thing back then: that Todor's own people had been prejudiced against themselves, brought up to regard themselves as second-class citizens, eager to appoint a Sass whenever and wherever possible in the belief that they were some superior race that would always make a better job of whatever they did than someone who actually grew up and belonged here in the homeland.

Today Todor had been out on the moors and tracked and shot a stag, and was dragging it back down the valley on horseback, still the best mode of transport in this territory despite all the technology which roamed over and above it now. His government drone, provided to him as standard issue for a Tracker in the Border Defence Force, was only allowed to assist him in his 'domestic' business such as deer culling, when its autonomous border duties went quiet. This occurred around midday today, as Todor knew it would from experience, when most of the people smugglers and refugees had given up or gone to ground until darkness fell again. Tonight would be Todor's first all-night shift since last week and he found himself looking forward to it more than usual. It was good money, but also he felt: good, noble work, that his forefathers would have been proud of him for.

Back at the cottage, Todor found that Zorana had the stock boiling already, must have glimpsed his figure with its spoil from the kitchen window even at great distance, rounding the head of the high pass. She was sharpening the knives, and they set about the deer carcass together in the shed with skill and alacrity born of long experience. They were accustomed to the rich brassy smell of blood and its constantly renewing and deepening stain upon the rough brown of their overalls, the good sight of it running in the ancient stone channels on the barn floor.

The radio was on when they sat down for dinner, as the sun was beginning to set behind the dense forest of pines in the foothills beyond their pasture. Drest was speaking, *President* Drest now as they would have to get used to calling her, expanding on her acceptance speech of last week and her many bold new plans for the homeland, how the property of Sassars was to be seized by the state at last, their bank accounts to be frozen. And the border skirmishes, the night incursions of refugees from their broken towns and cities to the south: this is where Todor most pricked up his ears, even laying his knife and fork down, leaving his fresh venison steaming on the plate, while he stood up to turn up the volume.

No more chickening around then, a strong stance at last . . . Todor said when the news story finished and he switched it to some traditional music, not wanting to spoil his mood or his dinner with any of the other less important tittle-tattle of the world's comings and goings for the day. Zorana had some news, she said, not unconnected with this. Her nephew and his wife and baby were selling their house down south and coming home, she said they'd told her today, inspired by Drest's victory, coming back across the border to resume their citizenship before any immigration clampdown the new administration might bring in could potentially complicate things. *Complicate?* Todor asked, helping himself to more carrots and turnips, *They're not Sass, why would they have any difficulty coming home to here?*

Well that's what I told them, and to quote your name at the border post if necessary, since I'm sure you'll be held in high esteem in official circles for the work you do, or will be, for the new regime. Todor nodded his head in silent agreement and in slow, secret, solemn pride. Zorana reached around for her photograph of the young family that she kept on the kitchen window sill and beamed at it happily as if she was face-to-face with her home-come relatives already.

THE NIGHT AIR was sharp and pleasingly chill when Todor stepped out a few hours later. A fifty percent likelihood of snow had been forecast for the night. He drove the first ten miles in his jeep to the remote ridge above Chatto, then released the drone from its place under cover in the boot and set it off to hover a thousand feet above him as he proceeded on foot. The moon, almost full, was rising up out of the lower lands to the south so that he might not even need his infra-red goggles until the cloud-cover thickened. He approached the edge of a vast pine forest that he knew well, the long lonely path through which he always enjoyed, sometimes sighting fox and deer along the way. When he emerged from its other side he knew he would have a full overview of the twenty mile stretch of border that had been assigned to him to patrol tonight.

Todor was not an ignorant, uneducated or uncreative man, whatever the prejudices towards him of city dwellers—those who he occasionally encountered when they ventured out to these parts in summer in search of relaxing holidays amid what they regarded as blissful emptiness, which in fact to Todor's eye was a place of business, always buzzing with unseen life. He had been a student once in his youth, in the great historic city sixty miles to the north, and had gone out with a girl who was at Art School, who had led him around various galleries and museums to share with him the source of her inspirations and aspirations.

One picture he had seen there often returned to his memory as he entered this and other similar remote forests along border country. It had been by some German Romantic painter of the 19th century, of a French Napoleonic soldier standing alone looking into the edge of a vast German forest. Angela, that had been her name, had explained that the painting referred not just to Napoleon's ultimate failure to conquer Germany, but also to the defeat of the Romans two thousand years earlier in the same impenetrable forests beyond the frontier of the River Rhine. Some people had been likening Drest to Hitler recently, but Todor considered the analogy unfair. The homeland had been enslaved to others for centuries, millenia, it had never had any colonies and empires of its own, other than in alliance with its pompous, militaristic neighbor. We weren't about to conquer anyone, let alone the world, only to *Get our own house in order,* yes that was the phrase that President Drest had used. She was like an empress ushering in some golden era the homeland had hitherto always been denied until now. Now was its moment at last.

These were Todor's forthright, uplifting thoughts at least, when the drone network, his and the others all 'talking' to each other, picked up the first infra-red targets of the night. Two human traces, his visor readout told him, as he paused to fold it down over his face, about as far from the electrified wire as he currently was, which was perfect timing.

A third trace could also be seen downhill from them in the other direction, clearly a guide, a people trafficker who had got them to this point, perhaps placed some bypass device on the fence at a point he had directed them to. Todor's drone overhead had been engineered for complete silence, deadly as a barn owl if it needed to be, although Todor usually preferred to conserve its battery and fire off any shots himself.

Leaving the edge of the woods, just before the moon vanished behind clouds and he had to pull his full infra-red headset down, he caught sight of the gnarled and twisting roots of some of the much older trees that pre-dated the current plantation, oak trees that probably carried the scars of bullets and swords from the skirmishes of previous centuries. Something about those roots made him shiver tonight, touching upon some buried memory perhaps. As he walked on it came to him. The burned-black bodies of women and children that he had witnessed at the aftermath of the massacre the Sassars had carried out in Freedom Square when the homeland resistance protested the attempt to suppress the independence vote. It had been a peaceful political demonstration, a party atmosphere almost, handmade banners swaying in the spring sunshine before the army had turned their tanks on them. Like wolves preying on sheep, foxes let loose in a hen house. That black day had marked the end of innocence, the start of the short and savage war. The memory was just what Todor needed at that moment, to set his pulse racing and his put his blood on the boil. He could see on his visor that the targets were running now, so he followed suit, aiming to reach the wire before them.

It was a simple trick that Berovic had taught him, that he said he often used on his stretch 50 miles west. Todor whispered into his mouthpiece to tell the drone to power down this section of the fence and wait on his signal to re-charge at treble strength. The Sassars would think they'd lucked out or found their guide's bypass section, and rather than hang about might just plunge right in there, try to scale or cut the ten-feet-high barrier. Todor was a quarter of a mile from them but his telephoto-toggle meant he felt near enough to touch them. A man and a woman, husband and wife perhaps. He didn't think of them as human, but as lower than animals, particularly at moments like these. He whispered the code, E52, and the drone switched the power back on, with one target at the top of the wire, the other half way down. They screamed and smoked in a brief flash of light then fell on the homeland side, which was always a relief to Todor. The drone could lift him to the other side if required, but it was against official protocols which meant he might need one of Gorgi's pals to fiddle the software afterwards. Gorgi, like Berovic, could be trusted, was an old solider too, in on the same racket as Todor. They didn't talk about it much when they met, no longer needed to. Men you fought beside in the civil war could be trusted unto death. If you talked about shit like this, the old team took care of you and you'd be found a month later with your tongue cut out in a ditch beside some lonely road miles from anywhere.

Officially . . . a word that Todor and the older guards laughed out of the side of their mouths at. Officially, you were supposed to arrest intruders like these, cuff them and escort them down to the nearest barracks, but nobody he knew did anymore, not with the smaller parties, the ones and the twos, the stragglers. The border force were overstretched these days anyway. The Sassar towns had been disintegrating into crime and starvation in the wake of the economic meltdown their once belligerent nation had brought upon itself with its flagrant defiance of international law, the atrocities it had sanctioned against Todor's people, the crippling UN sanctions imposed upon it in retaliation. Hell mend them. They should have stayed home and stewed in their own self-made disaster zone of a country that had turned its back on the rest of the civilized world, roasted their own dogs on bonfires, as far as Todor was concerned. For what they had done to his race, his country, not just in the recent war but for centuries of arrogant oppression and colonial exploitation: for this they could never pay dearly enough for him. They had forfeited their right to be human by de-humanizing others. What goes around. History had tipped against them now.

Todor even had a code for what happened next, one that he had programmed into his drone. He and the Owlbot worked together like a farmer and his trusty sheepdog. *D42* he whispered, then *G19*. He'd been reading for some time before the election that Drest might be planning to strengthen the border fence, replace it with a solid wall of concrete or steel. For that reason, he and Berovic and Gorgi had agreed a sub-routine for the drone to follow that would ensure it dug a grave pit three hundred yards from the border line, just to be on the safe side, clear of any possible future foundation excavation or trial cores.

When Todor reached the foot of the fence he saw that the male target was sprawled unconscious face down in the mud, upper limbs sprawled in ungainly pose, legs tangled upside down in the barbed wire above. He drew his rifle and fired three muffled shots at close quarters, one to the head, two to the back near the heart. Then something startled him. An object broke free unexpectedly from the female and snagged half way down the fence. The woman opened her mouth and began to say something. How he resented the inconvenient historic fact that they spoke the same language as he did. This of course being yet another dimension of their villainy, how they had driven the language of his forefathers underground, tried to stamp out their culture. He tried never to see the faces of the fugitives, let alone hear their voices speak. *Please . . .* was the only word she got out before Todor, almost reflexively, had fired a couple of shots into the center of her spread-eagled form. He saw that her long hair had fallen loose anyway, covering up her face like a drawn curtain.

Then the bundle on the fence began to cry out. What he had thought at a distance had merely been a pack on her back had been, it seemed, a papoose, a baby carrier. The sound shocked Todor to his core. In a flash he was remembering the sound of his own daughter crying when she was newborn and he thought of her far away from all this in the city to the north, safe and unaware, blind to all this darkness. He raised his gun. The child writhed, stretched out its little hand, recoiling from the harshness it found, the barbed wire like strange festive holly. Then he was remembering that other birth, of his own son, who had died in the civil war, before even his seventeenth birthday, before he'd even kissed a girl. Where was *his* son, *his* family?—the children he might have fathered, were he not now beneath the ground for ten long years? Todor looked down at his own finger on the trigger, wondering why he had not yet fired. He found himself moving closer, against his will. His limbs shaking. The sound, he had to stop the sound. It made no sense. He didn't need to get any closer, so why was he doing so? Babies all look the same. It would only grow up and produce more, over and over, the endless proliferation of their kind. Sound could travel so far in these hills at night. He had to stop it, terminate the unanticipated situation. He fired.

But the silence that came then was not what he expected. Not the silence of the hills and the moors that he thought he knew. His legs gave out under him and he knelt, sat down in the mud and stared into the distance to the west, where a patch of cloud was clearing and he could dimly see a twinkling of stars. It was the silence of the death of his own child, his own death, the laughing grin of a skull at all humanity, the ultimate, monstrous joke. He was a beetle, an insect, and nothing could stop the boot that was crushing us all. Truly, the devil walked upon the earth. His mother would be ashamed of him. This fact flooded in and alarmed his mind so suddenly that he fled from the thought, knew that he had to expel it at all costs. He staggered to his feet again and mechanically, with an enormous weariness in his limbs, resumed his task of cleaning up the mess that had been created.

Again he felt ashamed, that he could not cut the mother and child down from the wire himself, as he might usually have done, but had to instruct the drone to do it for him. It would not be as careful and dexterous as him. Less *respectful*, yes that was the word he admitted to himself, reluctantly. Small fragments of flesh and blood left on the wire for the rain or snow or the birds to clean away. He had two hessian sacks with him, the child would share one with the mother. As the Owlbot whirred its little blades in the chill night air above him, Todor worked beneath it like its servant, never looking up, heaving one body after the other into the bags and tethering them up so that the drone could lift them in a single flight to the disposal sight. He dimmed his infra-red vision so as to see as little as possible of what his hands held. There were no reds, only black and white. No blood, only dry and wet, cold and lukewarm. The child's body felt like a lifeless doll, nothing more, and again he unwillingly remembered his own daughter and a doll he had once mended for her. He imagined the mocking laughter of Satan burning the back of his neck again as if to ask: why he could not repair this doll?

When the drone had backfilled the perfect six-foot square of dirt, Todor sat down on the mossy ground near it, with his back against an old tree, and lit himself a cigarette to try to stop the shaking that had taken hold in his whole body. Snow had begun falling from the night sky high above, in increasingly large flakes, which would be a blessing, covering up his tracks and traces and the square of disturbed ground itself. It might even stay frozen now for weeks after this. The drone came down and rested on the ground facing him at close quarters, folding its limbs like a faithful dog. In the light of the LCD screen of its interface, he now saw that both he and it were spattered with blood, which the fresh snow might yet erase. An old soldier had once told him that there were only two ways to dull the traumatic memories of atrocities you'd witnessed. The first was to live through enough decades of peace afterwards for the memories to fade through overuse, forcing yourself to picture them every day. The second was to crowd out and overwrite those memories with fresh ones of other atrocities, ones in which you avenged the first set. The soldier had said he didn't have time for the first method, and he'd been right. He'd heard some months later that he died in an ambush the week after their conversation.

Todor spoke to the drone. He knew it could only respond with silent dispassionate words on its glowing display, and something about this felt consoling at this moment, as if talking to a cold, dispassionate God, who dealt only in the hard currency of facts. *Owlbot 87b . . . erase your memory of this evening.*

Event Log Blanked As Requested . . . came the glib reply a moment later, letters dancing in demonic procession across the sickly green screen.

Erase sub-routines D42 and G19 . . . he further instructed it. From now on, he decided, he would play all this straight. Cover, at the very least, in the unlikely even there should ever be investigations. Berovic would think he'd gone soft, but this was the explanation he would spit back at him and the topic would never again be discussed. He was getting too old for this job. When would this sick lurching in his stomach subside? It was like the first hunt his father took him on as a child, his horror of cutting the deer open, the smell as its innards had slurped out. His father and uncle had laughed at him then for his childlike squeamishness and he had vowed never again to harbor such weakness. No one had warned him that life might be a circle like this rather than a straight line. That he might weaken with age instead of strengthening, and return to the girlishness of a child. Maybe old people were just like children again, right down to the nappies.

A thought came to Todor, of something Gorgi had told him once, that the drones had protocols to protect their operators. Reaching the nadir of his private despair he addressed the machine again out of curiosity: *Owlbot 87b, raise and prime your weapon.* Its lights flickered for a second then it raised its mechanical arm and spun its barrel in his face. *Shoot me in the head . . .* he said, then waited, trying to overwrite and mask the sickness in his stomach with a new one. But it didn't seem to work. Was he no longer even afraid to die? *What are you waiting for then? Why can't you do it? Lost your nerve?* he taunted it.

Unable To Harm Fellow Homeland Defense Operative . . . came the answer at last. Grimly, he laughed out loud. So that was it then, the joke Gorgi wanted him to see. He was recognized by a robot as its brother, a cold metal machine. He got to his feet and dusted himself down, preparing for the long walk back down the hillside through the deep forest. A few minutes later the drone received a signal to join its fellows on another hunt further east and they parted company for the night, its compact rectilinear form unfolding its wings like a hellish bat and setting off undaunted into the flurry of weather overhead, its tiny red eyes glowing.

Walking alone back down the long track through the woods, he switched his headlamp on as the snow fell in thick flakes, its endless motion slow and hypnotic. He wondered at all the branches and fronds around him and reaching far above, arching over at times like the vaults of some enormous cathedral. The light on his helmet lit everything from below like a marvel as he moved through it, as if to remind him that there was no escape from his own view of the world and his own role and responsibility within it. Did he create this world by revealing it as he moved through it like this, like the captain of a ship? Or did it somehow create him, make his every action inevitable? What was the difference between a robot of metal and one of flesh? Glimpsing pairs of lights in the woods he switched the lamp off for five minutes and knelt down to watch a lone grey wolf crossing his path, stalking a deer it had seen on the other side. He could have shot either of them, but instead he felt a strange impulse to hail the wolf, address it as he would some fellow woodsman, share with it the food in his pocket, let it lick in curiosity all the blood off his hands. The wolf had no choice either.

RETURNING HOME AS THE FIRST dim glow of dawn was starting to emerge all around the horizon, Todor found himself half-heartedly preparing stories to tell Zorana to account for the excessive blood on his uniform. He would have to say it was from some wild animal he had shot, but since he had no meat with him would also have to say that it had only feigned death then wriggled away injured from his grasp and escaped before he could get a shot off. As it was, no such explanations prove necessary, since she did not even notice his clothes before he had taken them off and taken them to the laundry room. Zorana was too engrossed in putting up Christmas decorations, having heard the unexpected good news while Todor was away that her nephew had decided to come home even earlier than expected and intended to be dropping by their house late afternoon. Not having many visitors these days in their rural isolation, they usually left decorations until as late as possible, when in-laws and children might be coming round. *Why the change of plan?* Todor asked. *I thought they weren't coming for another two weeks at least?*

He was but they heard that new rules might class their baby as Sassar because he was born there, Zorana answered from above from where she stood on a chair, her head lost among the gaudy heaven of green, red and gold colored crepe and tinsel . . . *So Grigor said they were taking no chances, were going to go by some secret route over the border a friend of his knows rather than risk official channels and the sooner the better . . .*

What? Todor whispered, his voice gone unexpectedly hoarse. *What age did you say their child was?* His back was turned to her, and looking down at his hands, still shaking very slightly, he saw that he was absentmindedly holding a carved painted figure he had lifted up from the kitchen table, of the baby Jesus in his cot. It was from the little nativity scene that his great grandfather had carved back before the First World War, a beautiful thing that had been handed down in the family ever since. He recalled that the infant had once even had painted eyes and lips, as was the usual tradition, but saw that now the color had faded, as if the child was asleep. The heirloom could only grow more strange and valuable over time, provided it was cherished by each generation.

The Summer King's Day

Timothy Granville

———◆———

IN THE DISTANCE a bell started ringing. It came steadily closer, drawing shouts and the sound of beaten pots and pans from the sunlit town. Somewhere a child screamed.

"This must be it," said Emma.

Duncan didn't take his eyes from the end of the street. "Yeah."

She smiled uneasily, conscious of the crowd collecting around them. Ten minutes ago there had only been some knots of tourists, a pensioner or two waiting by the war memorial and the door of The George and Dragon. It had seemed like everything might be fine. Now Emma glanced again at Duncan's face and saw it was a mistake to come here. She could have cried.

Poppy was clinging to her leg. "Mama! Carra!"

She picked her up. "Don't be scared."

"Moosica! Moosica!"

"Yes, there is music. It might get loud. But remember it's just a game."

"The locals are taking it pretty seriously," said Duncan.

He was right. Further up the hill Emma could hear shrieks and catcalls and howls. A tarnished kitchen sink had appeared from somewhere and now a teenage boy was rattling a length of copper pipe around the basin. More people pressed into the steep cobbled street, beginning to jostle each other. The stupid thing was they were here to get away from crowds and noise, that was the whole point of choosing a place like Elveley. She hadn't known about all this when she'd booked the cottage. It was such strange luck that they should be here on this day.

Trying to dismiss the thought, she pressed closer to Duncan. "Are you OK?"

"Yeah, fine," he said, still without turning his head.

"We don't have to stay."

"It's fine. I said I wanted to see." The procession was coming their way now. The people that had been lingering in the sunshine at the top of the street were spilling down it, parting to reveal the bell ringer dressed like a Morris dancer and a tall figure walking beside him.

Poppy must have seen this too because she started yelling, "Ma! Ma! Ma!"

"That's right," said Emma. "It *is* a man."

Poppy looked at her in that wincing, hunching way that reminded her so much of Duncan. "Now don't be silly," she told her. "Mummy and Daddy are here. It's a game. It's a man playing dressing-up."

"And he really is taking it seriously," said Duncan.

"Yeah. What's his mask made of?"

"Some kind of burr, apparently. They stick them to a balaclava. There's a pamphlet about it in the cottage."

She caught his sidelong look at the people around them, the movement of his chest as he took a deep breath. Please, she prayed. Not now. Please can we have one good day together?

Poppy started up again. "Hem! Hem! Hem!"

"We're not going home just yet," said Duncan.

Emma stroked her head. "It's all right, poppet."

But she clearly wasn't the only child to find the approaching figure unnerving. Many of the younger ones watched from behind parents' legs or demanded to be placed on shoulders. A little boy burst into tears as his father tried to take a picture of him. The older children made more of a performance of fear, goading each other to rush up into the heart of the procession and then run away screaming again down the hill. It happened often enough that it might even have been part of the ceremony.

The figure came closer, stalking towards the three of them through the milling onlookers. Whoever was wearing the costume played his role well, moving deliberately and holding himself upright, ignoring the tourists' camera phones and the neighbors braying in his face. Still, Emma couldn't say that he looked much like a king. His body was hidden in a robe covered with bleached grasses and other dry things, with a shaggy cowl framing the burr mask. Sheaths of bark had made his hands into misshapen paws. The crown of wildflowers seemed a grotesque afterthought, a mockery like Christ's crown. As his head turned, Emma saw flashes of white skin showing through the holes in the mask but no eyes or mouth. She hugged Poppy against her side to reassure her.

Taking another glance at Duncan, she realized he was no longer watching the procession. He was staring down at the cobbles, his forehead knitted, his jaw set. The crowd kept shouting, the bell rang on and on. She wanted to touch him but so often it just made things worse.

"You're not doing this for me, are you?" she asked.

"I'll be OK. Leave it."

Poppy interrupted them, yelling, "Dink! Dink!"

"Are you thirsty?" Emma asked, before seeing the man running forwards from the crowd holding a glass. "Oh that's right, he's having a drink. It's a bit early, isn't it?"

"It's part of the ritual."

The figure's head went back and the second man guided the contents of the glass down a funnel into the mouth hole of the mask. There were hoots and cheers from the crowd.

"How long's he going to keep that up?"

"All day. He has to drink whatever's offered to him."

"Wow. He'll get smashed."

"Shashed! Sashid!"

Emma laughed, even Duncan managed a smile. "Yes, Poppy," she said. "Poor old Summer King."

"Don't worry about him," said a voice at her shoulder.

She found herself looking at a big white-haired man who had come to stand alongside them in the crowd. He must have been imposing once but now his back was rounding into a hump, forcing his head down towards her. A hearing aid coiled round each fleshy ear.

"Oh, hi," she said.

The old man stooped further until his eyes were at Poppy's level. "Who's this then?"

"This is Poppy. Are you going to say hello, poppet?"

"Who's this, eh? Who's this?"

Emma felt Poppy shrink in her arms. She tried raising her voice. "I think we're feeling shy today."

"He knows how to look after himself," the old man told Poppy. "And if he don't, he can't do much complaining about it."

"Oh? Why not?"

"Why not?" he said, seeming to notice Emma for the first time. "He's a quiet 'un, that's why not."

"Kiyet!" said Poppy, putting a finger on her lips. "Ssss!"

"Ah!" said the old man. He held up a thick finger of his own, his hand trembling. "You see *we* know. He can't say nothing all day, can he? Otherwise it's bad luck for Elveley."

"Really?"

"That's how it's always been. He's quiet, he sticks to the quiet places. You just stay away from him."

"She's a scaredy-cat. I don't think she's going anywhere near."

Emma glanced round, trying to check on Duncan. His eyes were narrowed and his forehead lowered as though facing into a wind. She followed his gaze and saw that the heart of the procession had almost drawn level with them. A cry went up from the bell ringer: "The Summer King is here! Let us show him our good cheer!"

The rough music of pots and pans swelled and Poppy let out a whimper. "Now what's all this fuss?" said the old man.

"It's probably a bit . . ." began Emma.

He cut her off. "There's no need to worry, is there? Not if you show some respect."

"Well, we're working on that."

But if the old man heard he wasn't in a joking mood. "They all forget. They can't even get him the proper ruddy flowers. But then things don't grow like they should no more."

He shook his head, muttering to himself. Then his face broke into an odd smirk. "Summer King! *We* know his real name, don't we?"

Emma was about to speak when the noise of the procession rose again. She turned and was confronted by the burr mask, only feet away, a bristling travesty of a face. At that moment a hiss escaped from Duncan.

"Hey? Are you OK?"

He gripped her arm, starting to pant. "I . . . No . . . "

"Remember to breathe. Do you want to go?"

"Wait, I . . . "

As he was holding on to her a middle-aged woman and a younger man approached them. "There you are Uncle John," said the woman, addressing the old man. "You had us worried."

The old man looked like Poppy when she was being told off, feigning interest in something at the top of the street. "I never asked no one to put themselves out."

"What have you been getting up to?"

"Getting up to, she says. I've been talking to little Cathie here."

The woman gave Emma a tight smile. "This isn't Cath, John. Michael, help your grandfather."

The two of them led the old man off into the crowd that was drifting downhill in the wake of the Summer King. Emma set out against the flow, steering Duncan away from the tolling of the bell.

Now the procession had passed Poppy found her voice, pointing after it and shouting, "Ma! Ma! Ma!"

"Yes, poppet," said Emma. "But it's all right. We'll all be all right."

BACK AT THE COTTAGE Emma fed Poppy and put her down for her nap. Once she'd stopped squawking and kicking the travel cot she went to find Duncan. He was lying down on the bed with his back to her and the curtains drawn.

"Would you like soup for lunch?"

She whispered it, thinking he might have dropped off. But he shook his head. "I'm not hungry, thanks. Could you give me a minute?"

"OK."

She shut the bedroom door and went through into the kitchen and stood at the window. Past the garden hedge a view of the surrounding countryside unfolded under a flawless sky. She tried to look out at it but her eye kept being drawn to a bluebottle still buzzing in a cobweb on the window frame, gathering the dusty mesh like a spool. She felt strange, apprehensive, as though there was something awful she had to face but she'd temporarily forgotten what. Panic could be so contagious. No, she couldn't think like that. At least it hadn't become a full-blown attack. At least the afternoon might still be salvageable.

"You need to eat," she said out loud.

She sat down with a plate of leftovers, half-listening to The World at One—more Australian wildfires, someone dead from heat stress in Birmingham. Then she remembered the pamphlet.

It was lying on the sofa in the living room: *The Elveley Summer King* by A.P. Wilsher. While she ate she read about the ceremony. It lasted all day and ended with the Summer King being driven beyond the bounds of the town and his costume burnt. There was some comparison to scapegoat customs in other folk traditions, to the Jack in the Green. No one seemed to understand why the Elveley ceremony took place today rather than in May or at harvest time. Emma looked for the Summer King's other name but couldn't see any mention of it. She found it hard to concentrate on the text though because her mind kept going back to the morning, the way Duncan's attack had started as the mask turned towards them. Or had she imagined that? She skipped forwards a couple of pages and met the stare of a grainy Summer King flanked by young men in bellbottoms, his eyes two shadows fringed with skin.

"Hello."

Duncan was standing in the kitchen doorway. "Hi," she said, smiling and closing the pamphlet. "How are you feeling?"

"A bit shaky. OK."

"Would you be up to going for a walk this afternoon? I thought we could drive out of town and find somewhere nice."

He shrugged. "I guess so."

"OK. Good . . . Are you going to have something first?"

"No, no."

"You should."

"I'm fine."

He crossed over to the sink. When he bent to drink from the tap Emma quickly tucked the pamphlet under one of the placemats.

POPPY WOKE UP in a boisterous mood. She thumped round the cottage pulling things off surfaces and refused to put on clothes or sun cream and gave them one of those awful shocks when both of them thought the other was minding her and they turned round to find her gone. Duncan had been packing the car at the time and had left the front door open. Emma rushed out of the cottage shouting her name, running round the empty garden and into the road, looking up and down it helplessly. Then Duncan called her back inside. He'd found Poppy behind one of the living room curtains tearing pages out of the guest book. She was so relieved she told her off more than she probably should have.

Just as they'd finished packing and had found the car keys and Poppy had finally got over her tantrum at being carried outside by Duncan instead of her, Emma saw Hugh the cottage owner appear at the gate. He waved and came striding up the drive towards them. She heard Duncan swear under his breath.

Hugh stopped by the car, hands on hips. "Hi folks. It's another scorcher, isn't it? Thought I'd pop over to check everything was all right."

"Great, thanks," said Emma. "It's such a lovely house."

"Nothing you need?"

"No, everything's great."

"Good stuff. The other thing I thought I'd mention is our little festival today. It is worth catching at some point. Really rather unique."

"Oh, we've seen," she said, trying not to look at Duncan.

"Excellent. And what did you think? All a bit pagan, eh?"

"Car!" said Poppy, waving her hand to mime a steering wheel. "Brum!"

Hugh smiled at her. "Is that right? Are you taking Mummy and Daddy for a spin? Well I hope you're not going far."

"Neh," said Poppy, less sure of herself.

"No, good. It's hardly the done thing."

"What do you mean?" said Emma.

"It's one of the rules of the Summer King's Day, no one's meant to leave Eleveley. They even put markers at the edge of town. Personally I think it's an excuse to get everyone to the pub."

Duncan suddenly spoke up. "And what happens if you leave?"

"Some terrible fate, obviously. But I expect it's different for us outsiders. Between you and me, I've broken curfew once or twice myself."

"Car! Car!" said Poppy.

"Yes, point taken young lady. You've got my number if you need anything. OK, bye."

"Bye," said Emma, and Poppy started to wave.

Hugh turned at the gate. He laughed and called back, "Enjoy your taboo trip."

They got into the baking car. As Duncan was doing up his belt he muttered, "Prick."

"She's learning words all the time."

He glanced in the rear view mirror. "Yeah. Sorry."

"Anyway, what's the matter? He was being friendly."

"I don't know. He winds me up. All that 'Hi folks' and 'Good stuff.'"

"Do you want to stay in this afternoon? We can."

"Do you?"

They looked at each other. Then Poppy started kicking the back of Duncan's seat. "Car! Brum! Brum!"

He sighed. "Sounds like we're going then."

"It does, doesn't it? All right my poppet."

THEY DROVE OUT of Elveley down empty roads, past empty pavements. As they were leaving the town Emma noticed the armfuls of foliage that had been lashed to two of the lampposts and a traffic bollard, but she decided not to point them out to Duncan. Soon the houses gave way to fields and rickety barns and distant hills tufted with trees. On an impulse Emma pulled off the main road and they found themselves traveling through riddled shade down a tunnel of overhanging branches.

"So where are we heading?" she asked.

Duncan was looking at his phone. "I don't know. We're not far from somewhere called Elveley Barrow. We could try there?"

"What is it?"

"Not sure. Nature. It's all just green on the map."

"Sounds perfect."

Following Duncan's directions Emma turned onto a lane which climbed a steep hill. At the top they joined an even narrower track gouged with ruts and potholes. When they came to a passing place Duncan said, "You might as well park here. We're pretty close now."

They got Poppy out of her car seat and set off along the track. Though she babbled to herself on Duncan's shoulders neither of the adults spoke. Thick hedges either side of them blinkered their view, the air was loud with crickets. After a minute they came to an overgrown stile.

"Here we go," said Duncan. "Holding on tight, Poppy?"

As Emma pulled herself up through the snarl of vegetation, she caught sight of the landscape beyond the hedge.

"Duncan!" she said. "Wow!"

They stepped down into a chirring meadow carpeted with tall grasses and wildflowers. It rose gently to the crest of a hill capped by a small wood. To their left over the shoulder of the hill there was a view of bluish fields and stands of trees and an occasional toy farmhouse in the valley below. They started in the direction of the wood along a faint path trampled through the grass. Apart from a plane laying silent vapor trails and one or two wheeling birds of prey, everything was still under the heavy heat.

"Tees! Tees!" said Poppy.

"*Trees*," corrected Emma. "Yes, that's where we're going. Isn't it lovely here?"

"Mmm," said Duncan. "I'm not used to all this sky."

She saw he was squinting at the ground. She took his hand. "Come on. It'll be fine under the trees."

"Tees!" said Poppy.

"Yes, there'll be *three* of us under the *trees*. You and me and Daddy."

"Ma! Ma!"

Emma glanced round the meadow. "What man?"

"Ma! Ma!"

"Are you saying Mama?"

But her eyes had narrowed. She turned to Emma, wincing, thrusting out an arm. "Beeg."

"Can you see where she's pointing?" asked Duncan.

Emma peered towards the wood. "Not really . . . There's no one there, Poppy."

They carried on walking. Poppy had gone quiet and was holding onto Duncan's hair with both hands. She often had these funny little outbursts, but this one had unsettled Emma. The landscape seemed different from her first delighted glimpse of it. The reaches of sky and open countryside left her feeling small, exposed. Dry chitinous noise filled her ears, the apprehension that had been creeping up on her in the cottage started to return. She kept having to look up, checking the meadow again and again.

She couldn't give in to worrying like this. She gripped Duncan's hand tighter, made herself smile. "This is nice. Thanks for letting us come."

They made their way to the edge of the wood and clambered up a bank into the trees. It was cooler in the shade, a breeze set the leaves shivering. A hidden bird sang overhead, another responded.

"Den! Den! Den!" said Poppy.

Duncan craned his neck up at her. "You want to get down?"

"All right. But stay with Mummy and Daddy."

They paused while Duncan lifted Poppy off his shoulders. "I wonder if this is the barrow," he said, nodding at the curving bank behind them.

"Why would there be a wood on it? Is that normal?"

He shrugged. "No idea."

Emma shook her head too. She was always a bit lost in the countryside, she didn't even know what kind of trees these were. As she was trying to guess she noticed that the nearest trunk had been carved with graffiti. There were the usual initials enclosed by hearts but also crosses, stranger marks. She traced one of the shapes dug into the smooth grey bark, then at some disquiet turned automatically to look for Poppy.

She was poking her head out from behind the roots of a tree, grinning at her. "What are you doing you little monkey?"

"Chass! Dada! Mama!"

Duncan was grinning too. "What, you want us to chase you?"

"Chass! Chass!"

"What? Daddy and Mummy? Chasing Poppy?"

"Duncan . . . "

But Poppy had already scampered off into the trees with a squeal, Duncan jogging after her. Emma started running too, afraid to lose sight of the bright orange dress and flowery sunhat. "Don't go far," she called, but the game had taken over now and neither of them heard. Poppy reeled between the grey trunks, disappearing and emerging again, trailing laughter. Duncan began shouting, "I'm coming to get you! I've nearly got you!" which led to more squeals. The thought struck Emma that they were practicing hunting and being hunted, that was what they were playing. Without meaning to they were teaching their little girl how to hunt and be hunted. It was in them, it was coming naturally.

Suddenly Poppy doubled back towards her, shouting, "Chass! Chass!"

"Are we chasing Mummy now, Poppy?" said Duncan.

"No, we're not," she said.

Duncan began to sprint. "Chase Mummy!"

"No!"

She screamed and ran, weaving between the trees to get away from him. Footfalls followed right at her back, she heard Poppy's ecstatic shriek. Then she stumbled and Duncan was on her, catching her by the waist. She overbalanced and they fell to the floor, laughing.

Poppy dived onto them. "More! More!"

After that they both chased Poppy and she chased them and then it was Duncan's turn again. Poppy was in heaven, filling the wood with her noise. Whenever they tried to say that they were too hot or needed a rest she came charging at them until they started playing again. It was so good to see her happy, to see Duncan looking relaxed for once. For a time Emma lost herself in the game, forgot about everything.

Then without warning Duncan pulled up mid-run, facing away from her. "Hello?"

She leant against a tree. "What is it?"

"Hello?"

The wood had become strangely still. The birds had stopped singing, the breeze had died. It was like the day was holding its breath.

Duncan glanced back. "Where's Poppy?"

The words made her stomach turn. "Poppy?!"

They found her almost immediately, sitting between two bloated roots at the foot of one of the oldest and most gnarled trees. Emma snatched her up and turned in the direction Duncan had been looking.

"What's the matter? Who was it?"

"There's someone here," he whispered.

"What?"

"There was someone else running. It wasn't just us."

"Are you sure?"

She watched the wood for any movement. Nothing stirred under the trees, but as her eye fell on one particular trunk she began to imagine there was someone standing behind it. Once the thought had entered her mind it became impossible to shake. She stared at the tree, expecting a figure to step out at any moment. Liquid rose in her throat and she had to swallow.

But this was mad. Duncan was working himself up, putting her on edge. He must have been affecting Poppy too because she wasn't making a sound, not even fidgeting.

"You're safe," she said, cuddling her.

"We should go."

Duncan's face was grey, there was a catch in his voice. "Duncan, calm down."

"We need to go now!"

He began dragging them away through the trees, breaking into a run as soon as he was sure they were following. Emma stumbled after him, hissing for him to stop, really worried now. He was leading them in the opposite direction to the car, apparently fleeing at random. Things were getting out of hand.

She caught up with him at the edge of the wood. "Wait," she said, clawing at his shoulder. "Please."

"OK," said Duncan, panting. "But . . . don't stop."

They trotted down the bank together, emerging into the sunlight and the fizz and hiss of the grass. The hill on this side sloped to a level expanse of meadow, then dipped again through fenced-off pasture. Emma felt the incline hurrying them away from the car, from any plan or logic.

"Where are we going?" she asked.

"We should never . . . have . . . left town."

Duncan was breathing hard, almost hyperventilating. His fringe was dark with sweat. "Listen to me," she said. "You need to stay calm, OK? You're having a funny."

He shook his head. "I saw . . . In there . . . "

Poppy was still so quiet. "Don't worry, poppet," she told her. "Duncan, please believe me. It'll pass."

Even as she said it though a doubt lingered. She'd felt strange in the wood. The back of her neck was tingling, she had the sense of being watched. Eventually she couldn't stand it any longer and glanced around. For a split-second there was something loping down towards them through the grass, but at her double-take the meadow was empty.

"What . . . is it?" said Duncan

Had he noticed her looking back? "Nothing."

"It's . . . following . . . "

"Just stop."

"Isn't it?"

"I mean it, you're scaring Poppy."

But she was scared too now. Panic was doing odd things to her, the body at her hip felt like no weight at all. The tingling had spread, she kept wanting to turn. She managed to last another few seconds, then despite herself she had to look. Once again she glimpsed a silhouette in the corner of her eye, stalking them, gaining ground. Then it vanished. It was nothing, nothing.

By this time they had come down the slope and were some way across the level part of the meadow. Emma spotted a footpath over to their right, a thin mark chalked across the hillside. Perhaps it would lead them back up to the road. As she was raising her arm to point it out she heard the high, eerie cry of a bird of prey. The next moment Duncan sank to his knees.

"Duncan!"

He was hunched over, holding his chest. Emma dropped onto the grass, putting Poppy down alongside them. She lifted his head. His eyes bulged at her, it looked like he was choking. "Breathe," she told him.

"I . . . can't . . . I . . . "

"I'm here," she said. "Breathe."

"This . . . is bad . . . "

"You're all right."

"No . . . I'm not."

Straight away she knew it too. He wasn't, none of them were. The hazy forebodings which had followed her out of the wood came rushing into focus. She froze, she saw Duncan do the same. They stared at each other.

"What's happening?" she asked.

"Listen."

"To what?"

But before he could reply she understood. There was nothing. A hush had fallen over the grass which had been shrilling on all sides of them. The meadow was silent.

Poppy, she thought, and turned. She wasn't there. On the ground where she'd left her she saw a bundle of wildflowers and creepers and other greenery. It had been shaped into a sitting human form, child-sized, with rudimentary head and limbs.

Hoping that Poppy might somehow be hiding underneath the plants she picked it up. But it was far too light and at her touch she saw it change, withering in an instant. It came apart in her hands, crumbling to a rain of desiccated stalks and seed heads.

"Poppy?!" she screamed.

"Where'd . . . she go?"

Emma spun on her heels, scanning the meadow. It stretched around her, sweeping up the hillside to the wood at its top. The grass was tall enough to hide Poppy, she could be anywhere. She felt sick. She took a few steps in one direction, then stopped and stumbled the other way. She could hear Duncan wheezing Poppy's name and her own voice saying, "No, this isn't happening, no." The world had turned brittle and thin.

Nothing seemed as solid as it should be.

Glancing towards the distant hilltop, she spotted something. A pale shape at the wood's edge.

"Up there."

"Where?"

She wasn't seeing things, the shape was moving. It looked like a very tall man walking away from her, wearing some kind of flowing clothes. Then she wasn't so sure. Was it just a tree hit by lightning? It was hard to make out with the sun in her eyes and the quivering heat. Then she saw the smaller shape alongside it.

"Poppy!" she screamed again.

The pale figure danced and twisted. It lost limbs and gained them. It was a tree, a man, a tree. It kept on leading the scrap of bright orange back inside the wood.

Ignoring Duncan's questions she began to run across the meadow. It was so far to the wood, she couldn't believe they'd come that far. The grass streamed past but it was like standing in a retreating tide, with only the illusion of movement. Though she ran and ran the distance hardly closed at all. The sky loomed over her, apart from her breathing and the swishing grass nothing made a sound. She felt transparent with fear for Poppy.

Up on the crest of the hill the pale figure was entering the shade. My baby, thought Emma. She didn't understand. How could she have left her behind? How could she not have known? Then the slope of the hill cut off her view. She was too far away. They were gone into the trees.

Somewhere above her a bird cried out. The vast afternoon filled with the sound of chirring.

ROADKILL

Elin Olausson

WHEN A CAR APPROACHES, things can go one of two possible ways. If Dolores is in a good mood, she puts on that smile-but-not-really-a-smile of hers and says that Christmas has come early. When she's down, she steps into her boots and heads out with the shovel and the lantern without saying a single word.

I know which Dolores I prefer, but it's not for me to pick and choose. I sit on my bed while the nightlight paints the world red, and I know that no matter which Dolores went out the door, the one who comes back won't be a lot of fun to deal with. Just like plenty of things aren't fun, and that's just the way it is.

Me and Dolores, we're the only ones left around here. Most people have moved to the big city, I guess, but I prefer it right where I am. Dolores is the same. She's got a shoebox in her closet; it's crammed with postcards from someone called Mike or Mitch or something like that. *Dolly*, the postcards hiss, *I'm waiting for you. I've found a place for us and the rent's practically nothing. Let me know when you're on your way.* There are other ones with just a sentence or a few words scribbled on them. *Things are mad here. Might be best if you stay with your folks for a while.* One has a kitten on the picture side and the words *love you* on the blank one. It's not signed, unlike the others—as if there was only one person in the world she'd expect to be loved by.

Dolores has never said a word about Mike or whatever his name is. She doesn't have to. She taught me to read when I was five, and I knew right away that it was a useful skill. It lets me in on all the little secrets Dolores doesn't want me to know, as long as I cover my tracks. I enjoyed reading the newspaper, back when we still got it. I was too small to get through anything but the headlines, but that was enough. From them I gathered that Mike was right about the outside world. *Things are mad here. Stay where you are.*

Dolores has saved some old newspapers and stacked them on top of the bookshelf. I don't think it's for sentimental reasons, because she's not that type. Maybe she likes to leaf through them and think that she dodged a bullet. That she's better off than Mike will ever be.

I sit at the kitchen table when she comes in after the chicken-feeding and shrugs her big coat off. I've tried it on—it's heavy, swallows me whole. Dolores enters the kitchen with her rubber boots still on and drops the chicken bucket in the corner. She's grim-faced and wiry, and I have a hard time comprehending that anyone has ever sent her love notes.

"We got us four eggs." She sets them down in front of me—they roll around on the table, shit-stained, a downy feather stuck to one of them. "You clean them up. I'm tired."

She leaves. I hear her move through the house, placing muddy footprints everywhere. It's been years since we bothered with cleaning. I watch the eggs, that one feather. If I had feathers I'd never want to part with them. I wouldn't fly away, but I'd like to be able to.

Holding an egg is a little like cupping a newborn chicken in your hand. One moves and squeaks and one is still, dormant, but they're equally fragile. Squeeze the egg too hard and it breaks, and you have goo everywhere. Squeeze the chicken . . . well. I take my time polishing the eggs, because I don't have much else to do. They're the same muddy tea color as my hair, and I'm not sure if I like it or not. It's a stupid comparison, just as stupid as dreams of flying.

"Done yet?" Dolores barks from the innards of the house. "Damn roof's leaking."

She doesn't have to give me direct orders. I know what to do. After leaving the eggs on the counter I wrap the raincoat around me and head outside. This coat fits me better than Dolores' one does, but it clearly used to belong to someone older. There's a tag in it, with a dotted line where you're supposed to put your name, but nothing has been written. I've thought of jotting down my own name there, but it might make Dolores angry. I'm not scared of her, but it's just not worth it. It's not as if any other kid will come by and take the coat by mistake.

The ladder leans against the house like it's asleep or drunk. Its legs dig themselves deep into the soggy ground, down to where the furry things live. I climb fast, because I always do, because I don't trust the ladder and I certainly don't trust the house. Dolores once told me that it was built by her great-grandfather. Which means it's ancient and should be dead, because everything else from that far back is. Up on the sagging roof, I slither with my belly pressed to the corrugated metal sheets, reaching for the hammer and nails that have been left up there since last time. It's not raining heavily, but the air is damp, icy needles stinging my hands. Dolores says winters used to be different. But when I ask her why, she refuses to answer.

The hole in the roof is tiny, but these things grow and spread. Before I get to work, I lower my face to the opening and peer down. Dolores lies on her mattress, face up but eyes shut. At first I think she's sleeping, but then I see her facial muscles twitch. She makes an ugly sound, and I tear myself from the spy-hole. Dolores has no business crying. We are the lucky ones. I hammer for a while, but I only use one nail—I can push the scrap of metal aside and spy all I want. Not that I want to look at her right now, when she's all snot and tears. I want to store this moment at the back of my mind and forget about it.

When I come back inside a while later she's in the kitchen, knife in one hand and an apple in the other. She chops it in pieces, shoving them into her mouth and chewing soundlessly. The pale flesh is streaked with maggot trails, running here and there like scabs. The knife slices through a live maggot, and I look away. In front of the sink I spot that feather from before. It's crumpled—one of us must have stepped on it. Just another speck of dirt on a filthy floor.

"I didn't ask for this," Dolores says, apple kernels dropping from her mouth into her lap. "We're just surviving. That's all we've ever done."

I don't know what she wants me to say, so I stay quiet. In fact, I'm not sure she's talking to me at all.

THE ONLY TIME she lightens up is when Gabriel comes. Angel-faced Gabriel with the star on his chest and hair the color of night. His headlights slip into our corner of the world like a whisper, a quivering promise of something shiny. Dolores never talks about Gabriel when he's not around, but those headlights approaching is the one thing that can make her untangle her hair and splash icy water at her face and armpits. She waits out on the porch while his car coughs and wheezes its way from the main road up to our yard. I'm forced to wait with her, whether I like it or not.

Today, he drives slower than usual and it takes forever before he's even off the main road. I'm cold, and I'd rather be in the red nightlight glow in my room.

"Can I go inside?" It's not as if I think she'll agree to it. Dolores never agrees to anything.

"You stay right here where I can see you." She says that, but she only has eyes for the car.

"I don't like Gabriel," I lie. I do sort of like him. He's too stupid for his own good, or he wouldn't come here, but my chest tingles every time he smiles.

"Shut up," Dolores mutters. "Who the hell asked you, anyway?"

I think about that maggot, sliced in half. Death can be hard but it's sometimes easy, too. Like putting your shoes on or swinging a lantern.

Gabriel parks the car right below the porch and steps into the mud, shutting the car door with a creak. The car is the same rusty brown as all the other cars I've seen, but Gabriel's jacket is summer sky blue. He raises his hand in greeting, and Dolores does the same. Her fingertips are angry red from the cold.

"Hey there!" Gabriel grins, wiping the curls out of his face. "Nasty weather today."

Dolores shoves her hands into her coat pockets. "Always is, this time of year."

"You might be right about that." He gives me a quick look, the kind that is accidental and doesn't mean a thing. "Everything all right out here?"

Dolores nods. "How are things in town?"

I cling to her words, like I do whenever she mentions *town*. Every time I try and ask her about that place, she tells me to be quiet. But when Gabriel comes, Dolores is the curious one.

"Well, we had an outbreak of flu recently, and plenty of kids got sick—"

"Dead?" Dolores asks, cutting through his words like she did that maggot.

Gabriel's eyes ghost across my face, then back to her. "Yeah. Some of them. It's a good thing you're out here, on your own. There's not much that can hurt you here."

His lips remind me of blood when you wash your hands of it. Trails of bloody water, painting the world pink.

"There's plenty that can hurt you," Dolores says. "No matter where you are."

"I guess that's true." Gabriel runs a hand through his hair. "So, did you . . . Were there any cars passing by recently?"

Cars—that's the reason he comes here. It's all because of the road and that gap in it that outsiders have no clue about.

"No." Dolores seems to shrink a size, and her charcoal eyes sting me like a mosquito bite. "Not since last time."

She's telling the truth for once. It's not often that a car comes by. Usually it's just Gabriel, which is good because he knows not to drive past the bend. The people in town probably know it, too. Gabriel has put up signs by the main road, but they are invisible at night just like everything else. Outsiders drive past our house and past the bend, and wherever they were heading, they're not going to get there. And that's just the way it is.

"That's a relief," Gabriel says. "Let's hope people stay away from now on."

"Yep."

Liar, I want to tell her. *That's not what you're hoping for.*

"So, do you want to come inside?" Dolores looks like a bird, with her twig legs sticking out from under the coat. If I were older, I might have been able to snap her in two.

"I'm not sure if I . . . " Gabriel's eyes flicker. I want him to leave, and not come back until I'm all grown and Dolores is gone.

"Busy?" Dolores' voice hardens. "Sure."

"Someone needs to take care of things," he says, heading for the car. "You know how it is."

She mutters something. I hear her mutter all the time, and it's never interesting.

"Take care now." Gabriel opens the car door and it whines, because it's dying just like the rest of the world. One day that car will refuse to move, and then Gabriel won't be able to visit again.

Dolores waves before disappearing into the house and slamming the door. I watch Gabriel struggle for several minutes before the car roars and jumps forward. He's off, and there's no telling when he'll come by again. I'm not old, but I suppose that all things really do come to an end and that one day, Gabriel's visits will, too.

Dolores lies on her bed, coat still on. I peek through the doorway and she flings something at me. A postcard, squeezed into a ball. "Get out of here!"

I want to pick it up and see which card it is, but she's too angry. "He'll be here again soon enough."

She glares. "Shut up about things you don't understand."

So I do. I go to my own room and close the door and then I sit there, in the red glow, sorting my collection. There's the doll's head, the plastic car, the three stuffed bears. The pearl necklace and the picture book about wolves.

"I understand," I tell them. "I understand everything."

DOLORES LOCKS HERSELF in her room the next day like a sulking child, and I climb up the ladder to spy at her. But she doesn't do anything, just lies on the bed with her arms hugging her legs. I watch her anyway, weighing the hammer in my hand. *Swing, swing.* If the hole was wider, the hammer might fall straight through.

"I hear you, Linda," Dolores says. "You really don't have anything better to do?"

I stay quiet, and she doesn't speak again. After a while I climb back down to the ground and wipe the grime from my jeans. Nothing has changed, really. I'm small and she's a grown-up, and I don't think Gabriel likes either of us. My thoughts skip up the ladder to where the hammer lies, sleeping. One day the roof is going to fall in on us and it won't matter a whole lot then what Gabriel thinks.

Dolores is up early the next morning. Her stomping boots force themselves into my dreams, and for a moment I feel like she's in my room, pacing the floor. The red glow is useless against her—but once I open my eyes there's nothing there. The doll's head lies on the nightstand, watching me with a glassy stare. It had a body when I found it, but it was too badly burnt. Just like the little girl in the backseat. I don't want ugly things, so I removed the head and left the rest where it was. The doll's hair is thick and golden, and when I wrap it around my index finger the head hangs upside down, swinging.

I play with the doll until my stomach turns noisy, then pull the knitted sweater on over my pajamas and head to the kitchen to look for food. Dolores sits at the table, chewing her nails. They're thick, caked with dirt, and I can't look away though I want to.

"What do you want?" she says, still chewing.

"Eat." I open the cupboard. Once I saw a live rat in there, but not this time. There's not much else either, except for a carrot that I grab and gnaw a big chunk off before Dolores can stop me. She doesn't seem to mind, though, so I keep eating.

"He doesn't know what it's like out here," she mutters out of nowhere. I don't have to ask who she's talking about. "It's easy for him . . . them. They've still got shops, and there's gas if you can pay for it. What the hell do I have? He's got no right to come here and lecture me about the damn cars." She gives me a hard look, and I realize that she hates me. "People like that don't know shit. Life ain't a fairytale, and there's no happy ending. You going to cry now?" She laughs hoarsely, removing her hand from her mouth. The skin around her nails is raw and bloody. "Cry all you want. It won't change a thing."

I always expected her to go crazy eventually, but it would be inconvenient if it should happen now when I'm still a kid. "Is this about Mike?"

Dolores stops laughing. Her glares are like filthy fingertips scratching my face. "That's my business. Not yours."

"Just wondering." I tell myself that I'm not scared of her. "He sent you a lot of stuff. What happened? Did he die?"

She scoffs. "Of course he died. That's what people do."

I guess that's true. The chickens die, too, and the strangers who don't know about the gap in the road. Everyone who lived in this house before us have died. According to the newspaper headlines, there used to be cities with millions of people. Most of those people died as well.

"Anyway, I don't want to talk about it." She stands, swaying for a moment before regaining her balance. "It's in the past. It's over."

As if things in the past can't hurt you. I go back to my room and drop the doll's head to the floor. My naked feet push her around, here, there, and no matter what I do she keeps smiling.

THERE'S A CAR that night. We both hear it, but Dolores reaches the front door first. She hides under her coat, shooting me a secretive look.

"I'll go out," she says. "See if they need help."

I don't like it when I have to stay inside. When she's been gone a while I sneak out on the porch and lean over the railing, listening for the crash. There's always a crash, because Gabriel's signs are useless in the dark. A crash, sometimes a blast, then nothing. It's not as if we want it to happen, it just does. And dead people don't need food or clothes or golden-haired dolls, so we might as well take what we need.

Dolores is gone a long while. I get bored and start playing with my hair, braiding and unbraiding it. The cold makes my fingers slow and clumsy. When Dolores comes I'm numb, but I don't let it show.

She puts the sack down in front of me and throws the shovel aside. I get down on my knees and rummage through the sack, weighing items in my hand. A tiny purse, sunglasses, three pairs of shoes. A pink dress, cool and silky against my dirty fingers.

"Merry Christmas," Dolores says. She grins, but her eyes are broken.

Later, in my room, I squeeze my pale limbs into the dress and twirl to imaginary music. The doll has no hands but she claps anyway, loud and clear, and the stuffed bears hum along. The floor is icy but the nightlight glows like fire. Through the music I hear the crackling of flames lapping, licking, eating.

GABRIEL PAYS US a visit a week later. He comes all the way up on the porch this time, the star on his chest blazing. His eyes jump from this to that, and to my sparkling pink dress more than once. I've worn it day and night ever since Christmas.

"There was this young family passing through town recently." He scratches his chin. His nails look soft and breakable, nothing like Dolores' claws. "Man, wife, a little girl. Looked like they had money. Wife was pretty, and that little girl was dolled up like a princess." He looks down at me again. Behind my back, Dolores tugs at my hair.

"We didn't see anything," she says. "Sorry you had to come all this way."

"Right." Gabriel glances toward his car. "Could I come in, maybe? Have a look around?"

Dolores makes a low sound in her throat, a growl that only I can hear. "Of course, officer. Do whatever you need to do." She pushes me out of the way. Her hands tell me to go straight to my room and hide away all my toys and pretty things. While I sit on the floor, shoving stuff under the bed, Gabriel follows Dolores through the other rooms. I listen to their voices, their noisy footsteps.

"It's messy," Dolores says. "Bet you've never seen a place as messy as this before."

"You have no idea what I've seen."

They reach her bedroom and the door clicks. She's shut it. I know she'll never tell me anything later, so I head outside and up the ladder, to the spy-hole. I'm quiet, ghost-like. I want to know.

Gabriel sits on the bed with the box of postcards in his lap. He's picking them up one by one, murmuring the words while Dolores stands, back turned to him.

"You could have had a different life," he says when there are no cards left unread. "Away from here."

Dolores' shoulders are shaking.

"The girl . . . Was he the father?" Gabriel's voice is as soft as a baby chicken. I'd like to snatch it out of his throat and store it in a jar.

"He came back," Dolores says. "He came to get me, but he didn't know what had happened to the road. The explosion woke me up. That's it. That's the story."

"I'm sorry." Gabriel stands. He's too tall for our house, he distorts the proportions. I wish he would leave. "That's a horrible thing to go through." He puts his arm around her shoulders, and she starts bawling. I grab the hammer. I squeeze it until my knuckles lose their color.

Dolores cries forever. I try to imagine the future, but I can't because there is none. Just me, just this house. I think about my mother and my father and about the fact that they are dead or soon will be. Then I climb back down with the hammer.

A CAR DRIVES down the road some weeks later, when the smell has taken over the house and the pink dress has turned grey and filthy like everything else. I watch the headlights come closer, closer, past the warning signs. The night is dark and I'm a little scared and very hungry. I hope they've got food in the trunk and that they'll die quickly.

"Stay here," I tell the doll's head and the bears and Gabriel and Dolores. "I'll be back soon." I grab the sack, the lantern, and the hammer. The red glow sings, following me out into the night.

It's Christmas.

It Looked Like Her

Gordon Brown

———◆———

It was a summer where bad things happened. A summer of scabs. Cicada husks clinging to window screens. Dead grass spreading across the lawns like gum cancer. Up the river, the poultry plant exploded. Not action-movie exploded. Actually exploded. With a teeth-rattling roar on a sweltering morning. With threads of oil-black smoke that smeared against the sky. In the weeks that came after, the tap water was thick and cloudy. When our parents lifted glasses against the lights, we saw pale things squirming in it. What came out of the shower burned our skin.

A lot of kids got sick. A lot of teachers got sick. They packed us into classes where we outnumbered them fifty to one. Sixty to zero. Our hot breath stuck to each other's skin. Braids pasted to the backs of our necks. Sweat pooling up in our training bras as the bands gnawed into our ribs. We knocked over the ant farm by accident, crushing glass and gravel and panicked black bodies underfoot. We spent days throwing up in corners. Getting carried home by our parents, cocooned on the couch, left alone with the TV while they screamed themselves raw at the county commission.

That's how we saw her.

THE CRIME PROGRAM told us in a low voice set to sinister violins that she was one they never found. Not in a trash bag. Not in a suitcase. Not in the woods or the walls or washed up in pieces. She was one who disappeared entirely. One who everyone said had been acting normally on the day it happened, or else had been acting strange.

It showed us her photos. Breathtaking—even if her face ended a little too abruptly. Even if she had a hook-shaped scar on her bare midriff. Even if her eyes seemed a little too large in her skull. A little too dollish, too Dali, but still—they followed us into our restless dreams.

We watched the interview with her father, crumpled and gray and scooped-out. Her friends, looking too much like all our aunts, staring blankly into the darkness off-screen. The parade of newspaper headlines from decades past: "Former beauty queen vanishes." "Confessed mass murderer recants admission." "Mother's last wish: 'to know.'"

There was footage of a desolate tree line. The grainy security film from some flickering motel. The lake where they found a body. Not hers—only wearing her clothes. Clutching a Chanel purse full of flashlights and batteries and dogfood and pliers. Cut back to her best friend saying, "I can feel it. She's still alive." Cut to the retired detective shaking his head.

At last, the ghost-colored lettering, telling you what number to call if you knew anything. Before that, though. What made us sit up. What made our crusted eyes split wide. What made the hairs on our arms dance on end. The final montage. The age-progression. The picture of what she might look like now. With the feathered hair shorn away. With the luster diminished. With wrinkles laced under those enormous green eyes.

There was a face we recognized.

WE AGREED. Over the phone, at first. In person, next. Congealing in the corners of too-full classrooms where we were instructed to keep ourselves until someone came to teach us. No one ever did. Under the tangled mess of hoarse shouts, we Frankensteined our fragments. Looking for the connective tissue. Making the pieces fit.

Where had we seen her?

In town. In line at the bank. At the other side of the grocery store. Picking like a vulture through the DVDs in the library. Hurrying home from the poultry plant. Working odd shifts. Swallowed up by the humid evening. Lost inside those shapeless jackets and overalls. Two cars ahead at the drive-thru, her window cracked, her voice too soft to be heard over the snarling engines.

Where does she live?

Not far from here. In that house on the outskirts. The one colored like concrete. With the curtains always drawn. With the iron skeleton of a bed frame rusting to nothing in the weeds. The place where the weeping willows leaned close to console each other.

What does she look like now?

Not as different as you'd think. Not as old as the TV show guessed. But not good. The skin is a little loose on her jaw. The hair is tarantula-black, not blonde. The lips are thinner. The glamor shot glow has long since evaporated, though she could still be pretty, if she actually tried. Some version of it, at least.

But there are things she can't hide.

The suddenness of her chin. The enormity of her eyes. The disquieting shade of green. Her height. Her age. The practiced, vampy way she tilts her head, and more importantly still, the things she doesn't do. Like speak to anyone. Or meet the cashier's gaze. Or haunt the bar with the other poultry plant workers, waiting for someone to tell them whose fault it was, how much money they'd get, when they could go back to work, or if they ever would.

What was missing?

How she got away from whoever took her. How long they had her. What they did. Why she hadn't told anyone. If she even remembered.

But more importantly:

What she'd done to draw their attention. To show she was a target. Someone they could take. Because there must've been something. There had to have been. When we figured it out, we'd know. Know beyond any doubt. Know that it was something she'd done to herself. That it couldn't happen to us.

We never meant to go farther than that. We swore to each other we wouldn't. Swore by the moon and our souls and our grandmothers' ghosts. It was enough just to know. To have solved it. To walk around with the secret radiating under our shirts like our very own sun.

We'd hold our heads high whenever we got lectured for some careless transgression. Shoulders-back, smirking, letting it bounce off us like the trivial whine that it was. We'd see each other in public and exchange slow, solemn nods. It tethered us together. It should've been enough.

We texted each other questions in the dead hours of the night. Theories to paint in the blank spots, at first. Then, questions to keep the investigation alive. All through the witching hours our cellphones buzzed like termite hives. Why had she picked this town? Because it was so much like the place she'd been taken from. No, because this is a place nobody would ever think to look. Is there a reward? We said we wouldn't tell on her. Nobody's saying they would tell on her—just curious to know. She wasn't kidnapped. How do you know? She ran away. The whole thing was faked. What about all the phone calls her mother got? The whispering on the other end? That was her. It's obvious. How come they found blood in the kitchen, then? How come the neighbors heard her scream? How did she get that hook-shaped scar on her stomach? Was it the scar that made them notice her? People like that, you know. The ones who aren't normal. They're easy to spot. Maybe that's why they go missing. But what if it's something else?

It wasn't our fault. The threads in the story looped in on themselves. Curved and dead-ended like ant farm tunnels. We couldn't go back. We couldn't go on. Not like this. Posing the same questions. Submitting the same speculations. We were starting to bicker. Starting to fray. We needed to do something. Something different. Something new.

That's how we started to follow her.

We were careful. Very careful. We learned what days she came into the library, what time she did her shopping. Then what books she checked out, what went into her cart. We'd contrive reasons to place ourselves in her path. Clustered outside the gas station when she came in for her narrow cigarettes, fidgeting in a nervous knot, flicking our switchblade gaze across her as she clutched her purse tighter. Down by the river, still scummed over from the explosion, ankle-deep in a carpet of dead birds and bugs, pretending to fish while she passed on the path above. We'd crane our necks. Trying to see if she still wore jewelry. If she'd gotten tattoos. If she knew that we knew. Of course, she did. She waited behind the sliding doors of the supermarket, waiting for us to disperse. She kept her eyes locked on the asphalt when she finally shuffled past us.

Of course, that's what goaded us on.

If it was late enough, we could walk behind her. Always keeping a few streetlights between us. Always pretending to be talking about palm reading or people we hated when she looked over her shoulder. But we'd never follow her past the tire shop. And then never past the church. And then never past the edge of town, where the pine trees pulled tight together and deer ticks swarmed in the tall grass.

Never to her house. Some things were too risky. Too risky, unless we had a good reason. Like a frisbee flung onto the peeling porch. If anyone asked, we could say we were just trying to get it back. Or maybe we were looking for a lost cat. We'd seen him come up this way. That's all we were doing.

But she kept the curtains closed behind those ash-black windows. What was she keeping in there? What if it was something? Something that would tell us more. Something that could tell us everything. It might not be. Possibilities are just disappointments that haven't happened yet. But what if?

What if a couple of us knocked on her door, asking for a glass of water? She'd have to invite us inside, wouldn't she? And what if one of us asked to use the bathroom while we were there? She couldn't say no to that. But instead of going to the bathroom, what if one of us crept to her kitchen to unlock the back door? What if one of us took slow, spaced-out sips and kept her occupied in the living room while the rest of us slipped in. Slipped up the stairs. Not touching anything. Just looking.

Just giving ourselves ninety-nine seconds before tiptoeing back down and out and promising never to do it again. It would be over. Over for good.

A PAIR OF US went up to her front door. Went up to her front door and waited two minutes while the rest of us slunk around to the back. We knocked, she didn't answer. We tried the bell, no sound came out. We knocked again. Louder this time. Sending dandruff flakes off the old panels.

Movement on our right. A curtain peeled back, held in place by a finger. An enormous green eye stared at us from the dark. So easy to imagine her—the old her—hidden away in the dark. The breathtaking girl from TV. We almost forgot to ask for water. When we did, she told us to wait. She'd bring it to us. She let go of the curtain and vanished. We hadn't planned for that.

We're not sure what happened next.

Maybe we'd taken too long at the front door. Maybe those of us who were waiting by the back mistook her footsteps for one of ours. Maybe she'd opened the door when they twisted the handle. Maybe it was never locked to begin with.

At the front, we heard her scream. Heard crashing. Heard her screaming again. Wet and wavering. We ran. Followed. Heard the shriek rise and stretch and suddenly vanish—the drumbeat of sneakers against hardwood rushing in to fill the void. Heard one of us calling—maybe out loud, maybe only inside our heads: *Don't let her get away.*

Into the dark house. Bodies without thinking. Without knowing. Puppeted by something awful. Irresistible. Through a cramped kitchen where the walls were coated with grease. Through a hallway where no pictures hung. Arriving at a living room lit only by the television playing a soap opera, where the rest of us had caught her.

We had hands over her mouth to keep her from screaming. Hands gripping her arms. Hands pulling her back so she couldn't kick. Instinctively grasping oily fistfuls of her hair as we dragged her to the floor. Catching some of her clothes without meaning to as we pinned her. Lifting the hem of her blouse.

The scar was there. Except no, it wasn't. A scar was there. Not hook-shaped. Straight. Running down the side of her belly in a salt-white channel.

It might've stretched over time. Things like that happen. They probably do. We'd think about it afterwards. Long afterwards. After we realized how tightly we'd been holding her. After we looked down and saw how deep our fingernails had dug into her skin. After we realized she wasn't struggling anymore, only shaking. After we finally released her. Slunk back. Left her lying there on the carpet. Motionless. Speechless. Soft, terrified sobs bubbling out of her throat. Cold dread crawling down the backs of our necks.

After we ran. After we split up. After we cowered in our rooms, beneath avalanches of stuffed animals, concocting alibis, excuses, plea bargains. Wondering which one of us we'd first pick to betray. Waiting for the phone to ring. The unbelieving stammer then shouts of our parents. The wail of the sheriff's sirens.

After none of that happened.

Hours passed. Days passed. Weeks. The summer ended. The poultry plant re-opened and no admissions of fault were made. We'd see each other in public and drop our eyes. We'd invent excuses not to go out, for fear of running into her. A few of us opened our mouths in the shower and made ourselves sick all over. We clawed fingers into our flesh to prove we hadn't held her that hard. Until bruises blossomed. Until we broke the skin. In class, we refilled the ant farm without speaking. In bed, we sweated through our rose-patterned sheets and spent the nights with chainsaw dreams. Once—only once—we woke up to the sound of our phones buzzing. A final message on the screen:

It really looked like her.

Little Gods To Live In Them

David Surface

It was before dawn when the noises started. Steady, rhythmic, so distant they were almost inaudible, but with a feeling of great pressure behind them, the way her own blood felt throbbing in her ears when she'd climbed too many stairs. Lying in bed alone in the dark, Jane pressed her fingers to her wrist to find her pulse. When she found it, she could tell that there were two separate rhythms; similar, sometimes overlapping, but not the same.

Downstairs, the noises were even louder. Pulsing, steady as a heartbeat, they rattled the dishes in her cupboard, and made the panes of glass in the window frames buzz like wasps.

Jane opened her laptop and saw that the community newsgroup was already crowded with questions. *What is that noise? Are you all hearing this? Is there construction going on somewhere? Has anyone called the police?*

When she closed her computer, the sound was still there, a steady, low-level throb, all the windows and hinges in her house humming like insects to its rhythm. The early morning light filtering through the windows seemed strangely muted, like there was something wrong with the sun.

Instantly, Jane remembered a morning when she was a young child, waking up and wondering why the house was so dark. She'd found her mother standing on a stepladder, covering the last window with a heavy wool blanket. Her mother had told her there was going to be a solar eclipse, that an eclipse was when the sun turns black in the middle of the day, and that it was very dangerous to look at it. Jane's mother reassured her that it was all perfectly natural, and that there was nothing to be afraid of. Jane did not believe it, and cried and begged her mother to make it stop. But her mother could not stop it—no one could. So Jane hid inside her darkened house while the sky outside turned black and poisonous. When it was over and her mother had taken all the blankets and towels down from the windows, Jane asked if it would ever happen again.

Yes, her mother said, *but not for a long, long time.*

Jane walked into her kitchen for another cup of coffee and saw a smear of red on the polished wood floor. Casper was watching from the marble island in the middle of the kitchen, sitting up straight and staring at her with his unblinking pale green eyes.

"Shit, Casper . . . what did you do now?"

A mourning dove, wings askew, lay in the corner by the dishwasher, a few torn-out feathers scattered around, its beady eyes already frosted-over.

"Goddam it, Casper . . . " she began, then stopped. What was the point? He was an animal, doing what animals do. Bringing his prize-kill home to her. Why should she expect him to behave any differently?

Jane got the broom and swept the dove into a dustpan. Casper, still staring at her from his perch, blinked once and yawned. She could see pieces of bloody feather still inside his mouth.

Jane took the dove outside and dropped it into the garbage can, making sure the lid was on tight. Away from the rattling and buzzing noises in the house, the pounding seemed to come from everywhere at once.

"You hear it too?"

Jane turned and saw her neighbor Maddy peering over her rosebushes.

Jane nodded. "Woke me up this morning at five-thirty. Probably some kind of construction . . . "

"What if it's not construction?" Maddy said.

"What do you mean?"

"I don't know . . . " Maddy paused for a moment, peering intently at the tree-line. "Like . . . sky quakes."

"*Sky* quakes?"

"They've been reported in India," Maddy said. "Along the Ganges River. The North Sea and Japan. New York too. In the Fingerlakes. They're like sonic booms. Always near water."

Jane kept her expression relaxed and attentive, the way she always did whenever Maddy was going on about things like crystals and auras and chakras, things Jane knew and cared nothing about.

"So . . . that's what you think it is? Sky quakes?"

Maddy frowned and shook her head. "Too rhythmic. And it's been going on for too long . . . "

Jane listened. The low, throbbing sounds she could feel in her bones were coming from somewhere behind the trees.

"Sounds to me like it's coming from the river," Jane said. "Let's go see."

Maddy's violet-colored eyes grew wide behind her huge glasses. "You mean . . . right now?"

"Sure," Jane said, forcing a smile she didn't feel. "No time like the present."

Maddy wouldn't come, so Jane climbed into the big white SUV and started down Route 9. She turned left onto Old Harbor Road and began the long slow drop down toward the river. The sound was definitely coming from that direction. She could tell, even with the windows rolled up. Trees crowded-in around her, thick and dark.

When she turned the corner, something huge and grey rose up in the road ahead. She slammed on the brakes and stared out the window at the thing in front of her. It was one of those concrete construction barriers, the largest she'd ever seen. At least ten feet tall, it stood grey and silent in front of her, blocking her way.

Pushing the SUV door open, she climbed out and walked up and down the length of the barrier, looking for the name of a construction company, a phone number, anything that could tell her who'd put this ugly thing in her way. But the grey wall rising in front of her was blank and immoveable as a granite cliff.

When Jane got home, she threw her keys onto the kitchen counter, closed her eyes and took deep breaths to calm the pounding of her heart. When she opened her eyes, she noticed something on the ceiling above her. At first she thought it was a spider web. Looking closer, she saw a fine web of cracks running through the plaster, cracks she knew had not been there yesterday.

The house was old, the oldest in town. Built in 1795, it satisfied her desire for stability and permanence, and she displayed the date proudly in big brass numbers over the front door when they'd first moved in. Robert had worried that people might mistake *1795* for the address. Over the years, it became a kind of joke she told at his expense, the kind that wives tell about their husbands. *Silly Robert. Silly man.* Now Robert was gone, but the house was still here. It was all she had left.

Jane listened to the distant steady pounding, anger rising in her chest. *A permit,* she thought. There had to be a permit somewhere for new construction. She opened her computer and spent a few minutes searching the town website, but there was nothing about a new construction project. If they were too lazy or stupid to update the website, she'd just have to go there and find out herself.

Jane was on her way to the town hall when she saw a large sign in the window of what had been a vacant store.

Universal Builders Association
Community Relations

Jane stopped to look more closely at the sign. Near the top was an abstract logo that looked like a cross between the towers and cables of a bridge and the wings of a bird in flight. No email, no website, but there was a phone number at the bottom.

Pulling out her cell phone, Jane punched in the numbers and waited. After two rings, there was a click and a warm male voice spoke.

"Hello, Mrs. Westmore. This is Bradley Smith, Universal Builders Community Relations rep for your area . . . "

"How . . . " she began, but the voice cut her off—she realized with a flash of annoyance that she was talking to a recording.

"I'll be glad to meet with you in person to discuss any questions or concerns you may have. I'll text you a suggested time and the address of a meeting place near you. If it's agreeable, simply reply yes, and I'll look forward to meeting you."

The phone buzzed in her hand. Jane was startled to see it was the address of her favorite coffee shop, just two blocks away. The meeting time—twelve PM, one hour from now.

JANE KNEW THE COFFEE shop was busy on Saturdays, so she arrived a half-hour early. At precisely twelve o'clock, the door opened and a tall man stepped inside. He was wearing one of those tan canvas coats with too many pockets, the kind of hunting-jacket designed for men who've never been hunting. When he saw her, his face lit up in a broad smile.

"Mrs. Westmore? Bradley Smith." It was the same warm, smooth voice she recognized from the phone message. He extended his hand and she took it. His grip was cool and firm.

"You . . . " she said, releasing his hand. "You're with Universal Builders?"

"Community relations." He smiled. "I'm like the unarmed emissary they send out front with a white flag. Pleased to meet you. May I sit?"

She didn't like his joke. It was inappropriate and made her think of invading armies. "So," she began, "your company is doing some kind of major construction by the river?"

"You mean the bridge."

"What bridge? I haven't heard anything about a new bridge . . . "

"Well, they put a lot of effort into keeping it quiet. Looks like it worked." He smiled. Again, his attempt at humor riled her.

"Why haven't I heard about this? Why all the secrecy?"

"Well," he smiled apologetically, "I'm not really part of all that. Basically, my understanding is that it's some kind of Homeland Security thing. Any major public work like this, especially where transportation is involved, nowadays they prefer not to spread the word too far and wide. It's just a whole different world we live in now, unfortunately."

She looked closely at this man sitting across from her with his long legs stretched out casually in front of him. The skin on his face was tight and tanned with wrinkles around his eyes when he smiled. It was the kind of face you get on ski slopes and sail boats, she thought. His jeans were faded, but his Italian loafers with their gold buckles and soft blood-red leather were the kind that cost a fortune.

"So, that noise I've been hearing," she said. "That pounding..."

The man nodded. "The pile drivers."

"It woke me up this morning. It rattles the dishes in my kitchen. And this..." She pulled out her cell phone and opened it to the photos she'd taken. "Those cracks. They appeared in my ceiling this morning."

The man stared intently at the photos for a few moments, a concerned frown on his brow. "Can you send me these?" he asked, handing her phone back to her.

"Then what?"

"I can have someone come to your house and survey the damage..."

"You mean you send someone who tells me what it's going to cost, then I have someone else look at it who tells me it's going to cost five times what your guy says. Meanwhile, you keep hammering those big holes in the ground and destroying people's homes..." Jane was horrified to feel tears rise into her eyes, and turned away to quickly wipe them away. When the man spoke again, his voice was low and gentle.

"No one's out to destroy people's homes, Mrs. Westmore. Why don't you let me talk to my people. Then we'll take it from there."

ON HER WAY HOME, Jane was embarrassed and furious with herself for crying in front of the man. All those lies about women using their tears to control men—they were meant to make women seem weak. Besides, it wasn't weakness that had made her cry. It was the frustration of losing control, of being outmatched by something bigger and more powerful than herself.

When Jane pulled up to her house, she saw Maddy kneeling on the ground by the side of the road, laboring over a small wooden structure, the size and shape of a child's doll-house.

"What's that?"

Maddy glanced up at Jane. Her eyes, behind her huge black glasses, were startled, then cautious. "Just something I've been working on..."

"Is that a dollhouse for your grandkids?"

Maddy went back to work, leveling the ground under the little house with a garden trowel. "No. It's a hokora."

"A what?"

"A hokora. A Shinto shrine."

Jane knew Shinto was some kind of Japanese folk religion. She examined the structure more closely. It was made of plywood that Maddy had obviously painted by hand in bright colors. It did not, in Jane's opinion, look very Japanese at all.

"What's it supposed to be for?"

"People in Japan have been building them for thousands of years," Maddy said, still digging and smoothing with her trowel. "For spirits to live in. Spirits and gods. *Little houses by the side of the road, with little gods to live in them.*"

"So," Jane said, "is it supposed to protect you or something?"

Maddy kept working, and didn't look up when she answered. "Maybe…"

Jane watched Maddy working on the little shrine for another moment, then went back to her house and poured herself a glass of wine. As she took her first sip, she glanced out the window and saw Maddy still working in the dirt. She wondered if Maddy knew how foolish she looked, a grown woman on her knees building a home for invisible spirits. She remembered the "prayer wheel" Maddy had made for her when Robert had first gotten sick. Jane had hung the ugly thing on her kitchen wall, so Maddy would see it when she dropped by for coffee. When Robert died, Jane took it down and threw it in the trash, the way she did with other things that didn't work.

IN THE MORNING, Jane found a thin layer of white dust on the kitchen floor. She glared at the cracks spreading in the ceiling above her, worse than yesterday.

Grabbing her cell phone, Jane called the number she'd called before. There was a click on the line, then that warm male voice that she recognized.

"Mrs. Westmore. What can I do for you?"

"Those cracks. The ones in my ceiling. They're worse now. They're spreading."

"Are you home right now?"

"Yes. You told me you'd send someone . . . "

Casper suddenly went stiff and stared wildly at the door, his green eyes flaring wide. Then he exploded into motion, running for the rear of the house, claws scrambling madly on the wooden floor. That's when Jane heard a soft knocking. Realizing it was coming from the front door, she walked over and opened it.

There was Bradley Smith, smiling down at her with his perfect white teeth. Her brain stopped working for a moment.

"Sorry to startle you," he said. "I was actually on your street, just coming up from the site, when you called. May I come in?"

"Yes. Yes, of course . . . " She moved aside to let him enter. She knew she was staring at him, but couldn't seem to stop. He stepped carefully over her threshold, looking around appreciatively. Inside her house, he looked even taller. She led him back to the kitchen and pointed to the cracks in the ceiling.

"They've been spreading," she said. She pulled out her cell phone, opened the first photo she'd taken two days ago and handed it to him. "Look . . . "

He peered at the photo, then at the cracks in the plaster. "Yes, yes, I see . . . " She watched him run his fingers along the thin cracks in the ceiling in a gesture she thought looked oddly tender. "You certainly have a beautiful home, Mrs. Westmore," he said. "I can see why you love it so much."

"So . . . ," she said, crossing her arms and making her voice as firm as she could make it. "What are you going to do about this?"

"Actually," he said, "I was wondering if I could ask you for a favor . . . "

"What do you mean?" she said uncertainly.

"I've been doing this job for a long time. And one thing I've learned is that people tend not to trust strangers. They're afraid of new things. But people here know you. They trust you. They respect you. So, I was hoping that you might be willing to help with that. Be my eyes and ears in this community. Find out what people are thinking, what they're saying. Any questions or concerns they might have . . . "

"It sounds like you're asking me to spy on people."

He threw back his head and laughed. "I guess it does sound like that, doesn't it? Technically, it won't be spying, because they'll know you're talking to me. You'll be their voice. The voice of the community. And I'm sure that the people I work for will be willing to offer you . . . certain valuable considerations."

Jane looked again at the cracks in her ceiling. She had always been good at finding the right people. Building relationships, forging connections. It was how things got done.

"All right," she said.

Bradley Smith's grin grew even wider. "Thank you, Mrs. Westmore," he said. "I'm very grateful. You won't be sorry."

THAT EVENING, AFTER she'd fed Casper, Jane poured herself a glass of wine, stepped out into her back yard and listened. There was no infernal pounding noise, only the screaming of the tree frogs. She stood there for a while, watching the light drain from the sky. She felt the pang at her heart a split second before she recognized what it was. *Happy hour.* The hour she'd always shared with Robert, when they'd both stood outside like this with their first glasses of wine, listening to the frogs, watching the night come on.

A hand touched her arm and she nearly dropped her wineglass. She turned and saw Maddy's eyes, wide and startled-looking behind her big glasses, staring up at her.

"Can you hear that?" Maddy said.

"Hear what?"

"That screaming."

Jane listened. "That's just the tree frogs."

"No," Maddy insisted, her hand still on Jane's arm. "Listen . . . "

Jane listened harder. At first, all she could hear was the tree frogs' usual high-pitched scratchy squeal. Then she heard it, something behind the noise, or inside of it, a wave of sound, darker and more full-throated. Nearly human.

"You know what that is?" Maddy said in her urgent whisper. "It's *people.*"

Jane listened. Then she heard it. Many voices, hundreds of them. One long, furious wail of grief and rage.

By 6:30 on Wednesday, her house was filled with people, some of whom she'd never met before, others she'd known for years. Their anxious voices filled the air, sometimes talking over each other, so that Jane had to raise her voice and remind them to take their turn.

"Carol Godfrey told me they're going to start tearing down houses," Debra Simpson said.

"They can't do that!" another voice spoke up.

"Yes they can," Eileen Benedict said. "Eminent domain. Look it up. They do it all the time."

"Does anyone even know who these people are?" Debra asked. "Nobody's talked with them."

"I have," Jane said, feeling the warm blood rush to her face. The frantic voices all around her fell silent. Faces turned toward her. It was Eileen Benedict who broke the silence.

"You have . . . " Her voice was level and flat, and sounded more like an accusation than a question.

"Yes. Community Relations. I got in touch with them two days ago."

A tidal wave of voices rose up, dozens of questions were hurled at her. Through it all, Jane was aware of Eileen silently glaring at her. When the other voices subsided for a moment, Eileen spoke.

"And just how long did you plan to keep this to yourself?"

"What do you mean?" Jane said icily. "I just told you, didn't I?"

Jane turned to the other faces filling her living room and began to explain that Universal Builders was building a new bridge, and had agreed to pay for any damages related to the project. Another surge of questions rose up. She did her best to address them, relishing this new feeling of power, all the while sensing Eileen's harsh, cold stare.

It was a sharp tapping noise that woke Jane this time. As soon as she entered the kitchen, she could hear that the sound was coming from outside. She peered out the front door and saw a figure kneeling at the edge of the road in front of her house. Pulling her bathrobe closer around her against the chill, Jane walked toward the figure and the steady tapping.

"Maddy . . . " Jane spoke in a harsh whisper, "what are you doing?"

Jane could now see that Maddy was nailing a roof onto one of those tiny wooden houses, just like the one she'd shown Jane in front of her own house. What had she called it? A hokora. A home for the gods.

"Is that . . . " Jane started, then paused, unsure of how to ask what she was wondering. "Is that for me?" Maddy nodded and kept tapping. "Is that . . . is that supposed to *protect* me or something?"

Maddy leaned back, apparently finished. She turned and looked up. For a moment, Jane could see the moon reflected in her glasses. Maddy spoke so softly that Jane had to strain to hear.

"I'm worried about you, Jane," Maddy said. "You think you know things. You're always so sure of yourself." For a moment, Jane thought she could see tears behind Maddy's thick glasses. "But you can't always know everything. I know you want to. But you just can't."

Jane was still trying to think of what to say when Maddy stood up, wiped her hands on her jeans, then walked back into her house, closing the door behind her. Jane stood looking down at the little wooden house, wondering what Maddy was trying to protect her from.

BRADLEY SMITH WAS WAITING for her in the back of the coffee shop. He sat across from her, fingers folded on top of his chest, looking at her expectantly.

"So," he asked, "how did the meeting go?"

"Well," Jane said. "Some of them were pretty agitated."

"Why?"

"They're afraid you're going to start tearing down houses."

"What did you tell them?"

She studied his face. It was unreadable as a mask. "Are you?"

"Am I what?"

"Are you going to start tearing down people's houses?"

She searched his face for some lurking trace of evil, some hint of deception, but could find none. His smile was as harmless and bland as the smile of a child's doll. Then she remembered Eileen Benedict's hateful stare.

"Something's bothering you," he said.

"Oh, it's just . . . It's just this woman. Eileen Benedict." Jane couldn't contain a shiver of anger.

"You don't like her," he said.

"Let's just say she can be . . . difficult."

"In what way?"

"She . . . " *Why should I be telling him this,* Jane thought. Then it was coming out, all the anger and frustration. "She keeps questioning every move I make. Accusing me of things. It's like I'm alway on trial with her."

"And that's very frustrating for you."

"Yes. Yes it is." She felt embarrassed at how quickly the anger rose up. "She undercuts everything I do. She practically accused me of being a liar. In my own house . . . " She noticed him staring at her intently. His blue eyes suddenly now looked green, the same color as Casper's eyes.

"I'm sorry to hear that," he said. "She shouldn't be trying to interfere with you like that. Not when you're trying to do something positive for the community . . . "

A darkness she'd not seen before had fallen over his face—then it was gone, and he was smiling again. "When are you going to be meeting with them again?"

"Tonight. At seven-thirty."

"Good. When you do, I want you to tell them something for me. Tell them they have nothing to be afraid of."

She wanted to ask what he meant by that, what good he thought it would do, but when she looked into his calm, earnest face, she felt her doubts falter.

"Just tell them that," he said. "You can say I told you. They have nothing to be afraid of."

WHEN JANE GOT HOME she went around tidying up the house, getting ready for the meeting. As she went into the kitchen to start the coffee, she saw a fresh smear of blood on the tile floor. *Casper. Damn it.* It was just like him to drag something in when she was trying to clean up. She saw him watching her from on top of the kitchen cabinet, his wide eyes following her every move.

"All right," she said, "where is it?" Casper blinked once and kept watching her.

When she found what Casper had brought in, lying halfway under the refrigerator, a strangled sound rose up in her throat. It was a human finger, the nail perfectly manicured and painted bright pink.

The doorbell rang. Jane kicked the ghastly thing under the refrigerator without thinking, then ran to the sink and clutched the countertop while she gagged, but nothing would come up. The doorbell rang again. Breathing faster, she ran some water over a paper towel, dropped to her knees and wiped up the smear of red. The doorbell rang again and she hurried to answer it, pausing in front of the hall mirror to check herself. Her face was ghastly white.

Jane took a deep breath and opened the door. Debra Simpson and Marlene Parsons stared at her, their faces filling with alarm.

"Jane, are you okay?"

"Yes, yes, yes . . ." the words poured out of her mouth. "Just a little . . . Come in. Come in . . ." She led them into the living room, her mind still reeling.

"Jane," Debra said, "are you sure you're okay?"

"Yes, yes . . . It's just . . . I just have to check on something . . ."

Jane ran to the kitchen, dropped to her knees by the refrigerator, and looked under it. Peering into the haze of dust and cat hair, she saw something. Grabbing a wooden spoon from the counter, she bent down, her stomach twisting, and scraped the thing out into the open. She stared at it, exposed to the kitchen light, trying to understand what she was seeing. It was a carrot, shriveled and dry. She pressed her fists into her eyes, then looked again, but it did not change back to the thing she knew she'd seen a moment before.

The rest of the evening was a blur. Faces filled her living room again; angry, frightened faces. Throughout it all, Jane was aware of one face that wasn't there. Eileen Benedict's. A few times while Jane was speaking in front of the crowd, she thought she saw Eileen in the corner of her eye, watching her with that same silent, judgmental stare, but when she turned to look, it was someone else.

"Jane? Jane . . ." Someone was calling her name. It was Debra, looking at her with a trace of the same concerned expression that she greeted her with at the door. "Did you speak with him again?"

"Did I . . . speak with who?"

"That man. The man from Universal Builders. Did you ask him

about what's going to happen?"

Jane thought of the thing under her refrigerator, and the bright pink fingernail she knew she'd seen.

"Jane," Debra said again, "what did he say?"

"He said . . . " Jane closed her eyes and swallowed, took another deep breath, then spoke again. "He said we have nothing to be afraid of." She looked at all the disbelieving faces staring up at her, then said it again. "He says we have nothing to be afraid of."

AFTER EVERYONE HAD GONE, Jane finished the last of a bottle of white wine, then opened another. She couldn't get the image of what she'd found on the kitchen floor out of her head. Or the empty chair where Eileen Benedict should have been.

Sensing she was being watched, Jane was startled to see a figure standing close by in the dark. "Jesus Christ, Maddy," she said, "Don't sneak up on me like that! I thought you'd gone home."

"I just . . . " Maddy paused for a moment. "I just wanted to make sure you were all right."

"Yes, I'm all right. Why shouldn't I be?"

"Jane," Maddy said after a long silence. "Are you afraid?"

Of course I am, she thought. *Of course I'm afraid. Aren't you?* Instead, she said, "No. Why should I be?"

"I don't know . . . It's just . . . it's what that man said. That we don't have anything to be afraid of. People don't usually say that unless there really is something to be afraid of, don't they?"

Jane felt fear rise in her throat, but it quickly turned to anger. "Are you trying to scare me? Is that what you're trying to do? Because if that's what you're trying to do, you can just fuck off right now."

Jane leapt up and left Maddy sitting there staring at her with her mouth open, a hurt look on her face.

Inside her house, she picked up the phone and called Eileen's number, wondering how she could possibly explain why she was calling. The phone rang once. There was a strange rhythmic pulsing on the other end, and a high pitched howling that sounded almost human. Jane dropped the phone and stared at it, half-expecting to see it breathe or crawl away.

Then she snatched up her car keys and headed out the door. Whatever was going on, she was going to see it for herself.

On her way to the driveway, Jane stumbled over something and almost fell. It was the *hokura*, the little wooden house Maddy had made for her. Anger flared inside, and she kicked the stupid thing, knocking it over on its side.

"No!" Maddy called out. "Jane, no!" She saw Maddy staring at her in horror, her hands clasped over her mouth, eyes wide with fright.

Fuck you, Jane thought as she kicked the thing at her feet again and again. *Fuck you and your crystals and your prayer wheels and your stupid little shrines.* She raised her foot and stomped on the little house again and again until it lay in little pieces. Then she climbed into the SUV and drove away, tires squealing on the asphalt.

Jane didn't realize how drunk she was until she found herself struggling to keep the vehicle going in a straight line. She knew Eileen Benedict lived just a few blocks away. Squinting her eyes, she rolled down the window, letting the cold air in her face start to wake her up.

When she came to the place where Eileen's house should have been, Jane slowed down and stopped in the middle of the road, trying to understand what she was seeing. There had been holes in her vision after cataract surgery, bright angular places where the light bent in strange, unexpected ways and hid things from her—that was what she saw now in the place where Eileen's house should have been, a fragmentation of the light. But this time she knew it wasn't happening inside her eyes; it was happening out there in front of her. A shifting rupture-like absence in the world.

The sun was starting to break over the trees as Janet drove fast toward the river. The pounding and shrieking was louder than ever. When the grey concrete barrier rose up in front of her, she slammed on the brakes, pushed the door open, and climbed down. The thing in the road was too high, so she plunged into the trees, looking for a way around it. The thudding noise was deafening now, almost pushing her backward with each concussion, but she kept going. Whatever it was, she was going to see it. She scrambled downhill toward the river, scraping her hands on the rocks and briars while the terrible sound grew closer. When she finally broke through the trees into the open, her eyes strained to take in what she was seeing.

The thing in front of her rose up from the shore in a massive arc, wide as the river itself. But instead of bending toward the other side, it kept reaching higher and higher until it seemed to break through the sky, hiding itself behind the grey cloud layer above. One moment it appeared to be made of metal, then of glass, then of light, then all three, breaking apart and coming together like sun-glare shimmering on the surface of the water. As she looked up, shielding her eyes against the blinding light, she saw that it was alive, or that something alive was joining itself to this colossal thing that broke the sky. Hundreds of wraith-like shapes rising like the bacteria she sometimes saw swimming across her own eyeballs. They were all screaming, although whether they were screams of agony or screams of joy, she couldn't tell.

Jane closed her eyes to shut out the sight. When she opened them again, she found herself in the coffee shop. All the tables and chairs were empty. No one was behind the counter, but she could hear the machines making their familiar ticking and hissing sounds.

The figure of a man stood in the back, silhouetted by light from the window behind him, waiting patiently for her. She walked closer to him.

"What . . . " Her voice caught in her throat. "What *is* it?"

"I told you," he said, his lean, impassive face half-hidden in shadow. "It's a bridge."

"Those . . . things. Those things in the air, screaming. What are they?"

"I like to think of them as travelers," he said. "It might help you to think of them that way too."

The light coming through the window was turning dim and strange. Something was passing in front of the sun. *Don't look,* her mother had warned her. *Whatever you do, don't look.* The thing that was not supposed to happen for a long, long time—it was happening now.

"Please," she said, "make it stop. Please."

He smiled down at her, a gentle, sad smile. "I'm sorry. I can't do that. I'm afraid it's out of my hands."

Jane felt the tears running down her face. This time, she didn't try to hide them or wipe them away. "Please . . . " she said again. "Please. Make it stop." She kept saying it, long after she knew it was no use.

She looked up into his face that was neither young or old, and saw it flicker. For a moment, she could see Robert's face. Then the eyes became a familiar emerald-green like Casper's, the long pupils widening to take her in. She heard him say other things, things she'd been told a long time ago. That it was not as bad as it seemed. That it was all perfectly natural. And that there was nothing for her to be afraid of. Nothing at all.

WE ARE THE GORILLAS

Douglas Ford

———◆———

WE ARE THE GORILLAS.

And I'm the only female gorilla.

We became the gorillas because Mr. Van Doren took one look at us, his third-period social studies class, and said, "You're all a bunch of gorillas, aren't you? Van Doren's Gorillas."

We all looked around the room, at Mr. Van Doren, at each other. What did he see? What did he mean?

Then something happened. It started with Mark Esper, a boy who sat in the back. I know Mark Esper from English class. He took up more room than anyone in our middle school. He stood so tall and his clothes never fit right, his shirts never really covering his big stomach. Also, I know from English class that Mark Esper can't read. But Mark Esper started it. He stuck his big fist up into the air and twirled it around like someone moving an invisible crank shaft. Mark Esper did this as he began making a barking sound. Pretty soon, other people began making the same fist motion in the air and making the same sound with their mouths. I, the only girl, the only girl gorilla, did it, too. I did it with all the boys, and the sound of our barking filled the classroom like a war cry.

We thought Mr. Van Doren would get mad. We knew what we did might cost us somehow.

But Mr. Van Doren surprised us all by smiling, his teeth big and white.

When we quieted down, Mr. Van Doren said, "That's right. Gorillas, all of you."

LATER, I LEARNED that gorillas don't bark. They hoot, though. I now know that what we did that day—and on many other days—is called *hooting*.

"A bunch of gorillas," Mr. Van Doren would say, handing back our tests, mostly D's and F's. We hooted when he said this, and we hooted when the teacher's aide came in one day and Mr. Van Doren said, "Look at these gorillas, will you? The computer sure was good to me, wasn't it? Putting all of them into one class like that."

We had no assigned seating, but we always sat at the same desks anyway. Except I gradually moved further back, one seat at a time so no one would notice, until I sat right next to Mark Esper. Mark Esper didn't seem to notice or care. I wanted to sit near Mark Esper when the hooting began. I wanted to help start it.

Mark Esper couldn't read, but I sensed another sort of intelligence, the way he kept his eyes level, as if he noticed and measured everything. He kept measuring Mr. Van Doren, and Mr. Van Doren had no idea.

The teacher's aide laughed uncomfortably when Mr. Van Doren called us gorillas. Pretty much everyone laughed the same way as the teacher's aide, even the principal, Mr. Garwood, a big, tall man with a bald head and a smile that never went away, even when someone sent you to his office for doing something bad. He would keep smiling as he showed you a big wooden paddle hanging from his wall and tell you how in the old days, he would have smacked your butt with it. "I'd even get to pull down your pants," he'd say, "even the girls." Just hearing him say that made you feel embarrassed and want to look away, but he would make you look right at him as he said it again. "I'd get to pull down your pants."

When the principal's bald head appeared in the doorway of our classroom, Mark Esper shifted in his seat. He normally sat so still and straight, but not so much with Mr. Garwood there. I could picture what Mark Esper would look like as a grown-up. He would have a chin that stuck out real far and lips that would curl around a cigarette. Some day he would punch guys like the principal in the stomach, but now, the principal had the upper hand. When Mr. Garwood came all the way into the classroom, smiling, Mr. Van Doren turned and looked at him as if he just noticed him for the first time. "Your computer was real good to me, Principal!" said Mr. Van Doren. He said it just like that, not even using Mr. Garwood's name. "You gave me a bunch of gorillas."

We hooted as usual, but I noticed that Mark Esper did not. He remained quiet, as everyone else made the noise. I watched Mark Esper sit as still and quiet as a statue, and I tried to match his quietness. I didn't hoot at all, except maybe once.

The principal smiled through the hooting. His eyes seemed to roam around the room, as if in search of something. When his eyes came to me, they stopped.

"You have one girl in this class, Mr. Van Doren," he said.

The room got quiet. No hooting. I thought maybe everyone remained quiet so I could say something. But I didn't. I didn't know what to say.

"Yes," said Mr. Van Doren finally. "That's right. Like I said, they're gorillas." Mr. Van Doren said this in a quicker voice than he normally used, like he wanted the principal to leave.

Some of us hooted, but it didn't get loud the way it did other times. Part of me didn't want it to get loud, but part of me did. It was like everyone hooted for me.

"Right, yes," said Mr. Garwood. "I see that." He looked at me the whole time, smiling.

Then someone used that word, the one I hated. I don't know who said it, someone from several rows away. "Dawg." Not *dog*, like you would for an animal, but *dawg*, the word for a girl who looked ugly.

Instead of hooting, laughing.

Even Mark Esper laughed a little.

The principal kept smiling.

I'm glad they didn't hoot. I like hooting. I didn't want that ruined.

MR. VAN DOREN TOLD us he had to assign us a project with research. "I don't want to do this," he said, "because I know how you'll all do. You all, just a bunch of gorillas."

After the hooting died down, he told us to get started with choosing our topic. We each had to do a presentation in front of the class on the history of something.

I decided to do the history of gorillas.

Later, I sat in front of a library computer, looking up gorilla history.

I couldn't find anything.

I asked the librarian for help. When I told her my topic, she looked at me in a funny way. Then she showed me a website full of pictures of men in army suits carrying guns through a jungle. I went back and asked for help again—"the history of *gorillas*," I said as clearly as possible—and she made the same sound my English teacher made when Mark Esper couldn't read out loud. "Gorillas don't have societies," she said, "so they don't have histories."

So fine, I thought, I'll just research gorillas.

And so much to learn!

Did you know that they live in groups, and each group has a leader? *One dominant male*, I read. A silverback. The big silverback protects the others, and if anything comes close to the group, the silverback chases it off.

I thought again of what Mark Esper would look like as a grown-up. Right now he had a head full of thick hair, so much that I bet the principal felt jealous of him. One day, I bet, Mark Esper would have silver hair. He wouldn't have a bald head like Mr. Garwood.

I read so much about gorillas that I had trouble writing it all down.

I'd write a little bit, then start thinking of Mark Esper, then write down a little more, and pretty soon, all my time was gone.

I almost didn't hear the bell and had to hurry.

Later that night, I stood in front of my mirror, naked. Hair had started appearing in some crazy places, not just *down there*, but up to my stomach and even on to my back. I think because I'd started thinking about gorillas all the time. I think because Mr. Van Doren called us gorillas. I think because I was becoming a gorilla for real.

The next day, Mr. Van Doren made us stand up and tell him what we planned to do our presentation on. Most people didn't know, so they didn't have much to say, including Mark, Esper. During his turn, the principal appeared and stood in the doorway, smiling as usual.

"How are your gorillas doing, Mr. Van Doren?" he said.

"Acting like gorillas," said Mr. Van Doren.

We hooted for Mr. Van Doren, but we didn't hoot for the principal.

Mr. Van Doren called on me next. "You're up, Kaleen, go ahead."

I didn't say anything at first. I planned to surprise Mr. Van Doren with my plan to do the history of gorillas. But the way the principal just stood there in the door smiling, waiting to hear my answer, something about that made me not want to say anything.

"So what's it going to be, Kaleen? Wakey, wakey," Mr. Van Doren said, snapping his fingers.

Finally, I spoke. "I don't know."

Mr. Van Doren almost looked disappointed, but the principal kept on smiling. "Even the pretty lass," said Mr. Garwood, "a gorilla."

Later, I wrote down more about gorillas.

Did you know that gorillas will hurt people? Did you know that some people—people called *poachers*—have scars on their stomachs where gorillas took swipes at them?

One person said the gorilla almost *disemboweled* him. *Disemboweled*. That means all your guts fall out.

That night, I stood naked in front of the mirror again, noticing how in just one day, more hair covered more parts of my body. (I don't want to tell you where—it's weird.) I looked at my fingernails, too. I knew why the hair kept coming in, so thick and dark. Because when I lay in bed every night, I wished for myself to turn in to a gorilla for real. I wished for my fingernails to grow out into big rounded claws for *disemboweling*, and I even stopped biting them all the time like I used to.

Standing there in front of the mirror and thinking about my future claws reminded me of something.

Something that made me worried.

The paper I was using to write down all my gorilla facts. I left it that day in the library.

I put on my clothes real quick.

Normally, with my clothes on, you couldn't see all the hair coming in. Now you could see a *lot* of the hair, so dark and thick. Some of it even made it to my face.

With Mom still at work and Dad asleep on the living room sofa next to some empty beer cans, I knew I didn't need permission to walk back to school this late. But I took a kitchen knife, the biggest one I could find, for safety.

I didn't know if I could find the door to the school open.

Also, I didn't know what sort of things might be hiding behind the trees and the cars.

I imagined poachers who looked like the principal. I hooted just like we do in class, a warning to stay away, or you might just get disemboweled.

By the time I got to the school, the darkness had spread everywhere.

I didn't think the big front door would open. I thought I might have to walk back home and hope I could find my notes the next day.

But it opened right up.

I went inside, everything so different from the daytime, with kids hanging around the lockers, talking and laughing. It felt so empty. I hooted, just to see if someone would hoot in return. The sound echoed, so loud to my ears. My hoot sounded deeper than any sound I ever made before.

I passed Mr. Van Doren's classroom, taking a quick look inside, just to see if I would see him sitting at his desk. Teachers hardly ever left their classrooms. If he sat in there as usual, I would hoot so he would call me a gorilla. But the room sat empty.

I found the library and could see the computer screens glowing through the glass of the door window. There in the light, I saw my notes sitting where I left them. Someone locked the door though, so I couldn't get in. At least I knew I could get my notes in the morning.

Then I had an idea. I knew from the times I spent in the principal's office, waiting for my Mom or Dad to pick me up after I did something wrong, that his office had a special door to the library. Should I try that one?

Did you know gorillas show no fear? I thought of that, still holding the big knife.

I went by the principal's office and saw light from under the door.

I tried that door, and I found it unlocked. From the other side, I could hear sounds. Something like smacking.

Did you know gorillas are curious? I am.

When I went inside, I found what made those sounds. I saw Mark Esper's bare bottom first, red and sore-looking, him bent over, with Mr. Garwood standing behind him, that big paddle upraised. I watched as he brought it down again, Mark Esper making a sound like it hurt. Not a big sound, like most people would make. Like I would make. A little one, like he didn't want to show the pain. The redness on his bottom showed it enough.

I couldn't see the principal's face, but I knew that if I could, I would see his smile, the one always there, like he knew things.

I knew things, too. I can't tell how I knew them. I just did. I knew that even though Mark Esper couldn't read that he would keep passing his classes if he would let the principal use that paddle he loved so much, the one he said nobody would let him use anymore. Mark Esper couldn't read—and that's ok, because gorillas can't read, though they can use sign language sometimes—and if he could read, he would know what I know. That the paddle had words burned into it: *Spare the rod, spoil the child*.

Mark Esper must've heard me come in because his necked turned slightly. He saw me, and I used sign language to tell him to keep quiet. I know how to do that. I don't know how to say, *Don't be embarrassed, I won't look at your bare bottom*, but if I could, I would have said that with my fingers, too.

Mark Esper can't read, but he understood what I said when he saw my fingers held to my lips. He might have understood the other thing, too.

Did you know that gorillas protect the others in their group? Did you know they have strong bonds, even when they act mean to one another sometimes, like when they laugh at the word *dawg*?

I snuck up, the knife still in my hand. I got up right behind the principal, just as he brought the paddle back for another swat.

Then he noticed me.

He swung around, looking at my face, like he recognized me and didn't recognize me all at once. Probably because of all the hair. It probably grew more as I walked through the school. I hooted once to help him know who stood before him. Because he stood still, looking surprised, I had time to use the knife, real swift and fast across his belly. I would use claws if they came in fast enough, but I had to use the knife, the biggest one I could find in my mom's kitchen, and his belly must have been soft because the knife went in so deep. Or maybe I've grown strong.

He looked down, still with a surprised look. The smile hung on his lips. Sort of. It looked different now. Probably how someone would look if they got *disemboweled*. The poacher didn't get disemboweled. But I used my new gorilla powers to make sure that Mr. Garwood got *disemboweled*.

He fell back, trying to grab something on his desk, dropping his paddle. I didn't know what the principal might be trying to grab, but Mark Esper did. Mark Esper pulled up his pants and grabbed the phone before Mr. Garwood could. He smashed it under his foot. Then Mark Esper took the other phone, the one the principal used to call my parents all the time, and he pulled it out of the wall. The principal's guts kept coming out, and he fell into a big puddle of his own blood. More kept coming out. His eyes got shiny, like glass, and Mark Esper and I both watched as his smile went away.

Nobody knew I came there that night.

And nobody knew that the principal kept Mark Esper there so late either, not even his parents, I guess.

Before we started walking out of the school together, I used the door from the principal's office to the library and grabbed my notes from the library, and we left quickly and quietly. I kept the bloody knife out the whole time, just in case he needed me to protect him some more, because my claws still hadn't come in. They would though. I told Mark Esper all about them until we came to his street and he had to turn and walk his own way.

I watched him walk a little way. He looked smaller than I remembered. Or maybe I'd grown larger.

Either way, we are the gorillas.
And I am the only female gorilla.
And my back now glows silver.

The Body Trick

Alexander James

———◆———

THEY STARTED, ELLEN remembered, one stifling afternoon, another day shut up indoors by their mother as she went out to work. They'd picked through the kitchen cupboards, trying spoonfuls of old herbs and coughing them up again in clouds. They'd wandered the dank confines of the garage, squeezing between the teetering stacks of boxes. They'd stood before the entrance to their mother's room and dared each other to step inside. They had done everything they could and they were thoroughly, deathly bored. The TV just played old cowboy movies they had seen a hundred times before, stuff from back before they were born. They passed a tumbler of wine back and forth between them as they watched from the carpet. Ellen was a few minutes younger, so she always had to drink second. Despite the yellowing leaves pawing at the patio door, it was a warm day, and as the sun dipped into the living room the atmosphere grew stuffy, the air caught up in pillars of falling dust.

In the many years since, Ellen had often attempted to make sense of what she had said next. She had searched in the silent and dark places inside herself for the source of the words that had risen up through her. Was it some throwaway joke from a variety show? Or a suggestion in one of their magazines, those with names like *Girls Chat* that their mother would always vet before she bought them at the newsagents? She was sure that the idea must have come from someone, or somewhere, else. It wasn't in her character.

"Let's play a trick on Mum, when she gets back."

Jess turned. Ellen knew her sister was leery of some kind of set-up, a ploy to get her locked in her room for another evening. Yet there must have been something about the way Ellen said it. A conviction. Because Jess replied, slowly, unsure what to make of her sister's sudden streak of malice:

"What do you think we should do?"

Ellen leaned in close and whispered her idea for the trick. She couldn't recall exactly what she'd said, what particulars she'd imparted to her sister. She only remembered her face changing as she spoke, first prickling in a flush and then creasing with giggles.

Jess leaned back, her mind working for a second. "Okay."

Would they use belts or knives? Or would they take out the left-behind tools, the pipe wrench and the hammer? Would their eyes be closed, or open? How much blood was too much?

It was important, they agreed, to get the details right.

The first trick was a simple one, and their most effective by far. They'd splayed themselves out on the linoleum, paring knives held loose as baby birds in their hands, identical crimson slashes circling their throats up to behind their ears. By the time everything was in place they didn't have to wait long. They heard their mother's car dragging over the gravel, the locks click-clacking on the front door, her swift trot into the kitchen. Neither of them could glimpse her face clearly, but the catch of her breath told them everything they needed to know. Time briefly stopped, the three of them frozen in tableau. Then Ellen began to shake with nervous laughter and it was over.

Of course, there were punishments, worse than the usual. Yet the chill and hungry night that followed had been worth it just to hear that gasp, to know that their mother's composure could be cracked if only for a second. Ellen replayed every detail behind her eyelids as she lay in bed. The lazy sun, the dancing dust, the cool floor against the backs of her arms, the gentle weight of the blade in her hand. She shivered, her stomach hollow, but took some small comfort in knowing that she wasn't alone. On the other side of the thin wall that separated them, Jess was no doubt entertaining the very same thoughts as her.

At least, that's what Ellen had assumed at the time. Perhaps her sister had been busy fostering more plans in the darkness, ideas for further tricks Ellen wasn't privy to. Or perhaps she hadn't been thinking of anything at all, her face slack, her eyes unblinking, her mouth half-open as if she'd been cut off mid-sentence. Practicing, even then. Yes. That would go some way towards explaining what happened later, albeit not completely. Parts would remain to Ellen forever out-of-focus like the shadows in her childhood bedroom, flickering in the streetlight's glare from hanging coats to cloaked figures and then to something in-between.

A FEW DAYS LATER they tried again, confident that this time around they could elicit a more drastic reaction from their mother. Yet when she returned that evening to find them in the hallway, eyes bloodshot, silk scarves screwed tight around their necks, she merely snorted softly.

"Who could do such a thing?"

She padded a circuit around them, to the kitchen for a dark bottle before heading upstairs. For a while they lay there, waiting for something to happen, but she didn't come back down. Ellen tilted her head to see Jess was still pretending. She waggled her fingers at her sister and watched as something gradually crept back into her face. Or maybe it was the opposite; something in there retreating, making room for Jess to return.

Eventually, their mother said and did nothing at all when she walked in on yet another gory diorama.

"Oh, I *am* tired," she would murmur to herself, her gaze gliding over their bodies, past all the meticulous details they had put so much work into; the carefully applied makeup they had re-purposed from her dressing table, the near-broken angles of their frozen limbs. She would go up to her bedroom, or back out to drive until the shrinking daylight had extinguished entirely. As the shadows stretched longer and longer across them Ellen would grow cold, but still she would wait, unwilling or unable to spoil what felt at the time a flawless imitation of death. Later, as they washed their faces and arms in the kitchen sink, Jess would accuse her of not trying hard enough.

"She'd believe it if it was just me. But with you here . . . you just look like you're having a nap."

"That's not true."

Such matters were always a contest to Jess. She was better at most things. She was smarter, and prettier, and then she was better at being dead. Ellen would try to still her breath, to slow her heartbeats down until they rang in her ears like the tread of an intruder, but she could never quite match the depths of her sister's trance. Jess wouldn't have looked out of place atop the tombs in their local church, back when they used to go every Sunday. So complete was her sister's repose that Ellen was never quite sure if she would stir back into life once the trick was over. Every time it seemed another second would need to pass before her eyes refocused and that familiar smirk crept over her features.

In hindsight, their attempts were mostly childish, steeped in a child's notion of death and violence, a collection of cliches absorbed sideways from the world despite their mother's best efforts to shield them. Plainly unbelievable. And yet there were inclusions Ellen couldn't account for, snatches of memory bizarre and grim which had somehow survived the abrasion of intervening decades. She remembered, among other things, them painting pools of purplish lividity onto their skin as part of the preparations for a trick, not a single word passing between them as they blended dark and clotted margins against still-living flesh. A child shouldn't know how blood really sinks and settles in the tissues of a cooling body. A child *wouldn't* know. From where was that knowledge granted to them, she wondered? What other details had she elided from their countless hours of craft?

It seemed for a while that their steady escalation of tricks would never end, peppered with increasingly ghoulish touches that went either unobserved or unmentioned by their mother. Until one afternoon, watching old movies as they always did, Jess didn't suggest any new ideas, and again the day after that. Ellen received a blank stare when she dared to broach the subject.

"Let's not," Jess said, eventually, turning back to the screen.

Ellen didn't push it. She'd assumed Jess had grown bored of their new hobby, as she often did, and up until that point been indulging her younger sister's whims in a bout of rare charity. Secretly, the prospect of a return to those long and aimless days filled her with relief. The preparation required for each trick had grown to become a chore, so exacting were Jess's demands for verisimilitude. Not to mention the very real pain involved. More than once had Ellen nursed a compressed nerve or throbbing bruise at the end of their antics, the result of an awkward position held far too long. Jess meanwhile arose with only the slightest hint of a grimace, as if she could've remained there for hours longer. Days, even.

Was that the first sign, Ellen asked herself, that her sister was changing? Or was it among the last, the shedding scraps of a transformation invisible yet total, waiting patiently to be recognized for what it was?

ON OCCASION THEIR MOTHER would take them to the supermarket. She needed to be seen out with them every so often. People might talk, otherwise. They might say things like *she was taking matters a bit too hard*, or that *the girls hadn't been at school for quite a while now, were they still unwell?* Comments of that nature.

Ellen tracked alongside the trolley as they navigated the gleaming rows, past all those signs stamped and slashed with yellow ribbons celebrating a never-ending sale. They didn't used to go to this supermarket, so far out of town. Other shoppers slumped past, trailed by children with crusted lips or circles around their eyes. She wasn't allowed to talk to those ones. Occasionally their mother would smile at an adult, mouthing a *hello* or a *good afternoon*. She had sent Jess for some tinned tomatoes and was in the midst of explaining to Ellen why tinned food was much safer—safer from what, exactly, she would not elaborate—when they heard the crash.

Jess was lying face down in the middle of the aisle, dented cans rolling to a stop around her. A pool of water, thin and pink, had begun to spread around her shoulders, soaking into her hair. A young assistant dithered before the scene.

"Oh my God," their mother said.

She hurried over and tried to drag Jess to her feet, to no avail.

"I'm so sorry. Really."

Eventually, she settled on propping her daughter up against the empty shelves. Jess's head lolled to one side, dripping, her eyes a thin crescent of white under half-settled lids.

"Miss. Is your daughter okay?" the assistant asked.

A crowd began to gather at the end of the aisle. Ellen took a step back into them, hoping she wouldn't be recognized. Someone in the mass clicked their tongue. *Is she all right? That's the Harrison girl, isn't it?* Another sighed. *Oh dear.* Children jostled for a view.

"Yes, yes. She's fine. She's just been . . . playing this stupid game, recently. Just a stupid game." Her mother's voice creaked at the end and Ellen found herself wincing at the sound.

"Right. Okay." The assistant's hands worked atop each other. "It's just . . . I wasn't sure she was breathing. When I found her."

At that the rumble of murmurs stopped, as if everyone had noticed at once how Jess lay so still and pale under the halogen bars, a body dredged from the deeps. Matted strands of hair clung to her face. It must have been only a few swollen seconds. Six, eight at most—far from the endless minutes of waiting Ellen recalled. For then her sister's ribs moved up and down, sharply, once, and the spell was broken.

"See? See. It's fine. She's fine. I'd like to pay now. Please. I'll pay for all of those, as well."

Their mother hid her face in her purse as she fretted and fumbled. Sensing that the drama had peaked, the watchers began to disperse, muttering their conclusions to each other. *Reckon she fainted? Hardly. Acting up. No wonder. Haven't you heard?* Some even braved the spill to grab what they could, paying no heed to the sopping figure still braced against the shelves, an unoccupied body.

There were consequences. Jess for what she had done, and Ellen for her assumed complicity. During the night, Ellen tapped on the dividing wall.

"Why didn't you tell me?" she asked, loud enough that she feared waking their mother, but there came no reply.

The next morning, they were taken to a doctor. What was his name?

Blackwell? Blackthorn? He spoke to Jess and Ellen separately in his office, a wood-paneled room that smelled of polish, and he wrote down all the things they said in a little notebook. He only asked a few questions, but once Ellen started talking, she found that she couldn't stop. She told him about everything, about the trick and her mother and Jess, and he didn't interrupt, only pursed his lips and wrote faster and faster in that little book of his.

"You didn't tell him anything, did you?" asked Jess when it was her turn to go in, the first words she had spoken to her sister since the supermarket.

"No," said Ellen. "Of course not."

Afterwards they sat in the waiting area, flicking through all the magazines they weren't allowed at home. The silhouettes of the doctor and their mother shifted behind a sheet of wire-laden glass. The only thing Ellen could make out was their mother shaking her head at each muffled remark, slowly at first, then with increasing vigor. As she drove them back home, she announced that they would not be returning to the clinic. Not while that man was still working there. Unbelievable, she muttered, what he was suggesting she do with her girls. *To* her girls. When Ellen asked, their mother only shook her head again and claimed the doctor had *got it completely backwards*. Funny how she could remember that perfectly, of all things, those exact words. Completely backwards.

FOLLOWING THEIR MEETING with the doctor, their mother's attitude underwent a marked change. Ellen came down on Monday morning to find her still in the house, making breakfast.

"Us girls have to stick together, don't we?" she said.

She had taken some overdue holiday at the encouragement of the company. That day they could get whatever magazine they wanted on their trip to the newsagents for bread and milk and wine. At dinnertime, their mother even remarked that the girls were looking much healthier. Perhaps their sickness was finally turning a corner, and a return to school could be considered. Assuming they'd fully recovered, she added, before she fixed them with a meaningful look. Ellen nodded. Jess looked down, pushed the food around on her plate.

After Jess's last trick some unspoken contract between the two of them had been violated. Their mother wasn't scared or shocked, only humiliated. More to the point, Jess had done it alone. Ellen had just been a prop, a dumb tool to be used like the scissors or knife or the hammer. If she could be a tool then she could be a target. She thought to confront her sister, but Ellen knew she would only laugh and ask if she could take a joke.

On Thursday, just as matters were beginning to settle into a routine of sorts, their mother received a call from her office.

"Stupid to think I could . . . look, I've got to go in. I don't care what you get up to, what kind of fight you've had," she said, as she grabbed her coat. "Just . . . amuse each other, for a while. Okay?"

Again she locked the heavy bolts on the front door, leaving them with only the other's unwelcome company.

The rest of the day juddered along restlessly, itching at them. A couple of flies had somehow gotten inside the living room. They droned loops above their heads, stopping to sip at the red-speckled rim of the tumbler before resuming their erratic flight. The girls were watching something about an explorer on the Nile. People running in and out of caves in cardboard costumes, golden statues, a monstrous figure in pursuit. During a quiet point, Jess leaned over and whispered something in Ellen's ear.

Ellen remembered nearly retching when she heard it, although only seconds later she couldn't recall what exactly her sister had said. Not even a snatched fragment, a few scattered words. The idea had sublimated in her mind as soon as it arrived, leaving only an oily, indelible residue. All that remained was a conviction that Jess was planning a horrible joke, a trick harsh and chemical.

"Why would we want to do that?" Ellen said. She shrunk away. "That's an awful idea. Really . . . awful."

"What?"

"That wouldn't even scare her. That would just . . . hurt her. Make her sick. Or—"

Jess rolled her eyes. "Fine. No need to get upset. It was just an idea. No worse than the one you told me." She turned back to the TV. "You aren't the only one who can have ideas, you know."

She knew Jess wanted her to ask, so she did. "What do you mean?"

"I mean your secret."

"What secret?" Ellen's face grew warm.

Despite her smirk a note of petulance quavered in Jess's voice.

"It wasn't your idea, was it? The trick. I know because you couldn't come up with any better ideas afterwards. Only boring stuff. Like you didn't know what made it so good."

"I didn't get it from anywhere. It came from me."

Jess continued, still staring at the screen.

"It's fine. I went and got more. When I started playing the trick by myself."

A pulse beat in Ellen's head.

"The further down I went, the more the ideas came up. Lots of them I forgot. Some of them gave me bad headaches. But I managed to remember a few. All I had to do was to not move. Not breathe."

Jess turned, her expression unreadable. A dark bruise had blossomed at the margin of her scalp, the first of a fading cluster that stretched beneath her hair. It didn't look fake.

"I learnt a lot about pretending. I was pretending at all the wrong things, like you. I fixed them, but now it's strange. Backwards. It's a lot easier *not* to breathe. You should try it too."

Ellen edged away from her sister, towards the doorway. Something was wrong, something she couldn't spot immediately.

"What?" she said. "No."

Jess blinked, one eyelid moving before the other. Ellen saw then that everything about her sister was a split-second off. Her speech, the movements of her hands and eyes and face. Every action carried a subtle and stilted delay, as if she had to remind herself to do them.

"Let me show you. It'll be funny. I'm getting really good at it now."

"But . . . " Ellen fumbled for an excuse, any excuse not to see what would happen next. "You've told me. How is the trick going to work if I already know?"

"You'll believe me anyway."

Before Ellen could say anything more Jess rose to her feet and began to sway from side to side. One half of her face fell slack and began to twitch. A low groan erupted from her as she shuddered, and then collapsed, bouncing her head off the patio door with a crack as she did so. Her arms and legs shot in and out at spasmodic angles, curling and buckling upon themselves, the limbs of a deep-sea creature pulled unwilling to the surface. Ellen leapt to her feet, backed into the doorway as her sister thrashed and gurgled for interminable seconds. Eventually, a final, awful rattle escaped from her sister.

The silence grew thick. Ellen tried to laugh. Her attempts were swiftly swallowed in the overstuffed cushions, the heavy fabrics draped over every sharp edge in the room. She willed herself not to cringe at her sister's twisted body, her glassy eyes. She wasn't going to fall for it.

Jess didn't move.

"Jess. Come on."

Still nothing. Ellen approached, nudged her sister with her toe. Nothing. She bent down next to Jess's body and, bracing herself, held her hand out over her sister's rictus mouth. Nothing. She kept waiting, for much longer than she could've held her own breath. Then, for longer than she thought anyone could.

"Jess?"

She took her hand away. A fly swooped low and landed on Jess's face. Ellen watched it rub its little claws all over her cheek, searching for something.

"Oh."

It crawled up and up, onto her open eye, her pupil.

Nothing.

"Oh. Oh."

Ellen jerked back. For a moment she stood there, stunned. What should she do now? Call their mother's office? An ambulance? What would she tell them?

She groped to the phone in the hallway, the walls swimming in and out with her heartbeat, blinking away the darkness boiling at the edge of her vision. It was only after she'd punched in the emergency number and it had rung out three times that there came a suppressed snort from the living room.

"I can't believe it. I really got you."

Jess was leaning in the doorway, her head silhouetted by the dying sun. The air turned soupy like in the worst kind of dreams, the ones where everything was the same but for the overwhelming wrongness in everything, infusing the world inside and out. Her face was shrouded, but Ellen could imagine her smile. Another trick. But it felt real. It *was* real.

"You did it," Ellen said. Somebody was asking questions on the other end of the phone.

"Ahhh. I told you, I'd gotten good at it. I've been learning."

"How can you *learn* that?"

Jess said nothing.

"You stopped breathing," Ellen said. "You hit your head. Hard."

"Huh. I didn't notice."

Ellen swallowed.

"This is stupid, Jess," she said, screwing her eyes shut.

"What?"

"I said . . . " Ellen felt the air being pushed out of her lungs. She tried to raise her voice. "It's stupid. It's not funny anymore."

Jess didn't reply.

"I don't want to play this anymore. I want to go outside, with all the others. I want to go back to school. I don't want to be stuck in here with you . . . "

The floor rushed up to meet Ellen, the canned voice of the operator a thousand miles away.

What had happened then? A few memories with ragged edges, all out of order. Ellen's days no longer belonged to her. She would blink and find herself no longer barricaded in her bedroom but instead standing opposite Jess, holding a knife or cudgel that wasn't there before, staring into her sister's greying face, at the dried red around her eyes or mouth. In the evenings, upon their mother's return, Ellen would venture downstairs to find her sister sitting at the dinner table. She would be transformed from earlier, her hair freshly combed, eyes now limpid and glittering, all traces of violence expunged.

Ellen choked down her food so she didn't have to witness Jess pretending to talk to their mother, pretending to eat. It was all a trick, a backwards trick, a trick where you already knew how it was done and that only made it worse. A trick that would be dropped the second they were alone again. After dinner she would go to bed early and read her magazines over and over until she didn't remember falling asleep, her final thoughts drifting to the thin wall that separated her from her twin, of what nameless processes might be taking place on the other side. It was just a matter of time until her sister would knock on that wall one quiet afternoon, with just them in the house, and ask her if she wanted to see another trick. A really scary one this time.

At least, that was how Ellen had assumed it would end. But Jess, as always, had other plans.

ELLEN'S MOTHER TOOK her to the funeral home before the ceremony. She had insisted on seeing Jess one last time. To be sure. She didn't know why she was surprised to see her father waiting at the entrance, leaning on his car. It made sense for him to be there. He looked different to how Ellen remembered him. More lines in his face. And he had a tan. She could smell coconut as he hugged her.

"Hello, princess."

She thought that he didn't look sad at all, just very tired. A dried-out man in a dark suit was waiting for them just inside the building. He led them through the tangle of antiseptic corridors while her parents talked in low tones just ahead.

"—how long has she been—"

"—so now you care—"

"—unfit. The school called me—"

—until they arrived at a chilled room in which lay Jessica, her limbs straightened out, her body nestled in mounds of shiny white satin. Ellen was given a step stool so she could lean over the box. They'd done a good job with her face. She had overheard what the hospital had said to their mother on the phone. About the discoloration. All those invisible wounds that had built up day after day. Nobody could have predicted it. It was nobody's fault.

The damage had been reduced to a faint shadow across her left temple and cheek. And she looked so content. Like she'd finally got what she wanted. Everyone believes you now, Ellen wanted to say. You can stop. You've won. As if it was ever a contest.

Ellen remembered thinking she should have been distraught, looking down at Jess's body. Only a queasy mix of guilt and relief bubbled in her stomach. If she had never whispered those things to her, her sister might still be around. She had . . . infected Jess, somehow, with what she had said. An idea which forgot itself.

She had waited at that moment for a voice or a concept to rise up in her as it had before, to leave some stain of knowledge upon her in its passing. More than that—she had willed it, invited it. *Tell me. Come back and tell me. Tell me what you told her.* Nothing. Silence in all directions within herself.

Wait. Was that a flicker across Jess's upper lip, a fraction of a flared nostril? The slightest quiver of her sunken chest, like she was stifling a laugh?

"She's pretending," Ellen said, turning to her mother.

Her mother looked up, eyes red and puffy.

"Ellen. This is not the time for your nonsense."

There was something in her mother's voice. Anger, Ellen had thought at the time.

"It's not nonsense. She's playing the trick again." She needed to make her understand. "On all of us. She's not dead. Not like that. She's pretending, only now she's stopped pretending—"

Ellen toppled off the step from the blow. Once she was on the floor, she found it very hard to get back up again.

"What on earth are you doing?" said her father.

Ellen didn't hear the argument. She pictured her lifeblood blooming out of a gash on her face, soaking through the thick carpet, dripping between the floorboards below. She imagined the expressions of her parents turning to horror when they realized what had happened, that their remaining daughter had joined Jessica thanks to their thoughtlessness, their preoccupations. She tried and tried to stop breathing but she couldn't help taking long low gulps as if minutes before she'd been drowning.

"I'm not a madwoman. It doesn't stop. Ever."

At that, her mother left. Others entered, a procession of shiny black shoes. "Leave her," someone said, not unkindly.

By the time Ellen could get up again the room had emptied. Jess was gone. Outside, her father was leaning against his car, smoking and chatting to a young woman in the passenger seat. Had she always been there? He opened the backseat door with a flourish when he noticed Ellen.

"There she is. Had a bit of a tizzy, didn't she? Just needed a breather. Come on, princess." He gave a wan smile.

They drove in silence for a while, past the bleached driveways, the endless bungalows. The woman—Ellen never found out her name—applied eyeliner in-between speed bumps, her mouth a goldfish O. Her father's gaze kept darting to meet Ellen's own in the rear-view mirror. Eventually, he said:

"Me and your mother thought it would be best if you got ready at my flat today. Maybe you could stay for a week or two after, as well. Just an idea, until things get back to normal."

Ellen nodded.

"Your mother . . . " Her father continued while they hung at a roundabout. The indicator click-clacked dryly, counting down. "She didn't mean to do that, earlier. Something very bad happened to her family. When she was younger. She, uhm. Well. I think all of this has reminded her."

"What was it?"

He grunted as he spun the wheel.

"I'm sure she'll tell you herself. When she's ready."

Her father's friend said something too quiet for Ellen to hear, and he shushed her sharply.

BUT UPON ELLEN'S return to her home several weeks later her mother mentioned nothing of Jess, nor of her own family. She was cordial and calm, treating her remaining daughter like a lodger who always paid the rent on time. And Ellen never asked her. Not when she went to a new school, not when she got a job as a typist and could afford to move out, not when she put down a deposit for a seedy flat with her new boyfriend, bump barely visible under her sundress. After that, when she had twins of her own . . . well, they had very little reason to be in touch with each other by that point.

So the years smeared by. Things came unstuck from the bottom of Ellen's soul and floated up into the pale light, matters better left forgotten. Some nights she would stare up at the ceiling, combing the inside of her head for any hidden cracks that could be prized open. On others she would hold her breath until dark stars unfurled before her eyes, filling her vision as she sank down and down.

She tried not to think of the past, even as her own life followed a trajectory she recognized all too well. Her daughters grew up. Grew to have secrets of their own. Ellen didn't try to shield them from the terrible things they would see and hear in the world, things that they might share with each other. Unlike her mother and her confused attempts, her dim recognition of the familial contagion, she had a plan for what would inevitably occur. What would need to be done.

Which is why, upon returning home late one evening to find her daughters slumped face-down in the hallway, Ellen didn't gasp, or shriek. She knelt down, took the blades from their limp hands into her own and she waited. She waited until the porch light shuddered into life and the breeze grew biting. She waited to see who would give up the trick first—who would be the first to laugh, to make something flutter and retreat from behind their features. Who would be the first to breathe.

FEED

Jason A. Wyckoff

———◆———

HER COUSIN HAD HURT her knee somehow. On display were two flash-whitened legs tapering to nubbin-sprouted feet made small from perspective. Beyond was near dark; the only definition was the division between two blocks, beige wall and walnut wainscoting, which told Nell her cousin was resting in her living room. She didn't know her cousin's house well, but she knew that much at least. A two-quart locking baggie filled with ice cubes slouched over a decorative tea-towel covering her cousin's knee. She wrote that the knee was bothering her again. Nell couldn't remember what the initial complaint was. What was wrong with her cousin's knee? She selected the 'Love' response to indicate her abiding support; they were cousins, after all. It was more personal than just responding with a 'Sad' face to indicate her empathy, which she might have done with a male co-worker or the like.

As the train dragged to a stop, Nell's left arm pressed into the partition, five down-sloping aluminum bars like a flattened ribcage. The train was headed downtown. Nell was on her way to the county recorder's office.

A news report about a woman trapped in a coma for ten years had terrified her, and she wanted to create a living will. She couldn't tell her brother or her friends; they would chide her she was far too young to worry about such things, but, in Nell's mind 1) she wasn't, or wouldn't be soon enough, and 2) why should she burden anyone else when she could make her own decisions (at such time as she still *could* make those decisions)? The car was over half-full already and no one moved to exit. The doors opened next to her and Nell smelled the familiar mix of oil and ozone from the station platform, a scent which evoked for her curious dual feelings of incubation and release. A few new bodies shifted past her peripherally, and then the doors shut.

As the train lurched forward once more, a man in a tight suit jacket and skinny tie removed his fedora, holding it upside-down in front of him. His wide smile showed bright, perfect teeth. He began to sing, "A Place Nobody Can Find." Nell loved that old song, but she was embarrassed because she didn't have any cash with her. Not wanting to seem ungracious, she thought it best just to look away. She watched a fifty-foot-tall marionette of a deep-sea diver navigate the streets of Montréal. It was truly an impressive spectacle. She wondered for a second if Doris from church had recorded the procession herself; but, no, she was only re-posting. Nell 'Like'd it.

There was a commotion towards the front of the car. The singer's performance faltered. He put his hat back on his head and joined the other riders who were shuffling towards the rear, grumbling. The cause was soon obvious: a rank scent assailed Nell's nostrils. It was not unusual to suffer the awful stench of a fellow passenger. Common BO was so prevalent there was little else to do than to scrunch your nose in disapproval and go on with your day. And the odor of urine, sharp or stale, greeted Nell upon entry to the train more often than she cared to guess. The body's other excretions were more likely to cause a ruckus such as this, but, awful as the smell was, Nell did not detect the fetor of vomit or shit. It was something more like vegetable rot tinged with the skunk of old decay (Nell recalled a shriveled snake she'd encountered mushed into the gravel drive at her grandparent's house). And there was a tempering earthy note which somehow kept the stink from being *too* objectionable.

Nell turned her head to see to whom the offensive odor clung, but her view was blocked by the protuberant backpack of a young man with a red beard.

Nell flinched and stifled an exclamation at the sight of a dead elephant. Two horrible, empty wounds flanked the poor beast's limp trunk. She scrolled swiftly past. Yes, she hated violence against animals too, and yes, she was livid with the perpetrators of this ghastly slaughter, but she didn't want to see those images in her feed. It wasn't a matter of shying away from them, she thought, but rather an aversion any right-minded person should feel. It seemed to her that anyone who would post such images was indulging a morbid, lurid fascination with the atrocities they professed to revile. Nell didn't look to see who'd linked to the article.

Not two flicks of her thumb later there waited a video of a man cutting an owl loose from a soccer net. That was much better of course; kindness towards animals was always to be commended. She 'Like'd the video, though not without some misgiving; she'd been wondering more and more recently if some of the animal rescues she'd seen might have been staged.

The bearded student holding the partition pole turned sideways. Nell could see past him now. The person responsible for the stench must have been the man in the heavy coat and hoodie slumped forward in his seat on the opposite side of the car near the front. There was no particular indication in his appearance that he should be the cause for the offense, nor any clue to the cause *of* it, but the empty seats beside and opposite indicated he was the source. There were other riders up that way, snuffling into the crooks of their elbows or pulling stretchy shirt collars up over their noses, but the majority by far was stuffed into the back half of the car.

She saw a post from another cousin more distant. He was sharing a link with the caption "Most People Won't Share This Soldier's Story," below a photo of a man perched at the edge of a butte, smiling at the camera, steady and sure atop the back-bent black metal 'blades' below his knees. Nell grieved for the soldier's sacrifice and spared a thought to commend him for his service but recoiled at the guilt-laden challenge of the headline. Was Nell supposed to count herself less of a patriot if she didn't share the politically charged article? She indicated she was 'Angry';

let her distant cousin interpret her response as directed to the nebulous 'Most People' whose modest social media presence he apparently considered a slap in the face to veterans.

Someone barked curses from the back of the car; several bursts of banging and rattling followed. Nell couldn't see through the crowd, but the inference was clear: the door between cars wouldn't budge. No one seemed inclined to try the forward exit. There would be no escaping the smell before the side doors opened at the next stop.

And the stink was getting stronger and more oppressive, saturating the enclosed air. Nell mused that a person's sense of smell usually adjusted quickly to suppress awareness of foul odors. This clearly was not going to be one of those instances.

Nell tried to distract herself: Brenda from high school, her chubby face flush, her brow ringed with sweat, held up a cheap plastic circle dangling from a cord around her neck. She'd just completed her first ever 5K run. She extolled the virtues of trying to get into shape, no matter how late in life you start. Respondents congratulated and encouraged her. Nell felt anything she might say would be both superfluous and, if she honestly assessed Brenda's physique, disingenuous. She chose 'Wow': declamatory yet non-committal. She pulled up Brenda's profile page. The next post down was a 'Throwback Thursday' pic. Nell remembered the photo from their yearbook. They had worn the same fright bangs and bell-flared shoulder-length hair. She selected 'Sad' because she thought that was funnier than just echoing back the expected 'Haha'. She looked at Brenda's friends and recognized a fellow classmate. She sent a friend request and continued searching. A few seconds later, she realized her mistake and gasped. The only personal interaction she'd ever had with Tim Gallagher was the day he forcibly groped her in a stairwell. Why had she sent the request? She went to cancel it, but she just ended up back on her feed with one new notification. She cringed to think he might have accepted—and so quickly.

Past the doors, a woman with clicking bracelets yelled and pointed at two young men across the aisle. She condemned their lifestyle and informed them that Jesus was going to cast them into a lake of hellfire because they had turned their backs on him. Both men were small, nearly boys, really. They were holding hands and ducking their heads. Nell saw that they were wearing yarmulkes, and she was unsure which 'choice' the woman objected to.

The proximity of the other passengers made her feel uncomfortably warm. Shouldn't they be at the next stop by now? It had never taken this long before. Yes, it seemed the train might be moving more slowly than usual, though it was almost impossible to be sure in the black of the tunnel.

Tim Gallagher was in her feed now. Nell saw a sunset from three days previous. It was an orange splash; no washes of purple or rose, no striations of wispy stratus clouds hugging the horizon or dividing the twilight. She 'Love'd it.

A groan indicating intense strain drew her attention towards the front of the car. A man on the bench opposite the slumped man was spreading his legs as far apart as he possibly could. Though no one shared the bench with him or made any indication towards claiming one of the empty seats, the man planted both hands on the edge of the bench, holding himself partially aloft as he tried to get his legs up to cover the two seats on either side, though he clearly lacked the flexibility to accomplish the 'splits'. His face was red; the veins in his neck protruded as he jerked his head, glaring in turn at every person in his line of sight.

Nell looked down as the person beside her pressed closer, mashing her into the divider. Margie from work had posted a photo of a casserole she'd prepared for her family. The melted cheese on top appeared greenish and separated into lumpy clots and runny grease. Even if the dish tasted good, how could anyone think the picture looked the least bit appetizing? Nell replied '!!!!!'. Her neighbor Gloria posted a picture of her father on his 92nd birthday, 'Still looks great!'—which was clearly inaccurate. His spittle-glossed mouth was slack and his yellow eyes stared blankly off-camera. Nell selected 'Haha' to let Gloria know she was in on the joke.

A burst of trebly heavy metal made her glance upwards. A woman with ratty blonde hair grimaced defiantly at no one. From the volume of the music leaking from her headphones, Nell wondered if her sour expression wasn't pain-induced.

Wait—had she replied 'Haha' to a picture of her neighbor's decrepit father? Nell tried to scroll back up, but no matter which direction she swiped with thumb or finger, her feed only moved downward. In fact, it seemed to be moving of its own accord, as though drawn by a slowly sinking counterweight.

A woman screamed. The sound directed Nell back to the slumping, stinking man. His shoulders had pitched back against the seat and dislodged the cloth hood. His head lolled. His skin was cracked and grey; his eyes were empty pits of black—or so Nell thought from a quick glance. The backpack swung into her face and she had to push it away. She thought there had been something else—a puff of fine ash or white pollen or spores billowing up from the man's mouth, clinging in a fine film to the ceiling, drifting towards the back of the car. Nell's hand jerked up with a feint before she remembered there was no 'stop' cord to tug: she was on a train, not a bus.

The singer with the hat was yelling at the screaming woman to shut up, but her squall continued unabated. The tinny rock music chitter-chugged along. Nell thought she must have been wrong. More people would react if she had seen what she'd thought she'd seen. They would have to. Why hadn't the train stopped? Had they gone through the next station already? There could be no doubt the train was moving; a sack-like person squeezing between the bearded man and the blonde rocker threatened to fall into Nell's lap as the train veered around a curve.

'Is this a ghost?' read a shivering graphic over black and white security footage. "I don't know!" Nell hissed, and when the person beside her jabbed her side with an elbow, she typed 'I DON"T KNOW!' and scrolled onward. The cousin with the injured knee posted a pic of her son's new tattoo: a stand of white-flecked, red-top Toadstools with the word 'MEME' in black-outlined bright yellow letters below it. Nell blinked in confusion. That couldn't really be what he'd had permanently inscribed on his flesh. She replied with a knife and an eggplant.

She sniffed and her sinuses tickled. She thought again of the hazy effluvium. Was her subconscious trying to tell her something? Was a psychotropic mushroom spore causing her to hallucinate? Had parasitic toxic fungi animated a man's corpse and impelled it to spread the infestation in a confined space? One hears so much about the dangers of climate change these days.

'Ashley's cheer squad finished last at regionals but the girls had a ton of fun!'

What was the point of sitting next to the doors if the train never stopped?

Tim Gallagher was proud of his new deck.

'maybe next year' Nell typed, forgetting she'd moved on from the previous post. The sack person swooned and sank onto her lap, forced back by a skirmish going on behind the wall of bodies. Nell peered forward. The dusty whitish film was on everything in the front part of the car. The overzealous manspreader was a broken statue, the hollow-eyed man a frost-crusted mummy. The boys were swatting at their heads, spitting, and wiping their yarmulkes on their coat sleeves.

Gold, cursive writing on a blue sky background reminded her 'Our Most Renewable Resource is Our Children,' or something like that; fine dust blurred her screen. She gave it three shit-piles. A faceless stick figure in a shaky border waved at her, captioned by the quote 'It's so hard to tell when their heads are twisted around'. Nell didn't know how to respond and moved on, but then it was the next post, as well, so she 'Like'd it, and then it was the next post again, and she 'Like'd it again.

She flinched at a sticky kiss on her cheek. The red-bearded student waggled his erect penis between the aluminum divider slats. Nell threw her shoulder up and twisted away; the amorphous shape hurled itself off of her legs and bulled towards the opposite doors, causing half a dozen people to topple in a thrashing heap. Tears streamed from behind the silted glasses of a young girl standing on the seat across from Nell. The singing man was holding one hand with the other, staring at a bloody gash in his palm.

'Nell changed her profile picture'—only she hadn't, and no photo appeared in the frame, only a targeted advertisement: 'Do You Have Mold?'

Maybe it *was* a psychotropic spore. Or—maybe it was all just in her head. Maybe unbearable situations caused the mind to imagine impossible things. Yes. Nell remembered that extreme stress or fear could slow one's perception of time. But it can't *alter* time, she thought. Either way, whether she was poisoning herself with her own panic or if she was inhaling airborne fungal spermatozoa, reality *must* reassert itself. No matter how long it had seemed, the distance between stations hadn't actually changed, and they had to reach the next one eventually. No, not eventually—very *soon*. Within the space of a scream. A scream could last no longer than a breath, but they couldn't be more than a breath away, not by now. So, no matter what she perceived, the truth would be revealed just as soon as her scream reached its terminus. All she had to do was start. Just start.

Nell opened her mouth and coughed. Glistening, dancing static bloomed in front of her eyes. She thought, 'Wow', and turned on her camera to share.

'Neath The Mirror Of The Sea

Rhonda Eikamp

———————♦———————

SHE SWAM THROUGH dreams of coral bones, dainty jellyfish, the choking salt. She rescued him and he wasn't dead.

When they pulled over to see where they were, Kylie rolled the window down. *Breathe.* The cries of grieving gulls dropped into the car. Leaning out, she glimpsed the deserted-looking beach, far down across the boulevard, a wet-gold strip. The air was crusty with salt. She wanted to wipe the air off her face. She'd forgotten how it was at the beach, the ubiquitous sand and salt, things sticking to your skin you could never wash away. A deeper salt inside made her shudder.

"This is it." Jeff glanced at the GPS, craned his neck to view the building. He whistled. "Nice. That's what—thirteen stories?"

"No one does thirteen stories." Kylie started the car back up. "Bad luck." An entrance to the resort's underground parking yawned dark as a sea cave. The condo resort was the best along the coast, voiceless on-line voices had assured them. Relax in sun-drenched luxury.

Jeff smiled and touched her hand. "I love your superstition." He hated it, she knew. Three years of therapy and then she'd married her therapist because the depth of his tolerance for her problems had seemed boundless. Because he asked, twice, and his eyes the second time had said she'd be killing something if she said no again. You're marrying your therapist? had been her mother's reaction, good luck with that. Jeff saved me after Mitch, Kylie had wanted to say. Swam through my nightmares, pulled me up gasping. It was love she felt, if love was wanting to breathe again. For two years now she'd breathed.

The air in the parking garage was even saltier. They found the main door and a buzzer. A woman's bubbly voice buzzed them into the building. "Go through the lobby, take the elevator to the sixth floor. We're check-in for guests up here."

The ground-floor lobby they walked through was deserted, a few armchairs artfully placed against a tile wall in aquamarine. A black mosaic shape had been worked into the blue tiles, a curling eel that stretched the length of the wall and ended beside the elevators in a toothy smile. A welcoming monster. Kylie avoided its gaze, and noticed Jeff notice.

The receptionist at the sixth-floor desk had black gelled hair and the saddest hazel eyes Kylie had ever seen.

"The lower floors are private condo owners," she told them. Her name-tag said Blaise. Past the desk, glass doors led to an infinity pool. Water, too close. Kylie's head swirled. What they were attempting washed over her, suddenly daunting. It was too early.

The sky beyond the glass had begun to darken with clouds. "Your rental's on the thirteenth floor." *Bad luck.* Blaise handed Jeff the key and he turned to the elevator.

Kylie's gaze was drawn to a large vase placed conspicuously on a table in the middle of the lobby. Violet at the base, rising in an organic curl that grew dark near the top and opened into a fish-mouth, jagged white glazing at the rim suggesting fangs. Around its middle a blond cherubic boy hugged the sea serpent as though riding it, his lower half seeming to fuse into its eely folds, his painted eyes wide.

Kylie turned back to the receptionist. "What's the worm downstairs?" she asked. Jeff threw her an odd look.

"The dark one?" Blaise's voice fell at the end, uninterested; it might have been her answer. She looked back down to her computer.

"We'll be going on up to our room," Jeff said too quickly.

There was sand on the elevator floor. It hadn't been there before, Kylie was sure. She swiped it with her shoe and thought of children trooping in from the beach, though they had seen and heard no one in the building except Blaise. Their apartment on the thirteenth floor was at the end of a long curved hall. Beach decor, airy colors. Jeff stood on the balcony and called to her to come look.

She had to stop her thoughts swirling. He'd want it.

"Please, Jeff. I'm taking my time."

He came back in and rubbed her shoulders. "Let's stay positive. Hey, swank, huh?"

"You know how to pick 'em."

"Your idea to come back to the area though." His hands on her were gentle and she couldn't stand it. She pushed them off softly.

"You said I might be ready."

"Ready for oceans, babe. A little exposure therapy." *Ready for seas of grief, tides of tears.* "Maybe not . . . the place it happened."

"Consult your therapist prior to any attempt at exposure therapy. I did."

He smiled, glancing around. "I give my seal of approval."

Kylie laid her cheek against his freckled face and for a moment the swirling stopped. You walk off a sea cliff, again and again, water effervescing around you as you drown, and find there's someone to catch you. Something solid, deep below the surface, lifting you.

Outside the open balcony door the surf made its growl heard.

A blond boy stood in the balcony door, watching her. He was dripping wet.

"I want to talk about Mitch while we're here," she whispered. "Maybe tonight?"

Jeff nodded. "Absolutely. Now, if it's all right with you, I'm gonna hit that beach."

SWANK AND SWANKER.

The condo resort hadn't been there five years ago, Kylie felt certain as she moved about the apartment alone, or maybe its skeleton had been, developers having just discovered the charms of this wilder stretch of coast, hotels popping up everywhere. She had checked herself and Mitch into a much cheaper place a mile down the boulevard, the downscaled luxury of cable and a pool to which Mitch had rushed out with his Nerf football as soon as they arrived and made instant friends, the way only nine-year olds could, after which Kylie had packed lunch and some towels and crossed the busy boulevard with him to the beach. Silt muddied the memories, caked her throat. She recalled how the sky had darkened for the afternoon, she remembered that, signal flags on yellow. They'd splashed and dunked and laughed. The water was filled with tiny jellyfish, harmless apparently, and Mitch, always the innovator, removed his swim goggles and scooped a jellyfish up in one lens, an exact fit, begging her to let him keep it. She'd told him no, it would die if you took it out of the sea.

The haze on the horizon was ripening. Alone in the condo, Kylie rubbed at the salt fear inside her veins, took a deep breath and stepped onto the balcony. She could look at the ocean. Big deal. Big salty deal. From here the water seemed nearer the boulevard than it had been, at places smashing against the bulwarks where cars passed, spume flying into the air over hoods like so many minnows. The flags were on yellow. The stretch below looked nothing like her memory from the cheap motel a mile south, though she hadn't seen that beach from on high like this. The height lent her thoughts distance. She tried to make out Jeff among the meager beach crowd. He ought to be just getting down there, not in the water yet, but details had become shimmery under the purplish-brown clouds moving in, sandy surfaces coruscating between light and shade. The condo building's infinity pool on the sixth floor caught her gaze, just below her, and she leaned with her arms on the rail to stare straight down at the turquoise water, repressing a shudder. Look, you can do this too. The pool was empty. Leaning further: other balconies to the right and down, innumerable it seemed, all deserted. A honeycomb of a building. Private residents on the first five floors, the receptionist had said. The well-off, Kylie supposed, who worked in the city over there behind the inland horizon all day, or worked at home but apparently never on their balconies. Couldn't stand the sound of the surf any more than she could maybe, the constant mushy pulse always slightly unpredictable, like a bad heart. Lives beating. She floated on top of an ocean of hidden life—squirmings and feedings—deep news going on beneath the casual swimmer, the tourist. Wrecks perhaps. Corpses. That was an elbow, for instance, she'd been looking at it for awhile, on one of the balconies far below, resting on a patio table, attached—presumably—to a reader or napper, everything else obscured by the angle. A delicate bare arm, possibly a child. Perfectly still.

Splashing and spluttering but the water wasn't deep, just choppy and Mitch had gone wild, laughing and choking, moving off after he abandoned the jellyfish. He was a strong swimmer for his age. She'd bought him a bodyboard, the price enough to make her single-mom eyes water. Mitch's dad was only a memory of a one-night stand but she'd taken responsibility, hadn't she, turned it into beauty, the beautiful son who was her life. Doing it alone, feeling alone too often. Moved off, away from people, away from her, and there was a long sequence Kylie could never recall afterward, flashes of the empty bodyboard rocking past, moments while she told herself other kids had a neon-red one like it. Screams. She was on the beach then somehow, watching a line of lifeguards perpendicular to the shore who dived under at a whistle again and again, moving slowly forward like the searchers through woods at a crime scene. There was something darker out there beyond the line, an impossibly large shadow beneath the water. It moved up and down with them, gleeful, teasing.

She watched the elbow for a long time. It didn't move.

After a while she went to look around the sixth floor.

The receptionist Blaise smiled up at her absently, touched her wet-gel hair. The emptiness of the resort had an echo-chamber quality. Through the glass door the undisturbed surface of the deserted infinity pool melded with the sky and sea beyond, as it was meant to. No lifeguard, the sign said.

Kylie stared again at the vase on the central table, the violet glaze that suggested the sheen of eelskin, twisting around itself up to that gaping mouth. No eyes or other features. Whatever creature the artist had imagined was a tube, gaping open at one end for feeding. The wide eyes of the cherubic boy riding it seemed to follow her, the ubiquitous gaze.

"Not their best."

Kylie started. The elderly man beside her looked too shabby for the resort. Gray three-day stubble, T-shirt and jeans with an oily green stain down one leg. A workman. "I like the floor myself." He gestured down.

She looked down and almost screamed. She was standing on the sea monster. A floor mosaic, a serpent of dark tiles swimming through the blue, curled about the length of the lobby, disappearing beneath a seating group. The same as the wall downstairs.

Breathe. "Must be a theme," she croaked.

"Sea things." The old man's speech was difficult to pin down. His eyes, like the ceramic boy's, moved with her but in a different way, never fastening entirely on her. Not right in the head. She started to leave.

"You've been here before."

A question? "Five years ago. I didn't stay in this place of course. It was built later."

"But your husband wanted you to come here now."

Kylie held her breath against her thumping heart. The man's not-straight-at-her pupils were depthless and unnerving.

"*I* wanted to come back to the area." My decision, that didn't need approval. "Jeff picked the resort. Something new."

"The resort's always new for those who've never been to it."

Of course it is. "I've had a . . . water phobia for a while." *Beach-sand-sea phobia. Why tell him this? Not a phobia. A post-trauma, a post-life, in which she could never move forward. Post-Mitch.* She suddenly wanted someone else there, anyone to hear this man, how he must have been watching her and Jeff arrive. Even Blaise with her disinterest, but the receptionist had vanished into a back office. They were alone.

The man looked away out the glass door, toward the pool and beach and sky, seeing things. "The son swam and swam," he said.

She hadn't heard it, couldn't have. He meant the sun, some passing remark about the weather. Her mind tried to reparse it but couldn't. She was obsessed, on edge here on the coast again, at the beach where it happened, with the salt forever in her eyes and ears. She'd misheard because his speech was odd, not as if from underwater, no not that; but dopplered, as if approaching from far away.

He turned back then, gave her a sad smile and walked away, patting the vase as he did.

Swam and swam. The line of lifeguards swam and dived and swam and then the whistle directing them had gone from two blasts to three. A man beside Kylie had said, You know that means they're going from rescue to recovery, and then Kylie was on her knees in the sand, sick, she was looking at her vomit as though it hid Mitch's body somehow, he was lost in the rills of sand there to the left, in that clump of seaweed. The blanket the cops had given her slid off her back and Mitch was hiding under it, playing a trick. The sky had darkened completely, she remembered that, violet-brown everywhere, as though to meet the colossal shape rising through the waves.

Because they never found the body, Jeff told her later. This is why you have these nightmares, can't move on. There's the guilt even though there's nothing you could've done, and then you weren't given the chance to see him dead, that closure, and so he stays alive.

But you didn't see him when he was alive, she replied. You didn't know him.

No, he said carefully, not understanding.

And that was it, the thing Jeff could never understand, even now, married to her—how Mitch was everywhere, always standing in the door, seated at the kitchen table with them. A blond cherub. Always wet. How she had gone back to the motel alone that night and there was a towel for him still in the beach-bag and his Nerf ball drying in the sink. How he was in the room with her and Jeff when they ate or talked or screwed. How having known and loved someone means they stay alive, forever.

She stumbled out of the lobby to the pool for air, *breathe*, the sky was violet-brown all over, *swam and swam*, but it was only a poolside sofa where she'd collapsed and managed to crawl, her face crushed into the synthetic brown fabric. Birds cooed, two women with soft hands and accents, who had come out of nowhere. They helped her sit up.

"You poor ting," said one.

"It's the son," said the other. "Too much son."

Please stop this. "I'm okay."

They were German, they told Kylie, and also not customary to so much of son. Slim, fiftyish women in designer swimsuits, both of them burned fuchsia. As they cooed over her, Kylie's college German came back, enough to trap a word here and there. *Zuviel. Unter dem Meeresspiegel.* Under the mirror of the sea.

"She is also always wanting too much of everything," the first woman said of her companion, smiling. "It makes us mad trouble. Look at us."

Sunscreen, Kylie thought. Don't you have that in Germany?

The pool's deserted surface sparkled with too much flatness. "Where are all the people?" Kylie managed to ask. The women exchanged glances. "The residents, from the lower floors. Surely they use the pool. The lobby, the elevator."

"Oh, you are never seeing them."

"But there was a man . . . "

It was part of the trauma, these feelings of insecurity, a kind of mania after Mitch's death, the sense of being followed by something colossal and yet invisible, that made her carry a gun in her purse and put more locks on her door back home. Even if her son's death had had nothing to do with crime—the world had become untrustworthy, life a monster that could rise up at any moment. It was only after she started seeing Jeff that her paranoia had ebbed.

Sounds came through. There were others at the pool after all, a family just starting to jump in, on the far side a laughing teenage couple, the boy enticing the girl toward the deep end. How had she not seen them before? Kylie couldn't look straight at them, their happiness. She found herself leaning into one of the German women.

Jeff came through the glass door from the lobby. He was as pink as the women.

"There you are." He glanced at the pool and the concern on his face loosened. "You made it to here. I'm proud."

She touched his red arm. "You forgot sunscreen. Mad trouble for you tonight, mister."

IN HER NIGHTMARES Mitch was always rolling, dreamily, down to where the light barely penetrated, unconscious or already dead, turning over and over without a struggle, until a shape rose from below, impossibly large, the soul of the black ocean, scooping him into its jaws, its teeth tightening while Mitch's eyes flew open in pain.

Kylie woke in the night with a sob. The clock said two-thirty. Jeff twisted to hold her in his arms out of habit, only half-awake.

"He was riding it this time," she told him. She tried to hold this new image in her head, the twist in her dream. Instead of the jaws snapping shut: a fierce joy of meeting, the uplift, her son hugging the worm's back while they sped through schools of shining butterfish and the water changed him. "Riding it. Happy."

"Your image of him. Changing because we came here." Jeff's words were muffled by the pillow. He'd be asleep again in seconds. "That's good."

Outside the window that Jeff had insisted on leaving open a slit, the surf boomed close.

IN THE MORNING Kylie took her coffee out onto the balcony with Jeff.

The boulevard was gone, covered in water.

The surf lapped at the shrubs that edged their building far below. "Is that the tide come in?" she gasped. A long grin of coastal water stretching north and south, all features of the road—the entire strip of businesses that had been there yesterday—erased. She set her cup cautiously on the balcony rail because her hand shook. Jeff looked confused. "The whole road—it's covered."

"Oh." He smiled. "There's no road on this side. You're turned around."

"We came in on it."

"We came in at the back."

"I stood here yesterday—" She tried to remember. A beach, sunbathers. An elbow. It was the side with the infinity pool, still there below her.

"Climate change isn't *that* fast." He hugged her. "Come with me today, Kylie. The beach is what the place is famous for, after all. You literally just step out the door and you're there."

You're there. She could feel how it would be to say yes, how happy it would make him.

"Not yet."

After breakfast he packed a beach-bag, waving the sunscreen to show her he wasn't forgetting, and she watched him go, then regretted it. It's what she'd come for, wasn't it? To beat back the tide that never ebbed, the hooks in her heart—only she'd imagined doing it with people around, strangers who would be going about their tourist business of having fun, helping her by having no idea what she was going through. Not this long hall of silent doors, then the empty elevator like this. Sand still on the elevator floor. There seemed to be more of it today. Down, past the sixth floor, then past those private floors, descending, never stopping.

By the time Kylie reached the ground floor she was shaking.

As she crossed the deserted ground-floor lobby to the main door, the eel on the wall watched her. Its mosaic mouth was wide-open, fanged, she didn't remember fangs. She'd find him, *him*, Jeff her husband, surprise him by lounging in the sand beside him. Just walk out, cross the road (*no, not a road, you'll just be there*). So simple. She threw open the glass door.

Water lapped at the bottom step and before she could think she'd stepped down in it. Dark, violet water, hungry at her skin. *You're there.* She couldn't see her sandals through it. From her calves the scream rose through her. Only knee-deep, but when she spun to step back up she fell forward, catching herself with her hands. They disappeared beneath the water to the wrists. Her palms scraped at the unseen concrete steps, silken algae sticking to her skin. The automatic-lock door had closed on her. Then she was up and pounding on the glass with green-slimed fists.

Just inside the door stood the German weird sisters, looking at her.

Kylie's heart was drowning. Salt channels pumping in the sudden silence, tiny creatures that would eat through her ventricles and leave her there. The ocean had come for her, the dark thing. She'd never make it out.

The women opened the door. "You wanting back in?" one asked. Kylie stumbled past and found a chair. "There is buzzer. Always buzzer to Blaise." From the wall opposite Kylie, the eel leered.

"It's not right," Kylie groaned. She beat her slimy hands against the upholstered armchair, trying to clean them. "Too close." The women frowned. *Right there.* Beyond the opaqued glass door stretched dark sky, a blackened sun. Gray gull shadows darted. When was a beach not a beach? "There was no one around and there should have been. I was trying to do it alone and he—" She caught herself. The women looked like they might start cooing again. Kylie could hear her own voice grow loud. "Why aren't there any people? Please just tell me that. Middle of the season, all this luxury. *Where are the people?*" Breaking on a hysterical note.

"We are people." *Of course.* Insulted, surely, but they didn't seem to be. Kylie turned away from them.

"There are many people here."

"We have seen little boys."

After a long time Kylie looked up. She was alone.

Go up, wait for Jeff. She was turned around, that was all, a different side of the building. In water you lose all sense of direction. You lose all sense. She was smart, drowned in grief, but she had sense. She could figure it out. You figure your life out, ride it, even when the monster rises.

In a niche beside the elevator was a door she hadn't noticed before. To the stairwell, she thought. Mitch stood in it looking at her. Burnished sand glimmered on his wet swim trunks.

When Kylie stood, he turned and faded into the dark behind him.

The stairwell. That's what she'd do—take the stairs up, knock on doors to all those private apartments, say she was lost. Make it make sense. Floor by floor. She'd make them show themselves. She'd see the people that lived there. Something delicate would open for her, with delicate elbows.

Stepping to the door she saw her mistake. The bare concrete stairs led downward, not up. A basement access, dark but for the light from the lobby falling in behind her. A steely thrum cut to silence as she descended. The steps ended in water. A machine room then, flooded by the rising tide. In the corner, just beneath the oily surface, floated a coiled shadow, viscid whorls knotted and moving across themselves. If she breathed it would rise, its mouth would open to devour her (*just a drowned pipe, a curve of an underwater hose*). Then she heard a murmured splash from the far corner and realized she had only been looking at its tail. The coil took up the whole room, larger than nightmare, and over there (*don't look*) a head rose toward her.

"You shouldn't be worrying so much."

The voice from behind Kylie freed her paralysis and she spun, half-stumbling back up the steps.

It was the shabby man.

He touched her arm, a tap, as though to affix her there, and gazed at the room beyond her with his sad smile. "Everything gets broken sometimes," he said in his broken cadence. "The salt gets in it."

She stepped close, heart pounding. Fuck his salt and his innuendos. *Look at me.* His wavering eyes wouldn't. "He's still alive, isn't he?" she hissed. "Tell me."

A noise of exhalation, of exhilaration, spewed from the water behind her. The man was still smiling, gaze split between her and the room.

"Tell me!" Nothing. Kylie shoved him away, hit the elevator button and stumbled in.

On the sixth floor she found Blaise. "Your basement's flooded."

"Oh, that can't be. If it was, we wouldn't have any lights up here, Mrs. Henderson. You wouldn't see anything." For once the receptionist glanced up from her computer screen. The effect of her sad eyes was disconcerting. "You wouldn't want that, would you?"

She'd scream, draw a crowd from the emptiness. Blaise glanced past her. "There he is. Your husband knows."

"Knows?"

Jeff had stepped from the elevator. His hair was wet from his beach morning. The sight of him left Kylie weak. Rock-solid, lifting her. His freckles, out in force from the day before. His quick smile.

"Hey, another disappearing act. I didn't find you in the apartment. Where'd you go this time?"

She took his solid arm, knowing he'd feel her shaking, but she didn't care. "Say you'll come with me," she whispered, not looking at Blaise.

IN THE ELEVATOR she punched every button for the lower floors, and watched in incredulity as the elevator passed them all by.

"See, it won't stop. It won't let us look!"

"Well, there's probably a code. They wouldn't want just anyone on the private floors, would they?" His voice had tipped from casual to uncertain. "Look, see there? There's a slot for key cards. Why in hell would you want to go there anyway?"

"Because—" The door opened on the ground floor.

Cold water poured in to their knees. Kylie barked out a scream and scrambled for the button. In the instant before the door closed, she held a glimpse of the flooded lobby—armchairs buoyed and tilted, just beginning to float. The swirl of violet sea, pumping.

The elevator ascended, water draining out through the door seam that hadn't shut properly. She braced against the back wall, panting. *It'll short out*, her heart said, *we'll be stuck here. Buoyed and tilted.*

Jeff was staring at her. "Jesus. I thought you were getting over this."

"That's not normal!" she screamed. "You can't say that's normal!"

"Kylie, it's just water."

"It shouldn't be in the building!"

"It's part of the experience. Don't you remember?" He reached out to hold her, a solid thing, and she batted his hands away. "We saw it on the website. Don't you remember?"

Of course. They'd seen water.

"You don't know what's going on here, Jeff!"

The elevator spilled them onto the thirteenth floor, the remnant of water soaking into the carpet. Kylie lurched down the hall to their apartment. Jeff followed and closed the door.

"OK, then tell me."

The breakwaters wouldn't hold. "Oh Jeff, Mitch is *alive*. They're hiding him from me. My son is here!" Wrecks hidden in her husband's eyes bobbed to the surface. *He knows.* "He swam and swam and made it out and they've been holding him prisoner."

"Kylie."

"He's down there, on one of the lower floors, Jeff! I saw his elbow!"

Wrecks soft with ancient moss, shattered crustaceans. "On one of the lower floors? Under the water?" Jeff rubbed his face and when he looked up again he was different. "I was afraid of this. I was so afraid, babe." She was too full of blood to scream anymore. "I was kidding myself you were ready. All my fucking fault." She'd slap him, make him understand, but her arms were made of sponge. "Wait here."

He went to the bedroom. Sick for air, Kylie stepped onto the balcony and grasped the handrail. Through the bottom strut, ripples of ocean water lapped over her flip-flops. The calm sea that started at her toes stretched to the end of the sky. Seagulls floated nearby, so close she might have touched them.

"Kylie." Jeff led her back in. He had a syringe. The liquid inside was cloudy as salt water.

"What is that?"

"I love you."

"What *is* it?"

"It's fluspirilene."

From beneath the front door of the apartment behind him a puddle inched toward them.

"The water's here, Jeff. On the thirteenth floor. Bad luck."

"It's supposed to be here, on the top floor." He rolled her sleeve up. "It's what they're famous for, you just don't remember. It's the most exclusive place in the world."

"You don't want me to find Mitch, do you? You're in on it with them, with the monster."

For a second he closed his eyes.

She knocked the syringe from his hand.

In the fight he held her, but she was strong. They fell against the couch. Shouts pounded the air, her husband's lie *Mitch is dead!* pummeling her, his fingers quick, grasping for the syringe on the floor, but she was quicker. Her hand was in her purse and then she had her gun out.

"All these years you wanted me to forget! Not find out—it's why I wasn't supposed to come here all these years!"

"Kylie—"

The shot cleaved the world into a before and after of noise.

In the red silence of his blood, a scratch came at the door and she went to open it.

They were all there. The old man smiled his sad smile. Blaise patted her wet hair. The German women were worse than pink, their sunburn sloughed away to reveal cheese-white skin pocked with holes in which tiny eels writhed. All the private owners from the drowned floors, stretching away around the curve of hallway. Whole families. Children, so many children. The teenage couple enacted their flirt game, caught in their night surf. Where the hall fell off into deeper water behind them, the violet worm coiled.

Mitch climbed off its back and waded toward her.

Kylie thought her heart would float away. "You're alive."

His blond hair was flaked with algae. "You took your eyes off me, Mom."

"I didn't mean to. I was alone, all the responsibility . . . " She knelt before him in the water, face to face. "But you're all right. You can come home with me now."

He came close. His spongy hand fumbled at hers. The stench was hellish, but she would clean him up, she would love him and take care of him and nothing would ever happen to him again.

"No, Mom. I'm staying here. We all live here. Lots of people to keep me company." He smiled back at the worm and then leaned toward Kylie to whisper in her ear.

"I love him more than I ever loved you."

"No—"

Mitch lifted her limp hand that still held the gun and placed the barrel against her temple.

"Mitch—please!"

"They watch over me so much better than you ever did. Bad Mom."

Red noise cleaved the world, a river of red that swam and swam into the salt, into the laughing violet mouth of the sea.

Clipped Wings

Steve Toase

———◆———

WE MADE SNOW ANGELS. It was a family tradition. After the first fall, whether blizzard or barely there, we would dress in waterproofs and troop out, lie down and wear away the flakes to the grass and dirt below. Feel the cold against our backs as the snow was pushed up, erupting over our collars and down our necks.

Jamie led the way, bundled up as warm as could be. Star Child. You know what I mean. So many layers his arms pointed out either side, legs so padded he struggled to bend his knees. We both watched him flop onto the whitened lawn, swiping his arms as best he could. Me and Sarah glanced at each and laughed, hiding it from the kid behind our scarves. We could see it though. See the humor in each other's eyes. We've always been able to do that. Always used to be able to do that.

Sarah walked over to Jamie, grasped the front of his coat like a handle and lifted him to his feet. Jamie shrugged off his mother's hand and stumbled through the snow, shuddering free the thin coating from his back.

We both took our turns of course, lying down and getting our own wings. Trying to dodge child fist-sized snowballs that turned back to ice blossom halfway through the throw. Most of those grounded celestial beings were the size of a six year old. Back inside with cups of hot chocolate we stood by the window and counted them. Four cherubs, two adults, Sarah and I agreed. Jamie counted more, said he saw thirteen in the garden below, but you can't go by a kid who has only just learnt his numbers. More full of imagination than facts.

The thaw came quick. It was that time of year when the days flipped on each other fast. By the next morning trampled grass was visible through the wings. Within a couple of days most of the snow had gone apart from thin ridges pushed up by scraping hands and legs.

At the end of the second day I realized I was wrong. Jamie wasn't right, but he was closer than me. Several more angels were visible on the grass than I remember him making, friction-shaped wings and gowns outlined in thin off-white ribbons. I ignored it and put it down to tiredness. Everything got put down to tiredness back then. Now there isn't any time to be tired.

"Have you seen this?"

I turned around from the hob, leaving the pan to take care of itself. Sarah stood in the door, arms folded as if the cold that got into her bones during the day still hadn't left. She nodded toward the hallway and I followed her, pulling the kitchen door behind me. We walked into Jamie's bedroom, the one with the best view of the garden. Sarah put a finger to her lips and took my hand, leading me between half finished Lego projects scattered across the floor.

"Not so much like angels anymore," she said. I walked up to the window and rested my hands on Jamie's head. He grasped my fingers tight, and stepped back against my legs. Sarah wasn't joking. The thaw had changed the garden again, decorating it with the grinning dead, wings changed to orbits, bodies to nasal cavities, and the ones engraved by me and Sarah already absent.

"The adults always go first," Jamie said, breathing the words onto the cold glass. He was wrong about that. I wish he'd been right.

The next morning, Jamie was up before us as if he smelt the ice in the air, even before his blinds were opened. Tying my dressing gown closed,

I watched him range across his frozen kingdom, pausing to catch flakes on his tongue then flop forward to scrape his way through the drifts. Climbing to his feet, he turned to each new figure, knelt by their shoulder and whispered to them. I wondered what secrets he was telling the faceless figures he felt he couldn't say to us.

By evening the snow was already fading, revealing more skulls staring up from the lawn. I tried to pay them no attention. Seeing Jamie stood looking over the streetlamp-lit garden, I couldn't help saying something.

"Will you be sad when they go?"

Jamie shook his head.

"No," he said, and I breathed out my worry. Children's fixations can be deep, the hooks sharp. "They won't go. They're here now. They'll stay, waiting for us."

When the melt erased his figures the next day I smiled to myself. Only when he wasn't around to see.

"You'll be able to make some more," I said, getting my reassurance in before his disappointment.

He paused and turned to me, a figure in each hand.

"They haven't gone, Daddy. You just can't see them anymore."

We had forgotten angels had fallen before, transforming the earth with their impact.

I'VE ALWAYS LIKED winter, the way the wind spikes branches with water splinters and how a warm cafe and hot chocolate can improve anything. That winter was different. I started checking the weather forecast every morning, sometimes every hour, just to reassure myself that the skies were clear.

"Can I play out in the snow, Daddy?"

We were painting at the big table and I glanced out of the window.

"It's not snowing sweetheart," I said, passing him a pot of blue so he could dip in his hand and bring a fat caterpillar to life with messy fingerprints.

"Not yet, but it will soon."

With my hands covered in poster paint I had no way to check the latest forecast.

"We'll see," I said, giving the holding pattern answer. I looked down at his paper. The white was infected with blue, but the pattern was clear. Four shapes that might have been winged figures, or might have been the jawless gaze of the dead. Two hours later the skies opened. Snow paled the garden like infected skin.

"You told me I could," Jamie said, already dressed for the weather.

"I said we'll see," I said, kneeling down and unzipping his coat. "It's still coming down."

The flakes swirled past the streetlights, galaxies dying to be lost in the climbing mounds.

"Daddy!"

I walked through to the hallway. Jamie sat on the floor, boots half on.

"I've told you before not to shout through the house," I said, changing the subject before we started "You'll disturb the neighbors."

"Help me, Daddy."

"Not now," I said, shaking my head.

"Please."

"Not now," I repeated, using the voice that stopped discussion dead.

"They say that I have to go outside."

"Who?"

"The angels. I have to go out. If I don't show them where to land, how can they visit?"

"Not now. It's nearly tea time."

"They'll be angry."

"I'll be angry, Jamie. That's the end of the matter."

With his snowsuit hanging half off, he stomped into his bedroom and slammed the door. I should have said something, but was trying too hard to stifle a laugh.

I DON'T KNOW how he reached the key to let himself out.

I ran out without a coat, my voice dragging me along.

"Jamie Cobb, what the hell are you doing out here?"

He didn't turn. Normally when I reached that level of rage, he cowered. I never hit him, never needed to. Raising my voice was enough.

As I got closer I realized he was talking, but not to me. Whispering and slurring his words so I could barely make it out.

"So when you fall, you're perfect and then you become changed?"

He paused, then nodded. "I make mistakes sometimes too."

"You've made one now," I said. "Get in that house straightaway and get ready for bed."

When he turned it was hard to concentrate on his protests, distracted by the snow smeared across his brows and cheeks. The inside shown on his skin like long healed scars.

"They'll follow me in," Jamie said, staring at the prone figures already starting to be covered by the next flurry.

"I don't care," I said. "Get in that house."

He shook his head and stayed exactly where he was, snowflakes still falling like the tumbling dead.

Inside I put him down, trying to ignore the bruises already blossoming down my sides.

THE NEXT DAY was kindergarten and I spent several hours sitting quiet, trying not to think about the rage he had held within those small limbs. He seemed calmer, but it felt like a covering in place. Like he wasn't happier, but masking his rage. Several times in the afternoon I walked across to the window and gazed down at the lawn. There was nothing to see anymore. The last of the snow had thawed during the morning, leaving the lawn bare and broken. Traceless of anyone. Still, I felt like the land itself was staring at me and retreated deeper into the house where there were no windows.

When I picked him up I wasn't surprised to find out his teeth marks were left in another child's arm. We sat at the small table in the teacher's office, Jamie looking at his feet while I listened to what had happened.

"And what do you have to say," I said, turning to him as best I could.

"They tried to stop me."

The teacher followed us out into the cloakroom, the conversation sliding easily from formal to relaxed. We'd always got on well and there was no distance between us now, because of the uncharacteristic violence from my son. I lifted his coat off the hook and went to button it up. The back was smeared with mud and grass-stains. The teacher passed me a handful of paper towels and I wiped my hands clean.

"We tried to tell him there was no snow, but it didn't seem to make any difference."

Jamie nodded as if agreeing.

"They don't need snow. That's just made up. They say that it's made up by grown-ups to stop them becoming parallel with fear."

I didn't correct him. Something in the certainty made me want to change the subject.

BACK HOME I CLEANED his coat the best I could, then hung it to dry in the bathroom, blades of mud-stained grass falling into the bath.

"Can I go and play football in the garden?"

He was standing at the door, his face pressed against the frame, with that expression he got when he wanted something but knew not to push it. I hesitated. Part of me wanted to wait until Sarah got home from work. That was still two hours away, and being cooped up inside with an annoying child was either going to end up in crossed words or a tedious television marathon. At that moment I wanted neither. He'd already been punished with a time-out at Kindergarten, as well as the glacial task of writing an apology, so what came next was conversation and understanding. For now, I didn't want to think about that. Maybe that was my problem.

"Get your old coat from behind the door, and if it starts raining, make sure you come back inside."

He didn't answer but I didn't feel the need to clarify. He was a sensible kid, and there were jobs to do. The next hour went quick, lost in tasks I barely remembered, until I remembered him playing outside. I walked through his bedroom and pulled the blind to one side.

He lay on his back amongst a crowd of scuffed turf figures, his arms and legs pivoting slowly into the dirt. As I watched he stood up, counted something on his fingers and moved to one of the few patches of grass still untouched. With a child's carelessness he slumped back to the ground and I struggled not to open the window as his head impacted with the churned mud. Lying down he began to stretch and compress his arms once more like he was signaling to the sky.

There was a moment of conflict. If I went and put my own boots on to go into the garden myself I'd lose sight of him. I was certain if I took my eyes off him then he would not be there when I opened the door. So certain I tasted my stomach in my throat. If I opened the window to shout, to fill the air with my fear as anger and turn his anger into fear, then I was just as convinced he would run. He knew not to open the gate, knew our rules were not to leave the garden, but somehow I felt like the rules had shifted. Like the world had shifted. Like if I didn't hold on to something I was going to fall and not stop falling.

Instead, I stood at the window and watched him smear the ground to wings that looked far more like skulls, and as he ran out of space they overlapped, glistening with damp and dirt, staring up at me as they surrounded my child.

I was still watching when Sarah walked from the bus, grabbed him by his coat and dragged him upstairs. Though I tried to duck back into the room, she still saw me watching.

The rest of the evening passed in silences as thick as glaciers and no-one was immune. I tried not to break anything. I tried.

"I didn't know how to stop him," I said, trying to be truthful.

Sarah didn't look at me, just shook her head.

"You go outside and you tell him to get back in, and you make sure he does what he is told."

"It's not always that easy."

She shook her head.

"It very much is."

Not wanting to get drawn in any more, I left the room to go to the kitchen and make a cup of tea or wash up or do something other than continue the conversation. The lightswitch felt damp and for a moment I almost withdrew my hand in case I got a shock.

The mud was all over the floor, thick and stippled with dead plants and stones. In the middle of the layer someone had frictioned an angel.

My first reaction was to go and drag Jamie out of his bed. Make him explain what he had done. My second was to clean it up, scrape it from the floor until there was no trace in the house. Instead I went with my third.

Sarah leaned against the wall, looked at the floor and looked at me. There was no way into Jamie's bedroom without stepping through the mess.

"Leave it there," she said.

"Leave it?"

"Don't touch it. In the morning, show him and make him clean it up."

"Maybe he wasn't responsible," I said.

"Did you do it?"

"No. Of course not."

"Then make him clean it up."

I DIDN'T MAKE him clean it up. Sarah left early. Jamie woke later, and when he did he stepped over the mess to go for breakfast as if there was a carpet of mud in the hallway every day. I stopped him, and turned him around to look.

"How did that get there?"

"Daddy, I told you that they would come inside if you didn't do what they asked. What they asked me to ask you."

"The angels?"

He shook his head, and stepped past me toward breakfast.

"They're not angels anymore."

I followed him, and watched as he ate, then he pushed past me again to get to the bathroom. From where I stood I couldn't see his face apart from in the mirror, a faint haze across the skin.

"You need to clean it up," I said.

"The sink?" This was always a bone of contention. A spray of spit on the porcelain, pitted with muesli and toothpaste.

"The mess in the hallway."

He shook his head.

"There really isn't any point, Daddy."

"Why's that then?"

"It will just be back again later."

Something in that certainty unnerved me and I left the room.

"Don't disturb it. They'll come back and there will be more."

After I dropped him off at nursery I realized I hadn't mentioned the biting to Sarah and wasn't sure what to do about that. Instead of messaging her at work, I went back home and started cleaning. Not just the floor, but every trace of mud in the house, disinfecting shoes and coats until there was no trace of the last few days.

That afternoon it started snowing again. Not gentle languid flakes, but skin burning blizzards. The type of snow that took sight and fingers. From inside I watched it coming down, knowing I would have to leave soon and pick Jamie up, but not quite wanting to coat up and venture outside. The clock crept closer and closer to hometime. With a nervousness I couldn't quite put my finger on, I ventured out into the storm.

In the Kindergarten Jamie was sitting on the bench in the cloakroom. An outsider might have thought he was just waiting for me. His expression told me different. So did the teacher's.

"Normally we have no problem letting them outside when it's snowing. An important part of our ethos is for the kids to play in all sorts of weather. Today was just too heavy."

"I know what you mean," I said, trying to wipe the condensation from my glasses. She seemed annoyed at the interruption.

"Jamie wouldn't take no for an answer. Every time I turned my back he was at the door. I ended up having to sit him in my office. Unfortunately that didn't go down too well."

She rolled up her sleeve. The bite was deep and livid. Not the slight pressure of an annoyed child trying to get their own way, but the bite of anger and rage. Uncontrolled.

I became the child by proxy, my own hands wrapping around each other as if to clean away some unseen mark. A cascading back in time when the guilt of my own transgressions weighed heavy, but I was no longer the child and I needed to shake off that burning embarrassment.

"I will make sure that Jamie has a consequence as a result of this," I said, trying to insulate myself with the formality of the words.

The teacher looked toward the window, the desk, and the door. Everywhere but straight at me.

"I'm afraid it's gone beyond that Mr. Cobb. We'll have to exclude Jamie until the end of the week."

I thought about saying something, then caught the disappointment in her eyes as she carried on trying to avoid my gaze. Like she'd lost something too.

"I understand," I said. "Do we need to have a meeting before he comes back?"

"I know this might disrupt things," she said.

"I work at home, it's fine," I said, trying to reassure her. Trying to make up ground. She caught my gaze. I realized that any connection or trust was shattered.

"Get your coat off and get to your room," I said as Jamie stood in the middle of the hall, dropping dried mud on the floor.

"I need to go outside," he said.

"I don't care what you want. You are going to go to your room, get changed and straight to bed."

There was a moment, just a single moment when the air seemed to thicken to freezing fog, like it would ice my lungs to powder if I tried to take a breath. Jamie stared at me, then turned his back and went to his bedroom.

"There will be other times."

Those were the last words he said.

That night Sarah ignored me. I watched her move around the apartment, transitioning from work to food to bath to bed and could count on one hand the number of words that passed between us. She didn't distance herself or ignore me. There was just a gap that I didn't feel I could bridge with words or touch, so I left it unbridged. Don't get me wrong, we slept in the same bed, we said goodnight, we hugged, then turned away from each other. When I woke in the morning she had already left for work.

I let Jamie sleep. Neither of us had to be anywhere, so I lost myself in YouTube rabbit holes and the endless scroll of social media. By ten I was ready for breakfast, so clicked on the kettle and went to wake him up.

It was hard to tell if the bed had been slept in, like all six year olds' beds are, but what was certain was that Jamie was no longer in there.

The panic was boiling water hot, scorching me to do something but I didn't know what to do. I glanced outside. The sky was a million individual frozen scars. I still wasn't dressed and to run out unprepared would only make me a casualty too. I don't know why I felt time was no longer of the essence.

I compromised, pulling on a pair of old jeans and my old work shirt, slipping on my winter jacket, and not closing the door behind me. At first the snow took my sight until I learned how to see through the wounds in the air.

Snow angels scarred the lawn, clustered and stark. Already the depressions were filling with more snowfall, and for a moment I pictured them rising from the ground and crowding me, smothering the world away with crumbling wings. With bare hands I started digging through the drifts, searching for my child. Searching for Jamie.

I heard his voice first, compressed by the weight of the fall, and dug through until I found his back. Lying face against the grass it was hard to hear what he was saying. At first I thought it was "Dad, come for me." That was wishful thinking. With reddened fingers I scraped him out, turned him over. Even then his arms didn't stop moving. A graze on his face was full of soil and gravel. Digging between his teeth I cleared out his mouth and leant close so I could hear the phrase he was repeating over and over. The first word wasn't Dad.

Inside, I called the ambulance first, then Sarah. The paramedics struggled to get through, the snow already overwhelming gritted roads, and while I waited I had no way to stop listening to him repeat the same phrase over and over again. At first I tried to use my own body heat to warm him, but the cold just seemed to leach into me while he got no warmer. Instead, I wrapped him in blankets, and hot water bottles. I didn't know best practice. I didn't know what to do. The door was still open and drifts were starting to collect inside as if the snow couldn't bear to be parted from him for too long. I couldn't bring myself to leave him to shut out the world.

When the paramedics did arrive they came straight in, taking over, asking questions I should have had answers for and I had none. They tried to clean up the cuts on his face and looked at me as if my lack of answers was an admission of guilt. I didn't need to admit guilt. I was swimming in it.

The ride to the hospital was in silence, apart from Jamie mumbling the same sentence through the frosted plastic of the breathing mask. When we pulled in at A&E they sent me to do the paperwork while they took him deeper into the building. Once I'd finish filling and signing I waited near the entrance for Sarah to arrive. That's what I told myself anyway.

An orderly took both of us down the corridors, following first one colored line then the other. The room was painted in rainbows as if the cheerfulness could draw anxiety out of the room.

Sarah ignored me and knelt beside the bed. Jamie was sleeping and still his mouth moved, chewing the same phrase over and over.

"He wants you," she said, not trying hard to hide her disgust.

"He doesn't," I said. For a moment I thought about telling her to listen closer, but stayed silent.

THEY DIDN'T LET us see him again for a week. We never found out whether it was the hospital or the social workers. When we were allowed into the ward we had to wait outside the room until the doctor arrived. Through the safety glass we saw Jamie curled up into himself. The doctor was younger than me, and sat on the edge of Jamie's bed. For a couple of minutes he looked at Jamie's notes, sighed then looked at us.

"The good news is that there isn't any lasting damage due to the hypothermia, but the time it took to get to him has caused other damage." Gently, he reached across and turned Jamie toward us. "We're not sure what he cut his face on, but the infection was serious. We've managed to treat it, but we couldn't save all the skin."

With the caring firmness only medical staff seemed to have, he lifted Jamie's head around, and pulled away the tape and cotton pad. Underneath the skin was worn away, exposing the muscle, four holes worn in his cheek in the shape of a figure with wings. I moved so it wasn't so obvious but that made it so much worse.

"Can you get him back?" Sarah said, holding Jamie's hand.

"We're not sure," the doctor said. "He's fallen so far into himself, we're not sure if we can reach him."

Jamie shrugged him off and rolled back into a ball.

The doctor smiled, trying to reassure us of something, and stroked Jamie's arm.

"Don't they just look like angels when they're asleep?"

The Cardboard Voice

Tim Major

———◆———

"Chocolate bourbons are the best I can rustle up at short notice," Julia said as she returned carrying a tray. She had placed twelve of the biscuits on a fine china plate, arranged like the markers on a clock face.

How smiled wistfully and patted his stomach. "I'm on a regime," he said. "None of the good stuff for me, and ten thousand steps a day to work off the calories I'm not even allowed to eat."

"On whose say-so?" Julia asked.

"It's a thirty-day challenge, on a forum." In response to Julia's quizzical expression, he added, "A sort of a club, with everyone egging each other on."

"It sounds like a mean-spirited club," she replied. She set the tray precariously on a footstool, and passed a cup and saucer to How. She took one of the biscuits and proceeded to separate its top part carefully, then scrape the chocolate fondant icing with her front teeth. She smacked her lips and then grinned to acknowledge her peculiarly childish habit. It was as if a much younger person were occupying her old body.

"So what do I call you?" she said. "You signed your message Lee, but on your program you call yourself How."

"You've seen my show?"

"Old people can use the internet too, you know," she retorted. "I didn't much like it, though. A bit whizzy for my tastes."

He nodded. "Everyone calls me How. It's from my surname. My name's actually Lee Howie."

"All right. How."

He sipped his tea, which was weak. "Thank you so much for agreeing to meet with me, Julia."

"I was intrigued. Maybe we'll both learn something. So, you're an expert in . . . forgery, is that right?"

How wrinkled his nose. "In a sense, I suppose. A very modern version of forgery. I'm an expert in what are known as deepfakes."

"Hence the title of your program. What was it? *Truly, Madly, Deepfake*—that's it."

How had long regretted the title, which had occurred to him when he was an entirely different person. Now the subject had become a serious matter.

"Doctoring photos, as I understand it?" Julia continued. "Like Stalin making 'unpersons' by removing them from photographs and from the official record. Orwell's ideas, brought grimly to life."

How blinked in surprise. "Well, yes. That's actually a really good early example. I'll be referring to it in my talk—the one I'm preparing at the moment. But all of that is just a prelude to the modern phenomenon. There are still plenty of doctored photos, but video is where it's at."

"You make it sound almost exciting."

"Well, yes." How leant forward in his armchair, which creaked under his weight. "I can't deny I find it fascinating. I wouldn't have dedicated myself to exposing deepfakes otherwise."

Julia polished off another biscuit at a leisurely speed. Why she remained so thin was a mystery.

"And yet, like Stalin, surely the most obvious applications are negative ones? People pretending to be other people . . . it hardly sounds like a development that's going to result in world peace."

How considered making a gesture towards the usual argument: that new technology was neither good nor bad, that any new development could be misused. But he sensed that Julia understood that already. She was far sharper and more engaged than he had anticipated.

"You're right," he said. "There'll be plenty of benign uses—bringing dead Hollywood stars back to life onscreen, broadcasting politicians' speeches in different languages, with them actually speaking those words. But yes, there'll be a swathe of negative uses too. I can't deny that's what I find morbidly fascinating."

"So . . . videos featuring those same politicians, apparently caught *in flagrante delicto*, resulting in an end to their careers. Famous people seeming to express wild viewpoints, and perhaps calling upon their adoring fans to perform radical actions. Respectable young women taking their clothes off. Am I close?"

"Very close. You're very well informed, or else very imaginative."

Julia waved a hand dismissively. "It's nothing new, only more convincing. You seem very confident in your videos, by the way. Less so in person."

"I suppose it's an onscreen persona. A façade."

She smiled. "And there you have it. We're all pretending, aren't we? Even without technology tinkering with our image."

How considered this. "And you, Julia—are you pretending, too?"

She laughed, leant back in her chair, sipped at her tea. Her thin eyebrows rose and fell rapidly as she savored the taste, and it occurred to How that this was a unique characteristic. There was more to fakery than a simple image—mannerisms were an equally identifiable characteristic.

"Oh yes," she replied cheerfully. "I've been faking it my whole life." She gestured at their surroundings: the two plush sofas and luxurious wing-backed armchairs forming a horseshoe shape, the art-deco lamps, the heavy, embroidered curtains that reduced the sunlight to meagre slivers despite it being midday. Then she looked down at herself; her Harris tweed skirt and her thin ankles. "None of this is *me*."

How cleared his throat. "So, shall we talk about something real? Your grandfather. I'm eager to hear the story."

She sighed and placed her cup onto its saucer.

"Grandad was a lovely fellow. Had us kids in hoots of laughter whenever we'd visit. Quite a dab hand at conjuring tricks, which is quite apt, isn't it? But of course you don't want to hear about his later life."

How offered a smile of encouragement.

Julia continued, "It was in 1931. Mid-February. Grandad, on behalf of the Producers Distributing Company, invited the four journalists to their London offices. Of course, they didn't call him Grandad, so neither should I when I'm telling this story. Eric Allan Humphriss—a grand name, isn't it? And yet I've always resented the surname attached to myself. Children in the playground called me 'Humpy'—and it was almost Grandad's undoing, too."

"In what way?"

"Sloppy fact-checking. When the story was reported, journalists kept spelling his name 'Humphries'. That's part of the reason I wanted to tell you the story: to avoid him being consigned to the dustbin of history. So, anyway, there's Eric, and there are the four journalists, in that office in London. Before starting work there, Eric had been an engineer at RCA, and had developed their wonderful Photophone technology. Have you heard of it?"

"I'm afraid not. I was never a film student."

She scoffed. "You don't need to be. It's just interesting, that's all. Anyway, what he invented was the ability to include the soundtrack to a film on the physical film itself. Talkies were in their very early days at the time, obviously, and synchronized sound was something of a holy grail. His clever idea removed any issues about starting the soundtrack for each reel at precisely the right moment. And of course the way he did it was to include an *image* of the sound. Just like you'd see nowadays. A . . . I'm not sure how you'd describe it."

"A waveform?" How ventured.

"Yes. Yes, a waveform. Or, to the untrained eye, a long blotch with wiggly tops and bottoms. And it worked wonderfully—any sound could be recorded and its shape captured on film, and then a projector could shine a light through that tiny strip of film and the amount of light getting through would reproduce the sound itself. Don't ask me how, though. Anyway, Eric didn't stop there. He was a perpetual inventor—you should have seen some of the toys he produced in his shed in later life! But back then, he realized that if a sound could be recorded and its shape contained on film, then it must be possible to create *new* shapes, and use those blotches to create entirely new sounds."

"And others did too, didn't they?" How said. "Composers created music by drawing shapes."

Julia nodded. "But like you, Grandad was fascinated by forgery. His obsession was to recreate the human voice. He worked and worked at it, studying the shapes of recorded voices, convincing himself that he could learn to read and produce all phonetic sounds in visual form. What a project!"

"And he achieved it? He demonstrated it to those journalists in 1931?"

Julia shrugged modestly, as though her grandfather's achievement were her own. "Near enough. He played the men a single phrase, which he had created from scratch as a result of his studies. And they were *dumbfounded*. I only wish I could have been there to see the looks on their faces."

How nodded eagerly. "And what was the phrase?"

Julia giggled, sounding more like a child than a septuagenarian. "He was a terrible joker, never behaving as you'd expect. But even so, I have no idea why he chose the words he did."

She watched How for several seconds, clearly enjoying the suspense.

"It was a deep male voice," she said. "The reports said it was as clear as a bell. And in this commanding tone it said, 'All . . . of . . . a . . . tremble . . .'"

How exhaled the breath he hadn't realized he'd been holding in. "'All of a tremble'?"

"All of a tremble. Goodness knows what was going through his mind. And to think he spent a hundred hours creating the shape."

"I'm sorry—what?" How exclaimed. "Did you say a hundred hours?"

"At least. Any good forger is prepared to put in the time." Her eyes gleamed. "Perhaps you don't appreciate how detailed it was. In order for the photograph on the film strip to capture all of the complexities of the human voice, Eric had to make it in ink at an enormous scale. Forty feet long!"

How puffed out his cheeks. "I had no idea. That's . . . that's incredible. I wish I could have seen it."

Julia's head tilted. "Well, I could show it to you."

How scrutinized her face. He imagined that there was a lot of Eric Allan in his granddaughter—the same love of tricks.

"You're teasing me, Mrs. Robinson," he said.

Julia wrinkled her nose. "You won't want to accompany me to the barn, then?"

JULIA'S THEATRICAL INSTINCT remained evident; she threw open the doors of the barn with a flourish, startling a young man wearing a flat cap who had been in the process of sharpening a pair of shears on a grindstone (an act that How could scarcely believe anybody performed in the twenty-first century). Then, in a windowless room at the rear of the barn, she insisted that How remain on the blank side of the long sheet of cardboard as he unfolded its panels like a dressing-room screen. It took him several attempts to prop it on its end, Julia watching on and barking instructions like a foreman on a construction site, and How winced as the lower edge scuffed on the uneven concrete floor strewn with hay.

"All right," she said finally. "You can come around to this side now."

When he stood beside Julia, he put his hand over his mouth.

"It's beautiful," he whispered.

"D'you think so? I always thought it looked like a conga line of slugs."

He shook his head empathically, but didn't reply. The cardboard stretched the full length of the barn wall, and at first glance, the waveform upon it did appear like a series of traipsing hunched figures, though How saw them more as a herd of elephants with each tail held in the trunk of the one behind. However, that was only a fleeting impression. The swells were all of different sizes, their contours varying; some sloping steeply to a vertex, others bobbing uncertainly, others with fuzzed exteriors like caterpillars. What struck How was the sheer detail of the inked peaks, revealing the steadiness of the hand that had painstakingly described each shape in minute detail. The more How looked at it, the more he felt as if he were parachuting towards this inky mountain range which grew larger and larger, enveloping him.

How swallowed noisily. He wiped his eyes. "I'm sorry," he said. "I hadn't expected to be so moved by it."

She laughed softly. "Grandad would be delighted. Though, of course, it was never intended as an artwork. Perhaps he'd be downhearted at the idea of it becoming nothing more than a funny-looking painting."

"But that's not what it is at all," How said sharply. "It's a code, a key, as much as it ever was."

"If you had the right sort of projector, I suppose that's true. But I certainly don't have one. You'd have had your work cut out finding one any time after the war."

How stared at her. "But it's a *waveform*. It's universal—your grandfather would have known that, and understood he was creating something that would last beyond any fleeting technology."

"You mean—"

He nodded excitedly. "Hold on."

He pulled out his phone and tapped its screen. "There. It's the modern mantra, Julia: *there's an app for that*. Welcome to the twenty-first century."

He opened the app, then flipped his phone horizontal and stepped back so that the image onscreen encompassed the entirety of the waveform. Julia waited patiently as he cropped the resultant image to include only the cardboard strip.

Once finished, his finger remained hovering over the play button.

"Could we pop back indoors?" he said. "My phone speaker's rubbish. I feel we should pay enough respect to your grandfather's work to listen to it in decent quality."

Julia took his arm and they walked together back to the large house.

They were silent until How blurted, "Would you consider selling it to me?"

"It's an heirloom. And what would you do with it, anyway?"

"I honestly don't know. It's just that . . . I don't know. My line of work is all digital, all abstract. Coming across an honest-to-goodness artifact like this, a slice of history . . . it feels important, that's all."

"Then it'll be here waiting, whenever you need to be overwhelmed all over again."

In the sitting-room How fiddled with the leads behind the amplifier and then angled the heavy wooden speakers so that they pointed at the middle sofa, where Julia sat.

"Gentlemen," he said in something approximating a stage magician's tone. "What you will hear today is a marvel the likes of which have never been experienced before. I have studied this phenomenon to the point where I can read the physical shape of a voice as readily as if they were words in a book. Today, I am able to present to you the first synthetic voice—a voice that is not a voice, and words that had never been spoken."

He bowed his head to the screen of his phone connected to the amplifier. He clicked play.

From the speakers came a sonorous, deep voice.

"*All . . . of . . . a . . . tremble . . .*"

It spoke more slowly than How had expected, and despite the slight flattening which conveyed a nasal tone to the voice, as though the man had a slight cold, there was also a surprising suggestion of humor to the delivery. Only now did it occur to How that the voice may actually be Eric Allan Humphriss's own voice—or rather, an ink approximation of an image of a true recording of it.

Another oddity was the clicking sound in the background, rather like the scuffing of a record player's needle: three dull staccato clicks that triggered something in How's mind, an association that remained out of reach.

He looked up to see that Julia was dabbing at her eyes with a handkerchief.

"My word," she said. "Wasn't that something?"

"Would you like to hear it again?"

"No," she replied hastily. "No. Just the once. I'd rather it be a once-in-a-lifetime experience. You don't get those often, at my age. But thank you, How. Thank you so very much."

They continued chatting, but How found himself surreptitiously checking his phone, and it was clear that Julia was tired after her emotional experience. Soon, he made his excuses and insisted he would see himself out.

He turned in the doorway of the sitting-room. "I should fold up the cardboard strip again. And would you allow me to bring it into the house rather than leave it out there in the barn? The thought of it amongst all that straw gives me the shudders."

She nodded, her eyes shining.

He went immediately to the barn. Before he folded up the cardboard strip he gazed at it for several minutes. He could see no evidence in the meandering waveform of the three clicks he had heard.

PREPARATION FOR THE TEDX talk occupied How entirely for several days. He paused only to record a new episode of *Truly, Madly, Deepfake* on the subject of Dr. Dre's "duet" with a computer-generated, apparently three-dimensional "hologrammatic" Tupac Shakur at the Coachella Festival in 2012—in reality an application of the "Pepper's Ghost" illusion first popularized 150 years earlier. But How felt his delivery seemed phoned in, and he struggled to maintain his screen persona despite the short running time. He was a different person now.

He didn't listen to Julia's waveform again, though he couldn't have explained why he was reluctant to do so.

"I THINK WE'RE GOOD," Gabrielle said, putting her camera on the coffee table in How's tiny apartment.

"You have enough shots in profile?" How asked. "They're just as important as front-facing ones, aren't they? Otherwise I won't be able to look left and right without introducing artifact blotches."

"Trust me," Gabrielle said. She tapped the camera. "I have enough images of you here to recreate you entirely, doing anything that may take my fancy. It's just as well you're a bloke, and an ugly bastard to boot. Anyone more attractive would be at perpetual risk of being inserted into porn vids shared on the internet. You should consider yourself lucky."

How snorted. "Talk about a back-handed compliment, Gab. And *you're* lucky that I trust you."

"You know, we could actually do that, you know . . . " Gabrielle said thoughtfully, rubbing her shaven head.

"Fake me into a porn clip?" How said, appalled.

"Yeah. I mean, wouldn't that be the most impactful demonstration during your talk? You'd be putting your money where your mouth is, highlighting the dangers of this new AI."

"Sure. But . . . "

He watched her carefully. Her expression appeared deadly serious.

Then, gradually, a grin formed.

"I'm yanking your chain," she said, rocking back in her seat gleefully. "You think anyone'd hang around to watch if you subjected them to *that*?"

He exhaled with relief. "Plan A, then?"

"Plan A. Putting together your avatar will be easy enough. Then we'll rig up the kit that'll allow you to manipulate the image in real time. Have you decided who you want to morph into for the showstopper?"

How scratched his temple. "I'd have said Barack Obama, if it hadn't already been done. It has to be somebody who commands respect, somebody who'd never say what I'll make them say."

"Before you get carried away, let me remind you it also needs to be somebody who's appeared in loads of video footage," Gabrielle said. "Ideally against a plain background, to save me some work."

"A newsreader?"

"They'll say whatever's put on the teleprompter."

"Some pop star?"

She chuckled. " 'Pop star'? Do you realize how out of date you sound, Mr. Finger-on-Society's-Pulse?"

He crossed to the kitchenette. "I'll keep thinking of ideas. As for now, fancy a drink and bit of fooling around for old time's sake?"

Gabrielle smiled indulgently. "I'll take the drink, but then I'd better turn in. Mind if I kip here tonight? Solo—if that doesn't offend you."

How did his best to adopt an expression that suggested no offense taken. "You can have my bed," he said. "I'm not tired yet, and the sofa'll do me just fine."

HE HAD NO IDEA what time it was when he woke with a start. The apartment was as close to pitch black as it ever got, the dim neon of the fast-food restaurants across the street lending the room an eerie glow.

What had woken him?

A sound.

He replayed it in his mind, then shuddered.

Three dull staccato clicks, just like he had heard on the waveform playback.

He reached up and fumbled for the light switch, then winced at the resulting brightness.

Then he stood to face the clock on the wall to his right.

It had once belonged to his father, an object so familiar that he barely even registered its presence. Now that he examined it properly, it seemed absurd, with its twee cottage roof and the little red hatchway above the clock face.

The cuckoo had never emerged from its housing, though How knew it was in there; he'd once levered the hatch open with a screwdriver. There was something wrong with the mechanism, and he'd never attempted to fix it.

According to the clock, it was one minute after three.

His hand trembled slightly as he nudged the minute hand backwards. The red hatchway shook a little with each click in place of a chime. Three dull clicks, each with a slightly delayed echo as the cuckoo struck the inside of the door.

The same sounds he had heard at Julia's house.

It didn't make sense. He darted into the hallway and rummaged in his jacket pocket for his earbuds, then returned to the sofa. He opened the waveform app, brought up the image of Humphriss's ink picture, then hesitated for several seconds before clicking play.

"All . . . of . . . a . . . tremble . . ."

This time, the voice elicited entirely different responses. The flattened tone evoked both mean-spiritedness and an image of somebody calling via an old phone line, like a kidnapper conveying demands in a Hollywood thriller. The suggestion of humor How had identified now seemed like mockery.

And though the clicking sounds were *precisely* the same as the vain efforts of the trapped cuckoo . . . there were only two of them.

"Is that really what I look like?" How asked. "What I act like?"

The How on the computer screen mouthed the same questions, aping his movements in real time. How raised his right hand and waved, and after only a fractional lag as the motion was captured by the camera rig jerry-rigged in the center of the lounge and then processed by the computer, the onscreen man waved too.

"'Fraid so," Gabrielle said. "You're a regular Frankenstein's monster."

How took a step forward so that his face was half a meter from the central camera. Looking out of the corner of his eye at the screen, he saw his face in close-up, eyes pointing to the left. It certainly was eerie, and he felt little connection with that person. But he had to admit that the detail was astounding. He could see the pockmarks on his face, and the skin on the bridge of his nose shone, and he saw the slight indents where his glasses had been pressing only minutes before. Only a slight rigidity to the lips, and a slight dullness in the eyes, gave the game away.

"Brace yourself," Gabrielle said.

He continued watching his doppelgänger as she knelt to tap commands into the computer keyboard resting on the coffee table.

Then, before he was ready, the How onscreen blinked and then became somebody else.

How stared at the new face on the screen, and the face on the screen stared to the left as if staring at *another* screen.

"Fucking hell," How said—

—and on the screen, David Attenborough mouthed those same words.

How clamped his lips together, then bobbed his head, then puffed out his cheeks. David Attenborough played the fool, copying his actions precisely. How stepped forward and back and marveled at the sense of controlling the old man, and the wry intelligence suggested by the crow's feet around his eyes, the flapping of his linen jacket as he moved.

"There's a *lot* of footage of David Attenborough available," Gabrielle said by way of explanation. "But of course you'd have to clear it with him before you use his likeness. There's no legal precedent, but if you're going to make an enemy, you don't want it to be the most loved man in Britain, do you?"

How shook his head, and the onscreen David Attenborough seemed to marvel at the idea too.

"Course, then there's the matter of the voice," Gabrielle said. "I'm a video lass. If you want audio to complete the illusion, that's a whole other area of AI. I took the liberty of sending a bunch of your online videos to a mate of mine who has some experience, and he's already done good work isolating your speech patterns, inflections, all that. Want to hear it?"

"No," How said sharply, even before her question had registered consciously.

"What about Attenborough? Waste of an opportunity, not using his voice. Seeing him speak in your unprepossessing monotone will undermine the effect."

How shook his head emphatically. "I don't want to fake the audio. Okay? I just don't."

EVENTUALLY, GABRIELLE COAXED the story out of him. She seemed almost disappointed when he had finished, though she accepted that the Humphriss story warranted mention in the TEDx talk.

She wouldn't let up until he agreed to play the waveform.

Again, her appreciation seemed mostly academic.

This time, How barely paid any attention to the voice itself, which seemed muted, indistinct. Nothing like as loud as the single dull click behind it.

HE INSISTED THAT HE wouldn't, that he would remain in the apartment, but when it came to it, going out for drinks seemed like a reasonable idea. As usual, it transpired that Gabrielle had merged two social plans into one, and when they arrived at the Moroccan-themed bar, a group of four of her friends were already waiting. One of them, a student named Iris, recognized How from his web videos, and she cornered him for most of the night. Whenever Gabrielle caught How's eye, she made a face, and How tried to respond in the same manner, but the alcohol had got to him immediately, and it was as if his face was made of rubber, refusing to comply with his commands.

At half past ten, after a stint of wild performative dancing on the tiny tiled square at the rear of the building, Gabrielle sauntered over to join How, who had been left alone when Iris had headed to the bar.

"You two getting on well, then?" she said.

"She's very nice," How replied.

"Just your type."

"Is she?" How genuinely wasn't sure what his type might be.

"Perky. Hopeful."

"You're not either of those things, Gab, and we had a good run."

She laughed raucously. "I'm not your type. Trust me. I know you better than you know yourself."

Iris returned carrying two mojitos and flashed an apologetic look at Gabrielle as she passed one of them to How. Gabrielle shrugged good-naturedly.

"Has he told you about the cardboard voice yet?" Gabrielle said to Iris. Then she was forced to say it again, louder and closer to Iris's ear, to be heard above the music and the hum of conversation.

Iris shook her head, then glanced expectantly at How.

He shook his head too. The motion seemed slightly delayed after his conscious command.

"Tell me," Iris said. Gabrielle was right: hopeful.

How told her the story.

And then he allowed her to convince him to play the recording. They took one earbud each, their heads pressed together as they stared at the phone screen.

There was no click.

ON THE WALK HOME, alone after Gabrielle had peeled off with some random and after How had waited with an offended Iris until a taxi arrived, he was a caricature of a drunk. His legs threatened to travel too fast or to slow, his torso teetering above them. A passing hipster wearing an oversized beanie hat recognized him and shouted a greeting. How tried to reply but his voice didn't seem quite his own, his lips oddly inert.

The heels of his shoes made continual dull clicks on the pavement.

He gazed idly up at the plume of smoke that hung above the shopfronts. It was far blacker than the sky poisoned with light pollution.

When he turned the corner and his apartment block rose into view, he was barely surprised to discover that it was on fire.

But it hurt.

Accompanied by a strange certainty that there was a lag between what was happening and the physical sensation, heat rose throughout his limbs and in his chest. He looked down, expecting to see his skin crackling, but there was nothing.

Sirens approached.

He was convinced of something impossible.

He was convinced that he was still inside the building. In his apartment, having successfully refused Gabrielle's invitation. Perhaps curled up in bed, ignorant of the fire.

But then—

He raised his hands, splaying his fingers so that the blazing apartment was only visible through the gaps.

The fingers seemed insubstantial, not quite solid.

He didn't flinch as the first of the fire engines swung into the forecourt and came to a halt. The firefighter that dropped from the cab shouted at How, "Get back there if you know what's good for you."

"Yes, I will," How replied, then frowned at the odd timbre of his voice. Then he smacked his stiff lips together, then reached up to knead the flesh of his cheeks. No part of him felt quite like himself.

Even so, he backed away as more firefighters emerged, and then he turned to leave, not knowing where he might go now. He wondered whether Gabrielle might still recognize him.

He walked away into the night, with the unsettling sense that each of his actions, each of his mannerisms, was something learnt, copied, unreal.

The Validations

Ashley Stokes

———◆———

A WOMAN WAS SILHOUETTED against the skylight at the top of the stairwell. I'd only just arrived in the lobby and couldn't tell how far up she was, four flights, five, maybe more. Dusk had fallen. It was murky up there. When I reached the upper levels, the woman had vanished. From behind one of the tall doors came a bird's high-pitched screech. I must have disturbed someone's exotic pet. Everyone who came up these stairs must unsettle whatever it was.

The apartment I'd rented was on the top floor. I checked the rooms, comparing them, favorably, to the photos on the website. The kitchen had a rustic-looking table a little too big for the space. In what would be my bedroom for the week, I hung up my clothes and kicked off my trainers. As I was logging on to the Wi-Fi, the bird screeched again downstairs.

I startled and dropped my phone. It lay between my feet, reverse-side up.

This had happened before, I realized. Not realized: felt. I *felt* that this had happened before. Not dropping the phone. If you are anything like me, you're always dropping your phone. I had been in this room before and underneath me the bird had screeched.

This wasn't déjà vu—seeing something again—but déjà vecu: living through something again. I wasn't living through anything again, was I? I'd not been to this room or even this city before. If a client came to me and explained that she frequently has sensations of living through recurring events, unless I had reasons to believe she's epileptic, I'd explain that déjà experiences are harmless memory anomalies. The past and the present can become momentarily confused. The mind plays tricks, essentially. You have to go to the wacky fringes of parapsychology to believe you're having premonitions, or inhabiting the life of someone else, living or otherwise.

I told myself I was tired after the flight and the faff at Schiphol. I certainly had never before heard a bird, or any other living thing make a noise as grating and ugly as the bird downstairs. I would have remembered.

Some poor soul lived in the same apartment as that shrieking thing. Probably the woman I'd seen as I arrived. When I pictured her now, she was disheveled, her hair back-lit, tendrilly, a mess. She glinted with rain, like she'd been caught in a storm.

I knew now. It was obvious now: The woman on the landing was you.

In the shower, I had a word with myself. I hadn't seen you. Of course, I hadn't. You couldn't be here. It wasn't unusual for me to sometimes think I'd glimpsed someone I'd once known. In crowds and queues, I often thought I recognized someone from medical school or various placements, an ex-colleague, a client, an old boyfriend, someone I'd treated, helped. The shower was powerful and hot. I felt scoured afterwards.

Trying to get the coffee machine to work turned out to be a knotty diplomatic issue involving side-deals and ultimatums. I did in the end manage to make an espresso and took it to the window. It was winter. The city was here. I would go out, have fun. I hadn't seen you in the stairwell. It was impossible. You know why.

AN HOUR OR SO LATER I thought I saw you again, this time close to the Piazza del Limbo. You were standing in yellow lamplight at a corner along the street. You wore a distinctive high-collared and long-tailed coat, not one I had seen you wear during our sessions. A gaggle of tourists swarmed around you. When they fanned out, you were gone.

The thing is: I *had* been thinking about you again. After I'd left the apartment, I'd wandered without a plan through narrow medieval streets. I pulled up short at the Piazza del Limbo. "Piazza" conjures space, a grand public square. The Piazza del Limbo is more like a yard between a church and a house. The only reason I lingered was to look up its history on my phone. In the Middle Ages, there was a cemetery here for children who died before they were baptized.

The site seemed suddenly the sort of place I ought to avoid while I was here. Before I'd started to work with you I was only dimly aware of the sad afterlives of unbaptized children in the Middle Ages. It was only because of you and Ella that I'd researched the Swedish folk tale of the changeling. Because of our work together I knew now that it was a common superstition in Dark Age Scandinavia that the bathwaters of not-yet christened children should not be thrown out so not to attract a troll. The unbaptized child must have upon it some 'article of steel,' a pin or needle attached to its swaddling clothes, or risk being replaced by a troll.

Telling you about this story had been an aside during a difficult session. It was only in hindsight that I realized I should never in a million years have mentioned this legend to you.

I SOON LIKED the cramped streets, that I could look up and between the gables to see the night and stars as a black, glittery river. I side-stepped couples holding hands and wove my way through groups of pedestrians, some clearly locals, some tourists. Without making a decision to do so I was looking out for the woman in the high-collared coat. She couldn't have been you. Even if you liked that sort of coat, you couldn't have afforded one.

The first time I met you, you were wearing a khaki parka with a fake fur hood, a white sweatshirt and jeans, and your hair was tied up in a ponytail. You looked like any of the young mums I might wander by in the street or the supermarket or sit next to in the salon, ride a cross-trainer besides in the gym.

You were an unusual referral. Ninety percent of my clients live with Alzheimer's, and the remainder are schizophrenics. Your condition is extremely rare anyway, but in the overwhelming majority of known cases, there's an overlap between Alzheimer's and your condition. Or there's an overlap with schizophrenia.

You were twenty-three. You don't have Alzheimer's. You're not a paranoid schizophrenic. You had no history, or family history, of mental illness. You had not suffered a brain injury or head trauma. You were not a user of LSD or ketamine. You had not been responsive to more routine therapies and treatments. You had not been responsive to antipsychotics or psychoactive drugs. This was your last chance. If my methods made no difference, Ella would be taken into care and you would probably be detained under the Mental Health Act. My methods, though, had never been tried with someone with your condition even in its less severe or transient forms.

The mental health trust had been insistent, in private, that I was not to blame, it was not my fault. I was aware that seeing you in the stairwell, and at the Piazza del Limbo were manifestations of guilt, or manifestations of grief, or the commingling of the two.

I entered an elegant and spacious square. The neon sign of a bar drizzled a red shine across the cobbles. Inside Bar Magica 1826 I found a table and ordered a glass of Ornellaia from a waiter. As I sipped, I wondered if a locally significant event had occurred in 1826. The date felt charged to me. I had recently come across it somewhere else. To try and understand your condition, I'd been looking for case studies and precedents, research that eventually led me to the Swedish story of the troll and the oven. In 1826—this was it—an Irish governess, Anna Roche, drowned a sick boy called Michael in the River Flesk, she said to drive the faerie from him. A court eventually acquitted her of murder. She was acquitted.

A click. Someone had placed another glass of red wine on my table.

I looked up at the waiter.

"I didn't order. Non l'ho comprato."

"The lady says, for you." He swished his hand. A slim woman with long black hair at a table close by looked up from her phone and smiled. On the next table to her, a young guy with a beard fell off his chair. The rest of his table screamed with laughter.

The woman went back to wiping her thumbs across her screen. She was mid-thirties, I guessed, maybe younger, and wore a tight black top. I waved until she looked up. I raised another toast and mouthed 'thanks.' She raised both her palms to the ceiling.

"It's the good stuff they don't tell you about." She was American, but not from the South or New York.

"It's really nice."

"Oh, you're British. You on your own? Wanna come join me, Moneypenny?"

I didn't feel I could say no, not that I had any particular reason to brush her off and it was better not to be sitting around drinking wine on my own in a strange city when I had not yet found my bearings. While she gestured for the waiter, I grabbed my coat and scarf and hung them over the back of the chair opposite her.

There was an uncomfortable pause while we waited for her wine to arrive. You might have got an inkling of this, but although I talk for a living, and rely on light conversation to put people at their ease, to make them feel that their inner world is real and valid, I sometimes find everyday social chat difficult, as if a casual natter has become loaded for me, that I can't trust it outside of the treatment room.

When the wine arrived, she said, "Yes, you're right, it's wonderful. Oh my, that's good."

"First time here?"

"First time out of the States, sister. I am . . . how shall I phrase this . . . envious, in love, my senses overloaded . . . and you are?"

"Martina."

"They call you Marti, or Tina?

"Martina, or Doctor Drax."

"Doctor Drax! So you're a Bond villain now?" She held out her hand. "Astrea. Astrea Themis."

"Now that's a glamorous name."

"It's not my name."

"It's *not* your name?"

"No one knows my name, my real name anyway."

"So what is it?"

"Like I say . . . no one knows. Wait until you hear what I do. You'll run away like all the others when you find out what I do."

I laughed. "You stole my line."
"You first then."
"Psychiatrist."
"Horror writer."

ON THAT FIRST MEETING, I did like her. She was from Nebraska and had a fourteen-year-old daughter called Georgia. I didn't ask about the father/partner situation, but she told me anyway. Met someone, got stupidly drunk and stupidly pregnant. He was criminally stupid or stupidly criminal, or dangerously dangerous or dangerously dim. Whatever, he was still smart enough to disappear in a puff of smoke because he could. She described this as Astrea Themis' creation myth, a story she also said was the basis for the first she'd written, *The Underkin*.

Her other stories, she said, had gone through three discreet phases. Firstly: Something is very wrong. Secondly: Something bad is going to happen. Then lastly: Something bad has already happened. The catastrophe is here. The revelation is upon us. I asked if writing stories was a coping strategy for her, a valve that released difficult feelings. She laughed, not nervously but as if this were a genuinely hilarious thought.

During a washroom break, I looked her up on my phone. She had published three books: *An Empty Mist*, *House of Skulls* and *The Underkin and Other Stories*. On my return, we had another glass of Ornellaia. Almost like we were competing in our little catastrophes and disappointments we laughed about how everyone she meets thinks she'll write him up in a story, and everyone I meet thinks I'll soon start seeing him as the subject of a future case study. We laughed less when I told her that I work mainly with people with Alzheimer's and people with an impaired or an affected perception of reality, that I practice validation therapies that are controversial in the wider field. I certainly didn't tell her about you. I didn't mention you at all.

It was only towards the end of the evening that she told me why she was here. She was giving a reading the following night before heading back to the Midwest the morning after.

"Libri Infernali. Via di Nerli. Say you'll come, please, Martina, please, please, please."

AS I WAS DRIFTING off that night, the bird downstairs shrieked again and livened me up. Unable to sleep, I tried not to think anything was odd about Astrea's insistence I come to her reading. The title of one of her books started to bother me. *The Underkin and Other Stories*. The idea, the suggestion of Underkin, made me itch. I tried to order the book using my phone, but it was unavailable in the UK and out of stock in the US. There was no descriptor and no reviews. I hoped I would be able to pick up a copy at the reading tomorrow.

The bird screeched below me. I couldn't imagine what sort of bird would make that noise. How did the person downstairs put up with it at night? Couldn't she put a cover over its cage, keep it quiet? None of the reviews of the apartment had mentioned a needy pterodactyl downstairs.

When it was not screeching, I was anticipating its screech. It must know I was awake. It timed its screech in line with the rhythms of my breathing and any relaxation of the tension in my muscles. I lay there, thinking about what it must look like. Inevitably, I started to think about the bird you had told me about.

We were still in our early phase. I was still trying to get to know you, and you were trying to get to know me. You often tried to steer the conversation away from you and over to me: Where did I go for lunch? Was I married? Did I have any children? Was I hooking up with anyone? You liked my top. You liked my boots. Where did I get them? This was fun, but I needed you to concentrate on yourself, on your wellbeing and your daughter's. The referral notes said you were parenting Ella alone. When I asked about the father, it's interesting that you chose to emphasize the bird. There had been a bird in the room on the occasion Ella was conceived.

You didn't know the father. You had been at a party at the flat of a neighbor you didn't know either. Some girl, bit gothy, alternative, friend-of-a-friend got you talking to a man who was very tall, like a headmaster, you thought, and not the sort of man you would expect at a party. You were drunk. Very drunk.

You remember very little of how you arrived in the bedroom or what happened there, but when you came to your senses, the Headmaster was gone. A repetitive click stopped. You had thought the click was the bed frame, a loose joint. Turned out to be a bird trapped behind the curtain.

It fluttered around the room once before escaping through an open window. You told no one about this, apart from me. It hadn't seemed important until after Ella was born, until she was about eighteen months and you started to feel suspicious, then certain.

I had started to sketch a possible hypothesis: Because for too long you had been batted about, not in control of your destiny, living in circumstances that would stress and demoralize anyone, you had smothered a part of yourself that was angry with yourself, and then angry with the Headmaster, and angry with Ella for being born and complicating things further. If you convinced yourself that Ella was not Ella but someone else, someone who had been delivered by not the smiling stork of baby cards and popular saying but an anti-stork, the dark stork, a black bird, it was therefore OK to be angry at Ella.

You could only cope with your anger if Ella was not Ella. You were never angry with Ella, only with the impostor who had taken Ella's place, the identical copy of Ella. To cope with trauma, sometimes we make a double of ourselves ("it wasn't me"). Sometimes we make a double of the other ("she isn't she"). Certainly, what you eventually did requires not just the doubling of the child but also the doubling of the mother. Double doubling.

It's all academic now.

You know that.

I know that.

I hardly slept that night. Every time I drifted off, the bird would shriek. Every time the bird woke me up I lay there and thought of you. You and Ella. You and your trapped bird.

THE FOLLOWING EVENING I made my way across the river to a district of shuttered windows and featureless squares. No one was about. All the bars and cafes were closed, I assumed because it was winter and we were away from the historic center. Libri Infernali was the one lit-up door in what was more alley than street.

I had imagined that Libri Infernali would be a poky bookshop like the ones I'd passed the night before near Piazza del Limbo but I entered not a book-lined niche but a long corridor. Six or so chandeliers led the way. Velvety, crimson walls glowed between almost bristling shadow. The corridor fed into a place that surprised me. I'd imagined a cupboard-like shop and not an incredibly creative use of urban space, a courtyard beneath an atrium roof, a pyramid of slanting glass panels. Red pennants and paper lanterns hung from a lattice of overhead beams. Dotted around were bookcases and armchairs, barrels converted into tables, and makeshift shelves of curios and figurines. At the back of a low stage at the far end, glass cabinets contained god knows what, I couldn't tell however much I squinted. The courtyard was packed with people.

All afternoon I had toyed with the idea of not coming. Having slept hardly at all, I felt jaded and underwhelmed as I'd shuffled around an art gallery. Astrea was leaving tomorrow. As I'd never see her again, I could easily give her reading a miss. My other fear was I'd be the only person there. She was hardly a household name. I couldn't even order her books from America.

Here they were, though, lined up in neat piles on a display table inside the doorway: *An Empty Mist*, *House of Skulls* and *The Underkin and Other Stories*. The first one had a swirl of mist on the jacket and the second a yellow skull, but the third, I don't know what it was, frozen sludge seen from above, scum smeared across a fly's eye, a skein of scratchy, scribbly typographic gestures that floated in the last glimmerings of the last dusk. Something like that.

There was an extremely tall bookseller behind the table, an old man with white mutton chop whiskers, in his seventies at least. In his black, floor-length gown, he looked like he should be prowling around a lecture theater in the mid-1800s, pontificating about The Great Hippocampus Question or the Devonian Controversy. He smiled and hobbled slightly forwards as if I was about to get my money out.

"Later," I said. "Dopo." I meant it. I didn't want to carry a book around all evening. I'd buy one on my way out. The audience was much older than I'd expected. I assumed a horror writer would attract a twenty-something crowd, not a parliament of white-haired gentlemen who looked like they belonged at a board meeting or in a council chamber. No one noticed me. They were all staring up at the atrium roof. Astrea must be arriving by helicopter. I hunted around for a glass of wine, but seeing no table or waiter, gave up. Determined to stay at the back, I would make eye contact with Astrea only the once, listen to the story and leave before she or anyone else could waylay me.

A little bell tinkled. The courtyard lights dimmed. A glow crept up the wall behind the glass cabinets at the back of the stage. Wearing a long black dress and carrying a book, you drifted across the stage to a mic stand. You took the mic in one hand and scanned the crowd, the faces. I tried to focus. It wasn't you. It was Astrea. Astrea looked in my direction and smiled as if greatly relieved to see me.

"Good evening," she said. "Buona sera. Welcome. Before I begin, can I just say how grateful I am that my good friend, Doctor Martina Drax is here this evening. Martina, thank you. Thank you. It's so good to see you. I need you here with me tonight."

White-haired men clapped. I didn't know what to do with my hands and tried to look at the scuffed tiles as if this had nothing to do with me.

Up on the stage, she announced, "I'm going to read from my story, The Underkin."

She held the book up and flipped it open with her thumb.

"We are far to the north. Deep winter. Freezing. The gale howls and rattles the timbers. Inside, the fire is bright and greedy. She lays the child on the blade of the shovel. The child is not her child, not since she tossed his bathwaters out into the snow, not since she forgot to place against him an iron pin, not since he conversed with eggshells and spoke with the voice of the Troll of Drang Isle. Only the fire will chase the troll from the bairn. That's what you made her believe. You made the sad girl consign her baby to the flames. You—"

OUT OF BREATH when I got into the building, I stood panting and sweaty in the lobby. Looking up, someone stared down at me. She faded backwards into shadow.

A door slammed.

The bird shrieked.

AFTER THE READING at Libri Infernali it took me twenty-four hours to talk myself out of flying straight back home and not let Astrea ruin my holiday. By dusk the following evening, I was starving hungry, having subsisted all day on crispbreads and marmalade I'd found in a cupboard in the kitchen. Outside, it was colder than it had been the day before, or the day before that. In Piazza del Limbo, lined up along one side of the church were little jars and vases, each containing a glimmering candle. They had not been there two nights ago. I wondered who cared enough for the dead, unbaptized children of seven hundred, eight hundred years ago, who cared enough to remember them now?

I thought about Ella, and I thought about you, if, where you are now, after what you did, you still think Ella was someone else, something other. I turned away from the candles and checked the street in case you were watching me.

If I were someone else, I asked myself, a client, a patient, a person with problems, how would I advise someone like me, someone seeing doubles, who believed a stranger had read out in public a text designed to expose and shame her, a story about something only she and one other knew about?

Only you and I know that I told you about the Swedish folktale. A trivial bit of chat, I had not made any reference to it in my clinical notes. I had not told the police. It was not like I'd encouraged you to do anything. Throughout, I had only not disagreed with you that Ella was an impostor. I'd tried to validate your feelings. Otherwise we would descend into rancor, into fighting. If we descended into rancor and fighting, as you had with anyone else who had tried to help you—neighbors, social workers, your GP, other doctors—Ella would be taken from you. I was trying to act agreeably until you reached your own moment of clarity and rebonded with Ella.

The lights in the little glass jars against the wall started to fizzle out. Rain pattered on the shoulders of my coat. I was sad about you again, as sad, if not sadder than I had been after your social worker told me what you had done to Ella. I still could not visualize it. How could anyone, apart from you? I felt wracked by the thought that I had missed some clue or behavior that would have given me powers of prediction. I should have seen it coming. Everyone says no one could have seen it coming. I was seeing you now. On the landing. In the street. On the stage in Libri

Infernali. Astrea Themis read the same story I'd told you.

I was exhausted. I had not seen you, no. These were illusions, anomalies. I should not validate them. I should not have validated your delusions. You do not have Alzheimer's. I should not have treated you as if you have Alzheimer's. You suffer from Capgras Syndrome. No one understands Capgras Syndrome. Joseph Capgras, who in 1923 first described the condition after treating a woman called—this can't have been her name, it must have been a nickname—Madam Macabre, he, Joseph Capgras, didn't understand Capgras Syndrome. No one knows how to treat it. I should never have agreed to treat you. I can't treat fate.

I ENDED UP in a tiny slit of a bar and ordered a platter of cheese and salami and a glass of Ornellaia. I drank the wine slowly. It struck me that Astrea Themis is a horror writer. The story of the changeling is one of the earliest horror stories. It's not *that* obscure. I'd found versions of it in several compendiums of Scandinavian folk tales. She could easily have read one of these books. She couldn't have found out about it from either of us. She had published, let alone written, *The Underkin* long before I'd started to treat you.

I shouldn't have bolted. If I'd stayed at Libri Infernali, I could have asked her where her inspiration came from. She was only being friendly, over-friendly, American-friendly when she'd mentioned me on the stage.

I needed to give myself a break here, you understand, and not beat myself up about this as well. I was raw, in pain. I was seeing you in dark passages and yellow light. I had failed everyone involved in this case. A child had died because of my mistake. Astrea's story was not only a coincidence but a horrible coincidence, the sort that impacts on someone suffering from guilt and grief and severe tiredness.

All day I had been holed up in the apartment waiting until I could be sure Astrea had left the city. I regretted that now. I wished I had a copy of *The Underkin and Other Stories* so I could analyze the story. I would have to go back to the shop. I would do so tomorrow.

I needed sleep. All through the night the bird had shrieked below me. During the day, it had carried on, every couple of minutes: *shriek-squeak, shriek-squeak*. Where before I'd expected a bird of paradise was down there, some parrot or toucan with a long beak and impudent stare, now I imagined a much bulkier bird, flightless, squat and spoon-billed, something supposedly extinct, a throwback so ugly you wouldn't eat it if you'd seen it alive, that waddled in and out of corners. When I went from room to room, from bedroom to lounge, from kitchen to bathroom, it followed my footfalls to screech up at me. It was right under me, in the apartment below.

THE NEXT DAY, rain lashed down. In other circumstances, it would have been nice to have holed up in the apartment with a plate of pastries and a book, drowsing on the sofa until the rain stopped. I trudged my way south in a grey squall. Libri Infernali was empty. Rain thrummed on its glass roof as I wandered the shelves. I couldn't find any copies of Astrea's books. I'd had it in my head that I would grab a latte here and read *The Underkin* on one of the armchairs until the rain stopped. I was obviously going to be disappointed and resigned myself to hunting down a second-hand copy online when I got back home. I should have left then. This was not my sort of place. I kept picturing in my mind's eye that group of old men in their old suits looking up at the pyramid-shaped atrium as if something was going to drift down from the sky.

Someone whispered my name, almost as if he was not trying to attract my attention but practicing the language. The extremely tall bookseller walked towards me. His gown rippled about his feet.

"How do you know my name?" I said.

"Last night," he said. "Our esteemed guest, she spoke of you."

"Ah, yes, I see—"

"The lady was . . . how do I say—"

"Maybe you can help me? I'm looking for one of her books. You had copies last night."

"Last night the lady was very disappointed that you did not stay. She very much wanted to talk with you."

"I was feeling unwell, Signor?"

"Gufo. Signor Gufo."

"I was feeling unwell, Signor Gufo. The next time you are in contact with Signora Themis, please pass on my apologies—"

"All the books have been sold. Last night. All sold."

He looked down on me, his eyes deep in his sockets. If anything, he seemed older and taller than he had last night.

"I'll find it elsewhere," I said. "Have a good day."

"She was upset, the lady. She needed talk with you."

"I hardly know her, Signor Gufo."

"She must talk to you because she has a daughter, and her daughter now does not say the lady is her mother. She thinks the lady is someone who pretends to be her mother."

"She didn't say that to me."

"She came here to ask for your help."

"That's highly unlikely."

I turned my back, this time determined to leave.

"The Underkin," Signor Gufo called after me. "They are few but many. Don't be—"

DO YOU EVER FIND yourself with nowhere to go apart from someplace you know you should avoid like the plague? Do you ever get like this? From Libri Infernali I hurried through the streets, heading for a collection of anatomical waxworks and stuffed animals I'd bookmarked as a potential rainy-day outing. In the museum, sodden, shivering, I drifted through halls filled with cases of pinned butterflies and mounted insects. I walked along lines of animal skeletons: elephants and rhinos, moose and reindeer, ostriches and emus. In front of a display of big cats, I tried to process what Signor Gufo had said: that Astrea Themis' daughter believes Astrea is not her mother but is someone else. That sounded a lot like Capgras to me. In fact, it sounded a lot like you if you and Ella had your roles reversed.

There was a remote chance that she could have found out about you. Your case had been widely and ghoulishly, in my opinion, reported in the tabloids. Newspapers can be read online. My name, however, had been kept out of it. When your case comes to trial and I give evidence, that may change, but at the moment there's no way someone in Nebraska could connect us, or assume I'm some sort of world expert on Capgras.

On another day, I may have enjoyed the anatomical waxworks in the next series of galleries, admired the craftsmanship and the spirit of scientific enquiry that had informed their commission. Today, the displays seemed less like a sensuous celebration of the human form and more like a vile diorama of flayed corpses. I don't think you would have had much time, either, for a specimen with her legs truncated at mid-thigh; or a man resting on his elbow, the fingers of his other hand gently stroking his exposed collarbone as if he were sunbathing without his skin; or two baby twins, the foot of one nudging the forearm of the other in the font-like bulb of the womb, both slick and gleaming, asleep among the fronds and tubes of their mother.

I was the only visitor today. Apart from the occasional click of my boots on the marble floors, the galleries were silent. We could sit in silence for ages, couldn't we? Over the last few months it has nagged and haunted me: Why after that excruciatingly long silence, that day your face was red with torment, did I choose to add what I momentarily thought was a subtle way of saying you are not alone, that yours is an old story and all stories have endings.

"You know you're not the first person to have these feelings," I told you. "In fairy tales, old stories, especially from Sweden, you know, the snowy wastes, pre-Abba, a woman who feels her child is an impostor would not have followed the proper Christian rituals."

"So?"

I was relieved. At least you said something. "She would then perform some superstitious claptrap because she didn't have the correct support."

"What claptrap?"

"I'm saying that you are not alone."

"Just tell me, Martina."

So I told you, about the shovel and the oven and how folk once thought that proximity to fire could drive out the troll. It was a church story designed to keep scared and simple people wedded to the new faith. No one had actually done it. I was trying to say that we don't need faith when we have solutions based on how our minds really work. If you had pressed me I would have said that the troll is inside you, not Ella, but you have the power to drive out the troll.

You didn't respond to the story, did you? You sat there with your arms folded and chewed your bottom lip. I changed the subject to how Ella was doing at nursery.

In the last of the rooms, four glass-topped cabinets containing god-knows-what were surrounded by display cases full of half-made people that swirled in my peripheral vision. I wanted to leave, however cold and wet it was outside. Ahead, at the far end, four standing figures, women, skinless, eyeless, their flesh extremely red, red-tending-to-black.

The one on the right side was very black and shorter than the others.

She was not behind glass. At first I thought something had been covered up with a black sheet. I blinked. A real woman was studying the red-raw figures. A woman with tendrils of sprawling black hair, in a high-collared, long-tailed coat that pooled around her ankles. I couldn't work out if the hissing in my head was my breathing or yours.

THE LAST TRUDGE up what now seemed like a hundred flights of stairs nearly killed me. By the time I reached the apartment, I thought my shins would explode and my feet catch fire. The bird started to shriek as soon as I'd locked the door behind me. Drenched, I slid out of my clothes. They were too wet to be packed, really. As I fitted them into carrier bags to keep the rest of my luggage dryish, I felt scared. I needed help. I'd thought I could deal with what had happened to you and Ella on my own, in my own way. I was hallucinating. I needed to go home and see someone, a trauma specialist like Ruth Burgess or Andy Hemp at the Cedar Centre. I had never asked for help before. I had never needed it. I had never needed anything. Everything I ever wanted I had worked for and towards and achieved. I had been happy. I had not been troubled. Now I was seeing things, couldn't sleep, couldn't let go, find closure.

At the kitchen table, I used my phone to book a one-way flight home for the early evening. I counted up the remaining time. An hour to pack and make myself look presentable and less like a drowned Victorian chimney sweep. An hour to get to the airport. A four-hour wait for the flight.

The bird started to shriek louder than it ever had before. It may as well have been in the room, under the table, screaming for me to explain myself. That bird had ruined my holiday, destroyed any chance I'd had of finding any peace. I could not process what had happened because of that bird. It knew... knew what it was doing.

I abandoned any idea of changing and sorting out my face and my hair. I could do something at the airport. I packed my bags and left the keys on the kitchen table. I sent the landlord a text, saying I was leaving ahead of schedule. There is a monstrous bird downstairs and it had spoiled my stay. Signor, seriously, I'm not joking. If I'd had a gun, I'd have gone down and shot its head off.

AFTER I'D SCHLEPPED my luggage down the first of the tight staircases, I came out onto the landing immediately below the apartment. There was a grainy, underwater quality to the grey light that drifted down from the skylight. Rain clattered on glass. I was sure there was someone along the landing, someone who shuffled off as soon as I arrived. A door banged behind her, followed by a muffled thud as if the door was on a latch and had not closed properly.

I peered over the railing. There seemed to be more landings than ever before. The lobby was such a long way down. I wondered what someone down there would see? If you were down there, what would you see of me?

Behind one of the tall, ornate doors the bird screeched, shrieked, screamed out like it needed me, that for dear life it didn't want me to leave. The door was ajar. A little light from outside escaped onto the landing.

I remember telling myself I should not hesitate here. I would drag my case past the door, schlepp the next staircase to the next level, to the lower levels beyond until I found the lobby that was a long way down. I would find the outside and the rain. I would walk to the nearby square and stand at the taxi rank. I would not try to enter the apartment behind the tall, ornate door. I would not check out the bird. I did not care what either it or its owner looked like. I would not complain to its owner. I would not wring the neck of that bloody bird. Would you understand if I'd done that? Would you want me to do it?

I jerked my suitcase strap.

I let go of the strap.

The case scuffed to a halt.

This was all wrong. This was not the way I should be handling anything, the big things or the small things. In the scheme of things, the bird was a minor annoyance, a pest, nothing to lose my cool over. Breathe, I told myself. Think about it. If I left without seeing the bird, it would balloon and distort and I would feel bullied and blind. You must understand this. You must understand how that feels, what can happen if you let such self-image issues persist and fester. If I didn't see what in reality was probably a cute, sweet-looking songbird, it would mutate in my imagination and never leave me. The bird would be inside me forever. I told myself that I did have the power to expel the bird.

I pushed on its door.

I announced myself.

The bird shrieked, a long wail, more like a fox in the night, or the yowl of a fighting cat.

IN A VIOLET SKY, violet clouds swirled beyond a skylight above me. Something was trapped in the curtains, clicking, scratching. Either side of me, Astrea Themis, her face like a skull wrapped in white tissue paper, and him, Senor Gufo, the giant in academic robes, and surrounding them the old men with their eyes lifted, as if they did not like to see, to witness. Someone else. Someone I couldn't see yet. I could hear him, though, the shriek of him. The shriek was him.

Did you hear him? Did you hear him screech like that? Can you still hear him? I still hear him. Asleep. Awake. Indoors. Outdoors. As I talk to my therapist. As I talk to my doctor, my solicitor and the officer in charge of the case and people from the embassy. Do you remember him, too? His head the head of a baby bird. The gaping mouth of a baby bird. Twitches. Prods. Jabs. Shrieks. I could still hear him when I surfaced in the waste ground near the railway station, soaked through, my passport and a one-way airline ticketed stuffed into a high-collared coat that hadn't been mine before. I can still hear him as if he's someone under my skin. Can you still hear him? Can I see you? Can we talk? I believe you now. I believe it. I understand: What they did to you. What they did to us. I will speak. I will tell the jury. I will tell the judge. I am a doctor. They will believe me.

A Perfect Doll

Regina Garza Mitchell

THE GIRL IS GOOD. The girl is perfect, inside and out. Dark hair and eyes, skin smooth and soft without a blemish except for a tiny birthmark on the inside of her left ankle. She is kind and smart. Obedient. The kind of little girl who sits with her legs crossed, whose dresses drape in neat folds over her legs. Everything they had hoped for.

The more she grows, the more enchanted they become.

"Can you believe it?"

"So perfect!"

"A living doll."

They taught her how to read and write and count, so it was only natural she would be homeschooled. Their house in the country was big enough. Acres of wildland all around helped her learn biology, plants and animals. She learns about gardening and agriculture from the small plots they cultivate and the books she is always reading. She does complex sums and multiplication tables by the age of six. By twelve she has blown through the advanced trigonometry and calculus courses intended for high-schoolers.

She reads incessantly, devouring Dickens and Austen with the same enthusiasm she shows for the old set of encyclopedias she found out in the garage.

Simply perfect in every way.

One day they watch her as she skips through the field picking wildflowers. Yellow, blue, and purple blooms she places into a vase to decorate the table.

"Perfection."

"But of course! She is like you."

They kiss and laugh.

Another birthday arrives, and they celebrate with a small party. They give her small dolls to play with, a tea set, and a teddy bear.

She is nearly too big for the flounced dress they buy her, but she is a good girl and wears it anyway despite the way it cuts into her armpits and stretches across her chest, the way it sets just at her knees. She acts happy, though, and does not cry until that night when the dress rips as she tugs it off. She feels, somehow, as though she did something wrong. She raises her chapped armpits hoping the fresh air will make the hurt go away and cries softly into her pillow so that they won't hear. What is happening to her?

She is no longer perfect.

She paces her room, imagining this is how a caged lion feels. The room that has always meant safety suddenly seems small and dark. She opens the windows hoping for a gust of wind to blow these feelings away. Instead, she lets in humidity that hangs pregnant in the air of the room, making even less space for her. She thinks of going for a walk outside in the dark. Alone. But she knows she shouldn't. They might hear. And she doesn't want them to know she is imperfect, that there is something different about her now. Something wrong.

That night she dreams of darkness and being stuck in the shadows.

SHE ACTS THE WAY she always has, smiles and laughs. Only now the happiness is pretend. For the first time in her life, they give her more space. She is allowed to take walks in the fields, picking flowers on her own. They don't hover with their smiles and cameras and comments.

Her clothes change from pretty dresses to oversized sweaters and plain t-shirts and loose, soft pants that tie with a drawstring. Oxfords and tennis shoes rather than shiny Mary Janes. She enjoys the new freedom, her ability to go wherever she wants, even into the woods that they used to warn her away from. But she is also lonely without their adoration.

"You're old enough now," they say. "You know what you should and shouldn't do."

She smiles and gives a little curtsy, but they have already started walking back toward the house.

She spends that day in the woods identifying as many mushrooms as she can: chicken of the woods, morel, oyster, puffball, and black trumpet. She even spies what she thinks of in her head as a gnome and fairy mushroom, a red-capped beauty with yellow spots she knows is really named amanita muscaria or fly amanita. But her usual excitement is dimmed by this feeling she has. A feeling of . . . loss. Sorrow. Something she has never felt before.

"I am alone," she says. "Abandoned."

The words make her feel better, and she spends most of the morning hiking around the woods, enjoying the spongy feel of the moss underfoot and trying to count the number of different varieties she spies on trees or the ground. She stops at six, unsure as to whether she has already counted reindeer moss or not and then wondering if reindeer moss counts as moss since it is actually a variety of lichen. This line of thinking stops the mantra running through her head: imperfect, different, alone.

By lunchtime she realizes that despite her anxiety, she has actually enjoyed herself. It is the first day of her life that she has not had to be perfect for anyone. Her hands are dirty, shoes and pants wet and streaked with mud. She has not thought of herself, of who or what she is supposed to be. Has not thought of *them*. Once she realizes that, however, the heavy feeling deep in her stomach returns. Was this what they wanted or will they be mad that she has done nothing but traipse through the wilds all day? Her stomach growls, reminding her that she needs food even if the thought of it brings a wave of nausea. She could eat mushrooms; she has learned from books which ones are poisonous and which are not. But most need to be cooked, and she also needs water.

She sighs and kicks her foot into the ground. It takes her the rest of the day to find her way out of the woods and back to the house.

They are not mad. They are . . . indifferent. They do not have a meal waiting for her and do not offer to cook. When she asks if they would like her to make sandwiches, they inform her that they have already eaten. She can make what she wants as long as she cleans up afterward. They go back to the den and close the door. She hears the murmur of their voices from behind the door, the soft tones that rise and fall. The faint click of keys as they type on the computer, something she is never allowed to touch.

She heads to the kitchen and grabs an apple, a crust of bread and some butter, a large glass of water. She brews tea as she eats. She takes the tea upstairs on a tray, a small thrill of fear in her stomach wondering if (hoping) they will stop her, get angry. React. But they remain locked in the den from which comes click of keys and soft rumbling of their voices.

THE PATTERN CHANGES. Some days she does her schoolwork, which they still oversee, though not as enthusiastically. It used to be a family event, everyone working and talking together. Now she is expected to do most of it on her own, reading and completing the assignments they task her with. She doesn't think they bother to look at it. They spend more time locked in the den.

One day they leave the door slightly open, and she sees the floor is covered in photographs. Pictures of her as a younger child, always clad in exquisite dresses, hair soft and neat, hands and legs neatly folded as though she is required to stay inside herself. In some photos she holds a doll. Otherwise, she is always alone. Always serious. She feels much older now, less delicate.

She begins to do small things to test her boundaries. Not wearing shoes outside. Cutting her hair into an uneven frizz that clouds around her face. Not bathing every night.

They don't seem to notice. Aside from occasional meals that they take together in silence, she might be living alone. An unwelcome ghost.

She now sleeps with the windows open, a small act of defiance against the usual rules. It might be too cold, too damp, too windy. A crisp wind wakes her before the sun rises. She will go out prepared today, with books to read, a notebook to write in, food, and water. It will be a day to herself, a *planned* day. She smiles as she gets up. It feels good to make a decision, not to float around hoping for relief. She will help herself like the heroes in the books that she reads.

She remains hopeful despite the uncertain start in the bath. Curly, dark hairs have grown, seemingly overnight, in her armpits. They smell, and she wrinkles her nose as she washes herself. Another change. She decides that she will just have to get used to the changes in her body and in her routine. It is something new, after all. An opportunity of some kind, or a test. She will face it without fear.

And then, another unexpected event. This morning they are not up and waiting. They have not brewed their usual coffee or made their usual breakfast. There is a note on the counter telling her they have gone out for the day and will be back late.

This has never happened before, and she feels the now-familiar thrill of fear and excitement. *What does it mean?*

HER BIRTHDAY COMES and goes with little fanfare. They are not quite standoffish, but they aren't the way they used to be either. Her present this year is a doll, even though she hasn't played with her dolls in years. This is a special doll. It is expensive, custom made to look exactly like her. Or at least the way she used to look. A miniature version of her. This explains the photographs, she thinks, and why they were so secretive.

They don't seem happy, exactly, but excited and nervous. After the celebratory dinner, she sits on the couch next to the doll.

"It's a perfect doll, isn't it?"

"The exact image."

"Perfect."

"Perfect."

Their voices seem to be fading out like the old radio she sometimes uses. Close and then far away. There is no static here, though, just . . . distance. She seems to be moving away from them somehow, falling or being pulled back by something. She struggles to stay awake and feels something soft placed over her face and held down by a large hand.

"Oh, make it quick, darling!"

"Yes, of course," the words said softly, with just a slight pant. "This takes effort, though. And we need to do it right."

"Yes, yes, darling. I know."

She doesn't realize how tightly she is clutching the doll until it is pried from her. She is still resisting, still fighting both the pressure on her physical body and the pull from what she senses is a deep darkness.

"Perfect" is the last word she hears, though she knows it is not spoken about her.

They take her limp body outside and drag it through the field, past the plots of vegetables they grow that she used to tend. Burrs snag on her clothes and in her hair. She is beyond feeling them or the scrape of the ground on her back when her shirt comes untucked, but she can see it as though she is aware of everything.

They pull her to the clearing they have made, the one lined with candles. They use a knife to make an opening and collect her blood in a large earthenware bowl covered with arcane symbols. They use a brush dipped in her blood to paint some of these symbols on the ground and on her body. As the moon rises higher in the sky, they finish. They place her body in a pentagram made from her blood and lay the doll on top of her. She tries to move, to shake it off, to scream, but she is so tired. Even though she cannot feel her physical body, she is weak from fighting the pull that threatens to take her to some other place. She struggles to get back into her own skin, to knock the doll off of her body. To do anything that will stop their heinous ritual, interrupt the foul words they are chanting that make her feel nothing but sorrow and despair. Instead, she watches as they produce a small wooden cask and remove several items from it. They place them around her in various places on the pentagram, all the while intoning strange words. Her baby teeth, clippings of hair from when she was a baby, pictures of her as a child. A breeze springs up as they chant, voices growing louder in competition with the wailing wind.

She feels another tug, this time toward her inert body. She is pulled in two directions, and she makes her decision. Pushes with all her might toward her body. She feels a sense of dislocation, reminding her of when she rolled out of bed as a child.

And feels the doll sucking her breath out of her own body and into its own. *No!* she tries to scream. *No!*

They continue their chanting as she grows smaller, drawn out of her own comfortable skin and into the small, plastic confines of porcelain and cloth. The tiniest thread remains between her new prison and her old body. She turns her doll head, severing the string, and she watches as her human eyes close, body sags. It shrivels in on itself as though whatever had been inside of her was now gone. Her very essence.

They continue chanting, shouting over the wind that has kicked up out of nowhere, smiles on their chapped faces. Meanwhile the wind cuts her human body, her old self, to pieces until there is nothing left except the confines of this new doll body. All she can do is look out of the tiny eyes and watch herself disappear.

As the last grains of her bodily dust are blown away, the wind calms. Their chanting quiets, and they eventually stop. A hand reaches down and picks up the doll. Its eyes remain open as it stares glassily ahead.

"Perfect."

"It is, isn't it?"

"It'll be great in her bedroom."

"I picked up the cutest duvet cover. Yellow roses and pale green leaves."

"She'll love it."

They embrace in the moonlight and break apart when they hear a movement behind them.

A little girl stands up in the clearing and walks toward them uncertainly.

"Darling!"

"Happy birthday, sweetheart! Come, come, let's get your cake."

"And don't forget this. The birthday girl must have her present."

Her small fingers grip the doll and she hugs it close before taking one of their hands.

The three of them smile before heading back to the house.

The girl holds the doll to her shoulder and then lets it hang from her hand, bouncing against her thigh. The doll is perfect except for its mouth, open in a silent scream.

Madam and Yves

Marc Joan

———◆———

WHEN YVES DIED, I purchased his Geneva apartment and all it contained, down to the last tortured limb. The brown decor, the twisted beasts and plastic chimaeras, and the face that awaited me on Melektaus' steel bed: all became mine.

Mine too—I later discovered—were the unborn ones, Madam and the other disciples, who sat in Yves' software like so many pluripotent cells poised to erupt into predetermined anatomy. But I knew nothing of such imps when I bought Yves' apartment, and all goods and chattels therein, from his grieving parents; I knew only that the apartment was all that remained to me of an enigmatic love—is that the word?—that I did not understand. Here, I thought, in this ugly flat in the ugliest part of Geneva, surrounded by uglier interiors and the persistent odor of unattended death, I would unravel the mystery of my obsession with Yves. I would find the answer, somehow, even if I had to raise his dead, autistic soul.

Perhaps that soul watches me now as, face-up on the printing table, I look around and about—and above, to where Melektaus' pursed mouth hovers (its heat makes the air tremble)—while the warm metal baseplate cushions my head. Perhaps it nods, as unsmiling in its eternal death as Yves ever was in his short life, and says: *Yes, Georges; this is the answer.* Perhaps that is why Madam grinds her polymer teeth; she too wants what may come, and my hesitation irks her. The brass neck of God's plastic children! But that will change.

I am overtaken by a jaw-breaking yawn; fatigue swells my eyes like cancer. Absurd to be awake . . . But there it is; one can forget how to sleep, it seems.

I swipe away my phone's screensaver; the app is still open. Centrally, it displays a touchscreen button: *PRINT,* it offers. Or commands. Madam cannot read, but she knows what it says, and mouths the word like a dead echo: *print*. This, I guess, is for the benefit of the others; I hear them click and shift, as if impatient. All right then: *PRINT.*

But wait! (My thumb stops its downward motion; the millimeter of air between skin and screen swells with possibility). Wait: I am not ready. Let me walk again the steps of logic that brought me here, to lie before Melektaus. I must be *sure*, before I start.

When I first approached Yves' apartment as its new owner, I'd come straight from the Hôpitaux. The smell of cut flesh and sodium hypochlorite had stayed with me, as though my skin had soaked up the theatre's odors and now released them by slow diffusion; my body begged to be clean. Repelled by the stink of the apartment block's graffiti-inked, urine-spattered lift, I opted for the three flights of stairs to my new accommodation, that first day. The climb will be symbolic, I told myself: an ascension, an *escape*, from the pit of despair that had held me since Yves' death. Thus I set my eyes to the future, to the resolution of my life's dark question; to an answer that, surely, came closer with each upward step. And yet, as I climbed higher, I fell further into the past. With each tread and riser, half-healed memories throbbed again. When I reached the top floor, they were as fresh as week-old wounds; when I pushed at Yves' door their scabs peeled off and they bled anew.

The unclotting of memories! As the echoes of the shut door died, I found myself remembering the small, wicked interest piqued by the first shared glance between Yves and I. As I continued into the hallway, I recalled the growth of my "small interest" into a desire that fed off itself, and the maturation of that desire into a compulsion that I could not explain. And finally, Madam, as I opened the living-room door, the scent of putrefaction broke through the chemical fragrance of carpet cleaner and reminded me again of the dead insularity of my new, *sans*-Yves, existence. My fists clenched on the pain of loss. Sweet Yves! Poor Yves! He'd lain there so long, in that hot summer.

Yes: poor, sweet Yves. But *why* Yves? Good question, Madam; why? At first, because of his vulnerability: the weak give off an erotic charge that galvanizes me like nothing else. And what weakness could be as vulnerable, as desirable, as mental impairment? Indeed, Yves' confusion in the face of normal life provoked a fierce need in me that I could hardly control. Later, however, this natural appetite was replaced by another, more troubling hunger. I cannot put a word on it, for I do not know what it is; so, yes, let us call it *love*. No physical outlet satisfied it; satiation was found only in the dull light of Yves' sidelong glances, in the knowledge that his absolute need to look at me was greater than his immense need to look away. As if to see my face were to brush with an ecstasy he could hardly bear! It gave me such a peculiar, oddly refined pleasure; I hardly knew how to manage it, and once it had gone, I did not know how to replace it.

Oh, the memories! Sometimes, Madam, I would torture him by leaving clothes on the floor, or by placing my toothbrush on the sink's edge instead of in its holder. He didn't dare complain; he'd frown and squirm until at last he could stand it no longer, and then put everything back in everything's place, as his autistic needs demanded. Such innocent pleasures I had from him; such a long time, eternity, to be bereft of them!

No, Madam; I will share no more memories with you. Those keepsakes are mine alone. Suffice to say I was unanchored, emotionally adrift, that first night alone in Yves' flat. Bereft of company—of *love*—I sat for hours, my mind bare of thoughts; I stood abruptly for no reason; I walked about with no purpose; I sat again. Eventually, I showered; I washed my clothes, and while they dried I paced nakedly around the flat, searching for clean bed-sheets. My investigations took me to the room we'd called the *salle d'imprimerie*, the spare bedroom where Yves had set up his computers and 3D printers; here I found the fruits of his fecundity, tidied away by, I presume, those who had cleaned the apartment after his death. Jumbled and tangled, Yves' creations lay in piles against walls, in secret heaps beneath the table, in little clusters on chairs: for all the world like the polymer evidence of some old slaughter done by some plastic Pol Pot. Prosthetic legs of various designs, adorned with the elaborate polypropylene filigrees that had become Yves' trademark; podiatric orthoses in rainbow-bright polyethylene; epoxy elbow sockets lined with Day-Glo foam; all the flotsam and jetsam discarded from his orthotics day-job and hoarded "just in case."

More interesting by far, however, and by far more numerous, were the creatures that Yves' own mind had spawned for Yves' own pleasure, each weekend and most evenings. Their numbers and diversity suggested a malignancy of the creative process: as if his Id had imagined a plastic teratoma that now budded off its own little monsters, without volition, without mercy, without end. Absurdly grotesque, each of them! But I inspected them all with due gravity, that first night, like the inheritor of a great estate meeting his retinue of servants. You know what I saw, Madam. A rabbit-like creature with carnivorous teeth and owl's claws. A bastardized arthropod composition, like a giant millipede, with a head at each end, twisting against itself in segmented agony. A legless pig-thing that writhed and glared from a shelf. The others. They were all here still, in Yves' apartment, waiting: as repulsive as the day he'd made them, yes, but retaining still their extraordinary energy. Indeed, some— those with faces fabricated from thermoplastic polyurethane—almost had expressions on their rubbery skin: thus, a doll-like creature with dog's breasts, her fecund pelvis perched on famine-child legs, grinned at me in a revolting parody of allure, while a many-armed, hairless ape, its chest split by some unidentifiable orifice, leered at my nudity.

I could have broken them, Madam; I could have broken them all. But I did not harm a single one. Am I not merciful? (She does not answer; her face is turned upwards, to Melektaus' nozzle, as if to bask in its blistering heat).

In fact, Madam, the only other thing I did that first night, before curling up on the familiar dents and tired springs of Yves' mattress, was to remove the opaque plastic dust sheet from Melektaus. I can't remember why. Perhaps it was a random impulse. Or perhaps Melektaus' pale shroud reminded me that, shortly before his death, Yves had said he'd started a *unique* 3D-printing project: "something special." He'd volunteered no details—and to ask would have been beneath me—so I knew nothing more than that; but his secrecy had irked me at the time, and perhaps that half-forgotten irritant gnawed at me still. It was as though something whispered that "something special" awaited me on Melektaus' fabrication bed. And so I lifted the dust sheet—the sugary odor of PLA polymer wafted up—and there it was! In gleaming ebony plastic, in the finest of detail, my own 3D-printed facial facsimile sat on Melektaus' steel base-plate, staring back at me with the knowing smile of Buddha. Yes, Madam; I looked at me looking at me, and saw that I was beautiful. True, my mask was unfinished—printing had reached only as far as mid-forehead—but still: how delightful! How "love"-affirming! *Thank you, Yves*. And thus comforted, I slept that night.

Yes, one hundred and eight nights ago, I slept a full night through. For the last time.

Oh, to have true rest again! I close my eyes; I float on an ocean of weariness, without seabed or shore, without object or end. To slip beneath its surface and sink, sink . . . But no! I feel a sharp pain, as if Melektaus had spat a gobbet of burning plastic into my face. Or—more likely—as if Madam had reached out with a tiny plastic hand and tweaked the tender flesh just beneath my eyelid. Oh, you may play now, Madam; but soon you too shall see the face of God. I glare at her, but her expression does not change. *Continue*, it says; *pray continue*.

All right; listen then. In the days following the discovery of my doppelgänger mask waiting within the framework of Melektaus, the despair that—since Yves' death—had seeped ever more deeply into my cleaved life threatened to engulf me. A growing sense of existing without purpose prompted a desperate search among Yves' tasteless possessions. After all, if there were any answer to the mystery that once lay between Yves and I, surely it would be found in Yves' Geneva flat, not in my suburban villa. So I looked in every corner of every room, Madam; I opened every drawer and every cupboard. Nothing of interest; nothing. I then turned to Yves' creations, the offspring of his unique monomania. I arrayed them around the *salle d'imprimerie,* first in order of size, then re-arranged them, again and again, in categories such as gender, number of limbs, and so forth. I interrogated them unceasingly. Still nothing. Still no answer to my question: *why in God's name had I loved Yves?*

If love it was; but what else could it have been?

I searched on, through ever later nights; I turned every page of every book, I looked beneath tables, behind cupboards, seeking always some clue, some scrawled indicator on some balled-up scrap of paper. I searched on, and on; I had no choice. But I found nothing, and eventually I had nowhere else to look but among his files. Yves being Yves, there was no diary, no collection of Word documents containing his ponderous thoughts. Only computer files, all of which pertained to his 3D-printing projects: hundreds of sparsely annotated CAD files and ancillary material. Hundreds of them!

So be it, I thought; needs must when the devil drives. I would have to dig my pit deeper still, it seemed, if I were to escape it. Those files became my life, Madam, evenings and weekends; I went through each of them in turn, in date order, from the earliest to the most recent, examining the blueprints of each part of each little monster. The tedium was ameliorated by a growing hope: by following the arc of Yves' creativity, I thought, surely I would find answers. And indeed, as long evenings of investigation turned into yet later nights succeeded by still earlier mornings, gradually, gradually, the feeling grew on me that there was something there, some hidden design. Something intangible; something that, at first, I could not quite discern.

Eventually I reached the last-executed file: Visage 1. The CAD files showed me representations of my own face, rotated this way and that, and the file execution icon detailed the most recent activity: *Print run suspended (feedstock interruption).* So that's why my face was unfinished. Simple to fix, however; I replaced Melektaus' spool of black plastic filament, switched him on and *voila!*—up popped a gratifying pop-up on the computer screen: *Press OK to resume printing.* I pressed; Melektaus whined and whirred; his nozzle tracked around in x and y and z dimensions and then lowered itself to the unfinished edge of the mask. There it began to extrude molten plastic in precise layers. Curls of smoke snaked up like the steam from a witches cauldron; dust burnt. Hallelujah! Yves' special project *would* be finished; I would be complete.

But listen, Madam: while I waited for my plastic face to grow, I found some *unprinted* Melektaus files in Yves' directory; Visage 1 was the last *executed* file, but not the *last* file. Indeed, there were eight never-printed files: Visage 2, and Golem 1 to 7. The apotheosis, perhaps, of Yves' productivity.

The first of these unprinted ones, Visage 2, was Yves' own face; but I felt no need to fabricate this unsmiling mask, the counterpart to my own. Not then. As for the others, Madam—even their sterile CAD outlines disgusted me. So I had no plans—as I say, not then—to print those unfulfilled concepts; none. Indeed, of all Yves' projects, it was my own dark mask that most interested me. It was as though my features had been caught in an instant of divine inspiration, of joy, and then cast in obsidian. I wanted more than anything to look, to *be*, the likeness of me that Yves had captured. It was as if he had made something that was more I than I, and I was both jealous and proud. As if he had seen me as I *ought to be*.

But there was something awry, Madam: many times, I tried on my mask, my black soul's face—*and it did not fit*. The internal contours were not made for my features; it was like wearing somebody else's worn shoe. Once, as if one could alter reality by pretending it to be otherwise, I wore it to the February Masquerade, by the shores of Lake Geneva. My costume was admired, true—black robes beneath a cape of peacock feathers—but even this satisfaction could not disguise the mask's discomfort, the infuriating knowledge that *it was designed for another*.

This puzzled me for weeks; I even began to doubt Yves' fidelity. But something about the quality of the mask's internal contours—their roundness, their lack of any significant defining feature—their *familiarity*—triggered a suspicion that grew slowly into certainty. I confirmed it by recourse to the CAD files for Visage 1 and Visage 2. And yes—there was no doubt: the exterior of Visage 1 mapped perfectly onto the internal contours of Visage 2, and vice versa. Yves had designed an Yves-mask that fitted my face like a glove, and a Georges-mask that would have sat over Yves' features, tight as a second skin. So that each could, truly, be the other's mirror. The vanity of love! But *why?*

You see, Madam, questions breed questions. In attempting to understand my own absurd obsession, I now found that I needed to dissect the obsessions of Yves' absurd mind!

It was at this point—burdened by the immense mass of a fatigue which grew each day—that I decided to print Golem 1 to 7. I had no clear idea whether or how their stunted bodies could address my questions; I only knew that I could not interrogate them in CAD format. To proceed, I had to give them physical form. And mark this, Madam—to construct your tribe took weeks of pain. Even now my arms are freckled with white pockmarks left by the molten polymer that Melektaus would spit at me, as if to sear the thousand and one names of a plastic deity into my skin. Nothing was easy: Yves had specified different polymers for joints, faces, teeth and skin; therefore, different polymer spools had to be hunted out and inserted as the fabrication progressed; and once the various components had been printed, and cooled, and the effects of warping, if any, remedied, why then I had to fit together the various pieces of each ugly homunculus. I expedited matters somewhat by downloading Melektaus' operator app to my phone, such that I could control printing remotely, between surgeries. This saved me valuable minutes, as the components of your foul anatomies could be cooling while I remodeled living flesh in the theatre, such that you were ready for my attention as soon as I got back each evening; but even so, it took more time than I wanted to give. And can you guess the identity of Golem 1, Madam? Can you?

Yes. It was you, Madam. I made you first.

The assertion enrages her. Soundless words come, and the anlagen of fury and disgust briefly shadow her features. I seem to hear again the grinding of her polycarbonate teeth. With her knees up to her chest, she pulls at labia already agonizingly stretched by what tries to escape her womb. It peers out from her and gurns, her brat-child-beast-thing, as if to mirror her printed pain. Madam's meaning is clear: *Liar! Who is the real Creator?*

And that, Madam, is near blasphemy. But I will answer your questions, just as your tribe has answered mine. Let me tell you your own story—you and the other disciples. The truth is this: your tortured limbs, your bizarre anatomies—you owe them all to me. I remember, even if you do not, pulling you all from Melektaus, piece by piece. The stigmata of your fabrication, Madam, still lay unhealed on my skin when I finally arrayed you and the others around the table, facing the machine from which you had emerged. You sat there like so many imps, quasi-homunculi waiting to draw breath; waiting for a touch from your Creator, a Word to signal the start of your quasi-lives.

She looks at her six brethren as if to garner support. And indeed, on their polyurethane faces too I perceive the simulacra of emotion: shades of anger, ghosts of hate. But you cannot hate away the truth, my little children. I was the Fabricator; I looked at my Fabrication, and it was good.

But still I needed to know: what was this thing that I could receive only from Yves, and no other? What was this thing that—by virtue of its very *absence*—took from me, night by night, more and more hours of rest? Day by day, therefore, I interrogated your silent faces; I questioned each of you, alone or in groups. I placed you here and there, around the apartment, and showed you the poses that most became you. Some of you I elevated with shallow titles, dressing you in gaudy fabrics cut from Yves' shirts, only to bring you down again. Look at Lord Ubu, in his yellow loincloth, sat in his armchair throne with Madam on his knee! Laugh at Cocu Ubu, tied to a table leg by that same yellow cloth, forced to watch while Madam disports herself with Pig-Man! You hiss at me now, Madam, but you must know I needed answers; I needed answers!

And an answer came, at least in outline, on a day when I had arranged you, Madam, and your golem comrades, in an admiring semi-circle around my plastic face, which towered over you like an Easter Island god, while behind my likeness rose the austere columns of Melektaus, as square as a Babylonian temple. At that time, Golem 3 was struggling, I believe, with his own crisis of faith: for, acting on signs of potential dishonesty in his narrow, squint-eyed face, I had melted together his hands to prevent any thoughts of thieving. A minute's work with a soldering iron, and now, with elbows crooked, and fused hands positioned beneath his chin, he had—sweet irony!—an attitude of unceasing prayer. In fact, I suspect he spent all his time not in devotion but in questioning the justice of his lot. Many times I told him that life's lottery, by its very nature, does not favor the deserving; many times I suggested that the justice or otherwise of this situation is a philosophical point; many times I suggested that he find solace in the adoration of my printed face, and many times considered the merits of removing his plastic eyelids that he might better gaze on the beauty of my black likeness.

And that, Madam, was how the answer began to reveal itself to me, for it was by the squint eyes of Golem 3 that I saw the truth. Something about his left cheek; something that made me look long and close at him, and then, with increasing excitement, examine the rest of you. I arranged you in different combinations, first this one next to this one, and then this one next to that. And at last I saw it, Yves' devilish inspiration: he'd hidden his own face among yours! Thus, Golem 2 had the top left part of Yves' forehead, Golem 3 had his left eye and cheek; Golem 4 had the left part of mouth and chin; and so on. He'd made you all in his own image—or rather, made his own image in all of you!

Who'd have expected dull, slow Yves to have such cunning? But he had: I verified matters by returning to the CAD files, and yes, the relevant co-ordinates of Visage 2—Yves' own face—were repeated in the relevant features of Golem 2 to Golem 7. (And you Madam, what part of Yves do you display? The protruding belly, perhaps, with its everted navel . . . and the ears, definitely. Slightly lopsided, slightly prominent. Yes, Madam; you too were made in his likeness).

From that discovery came sequelae that transformed my understanding of the absurd infatuations played out in Yves' ugly apartment—and that led me to the final answer. For now I saw why it was that, no matter how often I arrayed you before my dark mask, no matter how I wired your limbs into positions of prayer and adulation, no matter how I made your skin blacken and melt with a soldering iron or notched your limbs with a box-cutter—you *never worshipped me*. Not really. And how could you? Yves had made your CAD files with *his* image; you therefore sought to adore Yves, whom you thought to be your creator. To worship Yves, I realized, was a prerogative embedded in your plastic DNA. And I—who *actually* fabricated you—what was I worth? To you, polymer ingrate, nothing!

How can gods rest without adoration? If they are not worshipped, they are not gods. Without adoration, I am nothing; since Yves' death, I am nothing. You grin, Madam; you grin now as you did then. But all things must end. *Selah.*

From the point of that final discovery, sleep evaded me entirely. My surgery suffered; first, the avoidable deaths; then the inevitable investigations and the concern of colleagues; finally, the tribunals. Sick leave, extended and re-extended, until it metamorphosed into dismissal. Oh, lack of sleep—I swear, it can kill you, and I do not know why I am not yet dead of it. But I could *not* sleep, and *cannot* sleep. Until I am your God.

Yes. You, Madam, will sit on my right side, while all Golems chant, *Holy, holy, holy.* You see, now I have found the answer, my little friends; it was hidden in your misshapen faces. The image of the one who must be adored. And now I have the answer, I can proceed.

Print, then! I almost hear her thin scream. Patience, Madam! But the others are triggered, I believe, by her impertinence. Perhaps the interruption excites them; lying beneath Melektaus, with my eyes closed, I almost hear their little limbs bending painfully at rubbery sockets before their polymer flesh snaps back into its created position, the plastic surface of one nudging the plastic surface of another with a click and a clack. Small mouths fight their pre-ordained laughs and leers.

But destiny always wins. You must wait, little ones, for the great incarnation. I open my eyes, and see them sitting, artificially motionless, in feigned innocence. Their implicit disrespect irritates me; I reach out, grab the little creature with six breasts, tweak each of her nipples in turn, savagely, and pull her face into a representation of discomfort. *Pour encourager les autres;* and the others, perhaps, are duly enthused, for they remain in their created positions with their given expressions. Like so many disposable dolls.

So: here we are. My thumb remains above the *PRINT* button; I find no flaws in my reasoning. I see only what is to come: the blessed sleep of a much-loved god.

Is that why you giggle, Madam? You see where this leads? Giggle away: you will worship before long.

I adjust my position slightly; the table's hard surface resists coccyx and scapulae. Melektaus' brass nozzle gapes at me like the mouth of a parasitic worm; it is pursed as though to kiss or spit or suck. A wisp of steam escapes its meatus. The fabrication plate beneath the back of my head is now painfully hot, but let it be so—let it be worse—for God cannot become Yves without agonies! Via my smartphone screen, I check the loaded program one last time: Visage 2. Good.

Well, then. I am ready. Print. From my throat to my forehead, layer by plastic layer; give me the burning face of the Creator! What say you, Madam?

Print.

Yes, Madam. I close my eyes. Let flesh melt and fat bubble from bone, nothing can stop the sleep of a worshipped God. This, Madam, is the answer I have sought.

PRINT.

The Delf

Danny Rhodes

———◆———

SOMEWHERE BEYOND THE GLASS, beyond the foam and the spray, was the Irish Sea. Palmer sighed at the soporific, claustrophobic swelter of the ferry, at his fellow passengers all crunched into themselves, at those buried in coats, hoodies, scarves and, of course, masks. The TV on the wall was tuned to the news channel. He watched the red banner, the daily toll, the numbers repeating over and over. He shook his head.

The coughing and the sneezing. The swearing and the glaring. Everything set on edge. Everybody wary of everybody else. All of this offered the most rudimentary of insights into how it might have been, though things were worse then, of course, ones chances less favorable. He imagined the terror of those other times, the angst-ridden living whilst waiting for the first symptoms to display themselves, the panic and bewilderment when the symptoms came, the full-blown hell of the end.

He cleared his throat. The girl opposite stared in his direction. His eyes met hers. She looked away. As if the gulf between one person and the next wasn't already wide enough, as if society wasn't already broken, here they were. He turned back to the window, the squall grey sea. Somewhere beyond his vision was the dark shadow of the mainland. Things were worse there. The virus was more rampant.

The ferry rode the swell in a rolling motion, lulling him towards sleep. Perhaps he was dead already. Perhaps everybody on this vessel was dead.

PALMER FELT THE STIFFENING in his shoulders the moment he pulled into the gravel car park. All of the preceding week he'd expected them to cancel. Even as he'd driven east beneath Chester and Manchester then on through the peaks, he'd expected them to cancel. But they hadn't. He'd even stopped to call and check. No, they were eager for him to come regardless of events, eager for him to share his hypothesis. So here he was.

A coach full of primary school children was leaving as he parked. A group of boys waved at him from the rear window. When he raised an arm to wave back they mocked him and laughed. He waited for the bus to pull away, climbed out of his car and wandered in the direction of the museum building, a former chapel on the steep lane rising from the village center. A noticeboard outside announced details of his lecture, though the notice was, in fact, his own flyer, simply pinned and somewhat lost amongst various others. He wondered if anybody had seen it. He wondered if anybody would attend.

He stopped to take in his surroundings, the little stone Methodist chapel above the village rooftops, the wide expanse of the moor on all sides, the dry stone walls and stilted trees. He considered the timelessness of the place. It all added to the narrative, a setting like this. The one leant itself to the other.

He ascended the steps and opened the door. The female steward behind the counter looked up from the book she was reading. She peered at him through the Perspex shield that separated them.

"Anthony Palmer," he said. "I'm giving a talk here this evening."

"Ah, yes," she said without smiling. "The lecture."

An adversary then.

"I thought I'd pop in to let you know I've arrived," he said.

She looked at him.

"It starts at eight?" she asked.

She turned to the clock on the wall. It was just after one, but over the years he'd learned a thing or two about visits like these.

"That's right," he said. "I caught the early ferry. Plenty of time to prepare. I'm staying overnight in the village too."

"At the Hollies," she said. "I know. I booked it for you."

He nodded a thank-you but the steward simply glared at him. He had never really connected with women.

"It's just a theory," he said, in an attempt to soften things, to secure a more friendly footing. After all, he wasn't here to cause trouble, just to stir things up a little, maintain his notoriety.

"I understand they dismissed it," she said.

"Well," he said. "I've read *those* articles."

She pulled the visitors book towards her.

"There's always room for scholarly progress," he said.

He realized how patronizing he was sounding. Not that she was listening to him. She was too busy locking the book away and shutting the hatch.

"Time to close up," she said.

"At one o'clock?" he asked.

"Oh, we're not currently open to the public," she said. "Pre-booked school visits only. They just left."

"I saw them," he said.

"We have your event tonight and then who knows what will happen. Personally, I expect it will be the last for some considerable time."

And with that she showed him the door.

HE RETURNED TO HIS CAR, opened the boot, shifted aside his box of books and pulled out his satchel. Then he headed down the hill, trudged around for a bit, reminding himself of the various stone dwellings, the little plaques recording the many that had perished, their tragic stories. The village had a reputation see. It had become something of a macabre tourist attraction. Some might even say it exploited its history, exaggerated its stories to meet its own ends. Some might say.

But today the place was very quiet. Now and then he thought he spotted dim shapes in windows, but try as he might he didn't *actually* observe another living soul. He wrote in his notebook and considered the nature of the situation, the locals trapped as their predecessors had once been trapped whilst he, the outsider, roamed freely.

The Hollies. Quiet and peaceful, though the proprietor seemed vacant, unhappy to have him there. She was wearing a mask.

"You're not wearing yours," she said.

"I don't carry one," he said. "And I shan't whilst I have a choice."

For a moment he wondered if that might be a deal breaker, but the proprietor let him in anyway.

"I read your book," she said.

"Not so melodramatic as the myth," he said. "But researched all the same. And no less horrible a fate."

She looked at him. He looked back at her. It was hard to understand what a person was thinking when you could only see their eyes.

"You're my sole guest," she said as they climbed the steep staircase, her three steps ahead, maintaining her distance. "After you, there won't be anybody else."

She showed him to his room. Functional. Standard. Situated at the very back of the place along a dark corridor. A little stuffy. The smell of dried flowers. Potpourri at a guess. But at least the museum had provided this for him. Alongside the nominal fee it was something. Now, if only he could sell a few books.

"I've put the sandwiches you requested on the side," she said. "Under cellophane." And then she backed away.

When he was alone he went to the window. He moved to open it, but it was painted shut. That wasn't good. He thought about asking to move rooms but the proprietor had seemed impatient to be getting on, wary of his presence. He didn't want to be a nuisance. Complaints could be made when he was back at home. There was always time for complaints. He looked at the plate of sandwiches. White bread. No butter. No tomatoes. All seemed to be well, though the cellophane was tightly applied, stretched taut, unyielding when he pressed it.

Standing at the window, he heard the sound of coughing. Somebody in the corridor. There was a slowness about the person's movements, a sluggishness. Everything was drawn out. A door closed. He heard more coughing. That was what had changed. A cough was no longer ordinary but sinister and threatening. Other people were threatening simply for being. If one believed of course. If one didn't have an alternative postulation.

The window might not open but the view went some way to compensate, expansive and invigorating as it was. He looked out through the glass, down at the garden. A sheltered patio with chairs. A segment of well-manicured grass. Some nicely stocked bird feeders. A stone wall marking the property boundary. A stream running behind. Sheep in the meadow beyond the stream. The open moorland stretching away. He imagined the village as it had once been, isolated, deeply set in the landscape, how intimately connected its populace must have felt, and how ripe they were for contamination. A tight community. Large families in small spaces. Gatherings on a Sunday. Everything interwoven. But they drank the same water too and were susceptible to a great number of ailments. There were other explanations, other theories, like his own. It did not have to be *Yersinia Pestis*.

"Not a conspiracy," he whispered to himself, practicing his introduction. "A theory based on numerous lesser-known facts. Facts that have been blurred by time, airbrushed out of the more popular, more dramatic, narrative..."

He stopped as something moved beneath his window, too close to the house for him to see clearly. He heard the sound of coughing again, looked down over the ledge. The proprietor's husband? Most likely. But that cough wasn't good. It wasn't good at all. And now the closed window made him uncomfortable and claustrophobic. He took the sandwiches and his satchel out into the little garden, half expecting to meet the source of the cough on route, but he encountered nobody, simply sat at the table with his face turned to the low winter sun and drank in the calm until another cough, distant, barely discernible, interrupted him. He felt the curious sensation of being watched then, of being peeped at, examined. The feeling of eyes on him. Something peering over the stone wall. He looked down the garden and towards the gargling stream. There was nobody. He thought about the reception he'd received at the museum, the lonely walk amongst the cottages, the distant proprietor at the B&B, the mocking children. They all added to the layering effect. No wonder people were nervous. No wonder people were scared. Times like these. So unsettling regardless of what you believed and didn't believe.

He rummaged in his satchel, located his notes. He had travelled to disprove a proof, to question a fact, to replace a false-fact with new understanding. Moreover, he'd come to deconstruct a legend. The museum had the sole function of reaffirming the story of a village ravaged by plague, of the heroic self-sacrifice made by the villagers, of innumerable lives saved. But the story, he believed, was inaccurate, based on numerous falsehoods. It was a legend, a myth, ripe for a yarn. The truth, he argued, was opaque and untenable, so much so that really there was no such thing as truth at all. Or there were many truths. That's what his talk and his book were all about, the extraordinary power of stories, the constructed narratives that made up history and the lengths people would go to in order to preserve them.

He ate the sandwiches, flavorless, bland, and yet somehow still able to leave an odd taste in his mouth. But perhaps that was simply his imagination. He opened his laptop in order to distract himself, spent some time going over his slides. It was good, he understood, to have slides.

IT WAS ALMOST FOUR O'CLOCK when he finished. He sat for a moment, pondering his next move. He could wander down to the delf before sunset? Why not? Then he could have a little rest in advance of the lecture, prepare himself for the inevitable onslaught.

He returned his laptop to his room, passing the proprietor's door as he did. Silently, he pushed the door open, located a living room, a single, floral chair facing the TV. No sign of a husband. No sign of anybody at all.

He stepped out of the B&B. The little stone cottages sat squat and silent. He noticed the dark windows, felt the sensation of intrusion and trespass again, that curious impression of being scrutinized. Like a specimen. A lab rat. That sort of thing.

He followed the lane until it petered out, became a track that ended at a five-barred gate. A stone trough sat by the wall there. Full of water. Murky. Spotted with algae. He peered into it, stared at his dark reflection. And then he stood upright with a start. He'd seen, or he thought he'd seen, just for a second, the reflected image of another beside him. He turned around. There was nobody, just a pigeon on the stone wall, which broke into flight, flurried noisily away.

He stood in the silence the bird left behind, calming his beating heart. He *had* seen somebody. He was certain of it. A person at his shoulder. Sunken eyed. Sallow. Drawn. A sick individual. Somebody obviously suffering.

But he couldn't have. There was only the quiet afternoon, the distant cawing of a crow, the sound of a sheep bleating on a faraway hillside.

THE TRACK REDUCED to a footway beyond the gate. It sloped away on a gentle, downward curve, darkening under the line of trees bordering the adjacent field. He stood for a moment savoring the stillness of the place, the sombre afternoon light, the brooding aspect of the surrounding moors. Then he continued on down the path towards the delf, looking about him as he went. A lone tree on a hill. Someone was up there, right at the place where the land met the sky. A singular silhouette. A walker? A climber? Up there on the moor. Half-a-mile away beneath the tree. For a long minute the figure didn't move. Then it turned and started down the slope in his direction. The over-physical nature of the figure's movements, the expressive jerks and twists, alarmed him. Like something out of sorts, he thought. Something lost. Like something burdened with a body. He watched it until it disappeared beneath the brow of the nearest hill.

No matter. It was a walker, that was all. Someone returning to the village after a long day of solitude out on the tops. Descending was always awkward and ungainly. It forced a person to stretch and strain in ways their body wasn't used to. That made sense. That would explain it.

He walked on. The sky losing its luster now, the light leaking away, the weather turning as moorland weather often turns, as he knew it could turn. It might be wise to head back. But he'd come this far. To the delf. To the place where they'd gathered each Sunday in their tight family units, each isolated from their neighbor but intrinsically linked by the landscape, piety, and fate. By some sense of duty. A curious, unnatural looking place. Fissures of limestone. Crags and crevices. Everything jutting or oddly sunken. Hollowed out arches in the rock. Blackened fractures.

Dead branches like calcified arteries, brittle to the touch.

And miasma. Putridity. Evil air. Something like it was visible at the bottom of the slope. Down there by the gurgling stream. A thickness. An effervescence. The ground soft underfoot. Soft and softer. Stagnant water. A stink. Flies buzzing there. Thousands of flies. In winter? He wrote it all down in his little book, scratching the words with his stubby pencil. He'd never seen the delf quite like this, never quite felt it as he was feeling it now. There was something about the place. There truly was.

He looked up to see a figure on the opposite bank. Under the trees. Shrunken and grey. The same squat figure he'd seen on the moor? The same face he'd seen in the water trough? Surely not. The greyness unsettled him. The pallor of the skin. The figure was watching him. Just standing there. He stared at it. He wished it away.

But it didn't go away.

He blinked hard, fought to gather himself. When he opened his eyes the figure had disappeared. Just a shadow then. A trick of the lessening light. Ridiculous to imagine anything else.

There was nobody there.

There was nobody anywhere. Not in this place at this time. Only himself. And now he wished he wasn't. The air had turned cold. The sun was descending. But he was here. He would see this through. A quick circle. To remind himself. To describe later. A way to set the tone of his lecture, pull the audience along with him.

He reached the cave-like wounds in the earth, pushed through a narrow gap, curiosity getting the better of him. Not for the first time. Dark inside. He stood in the cloying grip of it, his eyes struggling to adjust to the lack of light. He touched the stone walls, felt the ageless cold and damp of the stone. He reached back across the centuries. Geographically, physically, nothing much had changed. It might, so easily, have been 1666.

And then he felt something moving in the fissure behind him, felt it before he saw it, a presence emerging from the gloom. He span around. A human shape was jammed in the space next to him. A face. A mouth. A dark, wet hole. Dismal troughs for eyes. Blood and saliva. Raw and festering pustules.

It came at him.

He raised his hands to defend himself.

Too late.

The thing coughed in his direction. He felt spittle strike his skin, his cheeks, his forehead. He closed his eyes. The thing coughed again. He smelt something rancid and rotten, reached out. His fingers touched it. They touched it!

A slick mass.

A putrid wetness.

He wiped his face with his forearm, opened his eyes. There was nothing there. But the spittle was still on his skin. He could feel it. It was there and he had to wipe it away.

He retched and backed out of the fissure into the waning light. The mist hanging heavy at the bottom of the cleft. The cold and empty isolation of his surrounds. The isolation threatening now, pressing upon him from all sides.

Irrational. Nonsensical. It hadn't happened. None of it had happened.

But he knew it had.

He reached the footpath, started up through the trees, stumbling a little, at odds with himself, felt the presence of others beneath the trees. Behind him. In front of him. All around him. Everywhere and nowhere. All at once. The sound of voices. Calling and repeating their calls. Disorientating. Disturbing. Behind that bush. Behind that rock. Beyond and behind. All around. Everywhere. Grey faces. Stunted forms. Young and old. Sick. Desperate. Lost. The suffering dead.

A mass. A congregation. Calling him back as if he were one of them.

He made his way up the track towards the village, looking over his shoulder the whole time, feeling but not seeing, knowing but not wanting to know.

He reached the five-barred gate, the cluster of dark windowed cottages. But that didn't make much difference. He felt as though every window was hiding a face, a hostile pair of eyes wishing him harm. The feeling didn't abate until he reached the B&B.

Or even there. He could feel the enmity towards him, the ill feeling, the want to have him away. He walked through the hallway to the little garden, gathering himself, focussing on what had really happened rather than what might have happened. Nothing had happened, he told himself. His imagination was to blame. He had been up since before dawn. It had been a long journey. He was tired. There was the virus, the gathering hysteria, the curious nature of the delf, a topography that leant itself to disorientation, especially at dusk. He had imagined it all. Of course he had.

He sat on the little chair in the garden, feeling washed out. The last dregs of sunlight wasted away beyond the hills. The moor retracted to a featureless layer of brushstroke shadow beneath the darkening sky.

He noticed a curious smell in the air. Something sweet. A smell he had never smelt before. Odd. Really odd. It added to his gathering delirium. He felt unwell. Not right. Not right at all. His heart was racing. Some sort of hypertension. A panic attack. Caused by stress no doubt. Caused by a lack of personal care.

He retreated indoors, called out for the proprietor but the proprietor didn't respond. He knocked on a couple of the downstairs guest rooms, hoping someone might answer, offer him a painkiller perhaps, a sympathetic ear. But nobody answered. There were no other guests. The rooms marked private were all locked. The kitchen was locked too. The tables in the breakfast room were empty.

He sat in the dining room, opened his laptop, sought the museum website, the information on his event, hoping to locate a contact there. He felt his forehead, noticed he was sweating, that he was running a temperature.

There it was. *Professor Anthony Palmer—The Story of a Plague Village, An Alternative Perspective.* Underneath it in red capital letters, two words.

EVENT CANCELLED.

No. He hadn't cancelled it. He was feeling unwell but there were a couple of hours yet. A lie down would remedy everything. Why had they cancelled it?

He picked up the phone and dialed the museum. Nobody answered. He put the phone down. The light from the hall was very bright. It hurt his eyes. He blinked. Blinked again. A sharp, biting pain was growing behind his eyes. Worsening. He felt weak. Suddenly weak. He had to climb the stairs using his hands and elbows, drag himself up each impossibly steep step, everything rotating now, everything swimming. A vortex.

Blinding pain. Pain like he had never experienced. A needle in his sinuses. The taste of blood in his mouth. He reached the landing and the dark corridor, crawled along it on his hands and knees as the corridor stretched away from him.

Somehow he made it to his door.

He reached for the handle, grasped it, lost it, reached for it again. He lifted the key from his pocket. He tried to locate the lock, missed it, missed it again. And again. Then, somehow, he located it, pushed the key into the lock, twisted it, leant his weight on the door, forced the door open. He fell to the carpet, felt the rough texture of the carpet against his cheek, hauled himself up onto his knees, crawled through the door, the sprung door resistant to him, the sprung door whumping against his hip, trapping his ankle, until it closed hard behind him. He crawled across the carpet to the sink, dragged himself upright, shaking, weak, feeble, legs like jelly. Through blurred vision he dared to look in the mirror. His sunken eyes. His drawn skin. His face in the mirror, blotched and bright. Red. Unnaturally red. Everything on fire. He bared his teeth, saw his bleeding gums. He coughed thick globules of blood onto the white porcelain. The white tiles were splattered with his blood.

No. He shook his head. This was too quick. Far too quick. It didn't happen like this. It couldn't happen like this. Not even if, even if...

But it *was* happening.

His rapid breathing. His stomach in knots. Abdominal pain like he'd never known. He dropped to his knees above the toilet, bent over the bowl. He felt the bile in his throat, the heat and the poison. He vomited. There was blood in his vomit. He pulled himself up. It was all he could do to kick his trousers off. He sat on the toilet, released it all. Like water. The foulest smell. He dropped off the toilet, crawled to the bed and collapsed there, a helpless sack of weak muscle and sweating flesh. He was shivering. Hot and cold. Feverish. Delirious. He tried to call out, could barely make a sound.

"Help me. Please help me."

Nobody responded. Nobody came.

He lay on the bed. Drifted. Everywhere and nowhere. All at once. Drifted in and out. Drifted to the delf, through the miasma, into the cracks and crevices. The wet walls. The dank air. The hollow echo of a sermon. Of a voice. Of many voices. A prayer for the dead and the dying. For the stricken. Or something else. Something that wasn't a prayer at all. Something of the darkness.

A face on his face. Blemished skin on his skin. The horror of it. The horror.

He drifted in and out.

There was vomit on the bed. On the carpet. He could smell his own defecation. His mouth tasted of iron and vomit.

At one point, a grey and shrunken shape entered the room. It picked up his satchel and scurried away. Or he dreamed such a thing. He could barely register any of it. Only the sickness inside of him.

He drifted in and out.

IT WAS DARK in the room. He heard the door click open. A shaft of light pierced the darkness. He opened his eyes to see a blurred silhouette looking down on him. But the blinding shaft of light was a knife behind his eyes that twisted and twisted deep into his perceptions of what was actually there.

"Please," he murmured.

The shape didn't move. A blurred image. A person in a surgical mask. Others behind. All in masks. All in masks.

A mumbled enquiry. A shake of the head. A whisper.

"Not quite. Not yet. Soon."

"Please," he croaked. Again.

But the shape wasn't talking to him.

He tried to raise an arm. He couldn't lift it.

The door closed. The dark folded upon him. Layer after layer of dark pressed upon him, pressed on his chest, pressed and pressed so that later, if it was later, when they returned, he could barely perceive their presence at all.

Or breathe.

"They'll put the village in quarantine," one said.

"Yes," said another. "But what a wonderful postscript to the story."

"Yes," said the first voice. "Yes."

Where the Oxen Turned the Plow

Charles Wilkinson

———◆———

UNEASY WEATHER FOR THE FIRST of August, though not wet enough for Mr. Fabyn to unfurl his umbrella. For the past fortnight summer has been in hiding, suspended above low cloud cover. He glances up. A soft prickling in the air implies imminent rain, yet all morning it has held off. There is sufficient wind to shake the leaves, but he can't tell which direction it's coming from; the trees swell and quiver, uplifting the foliage, as if the airstream is forcing itself from within, traveling up the trunk and along the branches, a symptom of some disturbance rising through roots from the depths of the earth.

Mr. Fabyn tries to ignore the ache in his knees, the hot wires that have replaced his ligaments, the rub and slippage of bone on bone. He walks along the track that crosses the field. At the far end, there is a style leading onto a row of converted farm cottages. Boundary Road. The house furthest away, right at the edge of the small town, is where he lives alone. When he returns, he'll have a hot bath and rub in the balm that he's bought at the chemist. Perhaps he will start reading the journals that he began writing ten years previously, not with any literary intent but as an *aide-memoire*. Clarity and precision were what he aimed for, with few if any stylistic flourishes. He'd watched his own father die from dementia, the memories erased almost methodically, as though the recent past was being deleted year by year. At the end there was hardly much more than the *tohu wa-bohu*, the flickering confusion when space was formless before the world began.

He thrusts his stick hard into the ground in front of him and pushes first one leg and then the other forward, ignoring a flash of pain, the unpleasant warmth of tender flesh.

As he approaches the perimeter, he spots a middle-aged woman in a brown dress climbing over the style. Under one arm, she's holding a small white dog with a pointy face.

"Good morning, Mr. Fabyn."

"Foul weather!" he says, gesturing at the tangled white and grey clouds.

As he turns round to watch her, she puts down her little dog, which looks lost in the open space, as if it has been bred solely for the drawing-room. Who is the woman? He's not given to greeting people by name, and so he's unworried that he doesn't know hers. But that she fails to appear even very slightly familiar is more alarming. She knows him from somewhere. Perhaps she'd served him in a café or stamped his book in the Library.

He climbs over the style, lowering himself gingerly on the far side. As always, he's careful to put less weight on the leg that hurts the most. He glances at his watch. His walk has taken him longer than usual, which means that if he goes into the village there's a risk of running into Harold Shenley, the one person he'd never have the good fortune to forget. As he draws level with the front gate of his house, he considers going back inside, but there's a small parcel to be sent. Why postpone the errand? After 10:00 am the possible presence of Harold—in the Post Office, convenience store, or holding court in the café—is a hazard to be endured. Should he take a more circuitous route to the main street? The morning is unpleasantly moist. The air clings to him. He has a dull ache in both legs as if the clouds have mixed their dampness into the marrow of his bones.

As he rounds the corner, he scans the road ahead for the shambling figure of Shenley, usually enveloped in a muesli-colored tweed coat and baggy, curd-soft corduroy. Most days he has a shoulder bag filled with miscellaneous pieces of stationery and items to be used in a medical emergency. He wears a flat blue cap that is indisputably not a beret, but looks as if it might have been bought on a two-day trip to Dieppe.

There is no one in the High Street. He straightens and massages his left knee. At some point, he must resign himself to an operation, but he has a fear of general anesthetics: how you recall counting and not reaching ten; then the awakening with no sense of the passage of time. Where have you been in between? For Mr. Fabyn such an experience is a dry run for death, the mind simulating extinction.

Apart from Mr. Crisp behind the counter, the Post Office is empty. He has a small mustache of the kind beloved by minor officials. As he looks up, his gaze is non-committal. There are customers whom he greets by their first names and who call him Gerald. Even after ten years living in the town, which is little more than a large village, Mr. Fabyn has been afforded no such courtesies.

"Someone's been looking for you."

"Oh? I think I can guess who that might be."

"Harold Shenley."

"Now, where did he spring from, I wonder?" Mr. Fabyn takes his parcel out of his overcoat pocket and pushes it across the counter. "He's only been here for six months, but already he's inveigled himself onto every committee in town. They say he even intends to run for the council."

"First or second class?"

"Oh . . . second. I mean . . . no one knows what he did before he came here or why he imagines he has some kind of divine sanction to order everyone's lives."

"He said that he wanted to speak to you. On a matter of importance."

"He only talks to me about the Anglo-Saxons. Charters and manorial rights. The way land was distributed, that sort of thing. A deluge of dullness. Have you heard him on the subject?"

"No. Is there anything else?"

Mr. Fabyn has been found guilty of a *faux pas*. Is it that as the postmaster Crisp must maintain an aura of impartiality? Hardly. The man's been heard to speak in unflattering terms of many council luminaries. No, it must be that Mr. Fabyn has tried to assume the local's mantle, with its right to belittle newcomers, when he is in fact still an outsider, even though he has lived in the town for a decade.

"That's all."

"You be sure you speak to Harold. I don't want him coming in here and saying I haven't passed his message on."

MR. FABYN LOOKS at the neat row of his journals, all bound in Moroccan leather and positioned on the middle shelf of his book collection. August sunlight plays on the spines, bringing out the deep reds, golds and russet browns. After a career in Further Education, with its attendant clamor of staff and students, Mr. Fabyn developed the passion for solitude that made him leave the city, where he'd worked for forty years, for retirement in a small town surrounded by rural wilderness. He'd always had an aptitude for living by himself. But he required occasional excursions to a pub or café, even though he was always content to sit in a corner seat by himself, immersed in a magazine or newspaper. To exchange a few banalities with a landlord or proprietor was sufficient human contact. He wanted to be present in but not part of the community; regarded as unfailingly polite, referred to with respect by either his first or second name, but known as someone who was not on a quest for emotional intimacy or even in need of much in the way of conversation.

He takes down the first of his journals, the one that he started in August a decade ago. As he'd made a pact with himself not to reread them until ten years had passed, it could prove instructive to see how much he recalls, an indication as to the extent the plaque is binding to his brain cells. With some dismay, he notes that his handwriting has deteriorated. But perhaps that earlier neatness was no more than the care that is always taken at the commencement of any project. He reads a few paragraphs and is relieved to discover that he remembers the events described clearly; only a few minor details elude him. Then for some reason he is unable to press on. Has he been subconsciously upset by the encounter in the

Post Office? How come Shenley was referred to as "Harold," while he was either nothing or a mumbled "Mr. Fabyn." Perhaps he is regarded not with respect but as someone who is remote, even haughty.

He recalls his first meeting with Shenley. As was his habit every other evening of a weekday, Mr. Fabyn was seated at the oak table by the bow window in the Hundred House, a large stone inn in the center of the town.

"You won't mind if join you."

He glanced up to see a flat beige face under a blue cap, worn so that it pressed down on a protuberant pair of large parsnip-colored ears.

"Well, I suppose . . . I don't think . . ."

"I'm Harold. At the bar, they tell me you are in possession of I Boundary Row otherwise known as Boundary Cottage."

"That's right."

"And your name is?"

"Fabyn."

"Well, Fabian. And let me say first of all that I'm sorry to disturb you while you're reading your book, but you're living in a place that's of personal interest to me. Not the house itself, you understand, but the land beneath it."

Mr. Fabyn did not repeat his name or bother to point out that he was reading a newspaper rather than book.

"Really . . . in what way?"

Shenley folded his hands and cracked his knuckles in a manner that implied he had much to say and might as well make himself comfortable. He began with the explanation of the name of the inn in which they were seated: how from Anglo-Saxon times the land was often divided into Hundreds. Disputes were settled at a "hundred house." He then went on to say that this system was by no means universal: in Kent they had "lathes," in Sussex "rapes;" the Danelaw preferred the term "wapenstake." This was followed by disquisition on the ways in which money was raised to support the church, the lord of the manor or his equivalent and the monarch. After about ten minutes, when the topic was toxic with tedium, Mr. Fabyn risked an interruption.

"No doubt this is all fascinating stuff. But your point is?"

"Boundary Cottage. That's the name of your dwelling."

"Yes, yes... I've already admitted that's correct."

"The boundary is in the wrong place."

Mr. Fabyn picked up his newspaper. "I'm afraid I have no idea what you mean."

A shadow fell across Shenley's face, wiping away any pretense of cordiality. His eyes hardened; for a moment, it looked as if he were about to shout or slam his hand down on the table in a spasm of rage. Then once again he cracked his knuckles, an action that served to relax him. "Fair enough... for now. But it's a matter we'll have to come back to. Well, Fabian, I'd better let you get on with your book."

Mr. Fabyn turns a page of his journal. He must try to put Shenley and his absurd antics out of his mind. The man is not worth a millisecond of anyone's thoughts. He tries to concentrate on his account of a bus trip that ended in a breakdown two miles from its destination. The disaster and the confusion it caused! He recollects it all with complete clarity. Then, towards the bottom of the page, there's a paragraph describing a rendezvous at three o'clock in the morning, an incident that might as well have been experienced by someone else, for he has not the slightest memory of it.

In the event, there was no replacement bus. I was fortunate to share a taxi with another passenger who lived not five minutes away from me. This enabled me to complete my tasks around the house and prepare for my appointment by the river at 3:00 am. I awoke as planned. The intense heat of the day had faded, leaving the night air comfortable and cool, silky on the skin. A giant moon blazed as if lit with white-hot coals from within. The stars seemed to multiply as I moved swiftly across the fields. It was a moment before I understood that the agony in my bones had gone. The moon like a magnet had drawn all the pain out of me, down to the last filing. Stonequick was already by the river when I arrived. The unexpected radiance of the night incised the dark waters, as if its resident god were initialing it in silver. We performed the ceremony and parted an hour before dawn.

Mr. Fabyn looks at the date: August 3rd. Yes, he remembers the ride back home in the taxi, but the remainder of this preposterous account could only be fiction. The handwriting was his, its size and slant following seamlessly from what was written before. But the florid style, overheated with imagery, was quite unlike the concise prose elsewhere. And surely he had never met anyone with the improbable name of Stonequick? He could only imagine this interpolation was an account of a dream, although not presented as such. Either that or it was copied from a book, but it was unrepresentative of the type of fiction he admired.

Outside, the sun has burnt through the early morning mist before breakfast. The temperature is rising. By noon the sky's blue-flame metal seems to return its heat to earth. The news bulletin says it will be the hottest day in August for twenty-five years. As he stands up, the room seems to tilt very slightly. He steadies himself before going into the kitchen to pour himself a glass of water.

IT'S MID-AFTERNOON BEFORE Mr. Fabyn ventures out. He's wearing a floppy white hat of the kind once beloved by cricket umpires. A heat haze blurs boundaries, fusing the far lines of hedges and fields, rising from the path in front of him with a shimmer, as if a revenant's hand has smudged the air. He sets off towards a copse in the middle distance, where shadows anchored on grass promise a cool haven. His bones still feel vulnerable, screwed together badly, like rusting bits of Meccano, but at least the heat and humidity have bandaged the pain, allowing him to move more freely. A swallow swoops past him, on its way to the river. Far above, the swifts surf high currents, their thin cries only just audible. There are no other walkers. In such hot weather, people must prefer the cool sanctuaries of their back gardens, the parasols by the pool.

As soon as he steps into the shade of the nearest oak tree, there's a rustling, a sense of ferns parting, small branches being pulled aside. Then Harold Shenley slithers himself sideways through a gap. He appears slimmer than on previous occasions; his features, seasoned by the sunlight, have lost their softness. Hatless, his head is revealed as bald, shiny and nut-brown. His clothes have shed their oatmeal pallor. Today he wears a dark brown jacket and an open shirt the color of soil.

"I was hoping to have a word," he says.

"I heard something to that effect."

"Saves me the bother of knocking on your door."

At first, Mr. Fabyn is tempted to tell the man he is in a hurry and then step back onto the path. But perhaps there is some merit in attempting to settle the matter, whatever it might be. At least Shenley will probably be less inclined to buttonhole him in the pub.

"Well, here I am."

"Fabyn, that would be your name, would it not?"

"Agreed."

"Not Fabian."

"What is it that you want to talk to me about?"

"An unusual name . . . Fabyn. French, is it?"

"Not as far as I'm aware. My father wasn't sure where it came from."

"It was the biggest disaster that ever happened to this country."

"What?"

"Those Normans. All their invading."

"If you say so. But I'm sure you want to do more than regret the Norman Conquest. It's a little late for that."

Once again, he senses Shenley's profound distaste for him, something akin to an instinctive revulsion. It's a moment before the man masters his emotions.

"These fields. Open. That's what they were in Anglo-Saxon times. Every farmer had a strip. Sometimes more than one. No hedges and fences."

"It's not my period, but I'm sure you're right. But what has this got to do with me?"

"My family farmed this land."

"I don't see how you can possibly be sure about that after all this time."

"Our strip . . . it runs from over there, right through that style. Then it ends on the other side of your house. That's where the oxen turned the plough."

"And so what are you saying?"

"Your house shouldn't be there, should it? Stands to reason. It's on our land."

It is hard to fathom how a man who appears so unremarkable could be filled by a force worse than folly—a delusion that must amount to outright madness.

"You have no evidence for this. In any case property rights have moved on since the seventh century."

"I know what's ours."

Mr. Fabyn shakes his head and turns back towards his house. He's so incensed at having to stand and listen to such arrant drivel that he barely notices the discomfort in his knees. And so suddenly he's back in his house and with no memory of having climbed over the style. Inside, the heat has been building up in his absence. He opens every window on the ground floor. There are dark cracks spidering across the plaster by the fireplace. Is the hot weather drying the house up?

Later that evening, he finds himself unable to go to bed. The heat of the day has hidden itself in every room in the house. He glances at his watch. It is still not too late to phone the one person in the village with whom he's on passable terms, a school teacher who'd retired from the local comprehensive a few years previously.

"Ah, Brian. I'm sorry to ring you so late, but you don't happen to know Harold Shenley."

"A little . . . why?"

"He's not from here, is he? You didn't teach him."

"No . . . but Shenley is a well known name in these parts. Some of his relatives passed through my hands."

"What were they like?"

"Farming people, mostly. Not that interested in what we had to offer. They were all going straight back to the land. Although come to think of it, there were a few who made careers in local government."

"And Harold. What do you make of him?"

A cough and a cautious silence. "He seems pleasant enough. He's trying to make a contribution to the life of the town."

"He doesn't talk to you about Anglo-Saxon history. Persistently and almost to the point of mania."

A puzzled pause and then another cough. "No, why on earth would he do that? I taught Physics."

The storm starts at ten o'clock. Mr. Fabyn watches it from his bedroom window. There's no rain, not even the sound of far off thunder. A tine of lightning. Then the sky flares to white: the sheet hanging for a moment behind crags of cumuli, edging the ridgeway with silver's counterfeit dawn. Not a faint rumble to count from till the next strike. The whole empire of evening stage-lit yet silent. The only show the flashes of atmospheric photography, the sky reprinted again and again in chiaroscuro. The display is imbued with strangeness, as if brought to him courtesy of a parallel world. Later he lies on his bed without sleeping. Every ten seconds the ceiling turns to snow.

We came out of the forest at midnight and made our way to the river. Even at that hour the August air was balmy. We stood for a while in a semi-circle, our arms raised. The moonlight unsheathed the water's silver. No one thought to utter a prayer or a few words of farewell. Even the shaman was silent. Then I moved down the bank, feeling the long grass, touch by touch, on my naked legs. I consigned my father's sword to the river, my gift to the god, inhabitant of this place whose genius is flow.

Mr. Fabyn rereads the lines, which are in his handwriting on a loose piece of notepaper that he'd found that morning in his desk. Apart from the month there's no indication of a date. He's never had either the aptitude or the inclination to produce a work of fiction. Yet surely this passage could not be describing an event in which he'd participated. And who is the narrator? Mr. Fabyn's father had been an actuary who would never have owned a sword, even for ceremonial purposes. Neither of them was acquainted with shamans. Had someone, a proficient forger perhaps, left this account in his desk in order to make him doubt his sanity? There had been no break-ins and the woman who cleaned for him was certainly not a candidate for such subterfuge. Is it conceivable that he'd composed these words in a trance?

He puts the paper back in the desk. There's something subtly unfamiliar about the room in which he's standing, as if its angles have been realigned overnight, not in a way that is immediately apparent, but as though affected by some unknown overnight force. Hidden beneath its appearance, hardly changed except for the cracks by the fireplace, which are deeper and darker, there's been a fundamental alteration of its geometry. Yet it's obvious that this cannot be the case. When did he begin to think like this? He grabs his stick and heads for the door.

Outside, the morning is liquid clarity, its colors freshened in the air cleared by the previous night's storm. He takes a deep breath. Thank heavens it's cooler today. A sense of normality seeps back. He's come out without having a specific purpose. It'll be an hour before the Hundred House opens and his knees feel too fragile for him to contemplate a long walk. It will be best to have a coffee in the café by the church.

As soon as he walks in, he senses the place is under new management. The primary colors, pictures of animals and red gingham table cloths have all gone. In their place are photographs in black and white, mostly of the town or long dead football and cricket teams. There's a dull green glow of unpolished copper; the ceiling and walls are sepia. No one is behind the counter, so he rings a little silver bell. Silence. At length, there's a shuffling from behind the kitchen door and then the unwelcome shape of Harold Shenley establishes itself four square in front of him. He's holding an enormous brown teapot and a plate thick with fruitcake.

"Sit yourself down. The milk's on the table. And you'll see the sugar if you look for it."

"I don't recollect placing an order."

"No need to apologize."

"Are you in charge here now?"

"Let's just say this concern has come back to the family. It should never have gone out of it, if you want my opinion."

"I was hoping for coffee."

Harold Shenley sets down the teapot and fruitcake and then subsides into the chair opposite. In spite of some residual August heat, he's wearing a thick woolen suit the shade of beef stock. His face is shiny and expressionless, varnished like a coffin lid.

"I'm glad you've popped in. Means I won't have to come round to yours later. Although when I say 'yours' it's with qualifications."

"If you're referring to my house, it's mine and free of any mortgage. Check with my bank and the land registry if you wish."

"Now the trouble with these registers and such like is that there are some things they don't take into account."

"Such as?"

"Blood."

"At least half of what you say is unintelligible."

"You're not eating your fruitcake. You might be glad of having put on a few pounds when winter comes."

"Is it your usual custom to plonk yourself down in front of your customers and talk nonsense?"

No flicker of offense on the man's wooden features. He leans forward very slightly, as if to impart a confidence. "I'm talking about bloodlines. They found a skeleton in the southwest. Six thousand years old. But kids in the local primary school had the same DNA or what not. That's heritage for you. Talk about coming from a place, eh!"

"And the relevance of this is?"

"*Your* house. It's a burden on *our* earth."

"There's more than one piece of fruitcake here. The bill, if you please."

It's some time before Shenley rises to his feet. He picks up the teapot and the plate with its uneaten slabs of fruitcake, straightens himself and then from on high looks down at Fabyn as if his antagonist were in the dock. "You'd be welcome enough in here if you were a tourist. Someone just passing through. But taking up residence . . . just like that. Now that's unforgivable. And a word of advice. I'd think about the meaning of Section 103."

ALL MORNING MR. FABYN phones his gas, water, and electricity suppliers to find out why he'd been disconnected. Even when he manages to get through, no information is forthcoming. As all his bills have been paid on time, there's no apparent reason for the cessation of services. At half past eleven the telephone line goes dead. Exhausted, he sinks into his armchair. That night he'd slept badly and even now the remnants of his dreams surface, faces refined to the lineaments of terror, swimming up from the seabed, pale and accusatory. At midnight, he'd stumbled out of bed, remembering how in his nightmare he'd been in a field, hammered into the earth as if he were gatepost. From his fixed position, he saw the oxen moving, heavy and inexorable, towards him. He was fastened to the very place where they will drive over him and turn the plough. Just before he woke up he understood that the figure walking beside the beasts could only be Harold Shenley, his hand on a halter.

Mr. Fabyn forces himself out of his armchair. He dislikes mobile phones: the insistent ringing and unwanted texts; the whole business model of the companies merely a license to take money from his account and move it into theirs; a free pass for fraudsters, both semi-legal and illicit. But somewhere he still has one, bought on a rare trip abroad and unused for many years. If he goes into the town he will be able to buy a new SIM card, something to resurrect the device for long enough to make his urgent calls.

The cupboard under the telephone must be the place to search first: a charger but no sign of a mobile; a stack of out-of-date directories and a copy of the Yellow Pages, with a sheet of A4 paper placed between its leaves. He takes it out. A neatly typed paragraph produced on a manual machine.

Yesterday, with the help of my fellow captives, I cleared a circular space in the woods. The glade with its oak trees and mistletoe is their shrine. The man I know as Stonequick is holding the golden sickle. That he is of their tribe is apparent from his ears. The depositions: every piece of silver I own I have consigned to water. The river god is not placated. Stonequick has dyed his skin, first brown and then a dark blue that is almost black. Now our tribes have stopped moving through forest, alert to the movements of the creatures we kill, and claiming nothing but spears and clothes as our own, we settle and plant, mark out the extent of our territories. We are learning to die for land.

Mr. Fabyn reads through the passage twice. A farrago of pagan claptrap combined with a half baked account of the transition from a hunter-gatherer society to farming. Who could be secreting this nonsense about his house? Perhaps a member of the Shenley family could have owned the building at some point. No doubt it could be worth going to the bank to check the deeds—or should he just change the locks? Either way he might as well have lunch in the Hundred House while considering the problem.

Once again the day's sun has dispersed the early morning cloud. Noon revivifies the heat haze, ascending from the tarmac in a blur of angelic wings. Light rebounds from white stucco and the concrete of the fire station. He takes off his jacket and flings it over his shoulders. Once he's ordered at the bar of the Hundred House he decides to go into the beer garden. All the tables are taken. As Mr. Fabyn steps from the path and onto the grass, he feels momentarily faint; a cold shiver courses under his hot skin. In the cool shade underneath the horse chestnut, his friend Brian is seated with a large man clad in a charcoal-colored suit. Mr. Fabyn takes a sip of his pint and weaves his way between the tables. Brian, a small man with thinning grey hair, glances up.

"Ah Fabyn. Very timely. You were asking about the Shenleys only the other day. Meet my friend and former pupil, Derek Shenley. Quite a bigwig on the council as well as an authority on his family's history."

In spite of his smart suit, white shirt and tie, jug-eared Derek has the weather-roughened features of a man well used to leaning against a five-barred gate. He's staring at Fabyn with a countryman's skepticism.

"Are you by any chance related to Harold Shenley?"

"Almost everyone round about here is."

"Really? I had the impression that he is a newcomer to the district."

"Harold?" Derek's face creases with incredulity and then the table rocks to his laughter. "Harold! A newcomer! Why he's only been around these parts for about six thousand years."

Even after having lived in the town for a decade, Mr. Fabyn still finds the local sense of humor impenetrable. But this ludicrous hyperbole has moved it to another level. "Has this . . . relation . . . of yours been in contact with you about my property?"

"What was your name again?"

"Fabyn"

"Umm . . . Fabyn. Now that's a name that's come to my attention. A small matter of an emergency demolition notice, if I'm not mistaken."

"What in heaven's name to do you mean by that?"

"Property in Boundary Road in danger of uncontrolled collapse."

"My house was in perfect order when I left it fifteen minutes ago."

"Are there any other Fabyns in Boundary Road?"

"No, not so far as I'm aware."

"You didn't see the surveyor?"

"What is going on?"

"A report of a dangerous structure within the meaning of Section 103. You'd better get down there quickly if you think there's been a mistake."

As Mr. Fabyn tries to rush off, willing himself to overrule a pain rippling down his right knee, he passes a waiter carrying a tray with his order on it. He's half way across the garden when he hears laughter from under the horse chestnut tree. The heat's hammering down, bouncing light off the pavements and the bonnets of parked cars. He reaches the High Street before he realizes that he's left his stick behind, propped up next to a chair in the garden of the Hundred House. It's too late to go back for it now. In any case, he's making good progress, pure panic impelling him through his pain. A woman he recognizes comes out of a shop. As he's about to nod, she raises the small white dog she's carrying so that it covers her face. A minute later he's on the path, a short cut leading to Boundary Road. A figure is flickering towards him from the far end. For a moment, peering through the shimmering heat, he imagines it's a naked man, his glistening skin dyed to a blue that's almost black. Then as they move closer to each other, the form in front of him wobbles in the hazy light before becoming Harold Shenley dressed in a tight-fitting dark suit. Inexplicably, the man is taller than before; his head appears stained and wet, as if raised from its long sleep in a peat bog.

"Why are you trying to have my house demolished? I know that you've been in touch with your cousins on the council."

Shenley stops and smiles, revealing a row of stony teeth, still almost perfect after the rot of centuries. "Youngsters!" he rasps, his tone fondly dismissive. "Do you think I'm the sort to wait for all their section this and section that?" Then before Mr. Fabyn can even think of detaining him, he moves on, his stride enormous and inevitable.

When Mr. Fabyn reaches Boundary Road there's a moment of relief. No sign of diggers, wrecking balls and men in hard hats and orange jackets. Then he realizes that there's a void at the end of the terrace where his house should have been, a new vista of the fields beyond. As he stumbles forward, he sees a flag-like strip of his bedroom wallpaper, adhering to the exposed wall of his neighbor's property. In front of him, there's a sinkhole or something worse, a kind of chasm that has opened up, ingesting his house without regurgitating a single brick. A space with not a beam or a tile left. He peers down. Strata after strata, leading to the level where the oxen turned the plough, and then deeper into the darkness of prehistory, right to the place where the jug-eared man, with the genes of the Shenleys, cleared the forest, tilled the ground, planted the first seeds on that spot, became the father of a long line of farmers.

Feast of Fools: A Heartwarming Holiday Romance

LC von Hessen

———◆———

A barren, borderless land of white. Blank, pristine; sterile as the inner walls of a sanitarium. The children of this land scoop white matter into a rotund effigy with a crude approximation of a face. Twigs and stones and the battered hat of an absent elder, presumed dead.

A rustic hamlet cobbled together from saccharine foodstuffs. Curve-handled stakes with the blood-and-bandage color scheme of antique barber poles. The populace is flattened, crumbling, coarsely-featured. A great hand reaches down from the sky, having partly decapitated one of the flattened folk as the rest inexplicably rejoice.

The cramped interior of a cottage. Three small men in identical skintight garments hunch over a table, toiling with wooden hammers. A tall, stout man in red looms over them, hands on hips, glaring down at their progress, grinning. And on the inside: *Ho ho how's that quota moving along, fellas?*

Sophie returns the card to Mrs. Garland's mantel. Mrs. Garland herself nudges through the crowd to hand Sophie a mug of undisclosed hot, murky liquid.

"C'mon, put some cheer in those veins! This oughta get those bones humming!"

The old lady grins at Sophie under a pair of felt reindeer antlers emerging from her helmetlike perm. Sophie smiles and nods and hopes, quite intently, that this drink will get her properly hammered.

Sophie is only in attendance at this party because her mother was eager to show off her big-city lawyer daughter to family friends in the old hometown, and it was better than being interrogated by Mom once again as to why she wasn't married yet *at her age*.

And thus Ms. Sophie Frost, Esq. stands in the corner of a living room in Jingletown, Missouri, occasionally jabbed in the shoulder by a dead pine tree bound up and strangled by strings of undulating lights and sagging under metal balls on hooks. All visible surfaces are enveloped in prickling tinsel and python-coils of red ribbon and artificial pine. Out the windows, the cookie-cutter suburban houses are blanketed in a blue-white snowfall, ground down to grime and slush in the street. The constant rumble of party chatter is buoyed along by an array of soporific mid-century crooners on the stereo that seamlessly meld into one another.

This is a land that has long become foreign to Sophie, a land where strangers automatically say *Merry Christmas* rather than *Happy Holidays*, where people stop swearing aloud when their kids are born unless it's at sports on television, where the names of their boy-children resemble the onomatopoeia from a comic book action bubble while the girls' names have grown extraneous vowels and consonants in a sort of linguistic lichen. In Jingletown, Missouri, Dirk and Brent will someday embark on awkward high school double-dates with Ashleighynn and Caeylagh to see PG-rated romantic comedies at the local multiplex, wondering what to do with their hands in the dark.

After all these years, Sophie figured, she would no longer be subject to constant suspicion and hand-wringing for her mere presence alone, that sarcastic teenage punk chick tainting the well of wholesome Jingletown youth: she was now a bona fide New Yorker™, which held its own cultural cachet of explainable Otherness.

Sophie hadn't been back to the old town since her father's funeral in her senior year of college, and that was a decade ago. She was not especially close to her family and, secular to a fault, was apathetic to holidays in general unless they involved some degree of indulgence.

This time last week, she was cracking open a bottle of Veuve with Janice, Edie, and Yukiko at the luxe Midtown condo of Janice's finance bro fuck buddy to celebrate Sophie's having recently made partner at Woynich Quine & Tillinghast LLP. Naturally the subject of this trip arose.

"'Jingletown;' god, that sounds like the worst, shittiest redneck strip club," said Edie. She comically shook her ample bust. "C'mon down to Jingletown!"

"Wouldn't it actually be 'Jiggletown'?" said Yukiko, tapping a line of ketamine onto the glass coffee table.

"Twerkberg," brainstormed Janice, lying back on the leather wraparound couch with a joint in hand. "G-String, um, Gulch."

"When I was a kid, we just called it J-Town," said Sophie. "For obvious reasons."

The town itself had an utter lack of shame about its name, which was splashed across countless billboards alongside copyright-infringing Norman Rockwell families. There was even a modified version of "Jingle Bell Rock" referencing the town's name that was ubiquitous on local radio from the day after Halloween, with various renditions performed by an array of local community theatre actors and children's choirs. In Sophie's professional opinion it was the corniest shit imaginable.

And the town's name wasn't even Jingletown's greatest embarrassment, at least in the eyes of its expats. That honor went to Ol' Granpappy, the holiday-themed eyesore that brought the town a piddling stream of tourist revenue each winter. The OG—as the kids called him in Sophie's youth—was a statue of a bald, fat, bearded man painstakingly whittled from a single huge log of wood by one of the town's settlers around 200 years ago and positioned thereafter on a pedestal in the town square. His ultimate provenance remained a mystery: he held a crushed amorphous object in his hands that could've been a hat or a pouch or his own moonshine-pickled liver and wore nothing but long johns under his riding boots, a caricature of a grizzled old prospector.

By the early 20th century, Ol' Granpappy's resemblance to archetypal images of Santa Claus was distinctive enough that an official town decree gave him a new paint job to enhance the effect. Ol' Granpappy had become Old Saint Nick.

Granted, this was not exactly an avuncular Kris Kringle but was, in certain respects, more akin to a Krampus, rivaling Nashville's infamously uncanny statue of Nathan Bedford Forrest. His expression was deeply unnerving, the way his lips lolled apart baring teeth and tongue as if about to bellow or snap his jaws, and his eyes stared widely with floating, unfixed pupils under bushy brows set at an angry slant. Moreover, the poorly-varnished wood was prone to warp and crack and rot over the years, riddled with trypophobic hole clusters made by various burrowing worms and larvae no matter how often enterprising citizens stopped them up with wood glue.

Nonetheless, this folk art oddity had long been Jingletown's pride. Instead of the Elf on the Shelf, small plastic effigies of Ol' Granpappy kept watch year-round in every home, on nightstands, beside cash registers, lying in gutters like deaths by misadventure.

Wally, a friend of Sophie's from high school, pulled a prank one summer in which he spray-painted the OG to look like a leather bear, complete with chaps, vest, and salt-and-pepper beard. They'd laugh and flash devil horns at the wooden man through the windows of Wally's car until the paint was scraped off by buzzkill adults.

Poor Wally never did get out. Not until he was in his mid-twenties and downed a fistful of pills in his dad's basement.

And thus Sophie was not enthusiastic about her mother's texts imploring a visit for Christmas after all these years: *The town has changed. I think you'll be pleasantly surprised! [winking smiley face]*

As of this Christmas party, the pleasantness of this alleged surprise had yet to reveal itself to Sophie. Certainly the landscape was not quite as she'd remembered: everything felt more jagged and cramped, beset with a certain shabbiness, as if left to rot in the elements over the past decade. The pastel houses punctuated with once-bold greens and reds were now streaked with rust from the nails holding strings of lights in place, the molded plastic snowmen and choirboys out front glowing dimly through grime settled into their crevices. As she walked into the Garland home and passed a motion sensor, Sophie was treated to a slow, dirgelike rendition of "Jingle Bells" courtesy of a dying battery.

After Sophie earned her Bachelor's degree from Columbia and permanently moved to New York, her widowed mother sold the family home and opened a bed-and-breakfast called Tinsel Town Inn—so named because there was already a competing Jingletown Inn—complete with chintz curtains, a year-round artificial tree, and a requisite rack of Ol' Granpappies in various sizes and color schemes for sale by the front desk. Sophie would be staying there for the long weekend.

Her mother took her for an obligatory stop at Herbie's Diner after the flight, where Mariah Carey on the tinny diner stereo competed with a barrage of folksy banter by waitress Joy, a busybody older woman in a hairnet and candy-cane earrings.

"Take all you want, honey: gotta feed that tapeworm! Say, you gotten hitched yet? Oh, don't worry: true love will find you in the end! Say, have you heard the news? Poor Ol' Granpappy is 'riddled with termites' or somethin' and *they* want to tear him down!"

"Who are 'they'?"

"Developers! The big corporate fatcats! I tell you, it's a darn, cryin' shame. But we'll fight it, just you wait. We'll take that case all the way up to *City Hall* if we hafta!" Sophie, who was admitted to practice law before the Supreme Court, stifled a laugh in her coffee mug.

Sophie's mother was not in attendance at Mrs. Garland's party. Not only did she have to man Tinsel Town Inn's front desk during its busiest season of the year, but she "didn't want to get in the way" as this would be "a young persons' party."

Could've fooled me, thinks Sophie. She's struggling to find anyone here who appears to be under 40. Except, of course, for the couples: visible by their matching baggy holiday sweaters and sweatshirts like Colgate grins in potato sacks at an exuberantly Caucasian costume party. She can't recognize anyone, much less tell them apart, between the women with cheeks coated in foundation the bright orange-peach of overripe fruit while sporting the distinctive bleached, layered, center-parted Stepford Wave haircut favored by modern Republican doyennes, and their boyfriends and husbands with puffy Spam-colored ex-jock faces, over-gelled hair, and beard growth of indifference or self-conscious machismo. Sophie is the only one in black, a smart pencil-skirted cocktail dress suitable for any office function, and one of the few non-blondes.

A pair of children breeze by underfoot: little girls, probably sisters, in matching velvet dresses, red and green. Sophie shrinks back, unsure how to behave: her few similarly-aged friends with kids wouldn't go out to drink at a crowded gathering of fellow adults without hiring a sitter. She was frankly indifferent to children and didn't want kids herself: not because it might kneecap her career, which it would, but much like fly-fishing or skydiving, child-rearing seemed a very intense hobby for *other people*. On that front, she was also fine with remaining single as long as she still got laid somewhat regularly, favoring casual hookups and friends-with-benefits who would politely leave afterwards so she could sleep soundly beside her Yorkie instead of tugging back the covers and tolerating snores and clenching her buttocks to restrain any audible farts.

"Jolly! Merry!" calls Mrs. Garland. "Look out for the Cratchit family, you two!" Her fingers fan over her heart. "My granddaughters," she tells Sophie, with an indulgent smile. "It's not a party without children!" Her sweatshirt features a cartoon reindeer with a red blinking nose dead center: *blink-blink-blinkblinkblink*. Sophie wonders if this means anything in Morse code.

"I wouldn't know, Mrs. Garland."

"Oh, just call me Carol." Her eyes widen in admiration. "Christmas in the Big Apple, *golly!* Stockings over a roaring fireplace in a big Manhattan penthouse..."

Mrs. Garland was not aware that residential fireplaces in New York City were almost all bricked up and plastered over like feckless Fortunatos unless one was an elderly decades-long resident and lived in some rent-controlled cavern of an apartment. Sophie's profession brought her adjacent to the wealthy, though she was not rich herself: she lived in South Brooklyn in a century-old one-bedroom with water-stained ceilings and German cockroaches, next door to a perpetually-closed Italian bistro that she strongly suspected of being a Mob front. She was considered fairly successful by New York standards since she could afford to live in such a space without roommates.

She sips her cloyingly-spiced drink.

"What is this? Cider? Wassail?"

"It's a Jingletown Jamboree! It's our special recipe." Mrs. Garland winks. "You can put that on your 'blog'!"

"Um, I don't work in media. I'm an attorney."

The old woman clutches her hand and says, with unexpected solemnity, "Well then, thank you for your service in keeping the peace and order."

"Oh, you think I'm a prosecutor. No: no, I'm not a criminal lawyer. Actually I work in tort law—"

"Did somebody say linzer torte?!" A grinning fortyish woman in an apron bursts from the kitchen with a pastry balanced in two oven mitts. The two little girls run past again: in the process, the girl in red stomps on Sophie's boot, leaving a mushy child-sized shoeprint on the black leather.

Fucking brat.

"Have you heard they want to tear down Ol' Granpappy?" Mrs. Garland sighs. "It just hurts my heart, is what." After no response from Sophie, an urgent conspiratorial whisper: "Say, could you help us out? With Ol' Granpappy? You know, look into the case. Just as a favor to the town. We have to save him."

Ugh. First of all, this sort of advice had a price tag. She was asking for a consultation. Second, Sophie wasn't licensed to practice in Missouri and would have to be admitted *pro hac vice* in a jurisdiction halfway across the country to argue this case: why couldn't they just ask someone local, who would be cheaper and better-informed about local zoning ordinances? Lastly, she didn't do property law, immediately recalling the prolonged migraine that was the real estate case in her associate days where the opposing counsel was this *pro se* asshole who built his entire argument around *Stambovsky v. Ackley*, and—

"Have you met my son, Rudolph?"

"No, I haven't." A couple of beats later she nearly laughs aloud: his name is *Rudy Garland!* Oh god! *There's no place like home!* Perhaps if she clicked the heels of her boots together, she would wind up back in Brooklyn. *I'll get you, my pretty!*

Sophie points to the muck left by the little girl's shoe. "Hold on, I need to go clean this up." She maneuvers to the snack table, grasping some napkins.

Bending down to wipe off the slush, Sophie faces a small army of knee-to-thigh-high statuettes of Santa, snowmen, Victorian carolers with blow-up doll mouths, standing forest-thick and obscuring the walls. On the lone visible shelf, a younger Carol Garland and her husband stand with their two sons—one sunny, one sullen, Goofus and Gallant—in front of their Christmas tree farm in a framed snapshot. One must be Rudolph, but who's the other son?

As she rises to toss out the napkins, a tall man trips over a decorative poinsettia, sloshing the contents of his Solo cup down the front of her dress. He looks dutifully horrified.

"Oh gosh, I'm terribly sorry, Miss, er—"

"Frost."

He brightens. "Oh, right, you're Holly Frost's daughter! I've heard so much about you!"

She appraises this man. Studiously scruffy and shaggy-haired, gently tanned and even-featured, strong jaw and light crow's feet, flannel shirt under a requisite holiday sweater, Santa hat that flops about like a jester's cap: he's an ad agency's pitch of a nonthreatening handsome man. He does nothing for her own libido.

"My name's Rudolph, but everyone just calls me Rudy."

. . . And your little dog, too!

He offers a handshake of middling firmness. "Can I help you get cleaned up?"

"It's black. It won't show anyway." She grabs more tissues to dab at the fabric.

He scratches the back of his head. "Gosh, I know you've been away for awhile, but have you heard the news about Ol' Granpappy?"

She nods.

"Well, I think there's a simple solution, and I'm gonna do it. I plan on building a gazebo to protect Ol' Granpappy from the elements. Heck, I'm designing it now! When I think of raising my daughters without him, well . . . gosh, I should go check on my girls. They love their linzer torte!" He smiles through his stubble and disappears.

Well, that was pointless.

But not, it seems, to everyone. The other guests around them have been watching this interaction with fixed grins and wide eyes. Sadie is reminded uncomfortably of something she cannot quite recall.

Mrs. Garland appears at her elbow, tugging her sleeve.

"That's my Rudy! He's single, you know. Thirty-nine years young."

"Sure. Good for him."

"Well, don't you see?"

She shakes her head.

"You're an at-*tor*-ney," the old woman over-enunciates. "Rudy's an *ar*-chitect. It must be fate: your jobs both start with an A!"

Sophie pictures herself with a bold, flaming Scarlet Letter arising from the wet patch on the front of her dress, sipping a Jingletown Jamboree surrounded by columns of fire and cartoon demons at a Christmas party in Hell.

"His wife died tragically when the girls were young," stage-whispers Mrs. Garland. "But he's ready to love again!"

"Wow, that's a little presumptuous. I've only just met the guy. And I'm only here for a few days, you know."

Mrs. Garland blinks in confusion. "But the girls—"

"Sorry, I don't date guys with kids. That's a hard dealbreaker for me."

"But you're young yet; you can still have children of your—"

"I just don't want kids. At all. It's just not for me."

"But they're the reason! For the Season!" At Sophie's impassive face, the old woman grows a cold smile. "Like so many young people nowadays, you don't *know* you're unhappy."

"I'm not looking for a boyfriend, Mrs. Garland." And even if she was, it wouldn't be Rudy. He was the human equivalent of leftover melon slices in a corporate fruit platter. She could not picture this man having an inner life.

"Thank heavens you still *smell* local." Mrs. Garland hisses, slinking away.

Sophie wishes, quite desperately, for a spritz of Chanel No. 5.

Unfortunately she's stuck at this party until her mother returns: a New Yorker dependent on public transit, she hasn't driven a car since high school. Dawdling on the landing by the front door, she's annoyed that her mother isn't picking up the phone. Maybe she'd been set up. And for fuck's sake, how many times had they played "Jingletown Rock"?

Funny, she hadn't noticed when she arrived, but the front door is flanked by a pair of man-sized nutcrackers hoisting candy-cane pikes. Their painted eyes stare her straight in the face.

Yeah, and fuck you, too.

Rudy Garland pops up again, like a recurring cold sore, with a cluster of mistletoe raised in one hand.

"Want to help me hang it?"

Her eyes flick up to the berries, down to his face. "Good luck with that," she says, flatly.

But he keeps trying.

"Say, what's your favorite Christmas song?"

"Wham's 'Last Christmas.' The lyrics are actually really grim and cynical." She'd been surprised as an adult to learn that the version on Jingletown radio only looped the chorus over and over for four minutes straight.

"Lennon and McCartney put out some classics," Rudy says, nodding. "I'm into Mannheim Steamroller; they're rockin.'"

Oh my god, this guy.

"Refill your drink?" He pats his stomach. "It's good for the Ophite Ganglion."

"The . . . what?" She wasn't sure she'd heard him under the soundtrack, *Jingletown chime in Jingletown time.*

"Ophite Ganglion!" Rudy grins.

"O-kayyy. What is that?"

"It's right by the liver. Helps with keeping functions regular!"

Sophie pulls out her phone.

"Oh, you won't find it on the internet. Most doctors don't even know about it 'cause it's been covered up since the Dark Ages."

Actually one of my friends is a Medievalist and she says they don't really use the term 'Dark Ages' any more, it's a misnomer, she thinks, before realizing that is hardly the biggest issue here.

"So you say there's a centuries-long conspiracy to keep the 'Ophite

Ganglion' out of anatomical texts. Where's your proof?"

His brow creases in confusion. "You just don't—"

"No, you need evidence for this. This organ would have been discovered in autopsies and dissections. It's not like the clitoris being left out of human biology textbooks in high school health class." Rudy's face glows pink. "This isn't some theological debate, for Christ's sake. You need hard evidence to support a stance like this."

Silently, Rudy retrieves an '80s-era Family Medical Guide from the living room, opening it to a bookmarked anatomical diagram where a wormy little thing affixed to the liver has been drawn in Sharpie.

"Oh my *god*. Are you being serious? Is this some elaborate prank?"

He bends down, quite solemn. "Do you . . . believe?"

"*What?*"

"Sophie, please, stop running. It's destiny."

No, Virginia, there ain't no sanity clause!

It was absolutely time to leave.

Sophie ducks into the back hallway, double-checking her phone to confirm there is no car service available here, hiding out on the pretense of a bathroom break. She locks the door, lifts the upholstered toilet lid, turns the requisite Ol' Granpappy to face the wall.

The OG is watching you pee! She starts cracking up. In a mad world, all one can do is laugh.

Exiting the bathroom, Sophie almost smacks into the enormous head of a dead caribou.

"That's an authentic reindeer."

A slim thirtyish man slouches in a nearby doorway. In the dim light, he's anemically pleasant-looking. He wears a suit: no stop-sign red or kelly green in sight. The twin tails of a dark paisley tie hang loose around his open collar.

She looks into the wall-mounted reindeer's cold glass eyes. "I didn't think they were so huge."

"Yeah, they're bigger than you'd expect, right? Same with moose." He points at the antlers covered in velvet fuzz. "That was a commission. I don't normally do animals of that size."

"You're a taxidermist?"

"Well, hobbyist, yeah. I don't hunt them, I just mount them. Wow, that sounds like a bad innuendo. Um. Anyway." He extends a pale hand. "Samuel Garland."

"Oh, are you related to—"

"Yeah, I'm the spare." He rolls his eyes. Sophie likes him already.

"Oh yeah? So what do you do around here?"

"Well, I was a humanities major, then a watchmaker for awhile. And then I was called to—to other things." He sounds resigned, bittersweet. "Actually, we've met before. Mr. Tanzer's sophomore Western history class?" At her blank look: "Remember that World War One reenactment we did in class where I was cast as Franz Ferdinand and you were Gavrilo Princip?" A wan smile.

She remembers.

"Oh, right, *Sam!*"

16-year-old Sam Garland wore thick glasses and braces and shirts that were a couple sizes too big, like he was trying to look more imposing, or perhaps wearing his older brother's castoffs. He and Sophie were in the same grade throughout high school, even the same gifted program, but rarely interacted due to the disparity in their schedules. They would trade sarcastic remarks before Mr. Tanzer's class, often peppered on Sam's end with tidbits of obscure history he'd dredged up. She'd enjoyed his company but wouldn't have considered him a friend, and had since completely forgotten his name and existence.

Half a lifetime later, he's gotten contacts, grown into his features, and started dressing in properly-fitted button-downs. Actually he's become, by Sophie's standards, quite attractive: she's always preferred shy, skinny nerdy guys to the buff, bellicose frat-bro types that surrounded her in law school. As they converse about anything but Christmas cheer, she tries to subtly gauge the length and girth of his flaccid endowment through his cheap shiny trousers. Perhaps this night could be salvaged.

"They're trying to set me up with your brother out there." She rolls her eyes. "You know, he was actually telling me about this fucking bonkers conspiracy theory about a secret bodily organ."

"Oh god, *really?* Fucking idiot." He covers his eyes and forehead with one hand, sighing deeply.

After a moment, he ventures a nervous question. "Listen, would you like to come see my model town? It's just down in the basement."

Of course she would.

They pass through two more giant nutcrackers on the way. Further taxidermy is affixed to the walls over the stairs: a double-headed crow, a rooster with snakes for feet.

"Yeah, it's just standard gaff. It's all surface," Samuel explains. "You just use the skin and skull and some fine bones in the paws or wings or whatnot. No muscles or full skeletons."

When lights flip on, Sophie realizes this was not merely a "come up and look at my etchings" pretense: he really did have a model town in the basement. A sprawling table hosting snow-covered houses with glowing windows, fake foliage, and tiny citizens, all rendered in intimate detail.

"Wow, this is fantastic. No model train, though."

"Nope, Jingletown's never had a train."

And so it is, down to the billboards, the omnipresent Christmas decor, the little Ol' Granpappy.

"That's three years of work and counting. I also sleep down here, so." This basement is a dim, wide room with wood-paneled walls, its small, high windows obscured by snow. Another pair of those garish giant nutcrackers blocks a door at the back, gawping like nosy chaperones. Sophie wants to blindfold them.

"Actually, since I moved back here, I've become sort of an unofficial town historian." Samuel tugs a bulging scrapbook from a nearby shelf. "Did you know Jingletown used to be called New Languedoc, after the home of the Albigensians? And before that, the original settlers called it Yalda-Bahuth, which is itself a corruption."

He points to mimeographed documents and yellowed pulp clippings taped into the book. "The names, I suspect, are a deliberate mask. Just like the oldest Christmas traditions themselves—tree decorating, gift-giving, feasting, singing—are a mask for Saturnalia, the pagan Winter Solstice. The liberation of the bound God of Death: Saturn the sickle-bearer, the chthonic enforcer, the dark tyrant, devourer of his own children.

"Ultimately lost, though, was the reversing of roles: menials served by masters, fools made kings. The empowered become subservient. Reason and order become madness in a mad world. And each year the cycle renews.

"But they could never fully tamp down the carnival. They had to mask it instead. And I wonder, what other masks..." He finally notices she's only half-listening and steps forward. "Sophie, I know you're well-educated. What do you know about the Demiurge?"

She shrugs. "Not my area of expertise. Some sort of philosophical concept?" She toys with the stray ends of his tie. "So you say you sleep down here? Want to skip out on the party?" She gently but firmly tugs the tie like a leash.

Poor Samuel is immediately flustered. "Wow. Gee. Uh, wow, I didn't expect..." He flushes, laughs nervously. "Uh, I don't know if it's allowed..."

She rolls her eyes. "Sam, you're a grown man. Are you married?"

"No..."

Sophie looks back at the town, the little Garland house. Out front is a miniature Mrs. Garland in her sweatshirt and reindeer antlers. "Is it a religious thing?"

He sighs. "... Actually yeah, kind of."

Miniature brothers: sunny Rudy and sullen Samuel.

"I mean, don't get me wrong; I, I *absolutely* would, but..." He mutters something barely audible that sounds almost like *my seed isn't strong enough*.

—And a little Sophie figurine in a black dress. The paint is dusty: Little Sophie has been there awhile. Amateur taxidermist Samuel Garland is now officially weird in a bad way.

"What the hell is all this? Have you been stalking me?" She thrusts Little Sophie in his face.

Clearly aghast and ashamed, Samuel freezes for several moments—until a curiously grim determination settles into his face and tone.

"Well, tell me this, Sophie: why *did* you come back this time? You don't give a shit about Christmas and you're not the type to be guilted into family functions. Why here, and why now? Right when the genius loci of our town's heritage is under threat? Right when you've become a person of status and importance, yet have no romantic or familial ties to the city?"

"Because *it pulls us back*. His tendrils, inside all this town's native sons and daughters. The Ophite Ganglion *does* exist, but *only* for those born to this town. The Worm turns within us all, and it pulls us all back here during the time of our Saturn Return. And you, a member of the Law, the discipline of Saturn: you were sent forth to bring us knowledge of the outer world."

The party above erupts into cheers and applause as "The Jingletown Rock" is cranked so loud it constantly clips and warps.

"Ol' Granpappy—as He's called nowadays—must remain to watch over us, buffeted from the adversarial forces He devises as shows of faith, and we in turn watch His perpetual decay. This, too, was preordained. Trapped here in the sarkic realm, we are only His archons; we must continue to enact the cycle, to triumph over the material secular. You and my brother—" He winces. "... We *tried* to make it happen organically, but..."

A frantic hollow clapping sound, as if emitting from the gnashing jaws of countless wooden men.

His face falls, somehow both resigned and alarmed. "The Conqueror Worm is awake. He is always watching. He sees, and knows."

A rumbling laugh from below. The floor quakes beneath her feet.

"I'm sorry, Sophie." Samuel clasps her hand, his voice very soft now. "I tried to get out once, too."

The nutcrackers draw back their sharpened peppermint pikes and the basement door bursts open.

NEXT CHRISTMAS, A CUSTOMIZED card appears on Carol Garland's mantel from a family of four: the gap-toothed moppets Merry and Jolly posing before the newest Mr. and Mrs. Garland. The latter wears a sweatshirt depicting a wrapped present, its bow positioned over her swollen belly, which she cradles protectively.

They stand beneath the town square gazebo that Rudy designed and built. They pose alongside Ol' Granpappy in his fresh coat of Santa paint. They grin into eternity.

There, you see? Fairy tales do *come true, and real love will find you in the end. Happy endings are possible if only you believe.*

ABOUT THE CONTRIBUTORS

CLINT SMITH is the author of the short story collections *The Skeleton Melodies* (2020) and *Ghouljaw and Other Stories* (2014), as well as the novella *When It's Time For Dead Things to Die* (2019). Of late, his stories are slated to appear in *Supernatural Tales* and *Vastarien: A Literary Journal*. Clint lives in Indiana, along with his wife and children, just outside Deacon's Creek. Read more at www.clintsmithfiction.com.

JOSHUA REX is a writer of speculative fiction and a Master of Arts (History) candidate at Bowling Green State University. He was born in Sandusky, Ohio and grew up between the Midwest and New England. He is the author of the collection *What's Coming for You* (Rotary Press, 2020) and the novel *A Mighty Word* (Rotary Press, 2021), and hosts The Night Parlor Podcast. www.joshuarex.com.

DOUGLAS THOMPSON's short stories and poems have appeared in a wide range of magazines and anthologies, including *Ambit, Albedo One, Chapman and New Writing Scotland*. Variously classed as a Weird, Horror, Sci Fi, Literary, or Historical novelist, he has produced 14 novels and collections of short stories and poetry since 2009, from various publishers in Britain, Europe, and America. His novellas, "The Drowned Labyrinth" and "Dreams of a Dead Country" will be published in Portuguese and German by Raphus of São Paulo and Nighttrain of Darmstadt respectively, in 2022. His latest novels *The Suicide Machine* and *Barking Circus* are available in paperback from Zagava of Dusseldorf. www.douglasthompson.wordpress.com.

TIMOTHY GRANVILLE lives in rural Wiltshire, UK, with convenient access to a range of disquieting earthworks. His stories have appeared in a number of magazines and anthologies, including *Oculus Sinister* from Chthonic Matter.

ELIN OLAUSSON is a fan of the weird and the unsettling. She has had stories featured in *Curiouser Magazine, Luna Station Quarterly*, and anthologies such as Dark Ink Books' *Unburied: A Collection of Queer Dark Fiction* and Scare Street's *Night Terrors Vol. 4*. Her first short story collection, *Growth*, will be released by AM Ink Publishing in 2022. Elin's rural childhood made her love and fear the woods, and she firmly believes that a cat is your best companion in life. She lives in Sweden.

GORDON BROWN grew up in the deserts of Syria and now lives in the deserts of Nevada. Since his arrival in the New World, his work has appeared in *McSweeney's Internet Tendency, Tales to Terrify, F(r)iction Online, The Ocotillo Review*, and elsewhere. He spends his time writing feverishly and looking after his cats, of which he has none.

DAVID SURFACE lives and works in the Hudson Highlands of New York. His collection, *Terrible Things*, was published by Black Shuck Books in March of 2020. His stories have appeared in *Shadows & Tall Trees*, *Nightscript*, *Supernatural Tales*, *The Tenth Black Book of Horror*, *Uncertainties III*, *Twisted Book of Shadows*, *Phantom Drift*, *Crooked Houses: Tales of Cursed and Haunted Dwellings*, and Ellen Datlow's *Best New Horror #13*. A novel co-authored with Julia Rust, *Angel Falls*, will be published by Haverhill House Publishing's YAP imprint in summer 2020. You can visit him online at www.davidsurface.net.

DOUGLAS FORD lives and works on the west coast of Florida, just off an exit made famous by a Jack Ketchum short story. He is the author of a recent collection of weird fiction, *Ape in the Ring and Other Tales of the Macabre and Uncanny*, published by Madness Heart Press, as well as the novel, *The Beasts of Vissaria County*, due out from D&T Publishing in 2021. His short stories have appeared in such venues as *Dark Moon Digest*, *Tales to Terrify*, *Weird City*, along with *The Best Hardcore Horror, Volumes Three and Four*. His novella, *The Reattachment*, appeared in 2019 courtesy of Madness Heart Press. Upcoming publications include *Little Lugosi: A Love Story*.

ALEXANDER JAMES is a writer of weird fiction and poetry based in West London. You can find more of his work at www.alex-james.com.

JASON A. WYCKOFF is the author of two short story collections published by Tartarus Press, *Black Horse and Other Strange Stories* (2012) and *The Hidden Back Room* (2016). His work has appeared in anthologies from publishers including Haverhill House Publishing, Plutonian Press, and Siren's Call Publications, as well as the journals *Weirdbook* and *Turn to Ash*, and previous volumes of *Nightscript*. He lives in Columbus, Ohio, USA. Married, with cats. www.jasonawyckoff.weebly.com.

RHONDA EIKAMP was born and raised in Texas and now lives in Germany, where she works as a translator for a law firm. She is primarily a writer of short fiction. In addition to Chthonic Matter's *Oculus Sinister*, her work has appeared in *The Dark*, *3Elements Literary Review*, and *The Fantastic Other*, with stories forthcoming in *Phantom Drift* and *Vastarien*. Her story "You Can Check Out Any Time You Like" from *Apparition Lit* was recently chosen for translation for the Spanish podcast Las Escritoras de Urras. A list of her stories available online can be found at www.writinginthestrangeloop.wordpress.com/stories.

STEVE TOASE was born in North Yorkshire, England, and now lives in Munich, Germany. He writes regularly for *Fortean Times* and *Folklore Thursday*. His fiction has appeared in *Nightmare Magazine*, *Shadows & Tall Trees 8*, *Analog: Science Fiction and Fact*, *Three Lobed Burning Eye*, *Shimmer*, and *Lackington's* amongst others. Three of his stories have been reprinted in Ellen Datlow's *Best Horror of the Year* series. His debut short story collection *To Drown in Dark Water* is now out from Undertow Publications. He also likes old motorbikes and vintage cocktails.

You can keep up to date with his work via his Patreon www.patreon.com/stevetoase, www.tinyletter.com/stevetoase, facebook.com/stevetoase1, www.stevetoase.wordpress.com, stevetoase.co.uk, and @stevetoase on Twitter.

TIM MAJOR lives in York, UK with his wife and two sons. His recent books include *Hope Island* and *Snakeskins*, Sherlock Holmes novel *The Back to Front Murder*, short story collection *And the House Lights Dim* and a non-fiction book about the 1915 silent crime film, *Les Vampires*. His short stories have appeared in publications such as *Interzone*, *Vastarien* and *Not One of Us* and have been selected for *Best of British Science Fiction*, *Best of British Fantasy* and *Best Horror of the Year*. Find out more at www.cosycatastrophes.com.

ASHLEY STOKES is the author of *Gigantic* (Unsung Stories, 2021), *The Syllabus of Errors* (Unthank Books, 2013) and *Voice* (TLC Press, 2019), and editor of the *Unthology* series and *The End: Fifteen Endings to Fifteen Paintings* (Unthank Books, 2016). His recent short fiction includes "Subtemple" in *Black Static*; "Replacement Bus Service" in *Out of Darkness* (edited by Dan Coxon, Unsung Stories), "Hardrada" in *Tales from the Shadow Booth Vol. 4*, edited by Dan Coxon; "Evergreen" in *BFS Horizons 11*; "Two Drifters" in *Unsung Stories Online*, and "Black Lab" in *Storgy*. Other stories have appeared in *Bare Fiction*, *The Lonely Crowd*, *The Warwick Review* and more. He lives in the East of England where he's a ghostwriter and ghost.

REGINA GARZA MITCHELL is a professor who sometimes finds the energy to write fiction. Originally from Texas, she now lives in the Midwest. She is the author of *Shadow of the Vulture* (Death's Head Press) and editor, with David G. Barnett, of *The Big Book of Blasphemy* (Necro Publications). She has published more than 20 short stories, most recently in *Space and Time Magazine* and *Campfire Macabre* (Cemetery Gates Media). You can find her on Twitter @garzamitchell.

MARC JOAN, a biomedical scientist, was raised in India and resides in England. Publications include ~25 stories. His first novel is scheduled for 2022. Competition results include: 2017/2018 *Aesthetica Creative Writing Award* (finalist); 2017/18 *Ink Tears Short Story Competition* (runner up); 2017/18 *Galley Beggar Short Story Competition* (special mention); 2017 *Brighton Prize* (long-listed); 2018 *BBC National Short Story Award* (last 60 from ~1,000 entries); 2020 *CRAFT Short Fiction Prize* (top 4%); 2020 *Punt Volat/Spencer Parker Memorial Award* (winner); 2020 *William van Dyke Short Story Prize* (long-listed); 2020 *Gatehouse Press New Fiction Award* (Highly Commended); 2020/21 *Aesthetica Creative Writing Award* (finalist); 2021 *Short Fiction/University of Essex International Short Story Competition* (short-listed: one of seven short-listed from ~780 entries); 2021 *Brick Lane Bookshop Short Story Prize* (long-longlist). www.marc-joan.com.

DANNY RHODES is the author of three contemporary novels, *Asboville* (2006), *Soldier Boy* (2009) and most recently FAN (2014). His short fiction has appeared in numerous publications in the UK and the USA including *The Horror Library*, *Black Static*,

Cemetery Dance Magazine, Stephen Jones' *Best New Horror* and *The Year's Best Dark Fantasy & Horror Vol 2* (Pyr Books). He is a lecturer in Creative and Professional Writing at Canterbury Christ Church University and for the Open University. Visit his website at www.dannyrhodes.net.

CHARLES WILKINSON publications include *The Pain Tree and Other Stories* (London Magazine Editions, 2000). His stories have appeared in *Best Short Stories 1990* (Heinemann), *Best English Short Stories 2* (W.W. Norton, USA), *Best British Short Stories 2015* (Salt), *Confingo, London Magazine* and in genre magazines and anthologies such as *Black Static, The Dark Lane Anthology, Supernatural Tales, Theaker's Quarterly Fiction, Phantom Drift* (USA), *Bourbon Penn* (USA), *Shadows & Tall Trees* (Canada), *Nightscript* (USA) and *Best Weird Fiction 2015* (Undertow Books, Canada). His anthologies of strange tales and weird fiction, *A Twist in the Eye* (2016), *Splendid in Ash* (2018) and *Mills of Silence* (2021) appeared from Egaeus Press. A full-length collection of his poetry came out from Eyewear in 2019 and Eibonvale Press will publish his chapbook of weird stories, *The January Estate*, in 2021. He lives in Wales. More information can be found at his website www.charleswilkinsonauthor.com.

LC VON HESSEN is a writer of horror, weird fiction, and general unpleasantness, as well as a noise musician, occasional actor, and former Morbid Anatomy Museum docent. They have recently appeared in *Vastarien, Nightscript 6, Planet Scumm, Oculus Sinister, Beyond the Book of Eibon*, and *Hymns of Abomination*, with previous works collected in the ebook *Spiritus Ex Machina*. An ex-Midwesterner, von Hessen lives in Brooklyn with a talkative orange cat.

C.M. MULLER lives in St. Paul, Minnesota with his wife and two sons—and, of course, all those quaint and curious volumes of forgotten lore. He is related to the Norwegian writer Jonas Lie and draws much inspiration from that scrivener of old. His tales have appeared in *Shadows & Tall Trees, Vastarien, Supernatural Tales*, and a host of other venues. *Hidden Folk*, his debut story collection, was released in 2018.

For more information about NIGHTSCRIPT, please visit:

www.chthonicmatter.wordpress.com/nightscript

Printed in Great Britain
by Amazon